Arethusa by F. Marion Crawford

I0682412

Francis Marion Crawford was born on August 2nd, 1854 at Bagni di Lucca, Italy. An only son and a nephew to Julia Ward Howe, the American poet and writer of 'The Battle Hymn of the Republic'.

His education began at St Paul's School, Concord, New Hampshire, then to Cambridge University; University of Heidelberg; and the University of Rome.

In 1879 Crawford went to India, to study Sanskrit and then edited The Indian Herald. In 1881 he returned to America to continue his Sanskrit studies at Harvard University.

At this time in Boston he lived at his Aunt Julia house and in the company of his Uncle, Sam Ward. His family was concerned about his employment prospects. After a singing career as a baritone was ruled out, he was encouraged to write.

In December 1882 his first novel, 'Mr Isaacs', was an immediate hit which was amplified by 'Dr Claudius' in 1883.

In October 1884 he married Elizabeth Berdan. They went on to have two sons and two daughters.

Encouraged by his excellent start to a literary career he returned to Italy with Elizabeth to make a permanent home, principally in Sant' Agnello, where he bought the Villa Renzi that then became Villa Crawford.

In the late 1890s, he began to write his historical works: 'Ave Roma Immortalis' (1898), 'Rulers of the South' (1900) and 'Gleanings from Venetian History' (1905). The Saracinesca series is perhaps his best work. 'Saracinesca' was followed by 'Sant' Ilario' in 1889, 'Don Orsino' in 1892 and 'Corleone' in 1897, that being the first major treatment of the Mafia in literature.

Francis Marion Crawford died at Sorrento on Good Friday 1909 at Villa Crawford of a heart attack.

Index of Contents

CHAPTER I

Carlo Zeno, gentleman of Venice, ex-clerk, ex-gambler, ex-soldier of fortune, ex-lay prebendary of Patras, ex-duellist, and ex-Greek general, being about twenty-nine years of age, and having in his tough body the scars of half-a-dozen wounds that would have killed an ordinary man, had resolved to turn over a new leaf, had become a merchant, and was established in Constantinople in the year 1376.

He had bought a house in the city itself because the merchants of Genoa all dwelt in the town of Pera, on the other side of the Golden Horn. A Venetian could not have lived in the same place with Genoese, for the air would have poisoned him, to a certainty; and besides, the sight of a Genoese face, the sound of the Genoese dialect, the smell of Genoese cookery, were all equally sickening to any one brought up in the lagoons. Genoa was not fit to be mentioned within hearing of polite Venetian ears, its very name was unspeakable by decent Venetian lips; and even to pronounce the syllables for purposes of business was horribly unlucky.

Therefore Carlo Zeno and his friends had taken up their abode in the old city, amongst the Greeks and the Bokharians, the Jews and the Circassians, and they left the Genoese to themselves in Pera, pretending that they did not even exist. It was not always easy to keep up the pretence, it is true, for Zeno had extremely good eyes and could not help seeing those abominations of mankind on the other side of the Golden Horn when he sat in his balcony on spring evenings; and his only consolation was to dream of destroying them wholesale, of hewing them in pieces by the hundred and the thousand, and of piling up pyramids of their ugly grinning heads. Why were they Genoese? Carlo Zeno would rather have taken a box on the ear from Sultan Amurad, the Turk, over there in Asia Minor, than a civil word from the least objectionable of those utterly unspeakable monsters of Genoese. 'Behold,' said Tertullian one day in scorn, 'how these Christians love one another.' Matters had not improved in eleven hundred years, since that learned Doctor of the Church had departed this life, presumably for a more charitable world; but Carlo Zeno would have answered that the Genoese were no more Christians than mules, and much less so than the pigs, which are all under the special protection of the blessed Saint Anthony.

At the very time, too, when my story begins, those obnoxious villains of Genoa were on the successful side of a revolution; for they had helped Emperor Andronicus to imprison his father, Emperor John, in the tall Amena tower on the north side of the city, by the Golden Horn, and to lock up his two younger brothers in a separate dungeon. It was true that Emperor John had ordered Andronicus and his little son of five to be blinded with boiling vinegar, but Genoese money had miraculously converted the vinegar into bland white wine, and had reduced the temperature from the boiling point to that of a healthful lotion, so that neither the boy nor the man were any the worse after the application than before; but Andronicus had resented the mere intention on the part of his father, and had avenged himself by taking the Empire, such as it was, for the present, while reserving the delight of murdering his parent and his brothers at a convenient season in the future.

All this was very well, no doubt, and Andronicus was undisputed Emperor for the time being, because the Genoese and Sultan Amurad were willing that he should be; but Amurad had not always been his friend, and the Genoese had not always had the upper hand of the Venetians; the wind might change in a moment and a tempest might whirl him away from the throne even more quickly than the fair breeze had wafted him towards it.

Zeno thought so too, and wondered whether it would please fate to make him the spirit of the storm. He cared very little about Handsome John, as Paleologus was nicknamed, but he cared a great deal for a possible chance of driving the Genoese out of Pera and of getting the island of Tenedos for the Venetian Republic.

And now he had transacted the business of the day, and had dined on a roasted palamit, for it was a Friday and the palamit is the best fish that swims, from the Dardanelles to the Black Sea; and Zeno would no more have eaten meat on a day of abstinence than he would have sat down to table with a Genoese. He had been brought up to be a churchman, and though the attempt to make a priest of him had failed for obvious reasons, he was constant in observing those little rules and regulations which he had been taught to believe conducive to salvation, seeing that he was of a rash temper, prone to seek danger, and never sure of coming home alive when it pleased him to walk abroad. He was not a quarrelsome man on his own account, but he had a most wonderful facility for taking up the quarrels of other people who seemed to be in the right. The more hopeless the just case, or cause, the more certain it was that Carlo Zeno would take it up and fight for it as if it were his own.

But now, if ever, he was peacefully inclined; for the palamit had been done to a turn by the Dalmatian cook; the salad which had followed it had been composed to his liking, with shredded red peppers, pickled olives, anchovies, and cardamom seeds, all mixed among the crisp lettuce; and the draught of wine that had finished the meal had gleamed in the Murano glass like spirit of gold, and the flavour of it, as he had thoughtfully sipped it, had made him think of the scent that still sunshine draws from fruit hanging on vine and tree. He sat in a deep chair on his covered balcony, and was conscious that for the moment peace and privacy were almost as delightful as the best fight in the world. It would have been impossible to say more than that.

The sun was low, for the spring days were not yet long, and the shadow of the city already fell across the deep blue water of the Golden Horn. Zeno gazed down at the moving scene; his keen brown eyes watched the boats gliding by and softened, for what he saw made him think of Venice, the lagoons, and his home. Of all people, the most incorrigible wanderer is generally the most hopelessly sentimental about his native place.

Zeno had brown eyes that could soften like a woman's, but they were much more often keen and quick, turning suddenly to take in at a glance all that could be seen at all, until they fixed themselves with a piercing gaze on whatever interested their owner most for the time being,—his friend, or his adversary, his quarry if he were hunting, a woman's face or figure. He was not a big man, but he was thoroughly well made and well put together, elastic, tough, and active. His small brown hands, compact and firm, seemed ready to seize or strike at instant notice—the ideal hands of a fighting man. There was the same ready and fearless look in his clean-shaven face and small, energetic head, and when he moved his least motion betrayed the same gifts. Women did not think him handsome in those days, when the idea of beauty in man or woman alike was associated with fair or auburn hair and milk-white skin and cherry lips. In fact, Carlo Zeno hardly showed his lips at all, his thick hair was almost black, and his complexion was already as tanned and weather-stained as an old sailor's. But like many men of action he was careful of his dress, and extremely fastidious in his ways. In the ranks, the greatest dandies are often the best soldiers, explain the fact as you will. Some officers say that such men are far too vain to run away. Many a French noble who perished on the scaffold in the revolution bestowed more of his last moments on his toilet than he devoted to his prayers, and died like a hero and a gentleman. There are defects, like vanity, which may sometimes pass for virtues. Carlo Zeno was one of those men whose outward appearance is little affected by what they do, on whom the dust and heat of travel seem to leave no trace; who are invariably clean, neat, and fresh, the envy and despair of ordinary people. His dark-red velvet cap was always set on his thick hair at the same angle, and its sheen was as speckless as if dust did not exist. The narrow miniver border of his wine-coloured cloth coat was never ragged or worn at the edges; the fine linen, gathered at his throat and wrists, never betrayed the least suspicion of dinginess; the mud of Constantinople never clung to the soft Bulgarian leather of his well-made shoes.

Just now, the latter were stuck out in front of him as he leaned back in his deep chair and stretched his legs, asking himself vaguely whether he could be contented for any long time with the quiet life he was leading.

As if in answer to the question, his clerk and secretary, an important little grey-bearded personage, appeared on the balcony at that very moment with a letter in his hand.

'From Venice, sir,' said Omobono—that was his name—'and by the handwriting and the seal I judge it is written by Messer Marco Pesaro.'

Zeno frowned and then smiled, as he generally did at the manifestations of Omobono's incorrigible curiosity. It was the only defect of a most excellent person who was indispensable to Zeno's daily life, and invaluable in his business. Omobono had the sad and gentle face of an honest man who has failed on his own account, but whose excellent qualities are immensely serviceable to stronger men.

Zeno took the letter and glanced towards the harbour, far to the right of his house. Omobono made a short step backwards, but kept his eyes fixed on the paper.

'No foreign vessel has anchored to-day,' said the merchant; 'who brought this?'

'The captain of a Venetian ship, sir, which is anchored outside, before the Port of Theodosius.'

Zeno nodded carelessly as he cut the string. The letter was written on strong cotton paper from Padua, folded six times and secured by twisted hemp threads, of which the final knot had been squeezed into red wax and flattened under a heavy seal. Omobono watched his employer quietly, hoping to learn that he had rightly guessed the correspondent's name. Zeno, intent on reading, paid no attention to the secretary, who gradually edged nearer until he could almost make out the words.

This was what Zeno read, in very long sentences and in the Venetian dialect:—

MOST BELOVED AND HONOURED FRIEND—I despatch this writing by the opportunity of Sebastian Cornèr's good ship, sailing to-morrow, with the help of God, for Constantinople with a cargo of Florence cloth, Dalmatian linen, crossbows, Venetian lace, straw hats, and blind nightingales. May the Lord preserve the vessel, the crew, and the cargo from those unmentionable dogs of Genoese, and bring all safely to the end of the voyage within two months. The cloth, lace, and straw hats are mine, the rest of the cargo belongs to Sebastian Cornèr, except the nightingales, which are a gift from the Most Serene Republic to his majesty the Emperor, together with the man who takes care of the birds. What I say of my share in the cargo, most noble friend, is not as in the way of boasting myself a wealthy merchant, for indeed I am by no means rich, though by my constant industry, my sleepless watchfulness, and my honest dealing I have saved a crust of bread. Nay, I say it rather because I come with a request to you, and in order that you may know that there will be money due to me in Constantinople for the sale of this cargo, through the house of Marin Cornèr, the brother of Sebastian, who will pay you on your demand, most beloved and honoured friend, the sum of three hundred gold ducats. For I feel sure that you will undertake the business I ask, for love of me and a commission of a lira of piccoli for each ducat. I desire, in fact, that you will buy for me the most handsome slave that can be had for the money I offer, or even, if the girl were surpassingly beautiful, for three hundred and fifty ducats. The truth is, most noble friend, that my wife, who is, as you know, ten years older than I, and impeded by rheumatisms, is in need of a youthful and accomplished companion to help her to pass the time, and as I have always made it my duty and my business to fulfil and even, as in the present case, to anticipate her wishes, I am willing to spend this large sum of money for the sole purpose of pleasing her. Moreover I turn to you, most dear sir and friend, well knowing that your kindness is only matched by your fine taste. My wife would, I am sure, prefer as a companion a girl with fine natural hair, either quite black or very fair, the red auburn colour being so common here as to make one almost wish that women would not dye their hair at all. My dear and honoured friend, the teeth are a very important matter; pray give your most particular attention to their whiteness and regularity, for my wife is very fastidious. And also, I entreat you, choose a slave with small ankles, not larger than you can span with your thumb and middle finger. My wife will care less about a very small waist, though if it be naturally slender it is certainly a point of beauty. In all this, dearest sir, employ for love of me those gifts of discernment with which heaven has so richly endowed you, and I trust you will consider the commission a fair one. Sebastian Cornèr, who is an old man, will take charge of the slave and bring her to Venice, if you will only see that she is properly protected and fed until he is ready to sail, and this at the usual rate. I have also agreed with him that she is not to be lodged in the common cabin with the other female slaves whom he will bring from the Black Sea on his own account, but separately and with better food, lest she should grow unpleasingly thin. Yet it is understood that his regular slave-master is to be responsible for her protection, and will watch over her behaviour during the voyage. This, my most worthy, dear and honourable sir and friend, is the commission which I beg you to undertake; and in this and all your other affairs I pray that the hand of Providence, the intercession of the saints, and the wisdom of the one hundred and eighteen Nicene fathers may be always with you. From Venice. Marco Pesaro to the most noble patrician, Carlo Zeno, his friend. The fourteenth day of March in the year 1376.

Zeno smiled repeatedly as he read the letter, but he did not look up till he had finished it. His eyes met those of his secretary, who was now much nearer than before.

'Omobono,' said Zeno gravely, 'curiosity is unbecoming in a man of your years. With your grey beard and solemn air you are as prying and curious as a girl.'

Omobono looked contritely at his folded hands and moved the left one slowly within the right.

'Alas, sir,' he answered, 'I know it. I would that these hands held but a thousandth part of what my eyes have seen.'

'They would be rich if they did,' observed Zeno bluntly. 'It is fortunate that with your uncommon taste for other men's affairs you can at least keep something to yourself. Since you have no doubt mastered the contents of this letter as well as I—'

The good man protested.

'Indeed, sir, how could I have read a single word at this distance? Try for yourself, sir, for your eyes are far younger and better than mine.'

'Younger,' answered Zeno, 'but hardly better. And now send for Barlaam, the Syrian merchant, and bid him come quickly, for he may do business with me before the sun sets.'

'He will not do business to-day,' answered Omobono. 'This is Friday, which the Muslemin keep holy.'

'So much the worse for Barlaam. He will miss a good bargain. Send for Abraham of Smyrna, the Jewish caravan-broker.'

'He will not do business either,' said Omobono, 'for to-morrow is Sabbath, and Shabbes begins on Friday evening.'

'In the name of the blessed Mark our Evangelist, then send me some Christian, for Sunday cannot begin on Friday, even in Constantinople.'

'There is Rustan Karaboghazji, the Bokharian,' suggested Omobono.

Zeno looked sharply at the secretary.

'The slave-dealer?' he enquired.

Omobono nodded, but he reddened a little, poor man, and looked down at his hands again, for he had betrayed himself, after protesting that he knew nothing of the contents of the letter. Zeno laughed gaily.

'You are a good man, Omobono,' he said. 'You could not deceive a child. Do you happen to have heard that Rustan has what Messer Marco wants?'

But Omobono shook his head and grew still redder.

'Indeed, sir,—I—I do not know what your friend wants—I only guessed—'

'A very good guess, Omobono. If I could guess the future as you can the present, I should be a rich man. Yes, send for Rustan. I believe he will do better for me than the Jew or the Mohammedan.'

'They say here that it takes ten Jews to cheat a Greek, and ten Greeks to cheat a Bokharian, sir,' said Omobono.

'To say nothing of those Genoese swine who cheat the whole Eastern Empire! What chance have we poor Venetians in such a place?'

'May heaven send the Genoese the fate of Sodom and Gomorrah, and the halter of Judas Iscariot!' prayed Omobono very devoutly.

'By all means,' returned Zeno, 'I hope so. Now send for the Bokharian.'

Omobono bowed and left the balcony, and his employer leaned back in his chair again, still holding the folded paper in his hand. His expressive face wore a look of amusement for a while, but presently it turned into something more like good-natured contempt, as his thoughts went back from his secretary's last speech, to Marco Pesaro and his letter.

This Pesaro was a fat little man of forty, who had married a rich widow ten years older than himself. Carlo Zeno had known him well before he had been married, a boon companion, a jolly good-for-nothing who loved the society of younger men, and did them no good by example or precept. His father and mother had both perished in the great plague that raged in the year when Zeno was born, and Marco had been brought up by two old aunts who doted on him. The result usual in such cases had followed in due time; he had spent his own fortune and what he inherited from his aunts, who died conveniently, and when near forty he had found himself penniless, a poor relation of a great family, none the worse in health for nearly a quarter of a century of gaiety and feasting, and in temper much inclined to lead the same life for at least another twenty years. The heart was young yet, the round, pink face was absurdly youthful still, but the purse was in a state of permanent collapse, without any prospect of recovery. Then Marco sold everything he had, down to the sword which he had never drawn, and the jewelled dagger which had never done any worse damage than to cut the string of a love-letter; he sold his last silver spoons, his silver drinking-cup and the gold chain and ball from his cloak, and with the proceeds he gave a dozen of his friends one last farewell feast. Then, on the following day, his spirit broken and resigned to his fate, he offered himself to the very rich, elderly, and devout widow who had been making eyes at him for six months, and he was promptly accepted. With some of her money he engaged in the Eastern trade, renounced the follies of his youth, and became a respectable merchant.

It was affluence, it was luxury, but it was slavery and he knew it, and accepted the fact at first with much philosophy. Surely, he said to himself, a good cook and a good cellar, with a fine house at San Cassian, and a virtuous, if elderly, wife ought to satisfy any man of forty. The rest was but vanity. Could anything be more absurd, at his age, than to go on for ever playing the butterfly—such an elderly butterfly!—from one pair of bright eyes to another?

But he had counted without the fact that the butterfly is the final development of its genus and cannot turn into anything else. It must be a butterfly to the end. Poor Marco soon found that his heart was as susceptible as ever, and could beat like a boy's on very slight provocation, but that unfortunately it was never his rich wife who provoked it to such unseemly and lively action. Yet her facial angle inspired him with a terror even greater than the attraction of a pretty face and a well-turned figure. She had a way of setting her thin lips over her prominent teeth which at the same time stretched the skin upon the bridge of her hooked nose while she looked at him from under her half-closed lids, that made his blood run cold, robbed the richest sauce of its delicious flavour, and turned the wine of Samos to vinegar in his glass. Daily, she grew older, sharper, more irritable; and daily, too, the heart of Marco Pesaro seemed to grow younger and the more to crave the companionship of a mate much younger still, or at least the near presence of those outward, visible, and tangible gifts of the gods, such as a deep warm eye, and a soft white hand, with which man has always associated the heart of woman.

Zeno guessed all this and the rest too; the letter he had received needed no further explanation, and for old acquaintance's sake he had no objection to executing the commission Marco had thrust upon him.

And now, all you who stop and gather round the story-teller in this world's great bazaar, to listen, if his tale please you, and to find fault with him if it does not, you cry out that if Carlo Zeno was really the hero history describes him to have been, he would have been very, very grieved at being asked to do anything so inhuman as to buy a pretty slave abroad to be sent home to a friend, even though the latter protested that the girl was to be trained as a companion for his wife. He would have been grieved and angry, he would have torn the letter to shreds, and would either not have answered it at all, or would have written to tell Pesaro that he was a brute, that men and women are all free and equal, and that to buy and sell them is high treason against the majesty of the rights of men.

But to those protests and outcries the story-teller has many answers ready. In the first place, no one had even dreamt of the rights of men in 1376; and secondly, the trade in white slaves was almost as profitable to Venice then as it is in 1906 to certain great states the story-teller could name, with the advantage that there was no hypocritical secret about it, and that it was provided for in international treaties, in spite of the Pope, who said it was wrong; and thirdly, heroes are heroes for ever in respect of their heroic deeds, but in their daily lives they are very much like the other men of their class and time, as you will soon learn if you read the life of Bayard, 'without fear or reproach,' written by his Faithful Servitor; for the faithful one set down some doings of the virtuous knight which a modern biographer would have altogether left out, but which were no more a 'reproach' to a man in the year 1500, than getting drunk was a 'reproach' in 1700, or than stealing anything over a million is a 'reproach' to-day; fourthly and lastly, if Zeno had virtuously refused to buy a slave for Marco Pesaro, there would have been no story to tell, and this seems an excellent argument to the story-teller himself.

Zeno's thoughts soon wandered from Pesaro and the letter, and followed the old thread of life in Venice, till it led his soul through the labyrinth of daily existence far out into the dreamland beyond; and the place of his dreams was a calm and resplendent water, where stately palaces rose through vapours of purple and gold against an evening sky. Over the lagoon came music of old chimes from San Giorgio, and the deeper bells of Venice answered back again; at the instant the sunset breeze floated off the land and breathed into the dyed sails of the Istrians without a sound, so that the boats began to move by magic, gliding out one by one with a soft, low rush, heard only for a moment, as of a woman's hand drawn across silk.

The mere thought of Venice called up the vision of her before the inward eye of his heart; for he loved his native city better than he had ever loved any woman yet, and much better than his own life. When he could think of Venice, until the broad expanse of the lagoon seemed to spread itself over the deeper and darker waters of the Golden Horn, and when he could fancy himself at home, he was supremely and calmly happy, and would not have changed his dream for any reality except its own.

CHAPTER II

Omobono had drawn on a pair of well-greased raw-hide boots that came half-way up his thin legs, and had wrapped himself in his big brown cloak before going out. On his smooth grey head he wore a soft felt hat, the brim turned up round the crown at the back but pulled out to a long point in front, and he carried a tough cornel stick in his right hand. He had been careful to leave in the strong box the purse that contained money belonging to his employer, and had but a few small coins of his own in his wallet to pay a ferryman if he should need one, or to give to a hungry beggar. Like most men who have failed to make money Omobono was very sorry for poor people, and did not believe that all beggars could be rich if they would work. But he was poor himself, and his charity was of the humble kind.

There was a fairly broad street behind Carlo Zeno's house, and here the early spring sun had dried the mud to something like a solid surface; but Omobono followed this thoroughfare only for a little distance, and then turned into a narrow and filthy lane that led to other lanes, and to others still beyond, all crowded with humanity, all dark and muddy, all foul with garbage, all reeking with the overpowering smell of Eastern cooking made up of garlic, frying onions, sour cream, oil of sesame, and roasting mutton where there were Jews or Mohammedans, or fried fish where Christians lived, since it was Friday.

The small wooden houses, black with smoke and the dampness of the past winter, overhung the way so that the opposite balconies of the second stories almost touched each other. Had the buildings been higher, scarcely any light at all would have reached the lower windows; as it was, a man with good eyes might just see to read at noon if he were not too far within.

Omobono evidently knew his way well enough, for he did not pause as he threaded the labyrinth, and only now and then glanced up at certain dingy signs that hung from the crazy wooden balconies, or from wooden arms that stuck out here and there like gallows from the walls. As he walked, he was chiefly occupied in not running against the people he met, and in not stepping upon the half-naked children that squirmed and squalled in the mud before every doorstep. For there were children everywhere, children and dirt, dirt and children, all of much the same colour in those dusky lanes. Near almost every open door the slatternly mother stirred a dark mess of some sort over a little earthen pan of coals, or toasted gobbets of fat mutton on a black iron fork, or fried some wretched fish in boiling oil. The Christian women were by far the dirtiest, and their children were the least healthy and the most neglected, for many of the little creatures had not a stitch of clothing on them. Most decent were the Mohammedans; they had already the bearing and the self-respect of the conquering race, and they treated their Greek and Bokharian neighbours with silent contempt. Did not Sultan Amurad, over there on the Asian shore, make and unmake these miserable little Greek emperors as he pleased? If he chose could he not take Constantinople and turn a stream of Christian blood into the Golden Horn that would redden the Sea of Marmora as far as Antigone and Prinkipo?

Omobono went on and on, picking his way as he might, and little noticed by the people. He was not by any means in the poorest quarter of the city, and no one begged of him as he went by. If he thought of anything except of not setting his booted foot down on some child's sprawling leg or arm, he thanked heaven and the saints that he had been born a Venetian, and had been washed and sent to school like a Christian boy when he was little instead of having first seen the light, or what passed for light, in a back street of Constantinople.

He turned another corner, entered a lane even narrower than those he had yet traversed, but almost deserted, and much less dark because one side of it was occupied by a wall not more than ten feet high, in which only one small door was to be seen. Along the top of the masonry all sorts of sharp bits of rusty iron and a quantity of broken crockery were set in mortar with the evident intention of discouraging any attempt to climb over, either from within or from without. The door itself was in good repair, and had been recently coated with tar and sharp sand by way of preserving it against the damp. A well-worn horizontal slit an inch long, and an upright one a foot higher up, showed that it had two separate Persian locks into which keys were often thrust.

Omobono rapped on the tarred wood with the iron-shod end of his stick and listened. He could hear a number of girls' voices chattering, and one was singing softly in a language he did not understand. He knocked again, a moment later the voices were suddenly silent, and he heard the clacking of heavy slippers on wet flags as some one came to open.

'Who knocks?' asked a deep and harsh female voice from within, in the Greek tongue but with a thick accent.

'A Venetian who has business with the worthy Karaboghazji,' answered Omobono in a conciliatory tone.

'Which Karaboghazji?' enquired the voice suspiciously.

'Rustan,' explained Omobono mildly.

From his voice, the woman probably judged that if he had come with any nefarious purpose she was more than a match for him. The door opened after some rattling and creaking of locks, and Omobono started in spite of himself. She was indeed a match for him, or for any other man who was likely to knock at the door. It was no wonder that the Venetian secretary drew back and hesitated before he spoke again.

The woman was a huge red-haired negress in yellow, fully six feet tall in her heelless slippers, and her black arms, bare above the elbow, were as sinewy and muscular as any fisherman's or porter's. Her thick lips were parted in a sort of savage grin that showed two rows of teeth as sharp and white as a shark's; her hair must have been just dyed that day, for it was as red as flame to the very roots, and it stood out almost straight from her shiny black forehead and temples; as she rather contemptuously scrutinised Omobono from head to foot the whites of her coal-black eyes gleamed in a way that was positively terrifying. She wore wide Greek trousers of blue cotton, gathered at the ankle, and a wadded coat of yellow, that hung down below her knees in loose folds, like a sort of skirt, but fitted tightly over her tremendous shoulders. This garment was closely girded round her ample waist by a red sash, in which she carried her armoury, consisting of a serviceable Arab knife with a bone hilt and brass sheath, and a small whip made of a broad flat thong of hippopotamus hide with a short oak stock.

This terrific apparition stood in the little vestibule holding the door open and grinning at Omobono. She had closed another door behind her before opening the outer one, for the slave-dealer's establishment was evidently managed with a view to the safety of his merchandise.

'And what do you want of Rustan Karaboghazji at this time of the afternoon?' enquired the negress. 'Who are you?'

'I am only a clerk,' answered Omobono in a deprecating tone, and shrinking a little under his cloak, as the awful virago thrust her head forward. 'I am the clerk of Messer Carlo Zeno, a rich Venetian merchant, who sends a message by me to your master—'

'My master!' interrupted the black woman, with a scornful laugh. 'My master, indeed!'

'I—I supposed—' faltered Omobono apologetically.

The negress moved a little and rested one huge hand on her hip, while she slipped the other slowly up the door-post till it was above her head. In this attitude she looked gigantic.

'You mean my husband,' she said, showing all her teeth. 'Rustan Karaboghazji is my husband. Do you understand?'

'Yes, Kokóna—I—I mean Kyría—yes, certainly! I should have known at once that you were the mistress of the house if you had not condescended to open the door yourself, Kyría.'

'And what would become of the cattle,' enquired the negress with a backward toss of her head towards the yard behind her, 'if the stable door were in charge of a slave? If your master—' she dwelt on the two words contemptuously—'wishes to buy of us, he will have to come here and choose for himself.'

'No, no!' answered Omobono hastily. 'It is another matter. I think it is a commission for a friend. It is something very especial. That is why I beg to be allowed to speak with the Kyrios, your husband.'

The black woman had listened attentively.

'At this hour,' she said after a moment's thought, 'Rustan is at his devotions.'

'I would not interrupt them for the world,' protested Omobono. 'I can wait—'

'No. You will probably find him at the church of Saint Sergius and Saint Bacchus. If he is not there, ask the sacristan where he is. My husband is a very devout man; the sacristan knows him well.'

'I hope,' said Omobono, whose curiosity scented a mystery, 'that the sacristan will not take me for an importunate stranger and send me on a fool's errand. If the Kyría would give me some sign by which the sacristan may know that I came from her—'

Omobono paused on this suggestion, hoping for a favourable answer. Again the big woman waited a moment before speaking.

'Ask the sacristan to direct you to find Rustan Karaboghazji, by four toes and by five toes,' she said at last. 'He will certainly tell you the truth if you ask him in that way.'

'By four toes and by five toes,' repeated Omobono. 'I cannot forget that. I thank you, Kyría Karaboghazji, and I wish you a good day.'

The negress nodded and showed her teeth but said nothing more, drew back and shut the door without waiting any longer. Omobono stood still a moment, listened to the slapping of the heavy slippers on the wet flags within, and then went away down the almost deserted lane, wondering much at the taste of the Bokharian merchant in marrying an African giantess. But soon his natural curiosity began to occupy itself more actively with the hidden meaning of the password given him by Rustan's wife; and, meditating on this problem, he made his way through the heart of the city, traversing many narrow and tortuous streets, till he suddenly emerged into a broad highway where marble buildings gleamed in the late afternoon sunshine, and richly dressed Greeks lounged in the wide exedræ and stately porticoes, discussing the affairs of the Empire in general and their neighbours' most particularly.

Omobono trudged along, past the corner of the wide Forum of Theodosius, once the centre of the city's teeming life, but now given over to the tanners and leather-dressers, for one end of it was used as a slaughterhouse and the hides had not to be dragged far to be cured; he walked on quickly, keeping to the left, and was soon in narrow streets again, where afterwards the Grand Bazaar was built, and where even in those days the Persian merchants and the jewellers, the dealers in fine carpets and Eastern merchandise, the perfumers, the Egyptian goldsmiths and the Bokharian money-changers had their homes and the headquarters of their business. Here Omobono exchanged greetings now and then with men of all nationalities except Genoese, and very few of these last were to be seen, for they kept to their own quarter beyond the Golden Horn, in Pera. But Omobono would not stop to talk, and the streets were clean here, and well kept, and the children were not to be seen, so that he could walk quickly, without picking his way.

On still, and farther on; through the almost classic Forum of Constantine, past the hill on which the bronze-bound porphyry column still stands, and down on the other side, keeping the Hippodrome on his left and diving into the Bokharian quarter, as different from the last through which he had come, as that had been from those he had passed before. For then, as now, Constantinople was a patchwork of divers nations and languages and customs, and their quarters were like distinct towns,—some filthy, noisy and unhealthy, some rich and stately, some quiet and poor, some asleep all day and riotous all night, others silent as sleep itself from nightfall till dawn, and noisy all day with the hum of business or the ceaseless hammering clang and clatter of workmen's tools.

Before Omobono emerged upon the little square which then surrounded the churches of Saints Sergius and Bacchus and of Saints Peter and Paul—the latter is now destroyed—he heartily wished that he had hired a horse and man at one of the street corners; but he forgot his weariness when his destination was reached, and he saw a little bandy-legged sacristan in an absurdly short cassock of shabby black and purple cloth, leaning against one of the columns of the portico.

Omobono ascended the broad steps that led up from the level of the street, as though he were going in, but just as he was close to the sacristan he stopped, as if without any premeditation, and made a gesture of salutation, smiling in a friendly way.

'Praised be our Lord,' he said, in the Greek manner.

'Our Lord be praised. Amen,' answered the sacristan indifferently, for it was the custom to do so.

'Could you inform me,' proceeded the Venetian clerk, 'whether that good man Kyrios Rustan Karaboghazji is now in the church at his devotions?'

The sacristan had a perfectly round head with a pair of very small round eyes; moreover, his snub nose was quite round at the end. He now pursed out his lips and made his mouth round, too, as if he were going to whistle. Intentionally or unintentionally, he made himself look like an idiot, and slowly wagged his bullet head as if he did not understand.

'The church is open,' he said, at last. 'You may see,'

Omobono now applauded himself for having asked and obtained a password, but he meant to be cautious in using it.

'Thank you,' he said politely, and he went on, into the church.

The sun was low and cast a rich light through the open door, full upon the grating and closed gate of the sanctuary, and the gilt and burnished bars reflected and diffused the warm rays, like a glory before the unseen high altar. Omobono glanced quickly to the right and left as he passed between the pillars, but he saw no one. Farther on, before him and under the wide dome, two women in brown were at their prayers, the one kneeling, the other prostrate, in Eastern fashion, her forehead resting on the marble pavement. There was no man in sight.

Omobono chose a clean spot, hitched up his cloak in front and knelt upon one knee. He crossed himself and said a little prayer.

'O Lord,' he prayed, 'grant wealth and honour to the Most Serene Republic and give Venice the victory over the Genoese. Bless Messer Carlo Zeno, O Lord, and preserve him from sudden death. Send bread to the poor. Give Omobono strength to resist curiosity. For ever and ever. Amen.'

It was not a very eloquent little prayer and it lacked the set forms of invocation and doxology which devout persons use; but Omobono had made it up for himself long ago, and said it every day at least once, for it precisely expressed what he sincerely wished and intended to ask with due humility; and he was a good man, in spite of his besetting fault, and believed that what he asked would be granted. As yet, Venice had not triumphed over those unspeakable dogs of Genoese, though the day of glory was much nearer than even the Venetians dared to hope. But so far Carlo Zeno had been preserved from sudden death in spite of his manifest tendency to break his neck for any whim; for the rest, Omobono had more than once been the means of saving poor people from starvation, though at some risk of it to himself, poor man; and as for his curiosity, he had at least kept it so far in bounds as never to read his master's letters until his master had opened them himself, which was something for Omobono to be grateful for. On the whole, he judged that his small prayer was not unacceptable, and he used it every day.

He knelt a moment after he had finished it, partly because he was a little ashamed of its being very short though he never could think of anything to add to it, and he did not wish people to think that he was irreverent and gabbled over a prayer merely as a form; for he was very sensitive about such things, being a shy man. And partly he remained on his knees a little longer because the gilded grating was very handsome in the light of the setting sun, and reminded him of the grating in Saint Mark's, and that naturally made him think of heaven. But presently he rose and went out.

The sacristan was still standing by the same pillar.

'Kyrios Rustan is not in the church,' said Omobono, stopping again.

Once more the sacristan seemed to be about to purse his lips into a circle, and to put on an air of blank stupidity, and the clerk saw that the time had come to use the password.

'I must see him,' he said, dropping his voice, but speaking very distinctly. 'I beg you to direct me by four toes and five toes, so that I may find him.'

The sacristan's face and manner changed at once. His small eyes were suddenly full of intelligence, his mouth expanded in a friendly smile, and his snub nose seemed to draw itself to a point like the muzzle of a hound on a scent.

'Why did you not say that at once?' he asked. 'Rustan left the church a quarter of an hour before you came, but he is not far away. Do you see the entrance to the lane down there?'

He pointed towards the place.

'Yes,' said Omobono, 'by the corner.'

'Yes. Go into that lane. Take the first turn to the left, and then the second to the right again. Before you have gone far you will find Rustan walking up and down.'

'Walking up and down?' repeated Omobono, surprised that the Bokharian should select for his afternoon stroll such a place as one might expect to find in the direction indicated.

'Yes.' The sacristan grinned and winked at the Venetian clerk in a knowing way. 'He is a devout man. When he has said his prayers he walks up and down in that little lane.'

The man laughed audibly, but immediately looked behind him to see whether any one coming from within the church had heard him, for he considered himself a clerical character. Omobono thanked him politely.

'It is nothing,' answered the sacristan. 'A mere direction—what is it? If I had asked you for your purse and cloak by four toes and five toes, I am quite sure that you would have given me both.'

'Of course,' replied Omobono nervously, seeing that the reply was evidently expected of him. 'Of course I would. And so, good-day, my friend.'

'And good-day to you, friend,' returned the sacristan.

The clerk went away, devoutly hoping that no unknown person would suddenly accost him and demand of him his cloak in the name of four toes and five toes, and he wondered what in the world he should do if such a thing happened to him. He was quite sure that he should be unable to hide the fact that he knew the magic formula, for he had never been very good at deception; and if the words could procure such instant obedience from such a disagreeable person as the sacristan had at first seemed to be, some dreadful penalty was probably the portion of those who disobeyed the mandate.

Thus reflecting, and by no means easy in his mind, the clerk crossed the square and entered the lane. He had supposed that it led to a continuation of the Bokharian quarter, but he at once saw his mistake. Even now a man may live for years in Constantinople and yet be far from knowing every corner of it, and Omobono found himself in a part of the city which he had never seen. It was in ruins, and yet it was inhabited. Few of the houses had doors, hardly any window had a shutter, and as he passed, he saw that in many lower rooms the light fell from above, through a fallen floor and a broken roof above it.

Yet in every ruined dwelling, and almost at every door, there was some one, and all were frightful to see; all were in rags that hardly clung together, and some could scarcely cover themselves modestly; one was blind, another had no arms or no legs, another was devoured by hideous disease—many were mere bundles of bones in scanty rags, and stretched out filthy skeleton hands for alms as the decently dressed clerk came near. Omobono stood still for a moment when he realised that he was in the beggars' quarter, where more than half the dying paupers of the great city took refuge amidst houses ruined and burnt long ago when the Crusaders had sacked Constantinople, and never more than half repaired since then.

The clerk stood still, for the sight of so much misery hurt him, and it hurt him still more to think that he had but very few small coins in his wallet. The poor creatures should have them all, one by one, but there would be few indeed for so many.

And then, as he took out a little piece of bronze money, he heard sounds like nothing he had heard before; like many hundred sighs of suffering all breathed out together; and again, like many dying persons praying in low, exhausted voices; and again, like a gentle, hopeless wail; and through it all there was a pitiful tremor of weakness and pain that went to the clerk's heart. He could do very little, and he was obliged to go on, for his errand was pressing, and the people were as wretched at one door as they would be at the next, so that it was better not to give all his coins at once. He dropped one here, one there, into the wasted hands, and went on quickly, scarcely daring to glance at the faces that appeared at the low doors and ruined windows. Yet here and there he looked in, almost against his will, and he saw sights that sent a cold chill down his back, sights I have seen, too, but need not tell of. And so he went on, turning as the sacristan had instructed him, till he saw a tall, thin man in a brown cloth gown edged with cheap fox's fur, and having a tight fur cap on his head. He was talking with an old beggar woman, and his back was turned so that Omobono could only see that he had a long black beard, but he recognised Rustan, the Bokharian dealer. The house before which the two were standing seemed a trifle better than the rest in the street; there were crazy shutters to the large lower windows, which were open, however; there was a door which was ajar, and an attempt had been made to scrape the mud from the threshold. For the street was damp and muddy after the spring rains, but not otherwise very dirty. There was no garbage, not so much as a cabbage-stalk or a bleaching bone; for bones can be ground to dust between stones and eaten with water, and a cabbage-stalk is half a dinner to a starving man.

In spite of the prayer he had recently offered up against his besetting fault of curiosity, Omobono could not help treading very lightly as he came up behind the Bokharian, and as the mud was in a pasty state, neither hard nor slimy, his heavy boots made hardly any more noise in treading on it than a beggar's bare feet. In this way he advanced till he could see through an open window of the house, and he stood still and looked in, but he made as if he were politely waiting for Rustan to turn round. Either the old beggar woman was blind, or she thought fit not to call the Bokharian's attention to the fact that a well-dressed stranger was standing within a few feet of him. The two talked volubly in low tones and in the Bokharian language, which Omobono did not understand at all, and when he was quite sure that he could not follow the conversation he occupied his curiosity in watching what was going on inside the house. The window was low, having apparently once served as a shop in which the shopkeeper had sat, in Eastern fashion, half inside and half out, to wait upon his customers. During half a minute, which elapsed before Rustan turned round, the clerk saw a good deal.

In the first place his eyes fell on the upturned face of a woman who was certainly in the extremity of dangerous illness, and was probably dying. She had been beautiful once and she had beauty still, that was not only the soft shadow of coming death. The wasted body was covered with nameless rags, but the pillow was white and clean; the refined face was the colour of pure wax, and the dark hair, grey at the temples, had been carefully combed out and smoothed back from the forehead. The woman's eyes were closed, and deeply shadowed by suffering, but her delicate nostrils quivered now and then as she drew breath, and her pale lips moved a little as though trying to speak.

There were young children round the wretched bed, silent, thin, and wondering, as children are when the great mystery is very near them and they feel it. In their miserable tatters one could hardly have told whether the younger ones were boys or girls, but one was much older than the rest, and Omobono's eyes fixed themselves upon her, and he held his breath, lest the Bokharian should hear him and turn, and hide the vision and break the spell.

The girl was standing on the other side of the sick woman, bending down a very little, and watching her features with a look of infinite care and sorrow. One exquisite white hand touched the poor coverings of the bed, rather than rested on them, as if it longed to be of some use, and to relieve the woman's suffering ever so little. But the clerk did not look at the delicate fingers, for his eyes were riveted on the young girl's face. It was thin and white, but its lines were beautiful beyond comparison with all that he had ever seen, even in Venice, the city of beautiful women.

I think that true beauty is beyond description; you may describe the changeless, faultless outlines of a statue to a man who has seen good statues and can recall them; you can perhaps find words to describe the glow, and warmth, and deep texture of a famous picture, and what you write will mean something to those who know the master's work; you may even conjure up an image before untutored eyes. But neither minute description nor well-turned phrase, neither sensuous adjective nor spiritual simile can tell half the truth of a beautiful living thing.

And the fairest living woman is twice beautiful when gladness or love or anger or sorrow rises in her eyes, for then her soul is in her face. As Omobono looked through the window and watched the beggar girl leaning over her dying mother, he hardly saw the perfect line of the cheek, the dark and sweeping lashes or the deep brown eyes—the firm and rounded chin, the very tender mouth, the high-bred nostrils or the rich brown hair. He could not clearly recall any of those things a few minutes later; he only knew that he had seen for once something he had heard of all his life. It was not till he dreamt of her face that night—dreaming, poor man, that she was his guardian angel come to reprove him for his curiosity—that the details all came back, and most of all that brave and tender little mouth of hers, so delicately womanly and yet so strong, and that unspeakable turn of the cheek between the eye and the ear, and that poise of the small head on the slender neck—the details came back then. But in the first moment he only saw the whole and felt that it was perfect; then, for an instant, the eyes looked at him across the dying woman; and in a moment more the Bokharian turned, caught sight of him and came quickly forward, and the spell was broken.

Rustan Karaboghazji held out both hands to Omobono, as if he were greeting his dearest friend, and he spoke in fluent Italian. He was a young man still, not much past thirty, with dark, straight features, stony grey eyes, and a magnificent black beard.

'What happy chance brings you here?' he cried, immediately drawing the Venetian in the direction whence the latter had come. 'Fortunate indeed is Friday, the day of Venus, since it brings me into the path of my honoured Ser Omobono!'

'Indeed, it is no accident, Kyrios Rustan—' began Omobono.

'A double fortune, then, since a friend needs me,' continued the Bokharian, without the slightest hesitation. 'But do not call me Kyrios, Ser Omobono! First, I am not Greek, and then, my honoured friend, I am no Kyrios, but only a poor exile from my country, struggling to keep body and soul together among strangers.'

While he talked he had drawn Omobono's arm through his own and was leading him away from the house with considerable haste. The Venetian looked back, and saw that the old woman had disappeared.

'I have a message from my master,' he said, 'but before we go on, I should like to—' he hesitated, and stopped in spite of Rustan.

'What should you like to do?' asked the latter, with sudden sharpness.

Omobono's hand felt for the last of the small coins in his wallet.

'I wish to give a trifle to the poor people in that house,' he said, summoning his courage. 'I saw a sick woman—she seemed to be dying—'

But Rustan grasped his wrist and held it firmly, as if to make him put the money back, but he smiled gently at the same time.

'No, no, my friend,' he answered. 'I would not have spoken of it, but you force me to tell you that I have been before you there! I take some interest in those poor people, and I have just given enough to keep them for a week, when I shall come again. It is not wise to give too much. The other beggars would rob them if they guessed that there was anything to take. Come, come! The sun is setting, and it is not well to be in this quarter so late.'

Omobono remembered how the sacristan had winked and laughed, when he had spoken of Rustan's walks in the dismal lane, and the Venetian now proceeded to draw from what he had seen and heard a multitude of very logical inferences. That Rustan was an utter scoundrel he had never doubted since he had known him, and that his domestic life was perhaps not to his taste, Omobono guessed since he had seen the red-haired negress who was his wife. Nothing could be more natural than that the Bokharian, having discovered the beautiful, half-starved creature whom Omobono had first seen through the window, should plot to get her into his power for his own ends.

Having reached this conclusion, the mild little clerk suddenly felt the blood of a hero beating in his veins and longed to take Karaboghazji by the throat and shake him till he was senseless, never doubting but that the cause of justice would miraculously give him the strength needed for the enterprise. He submitted to be hurried away, indeed, because the moment was evidently not propitious for a feat of knight-errantry; but as he walked he struck his cornel stick viciously into the pasty mud and shut his mouth tight under his well-trimmed grey beard.

'And now,' said Rustan, drawing something like a breath of relief as they emerged into the open space before the church, 'pray tell me what urgent business brings you so far to find me, and tell me, too, how you came to know where I was.'

Here Omobono suddenly realised that in his deductions he had made some great mistake; for if Rustan had been in the beggars' quarter for such a purpose as the Venetian suspected, how was it possible that he should have left any sort of directions with his wife and the sacristan for finding him, in case he should be wanted on some urgent business? Omobono, always charitable, at once concluded that he had been led away into judging the man unjustly.

'Messer Carlo Zeno, the Venetian merchant, is very anxious to see you this very evening,' he said. 'From his manner, I suspect that the business will not bear any delay and that it may be profitable to you.'

Rustan smiled, bent his head and walked quickly, but said nothing for several moments.

'Does Messer Zeno need money?' he asked presently. 'If so, let us stop at my house and I will see what little sum I can dispose of.'

Mild as Omobono was, an angry, contemptuous answer rose to his lips, but he checked it in time.

'My master never borrows,' he answered, with immense dignity. 'I can only tell you that so far as I know he wishes to see you in regard to some commission with which a friend in Venice has charged him.'

Rustan smiled more pleasantly than ever, and walked still faster.

'We will go directly to Messer Zeno's house, then,' he said. 'This is a most fortunate day for buying and selling, and perhaps I have precisely what he wants. We shall see, we shall see!'

Omobono's thin little legs had hard work to keep up with the Bokharian's untiring stride, and though Rustan made a remark now and then, the clerk could hardly answer him for lack of breath. The sun had set and it was almost dark when they reached Zeno's house, and the secretary knocked at the door of his master's private room.

CHAPTER III

When it was quite dark the old woman came back with something hidden under her tattered shawl, and Zoë drew the rotten shutters that barely hung by the hinges and fastened them inside with bits of rain-bleached cord that were knotted through holes in the wood. She also shut the door and put up a wooden bar across it. While she was doing this she could hear Anastasia, the crazy paralytic who lived farther down the lane, singing a sort of mad litany of hunger to herself in the dark. It was the thin nasal voice of a starving lunatic, rising sharply and then dying away in a tuneless wail:—

Holy Mother, send us a little food, for we are hungry!

Kyrie eleeison! Eleeison!

Blessed Michael Archangel, gives us meat, for we starve! Eleeison!

O blessed Charalambos, for the love of Heaven, a kid roasted on the coals and good bread with it! Eleeison, eleeison! We are hungry!

Holy Sergius and Bacchus, Martyrs, have mercy upon us and send us a savoury meal of pottage! Eleeison! Pottage with oil and pepper! Eleeison, eleeison!

Holy Peter and Paul and Zacharius, send your angels with fish, and with meat, and with sweet cooked herbs! Eleeison, let us eat and be filled, and sleep! Eleeison! Spread us your heavenly tables, and let us drink of the good water from the heavenly spring!

Oh, we are hungry! We are starving! Eleeison! Eleeison! Eleeison!

The miserable, crazy voice rose to a piercing scream, that made Zoë shudder; and then there came a little low, faint wailing, as the mad woman collapsed in her chair, dreaming perhaps that her prayer was about to be answered.

Zoë had shut the door, and there was now a little light in the ruined room; for Nectaria, the old beggar woman, had been crouching in a corner over an earthen pan in which a few live coals were buried under ashes, and she had blown upon them till they glowed and had kindled a splinter of dry wood to a flame, and with this she had lit the small wick of an earthen lamp which held mingled oil and sheep's fat. But she placed the light on the stone floor so shaded that not a single ray could fall towards the door or the cracked shutters, lest some late returning beggar should see a glimmer from outside and guess that there was something to get by breaking in and stealing; for they were only three women, one dying, one very old, and the third Zoë herself, and two young children, and some of the beggars were strong men who had only lost one eye, or perhaps one hand, which had been chopped off for stealing.

When the light was burning Zoë could see that the sick woman was awake, and she poured out some milk from a small jug which Nectaria had brought, and warmed it over the coals in a cracked cup, and held it to the tired lips, propping up the pillow with her other hand. And the sick one drank, and tried to smile.

Meanwhile Nectaria spread out the rest of the supplies she had brought on a clean board; there was a small black loaf and three little fishes fried in oil, such as could be bought where food is cooked at the corners of the streets for the very poor. The two children gazed at this delicious meal with hungry eyes. They were boys, not more than seven and eight years old, and their rags were tied to them, to cover them, with all sorts of bits of string and strips of torn linen. But they were quite quiet, and did not try to take their share till Zoë came to the board and broke the black loaf into four equal portions with her white fingers. There was a piece for each of the boys, and a piece for Nectaria, and the girl kept a piece for herself; but she would not take a fish, as there were only three.

'This is all I could buy for the money,' said Nectaria. 'The milk is very dear now.'

'Why do you give it to me?' asked the sick woman, in a sweet and faint voice. 'You are only feeding the dead, and the living need the food.'

'Mother!' cried Zoë reproachfully, 'if you love us, do not talk of leaving us! The Bokharian has promised to bring a physician to see you, and to give us money for what you need. He will come in the morning, early in the morning, and you shall be cured, and live! Is it not as I say, Nectaria?'

The old woman nodded her head in answer as she munched her black bread, but would say nothing, and would not look up. There was silence for a while.

'And what have you promised the Bokharian?' asked the mother at last, fixing her sad eyes on Zoë's face. 'Did ever one of his people give one of us anything without return?'

'I have promised nothing,' Zoë answered, meeting her mother's gaze quietly. Yet there was a shade of effort in her tone.

'Nothing yet,' said the sick woman. 'I understand. But it will come—it will come too soon!'

She turned away her face on the pillow and the last words were hardly audible. The little boys did not hear them, and would not have understood; but old Nectaria heard and made signs to Zoë. The signs meant that by and by, when the sick woman should be dozing, Nectaria had something to tell; and Zoë nodded.

There was silence again till all had finished eating and had drunk in turn from the earthen jar of water. Then they sat still and silent for a little while, and though the windows and the door were shut they could hear the mad woman singing again:—

Eleeison! Spread heavenly tables! Eleeison! We are starving! Eleeison! Eleeison! Eleeison!

The sick woman breathed softly and regularly. The little boys grew sleepy and nodded, and huddled against each other as they sat. Then old Nectaria took the light and led them, half asleep, to a sort of bunk of boards and dry straw, in a small inner room, and put them to bed, covering them as well as she could; and they were soon asleep. She came back, shading the light carefully with her hand; and presently, when the sick woman seemed to be sleeping also, Nectaria and Zoë crept softly to the other end of the room and talked in whispers.

'She is better to-night,' said the girl.

Nectaria shook her head doubtfully.

'How can any one get well here, without medicine, without food, without fire?' she asked. 'Yes—she is better—a little. It will only take her longer to die.'

'She shall not die,' said Zoë. 'The Bokharian has promised money and help.'

'For nothing? he will give nothing,' Nectaria answered sadly. 'He talked long with me this afternoon, out in the street. I implored him to give us a little help now, till the danger is passed, because if you leave her she will die.'

'Did you try to make him believe that if he would help us now you would betray me to him in a few days?'

'Yes, but he laughed at me—softly and wisely as Bokharians laugh. He asked me if one should feed wolves with flesh before baiting the pit-fall that is to catch them. He says plainly that until you can make up your mind, we shall have only the three pennies he gives us every day, and if your mother dies, so much the worse; and if the children die, so much the worse; and if I die, so much the worse; for he says you are the strongest of us and will outlive us all.'

'It is true!' Zoë clasped her hands against the wall and pressed her forehead against them, closing her eyes. 'It is true,' she repeated, in the same whisper, 'I am so strong!'

Old Nectaria stood beside her and laid one wrinkled cheek to the cold wall, so that her face was near Zoë's, and they could still talk.

'If I refuse,' said the girl, quivering a little in her distress, 'I shall see you all die before my eyes, one by one!'

'Yet, if you leave your mother now—' the old woman began.

'She has lived through much more than losing me,' answered Zoë. 'My father's long imprisonment, his awful death!' she shuddered now, from head to foot.

Nectaria laid a withered hand sympathetically on her trembling shoulder, but Zoë mastered herself after a moment's silence and turned her face to her companion.

'You must make her think that I shall come back,' she whispered. 'There is no other way—unless I give my soul, too. That would kill her indeed—she could not live through that!'

'And to think that my old bones are worth nothing!' sighed the poor old woman; she took the rags of Zoë's tattered sleeve and pressed them to her lips.

But Zoë bent down, for she was the taller by a head, and she tenderly kissed the wrinkled face.

'Hush!' she whispered softly. 'You will wake her if you cry. I must do it, Ria, to save you all from death, since I can. If I wait longer, I shall grow thinner, and though I am so strong I may fall ill. Then I shall be worth nothing to the Bokharian.'

'But it is slavery, child! Do you not understand that it is slavery? That he will take you and sell you in the market, as he would sell an Arab mare, to the highest bidder?'

Zoë leaned sideways against the wall, and the faint light that shone upwards from the earthen lamp on the floor, fell upon her lovely upturned face, and on the outlines of her graceful body, ill-concealed by her thin rags.

'Is it true that I am still beautiful?' she asked after a pause.

'Yes,' answered the old woman, looking at her, 'it is true. You were not a pretty child, you were sallow, and your nose—'

Zoë interrupted her.

'Do you think that many girls as beautiful as I are offered in the slave market?'

'Not in my time,' answered the old woman. 'When I was in the market I never saw one that could compare with you.'

She had been sold herself, when she was thirteen.

'Of course,' she added, 'the handsome ones were kept apart from us and were better fed before they were sold, but we waited on them—we whom no one would buy except to make us work—and so we saw them every day.'

'He says he will give a hundred Venetian ducats for me, does he not?'

'Yes; and you are worth three hundred anywhere,' answered the old slave, and the tears came to her eyes, though she tried to squeeze them back with her crooked fingers.

The sick woman called to the two in a weak voice. Zoë was at her side instantly, and Nectaria shuffled as fast as she could to the pan of coals and crouched down to blow upon the embers in order to warm some milk.

'I am cold,' complained the sufferer, 'so cold!'

Zoë found one of her hands and began to chafe it gently between her own.

'It is like ice,' she said.

The girl was ill-clothed enough, as it was, and the early spring night was chilly; but she slipped off her ragged outer garment, the long-skirted coat of the Greeks, and spread it over the other wretched coverings of the bed, tucking it in round her mother's neck.

'But you, child?' protested the sick woman feebly.

'I am too hot, mother,' answered Zoë, whose teeth were chattering.

Nectaria brought the warm milk, and Zoë lifted the pillow as she had done before, and held the cup to the eager lips till the liquid was all gone.

'It is of no use,' sighed her mother. 'I shall die. I shall not live till morning.'

She had been a very great lady of Constantinople, the Kyría Agatha, wife of the Protosparthos Michael Rhangabé, whom the Emperor Andronicus had put to death with frightful tortures more than a year ago, because he had been faithful to the Emperor Johannes. Until her husband had been imprisoned, she had spent her life in a marble palace by the Golden Horn, or in a beautiful villa on the Bosphorus. She had lived delicately and had loved her existence, and even after all her husband's goods had been confiscated as well as all her own, she had lived in plenty for many months with her children, borrowing here and there of her friends and relatives. But they had forsaken her at last; not but that some of them were generous and would have supported her for years, if it had been only a matter of money, but it had become a question of life and death after Rhangabé had been executed, and none of them would risk being blinded, or maimed, or perhaps strangled for the sake of helping her. Then she had fallen into abject poverty; her slaves had all been taken from her with the rest of the property and sold again in the market, but old Nectaria had hidden herself and so had escaped; and she, who knew the city, had brought Kyría Agatha and her three children to the beggars' quarter as a last refuge, when no one would take them in. The old slave had toiled for them, and begged for them, and would have stolen for them if she had not been profoundly convinced that stealing was not only a crime punishable at the very least by the loss of the right hand, but that it was also a much greater sin because it proved that the thief did not believe in the goodness of Providence. For Providence, said Nectaria, was always right, and so long as men did right, men and Providence must necessarily agree; in other words, all would end well, either on earth or in heaven. But to steal, or kill by treachery, or otherwise to injure one's neighbour for one's own advantage, was to interfere with the ways of Providence, and people who did such things would in the end find themselves in a place diametrically opposite to that heaven in which Providence resided. Of its kind, Nectaria's reasoning was sound, and whether truly philosophical or not, it was undeniably moral.

Zoë was not Kyría Agatha's own daughter. No children had been born to the Protosparthos and his wife for several years after their marriage, and at last, in despair, they had adopted a little baby girl, the child of a young Venetian couple who had both died of the cholera that periodically visited Constantinople. Kyría Agatha and Rhangabé brought her up as their own daughter, and again years passed by; then, at last, two boys were born to them within eighteen months. Michael Rhangabé's affection for the adopted girl never suffered the slightest change. Kyría Agatha loved her own children better, as any mother would, and as any children would have a right to expect when they were old enough to reason. She had not been unkind to Zoë, still less had she conceived a dislike for her; but she had grown indifferent to her and had looked forward with pleasure to the time when the girl should marry and leave the house. Then the great catastrophe had come, and loss of fortune, and at last beggary and actual starvation; and though Zoë's devotion had grown deeper and more unselfish with every trial, the elder woman's anxiety now, in her last dire extremity, was for her boys first, then for herself, and for Zoë last of all.

The girl knew the truth about her birth, for Rhangabé himself had not thought it right that she should be deceived, but she had not the least recollection of her own parents; the Protosparthos and his wife had been her real father and mother and had been kind, and it was her nature to be grateful and devoted. She saw that the Kyría loved the boys best, but she was already too womanly not to feel that human nature must have its way where the ties of flesh and blood are concerned; and besides, if her adoptive mother had been cruel and cold, instead of only indifferent where she had once been loving, the girl would still have given her life for her, for dead Rhangabé's sake. While he had lived, she had almost worshipped him; in his last agonies he had sent a message to his wife and children, and to her, which by some happy miracle had been delivered; and now that he was dead she was ready to die for those who had been his; more than that, she was willing to be sold into slavery for them.

She stood by the bedside only half covered, and she tried to think of something more that she might do, while she gazed on the pale face that was turned up to hers.

'Are you warmer, now?' she asked tenderly.

'Yes—a little. Thank you, child.'

Kyría Agatha closed her eyes again, but Zoë still watched her. The conviction grew in the girl that the real danger was over, and that the delicately nurtured woman only needed care and warmth and food. That was all, but that was the unattainable, since there was nothing left that could be sold; nothing but Zoë's rare and lovely self. A hundred golden ducats were a fortune. In old Nectaria's hands such a sum would buy real comfort for more than a year, and in that time no one could tell what might happen. A turn of fortune might bring the Emperor John back to the throne. He had been a weak ruler, but neither cruel nor ungrateful, and surely he would provide for the widow of the Commander of his Guards who had perished in torment for being faithful to him. Then Zoë's freedom might be bought again, and she would go into a convent and live a good life to the end, in expiation of such evil as might be thrust upon her as a bought slave.

This she could do, and this she must do, for there was no other way to save Agatha's life, and the lives of the little boys.

'A little more milk,' said the sick woman, opening her eyes again.

Nectaria crouched over the embers, and warmed what was left of the milk. Zoë, watching her movements, saw that it was the last; but Kyría Agatha was surely better, and would ask for more during the night, and there would be none to give her; none, perhaps, until nearly noon to-morrow.

Nectaria took the pan of coals away to replenish it, going out to the back of the ruined house in order to light the charcoal in the open air. The sick woman closed her eyes again, being momentarily satisfied and warm.

Zoë sank upon her knees beside the bed, forgetting that she was cold and half-starved, as the tide of her thoughts rose in a wave of despair.

The fitful night breeze wafted the words of the mad woman's crooning along the lane, 'Eleeison! Eleeison!'

And Zoë unconsciously answered, as she would have answered in church, 'Kyrie eleeison!'

'Blessed Michael, Archangel, give us meat, we starve!' came the wild song, now high and distinct.

'Kyrie eleeison!' answered Zoë on her knees.

Then she sprang to her feet like a startled animal. Some one had knocked at the door. With one hand she gathered her thin rags across her bosom, the other unconsciously went to the sick woman's shoulder, as if at once to reassure her and to bid her be silent.

Again the knocking came, discreet still, but a little louder than before. Nectaria was still away and busy with the pan of coals, and the sick woman heard nothing, for she was sound asleep at last. Zoë saw this, and drew her bare feet out of her patched slippers before she ran lightly to the door.

'Who knocks?' she asked in a very low tone, clasping her tattered garment to her body.

The Bokharian's smooth voice answered her in oily accents.

'I am Rustan,' he said. 'I am suddenly obliged to go on a journey, and I start at dawn.'

Zoë held her breath, for she felt that the last chance of saving her mother was slipping away.

'Do you hear me?' asked Rustan, outside.

'Yes.'

'Will you make up your mind? I will give half as much again as I promised.'

The girl's face had been pale; it turned white now, for the great moment had come very suddenly. She made an effort to swallow, in order to speak distinctly, and she glanced towards the bed. Kyría Agatha was in a deep sleep.

'Have your brought the money with you?' Zoë asked, almost panting.

'Yes.'

The hand that grasped the rags to keep them together pressed desperately against her heart. While Rustan could have counted ten, there was silence. Twice again she looked towards the bed and then, with infinite precaution, she slipped out the wooden bar that kept the door closed. Once more she drew her rags over her, for they had fallen back when she used both her hands. She opened the door a little, and saw Rustan muffled in a cloak, his eager face and black beard thrust forward in anticipation of entering. But she stopped him, and held out one hand.

'My mother has fallen into a deep sleep,' she said. 'Give me the money and I will go with you.'

Without hesitation Rustan placed in her outstretched hand a small bag made of coarse sail-cloth, and closely tied with hemp twine.

'How much is it?' she whispered.

'One hundred and fifty gold ducats,' answered the Bokharian under his breath, for he knew that if he did not wake the sleeping woman there would be less trouble.

At that moment Nectaria came back from within, with the pan of coals. Zoë caught her eye and held out the heavy little bag. The woman stared, looked at Kyría Agatha's sleeping face, set down the pan upon the floor, and came forward.

'He has brought the money, a hundred and fifty ducats,' Zoë whispered, forcing the bag into Nectaria's trembling hands. 'It is the only way. Good-bye—quick—shut the door before she wakes—tell her I am asleep in the straw—God bless you—'

'Eleeison! Eleeison!' came the wail of the mad woman on the wind.

Before Nectaria could answer Zoë had pulled the door till it shut behind her, and was outside, barefooted on the hardening mud, and scarcely covered. She said nothing now, and Rustan was silent too, but he had taken one of her wrists and held it firmly without hurting it. The fleet young creature might make a dash for freedom yet, foolish as that would be, since he could easily force his way into the ruined house and take back his money if she escaped him. But he had nearly lost a young slave once before, and he would risk nothing, so he kept his strong hand tightly clasped round the slender wrist, though Zoë walked beside him quietly in the deep gloom, thinking only of covering herself from his gaze, though indeed he could scarcely see the outline of her figure.

They went on quickly. For the last time, as Rustan led her round a sharp turn, she heard the wild cry of the poor mad creature she had listened to so often by day and in the dead of night. Then she was in another street and could hear it no more.

She was not allowed time to think of her condition yet. A few steps farther and Rustan stopped short, still holding her fast by the wrist, and she saw that they had come upon a group of men who were waiting for them. One suddenly held up a lantern which had been covered, and now shed a yellow light through thin leaves of horn, and Zoë saw that he was a big Ethiopian, as black as ebony. She drew her tatters still more closely over her with her free hand and turned away from the light, as well as Rustan's unrelaxing hold would allow.

A moment later some one she could not see threw a wide warm cloak over her shoulders from behind her, and she caught it gladly and drew the folds to her breast.

'Get into the litter,' said Rustan, sharply but not loudly.

There was nothing soft or oily in his tone now. He had bought her and she was a part of his property. Four men had lifted a covered palanquin and held it up with the small open door just in front of her. She turned, sat upon the edge, and bent her head to slip into the conveyance backwards, as Eastern women learn to do very easily. Rustan held her wrist till she was ready to draw in her feet, and as he let her go at last she disappeared within. He instantly closed the sliding panel and fastened it with a bronze pin. There were half-a-dozen round holes in each door to let in air, not quite big enough to allow the passage of an ordinary woman's hand.

Zoë sank back in the close darkness and found herself leaning against yielding pillows covered with soft leather. The palanquin began to move steadily forwards, hardly swaying from side to side, and not rising or falling at all, as the porters walked on with a smooth, shuffling gait, each timing his step a fraction of a second later than that of the man next before him; lest, by all keeping step together, they should set their burden swinging, which is intolerable to the person carried.

Four men carried the litter, a fifth, armed with an iron-shod staff, went before with the lantern, and Rustan followed after. There was nothing in the appearance of the party to excite surprise or curiosity in a city where every well-to-do person who went out in the evening was carried in a palanquin, and accompanied by at least two trusty servants. For that matter, too, Rustan's business was perfectly legitimate, and it concerned no one that he should have a newly bought beauty carried in a closed litter from a distant quarter of the city to his home.

It was true that he had no receipt for his money, acknowledging that it was the stipulated price paid for a full-grown white maid between eighteen and nineteen years old, with brown eyes, brown hair, twenty-eight teeth, all sound, and a pale complexion; who weighed about two Attic talents and five minæ, and measured just six palms, standing on her bare feet. In strict law, he should have had such a document, signed by the father or mother or owner of the slave, but he knew that he was quite safe without it. Like all Bokharians, he was a profound judge of human nature, and he was quite sure that having once submitted to her fate Zoë would not cheat him by claiming the freedom she had sacrificed; moreover, he knew that the adopted daughter of Michael Rhangabé who had died on the stake in the Hippodrome as an enemy of the reigning Emperor, would have but a small chance of obtaining justice, even if she attempted to prove that she had been carried off by force. Rustan Karaboghazji felt that his position was unassailable as he followed the litter that carried his latest bargain through the winding streets of Constantinople towards the narrow lane, one side of which was formed by that mysterious wall which had but one door in it.

He was well pleased with his day's business, for he was quite sure that he had netted a handsome profit. Under his cloak he held a string of beads in one hand, and as he walked he made the calculation of his probable gains, pushing the beads along the string with his thumb. He had paid one hundred and fifty gold ducats for Zoë; but fifty of them were at least a quarter of their value under weight, so that the actual value of the gold was one hundred and thirty-seven and a half ducats. He was quite sure that Zeno would approve the purchase on a careful inspection, and that he would be willing to give three hundred and fifty sequins, though the girl was a little over age, as slaves' ages were counted. She should have been between sixteen and seventeen, yet she was exceptionally pretty, and spoke three languages—Greek, Latin, and Italian. If Zeno paid the price, the clear profit would be two hundred and twelve and a half ducats. The beads worked quickly in Rustan's fingers, and his hard grey eyes gleamed in the dark. Two hundred and twelve and a half on one hundred and thirty-seven and a half, by the new Venetian method of so much in the hundred, which was a very convenient way of reckoning profits, meant one hundred and fifty-four and a half per centum. The beads worked furiously, as the merchant's imagination carried him off into a mercantile paradise where he could make a hundred and fifty per cent on his capital every day of the year except Sundays and high feast days. This calculation was complicated, even for a Bokharian brain, but it was a delightful one to follow out, and Rustan's blood coursed pleasantly through his veins as he walked behind his purchase.

He had lost no time after he had left the beggars' quarter late in the afternoon, by no means sure that Zoë meant to surrender at all, and very doubtful as to her doing so within the next three days. Yet he had boldly promised that Carlo Zeno should see her on approval on the following morning. After all, he risked nothing but a first failure, for if he did not succeed in buying Zoë in time he could nevertheless show the Venetian merchant some very pretty wares. Zeno was not a man to waste words with such a creature as a slave-dealer, and the interview had not lasted ten minutes. It had taken longer than that to weigh the ducats in order to be sure that a certain number of them were under weight. The only thing Rustan now wished was that he had put many more light ones into the bag, since it had not even been opened; for he had naturally expected to be obliged to count them out before old Nectaria, who had a born slave's intelligence about money.

Inside the litter the girl lay on her cushions in the dark, wondering with a sort of horror at what she had done. She had thought of it indeed, through many days and sleepless nights, and she did not regret it; she would not have gone back, now that she had left plenty and comfort where there had been nothing but ruin and hunger; but she thought of what was before her and prayed that she might close her eyes and die before the morning came, or better still, before the litter stopped and Rustan drew back the sliding door.

In an age and a land of slavery, the slave's fate was familiar to her. She knew that there were public markets and private markets, and that her beauty, which meant her value, would save her from the former; but to the daughter of freeborn parents the difference between the one and the other was not so great as to be a consolation. She would be well lodged, well covered, and well fed, it was true, and she need not fear cruel treatment; but customers would come, perhaps to-morrow, and she was to be shown to them like a valuable horse; they would judge her points and discuss her and the sum that Rustan would ask; and if they thought the price too high they would go away and others would come, and others, till a bargain was struck at last. After that, she could only think of death as the end. She knew that many handsome girls were secretly sold to Sultan Amurad and the Turkish chiefs over in Asia Minor or in Adrianople, and it was more than likely that she herself would fare no better, for the conquerors were lavish with their gold, whereas the Greeks were either half-ruined nobles or sordid merchants who counted every penny.

The men carried the litter smoothly and steadily, never slackening and never hastening their pace. The time seemed endless. Now and then she heard voices and many steps, with the clatter of horses' hoofs, which told her that she was in one of the more frequented streets, but most of the time she heard scarcely anything but the shuffling walk of the men in their heavy sandals and the firmer tread of Rustan's well-shod feet where the road was hard. She guessed that he was avoiding the great thoroughfares, probably because the people who thronged them even at that hour would have hindered the progress of the palanquin. Zoë knew as well as the dealer that there was nothing as yet in the transaction which need be hidden; possibly, if she were afterwards sold to the Turks, she would be taken across the Bosphorus secretly, for though there was no law against selling Christian girls to unbelievers the people of the city looked upon the traffic with something like horror, and an angry crowd might rescue the merchandise from the dealer's hands. Zoë did not expect that rare good fortune, for Rustan was not a man to run any risks in his business.

As she lay among her cushions, dreading the end of the journey, but gradually wearying of the future, her thoughts went back to the first cause of all her misfortunes, of Michael Rhangabé's awful death, of all the suffering that had followed them. One man alone had wrought that evil and much more, one man, the reigning Emperor Andronicus. Zoë was not revengeful, not cruel, very far from bloodthirsty; but when she thought of him she felt that she would kill him if she could, and that it would only be justice. Suddenly a ray of something like hope flashed through her darkness. Nectaria had told her how beautiful she was; perhaps, being so much more valuable than most of the slaves that went to the market, she might be destined for the Emperor himself. It was just possible. She set her teeth and clenched her little hands in the dark. If that should be her fate, the usurper's days were numbered. She would free her country from its tyrant and be revenged for Rhangabé's murder and for all the rest at one quick stroke, though she might be condemned to die within the hour. That was indeed something to hope for.

The litter stopped and she heard keys thrust into locks, and felt that the porters turned short to the left to enter a door. Her journey through the city was at an end.

CHAPTER IV

Rustan stayed behind to shut the outer door, and Zoë felt that she was carried as much as twenty paces forward and upwards before the bearers stood still at last. Then the sliding panel opened, letting in light, and a strange voice told her to get out. She turned inside the palanquin and thrust out her naked feet. As she put them down, expecting to touch bare earth or a stone pavement, they rested on a rough carpet; at the same instant she sat on the edge of the litter bending her head to get out of it and looking round curiously.

Rustan was not there, and in his place she saw a huge young negress with flaming red hair and rolling eyes, who roughly ordered the porters to take away the palanquin and at the same time caught Zoë's wrist, whether to help her to stand upright or to secure her person it was hard to say. The girl was much more fearless than Omobono, the Venetian secretary, and she was not frightened by the gigantic woman's appearance, as he had been. In getting out she had managed to gather the cloak round her, so that the men should not see her in her rags; for there was light in the large room where she found herself, and now that she could look about her she saw a dozen or more girls and young women standing in small groups a few paces behind the negress. They surveyed the new arrival curiously, but with different expressions. Some seemed to pity her, others smiled as if to welcome her; one good-looking girl had noticed that she had no shoes, and her lip curled contemptuously at such a proof of abject poverty, for she herself was the daughter of a prosperous Caucasian horse-thief who had brought her up in plenty and ease in order that she might fetch a high price. The bearers had now left the room and there were no men present. Zoë vaguely wished that they would come back, even the black bearers of the litter, for she felt a very womanly woman's distrust of her own sex, where so many who were strangers, and possibly not well-disposed to her, were gathered together to look at her.

The negress surveyed her critically by the light of the large bronze lamp that stood on a stand beside her, and showed her sharp teeth in an approving smile that made her thick upper lip roll upwards on itself. She took the cloak from Zoë's shoulders and scrutinised her half-clad figure, till she blushed red. Then the daughter of the Caucasian horse-thief laughed rudely, and some of the others tittered while the negress gently pinched Zoë's bare arms and neck to judge of their firmness and of her general condition. Apparently the examination was tolerably satisfactory, for the woman nodded and grinned again. As yet not a word had been spoken since she had dismissed the bearers, but now she turned towards the other girls and called two of them.

'Lucilla and Yulia, you shall wait on her,' she said in Greek. 'The rest of you, to bed! It is already three hours of the night.'

Two dark-skinned girls in coarse blue linen clothes came forward with alacrity, evidently much pleased at being chosen for the office. They were ordinary slave-girls of fourteen or fifteen years, who would be sold for house-work, and had no pretensions to good looks. Their tightly plaited black hair was compressed into the smallest possible space at the backs of their heads, and they wore small red caps, coarsely embroidered, but neat and fresh. Their faces were much alike though they were not sisters. Zoë saw instantly that they were children of slaves of nondescript breed with a small admixture of African blood, of the race that swarmed in Constantinople.

'Go to bed, I say!' cried the negress to the others, seeing that some of them were inclined to linger. 'Be off!'

They saw her hand move towards the whip in her girdle and they ran for the door, crowding on each other like sheep at the gate when the dogs drive them into the fold. Having produced this desired result, the negress turned to Zoë again, and her manner suddenly became caressing and almost fawning.

'You are mistress here, Kokóna,' she said. 'These two girls shall wait on you while our humble roof is honoured by your presence. If you have the slightest cause of discontent with their service, only tell me, and they shall be taught their duty.'

Again her hand went significantly to her girdle, and she rolled her terrible eyes. The two maids shrank visibly at a threat of which they had already felt the meaning.

Zoë was not so dull as to misunderstand the negress's manner. The favourite slave of some high and mighty personage, of the Emperor himself, perhaps, would have power, if only for a time, and the wife of Karaboghazji lost no time in making a bid for such patronage.

'I am a slave, as these girls are,' Zoë answered, laying a kindly hand on the shoulder of the one nearest to her.

Both maids gazed up into her face with a sort of wondering gratitude.

'I am here to be sold, just as you are,' Zoë added, returning their look. The negress laughed loudly, for she was evidently in a good humour.

'Also the noble peacock and the sparrow are both birds, though the feathers are different!' she cried. 'But the Kokóna is hungry and cold,' she continued, in a tone of servile anxiety for Zoë's comfort. 'Will she not perhaps take a bath and change her clothes before supper? Everything is ready.'

'I have supped,' answered Zoë, who had eaten a piece of black bread, 'but as for clothes, I should like to put on the cloak again, for I feel cold.'

She had hardly spoken before the two maids had wrapped her in the warm mantle.

'Thank you,' she said to them, and she turned to the negress. 'You seem to be mistress here. May I go to bed now?'

'Yes, I am the mistress,' answered the African woman, all her teeth gleaming in the lamplight. 'I am Rustan Karaboghazji's wife, Kokóna.'

Zoë could not repress a movement of surprise. The negress laughed.

'Rustan is a wise man,' she said with a tremendous grin. 'It is cheaper to marry one woman with a strong hand than to keep a couple of smooth-faced thieves for gaolers, as most of the people in our business do. If the Kokóna will please to follow me I will show her the room I have prepared.'

Zoë bent her head and followed, for the negress was already leading the way. They entered a room of fair dimensions which had evidently been got ready with considerable care, for it contained everything that a woman accustomed to comfort could require. A good Persian carpet covered the floor; a narrow, but handsomely chiselled bronze bedstead was furnished with two mattresses, spotless linen, and a warm coverlet of silk and wool; on a marble table stood a little mirror of polished metal, before which lay two ivory combs and a number of ivory and silver hairpins and other little things needful for a woman's toilet; there stood also a gilt lamp with three beaks, which shed a pleasant light upon everything; a low curtained door at the end of the room gave access to the small bathroom, where another little lamp was burning. The negress drew the curtain back and showed the place to Zoë, who had certainly not expected to spend her first night of slavery in such luxurious quarters. Rustan's wife opened a large wardrobe, too, and showed her a plentiful supply of fine linen and clothes, neatly folded and lying on shelves. In the middle of the room a round table was prepared with three dishes, one containing some small cold birds, another a salad, and a third mixed sweetmeats, and there was also wine and water in small silver flagons, and one silver drinking-cup. It was long indeed since Zoë had seen anything like this, and her eyes smarted suddenly when she realised that the slave-dealer's prison reminded her faintly of her old home. For it was a prison after all; she guessed that beyond the shutters of the closed window there were stout iron bars, and as she had entered she had seen a big key in the lock on the outside of the door.

'It is late,' said the negress, when she had shown everything. 'The girls will sleep on the floor, for the carpet is good and there are two blankets for them, there in the corner. Good-night, Kokóna. By what name shall I call the Kokóna? The Kokóna will excuse her servant's ignorance!'

Zoë hesitated a moment. She had not thought of changing her name, but now she felt all at once that as a slave she must cut off all connection with her former life. What if the personage who was to buy her should turn out to have known her mother, and even herself, and should recognise her by her name? A resemblance of face could be explained away, but her face and her name together would certainly betray her. It was not so much that she feared the open shame of being recognised as Michael Rhangabé's adopted daughter; she had grown used to the meaning of the word slavery during those last desperate days. But people would not fail to say that Kyría Agatha had sold her adopted daughter into slavery in order to save herself and her own children from misery. Zoë could prevent that, and she only hesitated long enough to choose the name by which she was to be known.

'Call me Arethusa,' she said.

Her thoughts had flown back to the deed of justice she meant to do if she should ever be near the Emperor Andronicus; and if Areté had come later to mean virtue, it had meant courage first, manly, unflinching courage; and as Zoë was only a Greek girl and not a German professor, she naturally supposed that Areté was the very word from which Arethusa was derived.

'It is a fine name,' observed her gaoler obsequiously.

'And what shall I call you?' asked Zoë.

'I am Kyría Karaboghazji.' The negress tossed her flaming head and smiled with satisfied vanity. 'My husband calls me Zoë,' she added, with an amazing smirk, and some affectation of shyness.

'Zoë!' The high-born girl repeated her own name in genuine astonishment.

'Yes,' replied the negress. 'Rustan is very affectionate. He says that I am his Zoë, his "life," because he would surely die of starvation without me!'

'I see,' said the Greek girl.

She would not have believed that before lying down in her prison that night she would be forced to make an effort to suppress a laugh.

'And now it is growing late,' said the negress again, 'and Rustan is wondering why I do not come to comb his beard and smooth his pillow, and prepare his drink for the night. Good-night, Kokóna Arethusa! May Holy Charalambos send you dreams of delight!'

'And to you also, Kyría Karaboghazji,' Zoë answered, though the form of the woman's salutation was new to her.

The negress went out, still much pleased with herself, and swaying her massive hips as she walked. She shut the door, and Zoë heard the big key move in the lock.

The two slave-girls had stood at a respectful distance throughout the conversation, their hands crossed submissively and their eyes bent on the floor, for Rustan's wife had already taught them manners in order to improve their price. But she was no sooner gone than they looked at each other, and their lips began to twitch nervously; in another moment they were both seized with a convulsion of silent laughter. They shook from head to foot, they held their sides, they bent and swayed, and twisted their hands together, but not a sound escaped their lips. Beyond this, they could not control their mirth, and while they laughed they looked anxiously at Zoë.

She herself could not help smiling when she thought of the negress's enormous self-satisfaction, but presently she shook her head at the girls and laid her finger on her lips. Their amusement subsided quickly, for though she seemed kind, they knew what they had to expect if one word from her should expose them to the negress's displeasure.

Zoë was very tired, now that the great sacrifice was made, and she let the slave-girls help her as much as they would. They even made her eat something and drink a little water. Now and then, when they looked up at her, she patted them on the shoulder and smiled faintly, but her thoughts were far away in the ruined house in the beggars' quarter. When the girls had helped her in the bath and had dried her feet that had been stained with mud and blue with the cold, they chafed them with their hands and kissed them.

'They are like two little white mice!' said Yulia, laughing softly.

'No, they are like young doves!' said Lucilla.

And they each slipped one of her feet into a slipper of deerskin; and then they clothed her for the night, in fine dry linen and a small green silk jacket. They were skilful with their hands though they were still so young, and she let them do what they thought she needed, and lay down at last, to be covered and tucked in as warmly and comfortably as when Kyría Agatha used to put her to bed, before the boys had been born and had taken her place.

In a few minutes the little maids had put out the lamp, leaving only the small light in the bath; then they noiselessly devoured all the sweetmeats left on the table, after which they curled themselves upon the carpet under their blankets and were asleep in a moment, like young animals.

For a few moments Zoë still tried to think; tired though she was, she hated herself for being able to rest in such comfort while Kyría Agatha was perhaps awake under her pile of rags, and Nectaria was hugging the straw to keep a little warmth in her old body. But then she thought of the morrow, and of all that Nectaria would do with the gold for the sick woman and the little boys, and in this soothing reflexion she was borne softly away out of this world of slavery, through the ivory gates to the infinite gardens of dreamland.

She was waked by the sunshine streaming into the room through the window, and as she opened her eyes she saw the iron bars, and remembered where she was. She sighed, for she had been happy in her sleep. The girls were sitting cross-legged on the carpet, side by side, at a little distance, silently awaiting her pleasure. She turned her head on the pillow and lay on one side, looking at their small dark faces; but she did not speak to them yet. They were very much alike, she thought, commonplace girls, differing so little from thousands of other young slaves in the great city, that it would be hard for her to recognise them, if she should not see them for a few days. They would be disposed of soon, of course, for there was always a demand for healthy young house slaves who had been properly taught. She envied them their homely features, their coarse black hair, their angular figures, their sallow cheeks, and their cunning little black eyes. They could only be sold as workers. All her life Zoë had heard the price of house-slaves discussed, even more freely than the price of clothes or jewels, and she knew that neither of the girls was worth more than five-and-twenty ducats. She wondered what Rustan meant to ask for herself; he would certainly not demand less than double the sum he had paid.

While she was reflecting on these questions, and wishing all the time that she might have news of Kyría Agatha during the day, the big key moved in the Persian lock. The two girls sprang to their feet and stood in a respectful attitude, Zoë turned her eyes as she heard the sound, the door opened, and the negress's flaming head appeared in the sunlight. She saw that Zoë was awake, and she entered the room, shutting the door behind her. She greeted her valuable prisoner in the half-familiar, half-obsequious tone she had adopted from the first, asking her how she had slept, and whether the little maids had done their duty. The latter question was accompanied by a fierce look at the two girls. Zoë answered that they were most skilful and well behaved. The negress looked at the remains of the supper on the table.

'So the Kokóna Arethusa is fond of sweetmeats,' she observed. 'She eats only a mouthful from one bird and all the sugar-plums!'

Zoë was on the point of uttering an exclamation of surprised denial, when she met the terrified eyes of the two slave-girls and checked herself with a smile.

'I am very fond of sweets,' she answered carelessly.

The black woman seemed satisfied and turned from the table. She opened the wardrobe next, and selected what she considered the handsomest of the dresses that lay folded on the shelves within. Zoë watched her curiously. She unfolded garments of apple-green silk, and one of peach-coloured Persian velvet embroidered with silver, with a sash of plaited green silk and gold threads. The two girls took the things from her and laid them out.

'Surely,' Zoë said, 'you do not wish me to wear those clothes!'

'They are very good clothes,' observed the negress coaxingly. 'Look at this velvet coat! There are even seed-pearls in the embroidery, and it is quite new and fresh. My husband bought it from the Blachernæ palace, when Handsome John was imprisoned. It belonged to one of the favourite ladies. The slaves who ran away stole all the things and sold them.'

'I would rather wear something plainer,' said Zoë; but at the mention of the captive Emperor her brown eyes had grown very dark and hard, and her voice almost trembled.

'Kokóna Arethusa must look her best this morning,' objected Rustan's wife. 'She will receive a visit.'

Zoë started a little, and instinctively drew the bed-clothes up to her chin.

'Already!' she exclaimed in a low tone.

The negress grinned from ear to ear.

'The Kokóna will perhaps not spend another night under our humble roof,' she said. 'I do not know anything certainly as yet, because the customer has not seen you,' she continued more familiarly, 'but Rustan has consulted the astrologer, who says that these are fortunate days for our buying and our selling. So I do not doubt but that the customer will be pleased with your looks, Kokóna, for indeed, though I do not wish to flatter you, we have not entertained such a beauty in our modest home for a long time!'

All this was, of course, intended to put Zoë in a good humour, in order that she might produce an agreeable impression on the expected purchaser. Rustan had once missed a very good bargain because the merchandise had burst into tears at the wrong moment.

'What sort of person is the customer?' asked the girl. 'Do you know who he is?'

She asked the question quietly, but she held her breath as she waited for the reply.

'I forget his name,' answered the negress after a moment's thought. 'He is a foreigner, a rich young merchant who lives in a fine house by the Golden Horn.'

'A Christian, then?' Zoë asked, controlling her voice.

The other pretended to be shocked.

'Does the Kokóna Arethusa believe that Rustan would be so wicked as to sell a Christian maid to the Turks? Rustan is a very devout man, Kokóna! He would not do such an irreligious thing!'

Zoë remembered the allowance of three copper pennies daily, and how he had driven her to sell herself for Kyría Agatha's sake; but she did not care to impugn Rustan's piety.

'So the astrologer says that I shall be sold to-day,' she observed with an affectation of carelessness, though her heart was sinking, and she felt a little sick. 'Is he a great astrologer?'

'He is Rustan's friend, Gorlias Pietrogliant,' answered the negress, who was now turning over certain fine linen in the wardrobe. 'Yes, he is a good star-gazer, especially for merchants. He is very poor, but many have grown rich through consulting him.'

She found what she wanted, and held up a beautifully embroidered garment of linen as fine as a web.

'And if you are so fortunate as to go to the rich merchant's house,' she added, 'you may win favour of him by telling him to consult Gorlias about his affairs whenever he is in doubt.'

'Gorlias.' Zoë repeated the name, for she had never heard it.

'Gorlias Pietrogliant, who lives near the church of Saint Sergius and Saint Bacchus. Every one in that quarter knows him.'

'I shall remember,' Zoë said.

She understood at last why Rustan had been in the habit of going often to that church, where she had been kneeling in a dark corner when he had first seen her. Thence he had followed her to the ruined house. But she did not know that it was part of his regular business to frequent the churches of the poorest quarters, because it was there that starving girls were most often to be seen, praying to heaven for the bread that so rarely came from that direction. Many a good bargain had Rustan made by following a poor little ragged figure with a pretty face to a den of misery, and he was a perfect expert in doling out alms until his victim yielded or was forced to yield by her parents, for a handful of gold; nor has his method of conducting the business greatly changed, even in our own day, excepting that the slave-dealers themselves are mostly women now.

Having selected all the garments necessary for Zoë's costume, the negress bade one of the slave-girls take away the remains of the supper and bring what was already prepared for the morning. The maid obeyed, and was not gone two minutes. She brought in a bowl of cherries, with white bread and butter and fresh water, all on a polished tray of chiselled brass.

'Fruit is better for the health than sweetmeats at this time of day,' observed the mistress of the house. 'By and by, at dinner, the Kokóna shall have all she wishes.'

The little slaves looked at Zoë furtively and she smiled.

'Yes,' she said, 'fruit is much better in the morning.'

Rustan's wife came and stood beside the bed and scrutinised Zoë's face.

'I think,' she said critically, 'that as the customer is a foreigner, it will be better not to paint your eyes. The natural shadows under them are not bad.'

'I never painted my face in my life!' cried the girl, rather indignantly.

'And the Kokóna is quite right!' answered the negress, anxious to keep her in a good humour. 'Besides,' she continued, fawning again, 'I am here only to do your bidding and to wait on you to-day. Will it please you to bathe now? I shall wait on you myself.'

'The little maids are very quick and clever,' objected Zoë, who hardly looked upon the strapping African as a woman.

'No doubt, Kokóna, but this is a part of our business, and I do it better than they.'

'I would rather let them help me, if I must be helped,' said Zoë. 'But, indeed, I am quite used to dressing myself.'

'And pray,' argued the negress, grinning and growing familiar again, 'how could Rustan give his customers a written guarantee, unless I assured him, that there is no cause for complaint, no blemish, no scar, no hidden deformity, no ugly birthmark?'

Zoë turned her face away on the pillow.

'I had not thought of that,' she answered.

'Heaven forbid that I should myself,' returned the woman, relapsing into her obsequious manner again, 'if it were not to save the young Kokóna from any trouble or annoyance with our customer! If it will but please her to call herself my mistress and me her slave, she shall not be disappointed. If I am rough or clumsy she shall box my ears whenever she pleases, and I shall not complain!'

The little maids devoutly wished that Zoë would avail herself of their tyrant's extraordinary offer, but they dared not smile. She still turned her face away and was silent.

'See!' coaxed the African. 'I take off my coat!' She suited the action to the word and divested herself of her outer garment, which was the long coat and skirt in one, worn only by free women. 'I cover my head, in the Kokóna's presence!' She quickly flattened her wild red hair under a kerchief which she knotted at the back of her neck. 'I roll up my sleeves! Am I anything but a slave, a bath-woman? Why will the beautiful Kokóna not let me wait on her?'

Zoë turned her eyes and saw the change, and suddenly her objection vanished; for Rustan's wife looked precisely like the black slave-women who used to attend the ladies in the Roman bath in Rhangabé's palace. The association of ideas was so strong that the young girl could not help smiling faintly.

'As you please,' she said, raising herself upon one hand and preparing to get up.

CHAPTER V

Carlo Zeno's interview with Rustan had been short and business-like, as has been said. It was indeed not at all likely that a man of the Venetian's temper and tastes would talk with a Bokharian slave-dealer a moment longer than necessary.

Rustan, on hearing what was wanted, declared that he had the very thing; in fact, by a wonderful coincidence, it was the very thing in the acme of perfection, a dream, a vision, fully worth four hundred ducats, and certainly not to be sold for three hundred; it had fine natural hair that had never been dyed; its teeth were twenty-eight in number, the wisdom teeth not having yet appeared, and Rustan would wager that Messer Carlo could not find a single pearl in all Constantinople to match one of those eight-and-twenty; its ankles were so finely turned that a woman could span them with her thumb and forefinger. Rustan felt safe in saying this, for his black wife's huge hand could have spanned Zoë's throat; also it had a most beautiful and slender waist, which, as Messer Carlo remarked, was certainly a point of beauty. Moreover, Rustan would deliver a signed and sealed certificate with it.

For Zeno was conscientious, and held Marco Pesaro's letter in his hand while he questioned the Bokharian in regard to the various points in succession, lest he should forget any one of them. He did not in the least believe a word that Rustan said, of course. The East was never the land of simple, trusting faith between man and man. He would even have wagered that Rustan had nothing in his prison of the sort Pesaro wanted, and at the moment of the interview he would have been quite right. But he was tolerably sure that if he insisted on having the best, the best to be had would be forthcoming in a week at the utmost. Satisfied with this prospect, he dismissed Rustan and thought no more about the matter, except to wish that Marco Pesaro had not troubled him with such an absurd commission.

A fine young gentleman of later times would probably have thought few quests more amusing than this, and would have dreamt that night of the beauties he intended to see before at last deciding upon the purchase. Doubtless, there were young Venetians even then in Constantinople who would have envied Zeno the amusing task of criticising pretty faces, hands, and ankles.

But he was not of the same temper or disposition as those gay youths. He could not remember that any woman had ever made a very profound impression on him, even in his boyish days. When he was in Greece, it had been suggested to him that he might as well marry, like other young men, and he had allowed himself to be betrothed to a sleepy Greek heiress who had conceived an indolent but tenacious admiration for his fighting qualities; but it had pleased the fates that she should die before the wedding-day of a complication of the spleen superinduced by a surfeit of rose-leaf jam and honey-cakes. He was rather ashamed to own to himself that her translation to a better world had been a distinct relief to his feelings, for he had soon discovered that he did not love her, though he had been too kind to tell her so, and too honourable to think of breaking his promise of marriage.

He did not despise women either; indeed, his conduct in the affair of his betrothal had proved that. Now and then he had paused in his restless career to think of a more peaceful life, and in the pictures that rose before his imagination there was generally a woman. Unhappily, he had never seen any one like her in real life, and when he was tired of dreaming he shrugged his shoulders at such impossibilities and went back to his adventurous existence without a sigh. Yet it might be thought that although he did not fall in love he might now and then spend careless hours with the free and frail, for he made no profession or show of austerity, and whatever he really might be, he did not aspire to be called a saint. He had been a wild student in Padua once, and had drunk deep and played high, until he had suddenly grown tired of stupid dissipation and had left the dice to play the more exciting game of life and death as a soldier of fortune under a condottiere, during five long wandering years. But at the core of his nature there was something ascetic which his comrades could never understand, and at which they laughed when he was not within hearing; for he was an evil man to quarrel with, as they had found out. He never killed his man in a duel if he could help it, but he had a way of leaving his mark for life on his adversary's face which few cared to risk.

And now it was long indeed since his lips had touched a woman's, for his character had taken its final manly shape, and the only folly to which he still yielded now and then was that of risking his life recklessly whenever he fancied that a cause was worth it; but this he did not look upon as madness, still less as weakness, and there was no one to argue the question with him. His honest brown eyes softened sometimes, almost like a woman's, but only for pity or kindness, never for word or look of love.

He rose in the bright spring morning just before the sun was up, and went down the steps at the water's edge below his house and swam far out in clear water that was still icy cold. Then he dressed himself completely as strong and healthy men do, who hate to feel that they are not ready to face anything from the beginning of the day. But while he was dressing he was not thinking of the errand that was to take him to Rustan's house an hour before noon. Indeed, he had quite forgotten it, till he saw Omobono folding Pesaro's letter in his neat way in order to file it for reference. As the secretary knew what it contained, and had been actively employed in the matter to which it referred, he had thought there could be no great sin of curiosity in reading it carefully while his master was at his toilet. It would have been wrong, he thought, to find out what was in it before Zeno himself had broken the seal, but since it was open, it was evidently better that the secretary should understand precisely what was wanted of his employer, for such knowledge could only increase his own usefulness. For the rest, he vaguely hoped that Zeno would take him into close confidence and ask his opinion of any merchandise he thought of buying; for Omobono had a high opinion of his own taste in beauty, and had wished to pass for a lively spark in his young days.

But Zeno evidently considered himself qualified to decide the matter without help, for when it lacked an hour of noon he set his secretary at work on a fair copy of a letter he had been preparing, ordered his horse and running footman, and went upon his errand without any other attendant or companion. Omobono looked out of the window and watched him as he mounted, innocently envying him his youth and strength. The greatest fighting man of his century moved as such men generally do, without haste and without effort, never wasting a movement and never making an awkward one, never taking a fine attitude for the sake of effect, as the young men of Raphael's pictures so often seem to be doing, but always and everywhere unconsciously graceful, self-possessed, and ready for anything.

He rode a half-bred brown Arab mare, for he was not a heavy man, and he preferred a serviceable mount at all times to the showy and ill-tempered white Barbary, or the rather delicate thoroughbred of the desert, which were favourites with the rich Greeks of Constantinople. He was quietly dressed, too; and his bare-legged runner, who cleared the way for him when the streets were crowded, wore a plain brown tunic and cap, and did not yell at the poorer people and slaves or strike them in passing as the footmen of great personages always did. Zeno had picked him out of at least a hundred for his endurance and his long wind.

So they went quietly and quickly along, the man and his master, following very nearly the way which Omobono had taken on the previous afternoon, till they came to the long wall crested with sharp bits of rusty iron and broken crockery, and stopped before the only door that broke its blank length. Zeno looked at the defence critically, and wondered just how great an inducement would make him take the trouble of getting over it, at the risk of cutting his hands and tearing his clothes. Before any one answered his footman's knock, he had decided that it would be an easy matter to bring his well-broken horse close to the wall, to stand on the saddle, draw himself up and throw a heavy cloak over the spiky iron and the sharp-edged shards with one hand while hanging by the other. The rest would be easy enough. It was always his instinct to make such calculations when he entered or passed by any place that was meant to be defended.

This time the door was opened by Rustan Karaboghazji in person, and he bowed to the ground as Zeno got off his horse and stood beside him. Still bending low he made way and with a wide gesture invited his visitor to enter. But Zeno had no intention of wasting time by going in till he was assured that there was something ready for his inspection in the way of merchandise.

In answer to his question Rustan turned up his face sideways and smiled cunningly as he gradually straightened himself.

'Your Magnificence shall see!' he answered. 'Where is the letter? Every point is perfect, as I promised.'

'Were you really speaking the truth?' laughed Zeno. 'I expected to come at least three times before seeing anything!'

Rustan assumed an expression of gentle reproach.

'If your Splendour had dealt with Barlaam, the Syrian merchant, or with Abraham of Smyrna, the Jewish caravan-broker,' he said, 'it would have been as your Greatness deigns to suggest. Moreover, your Highness would not have been satisfied after all, and would have come at last to the house of your servant Rustan Karaboghazji, surnamed the Truth-speaker and the Just, and also the Keeper of Promises, by those who know him. It must have been so, since there is but one treasure in all the Empire such as your Mightiness asks for, and it is in this house.'

Zeno laughed carelessly, and entered.

'Your Unspeakableness is amused,' said Rustan, fastening the outer door carefully with both keys. 'But if it is not as I say, I entreat your High Mightiness to kick his humble servant from this door to the Seven Towers and back again, passing by the Chora, Blachernæ, and the Church of the Blessed Pantokrator on the way.'

'That would take a long time,' observed Zeno. 'Open the door and let me see the girl.'

'Your Grandeur shall see, indeed!' answered Rustan, smiling confidently as he led the way. 'Rustan the Truth-speaker,' he continued, as if to himself while walking, 'Karaboghazji the faithful Keeper of Promises!'

He gently caressed his beautiful black beard as he went on. He took Zeno through the small part of the house which he reserved for his own use, far from the larger rooms where he kept his stock of slaves. In an inner apartment they met the negress, resplendent in scarlet velvet and a heavy gold chain, her red hair combed straight out from her head. When Zeno appeared, she at once assumed what she considered a modest but engaging attitude, crossing her great hands upon her splendid coat, and looking down with a marvellous attempt at a simper.

Rustan stood still and for a moment Zeno thought that the dealer had ventured to jest with him, by showing him the terrific negress in her finery as the incomparable treasure of which he had spoken. But Rustan's words explained everything.

'My Life,' he said, speaking to his wife in a caressing tone, 'is the girl ready to be seen?'

'As my lord commanded me,' replied the negress, keeping her hands folded and bending a little.

'This lady,' said Rustan to Zeno, 'is my wife, and my right hand.' He turned to her. 'Sweet Dove,' he said, 'pray lead his Magnificence to the slave's room. I will wait here.'

Zeno seemed surprised at this arrangement.

'My wife' explained Rustan, 'understands the creatures better than I. My business is buying and selling; it is her part to keep the merchandise in good condition, and to show it to the customers who honour us.'

He smiled pleasantly as he said this, and remained standing while Zeno followed the negress out of the room. As he walked behind her he could not help noting her strong square shoulders, and the swing of her powerful hips, and her firm tread, and he conceived the idea that she would be a match for any ordinary man in a tussle. He was certainly not thinking of the slave-girl he was about to inspect.

Another door opened, and he was in a room flooded with sunshine and sweet with spring flowers; he stopped, and unconsciously drew one sharp breath of surprise. Zoë had been sitting in a big chair in the sun, and had half risen as the door opened, her hand resting on one of the arms of the seat. Her eyes met Zeno's, and for a moment no one moved. If Rustan had been present he would have raised the price of the merchandise to five hundred ducats at least; the black woman only grinned, well pleased with the appearance of the girl whom she had herself dressed to receive the customer's visit of inspection.

Zoë's hand tightened a little on the arm of the chair and she sank quietly into her seat again as she turned her eyes from Zeno's face, forgetting that she had promised herself to stand erect and cold as a slave should when she is being exhibited.

If the Venetian still doubted that by some mysterious chance of fate the girl he had come to buy at the slave-dealer's was as well born as himself, her movement as she sat down dispelled his lingering uncertainty. He had entered the room carelessly, still wearing his cap. As Zoë resumed her seat, he took it from his head, bowing instinctively, as he would have done on meeting a woman of his own class. A faint colour rose in the girl's cheeks, as she looked at him again.

Rustan's wife laughed silently, standing a little behind him. Zoë spoke first.

'Pray, sir,' she said, 'be covered.'

'His High Mightiness uncovers his head for coolness,' said the negress.

Zeno gave her a sharp glance and then turned to Zoë.

'It is not possible that you are a slave,' he said, coming a little nearer and looking down into her face.

But she would not meet his eyes.

'It is the truth, sir,' she said. 'I am a slave and any one may buy me and take me away.'

'Then you have been carried off by force,' Zeno answered with conviction, 'in war, perhaps, or in some raid of enemies on enemies. Tell me who you are and how it happened, and by the body of blessed Saint Mark, I will give you back free to your own people!'

Zoë looked at him in silent surprise. The negress answered him at once, for she did not like the turn affairs were taking, and though she had never heard of Carlo Zeno, she judged from his looks that he was able to make good his promise.

'Your Splendour does not really believe that my husband would risk the punishment of a robber for carrying off a free woman!' she cried.

'I am a slave,' Zoë said quietly. 'Only a slave and nothing else. There is no more than that to tell.'

She drew one hand across her brow and eyes as if to shut out something or to drive it away. Zeno came nearer and stood alone beside her.

'Tell me your story,' he said in a lower tone. 'Do not be afraid! no one shall hurt you.'

'There is no more to tell,' she repeated, shaking her head. 'But you are kind, and I thank you very much.'

She raised her clear brown eyes gratefully to his for a moment. There was sadness in them, but he saw that she had not been weeping; and like a man, he argued that if she were very unhappy she would, of course, shed copious tears the live-long day, like the captive maidens in the tales of chivalry. He looked at the beautiful young hand, now lying on the arm of the chair, and for the first time in his life he felt embarrassed.

The negress, who was not at all used to such methods in the buying and selling of humanity, now came forward and began to call attention to the fine quality of her goods.

'Very fine natural hair,' she observed. 'Your Gorgeousness will see at once that it has never been dyed.'

She took one of Zoë's plaits in her hand, and the girl shrank a little at the touch.

'Let her alone!' Zeno said sharply. 'I am not blind.'

'It is her business to show me,' Zoë answered for her, in a tone of submission.

'It shall not be her business much longer,' replied Zeno, almost to himself.

He suddenly turned away from her, went to the open window, and looked out, laying one hand on the iron bars. It was not often that he hesitated, but he found himself faced by a very unexpected difficulty. He was executing a commission for a friend, and if he bought a slave with his friend's money, he should feel bound in honour to send her to her new master at the first opportunity. On the other hand, though it was perfectly clear from the girl's behaviour that she expected no better fate, he was intimately convinced that in some way a great wrong was being done, and he had never yet passed a wrong by without trying to right it with his purse or his sword. Clearly, he was still at liberty to buy Zoë for himself, and take her to his home; yet he shrank from such a solution of the problem, as if it were the hardest of all. What should he do with a young and lovely girl in his house, where there were no women, where no woman ever set foot? She would need female attendants, and of course he could buy them for her, or hire them; but he thought with strong distaste of such an establishment as all this would force upon him. Besides, he could not keep the girl for ever, merely because he suspected that she was born a lady and was the victim of some great injustice. She denied that she was. What if she should persist in her denial after he had bought her to set her free? What if she really had no family, no home, no one to whom she could go, or wished to go? He would not turn her out, then; he would not sell her again, and he should not want her. Moreover, he knew well enough that it was not his nature to go on leading the peaceful life of a merchant much longer, even if the threatening times would permit it. He had always been as free as air. As he was now living, if it should please him to leave Constantinople, he could do so in twenty-four hours, leaving his business, though at a loss, to another merchant—for he had prospered. But it would be otherwise if this girl were in the house, under his protection, and it never occurred to him, after he had looked into her eyes, that she could live under his roof except in order that he might protect her—protect her from imaginary enemies, right imaginary wrongs she had never suffered, and altogether make of her what she protested that she was not.

It was absurd to think of such a thing, and having come to this conclusion in a shorter time than it has taken me to describe his thoughts, he turned abruptly with the intention of buying her for Marco Pesaro's account.

Unfortunately, when he saw her face he could not do it.

'I will send a palanquin for you in an hour,' he said hurriedly, and he made for the door in evident anxiety to get away without exchanging another word with Zoë.

The negress followed him quickly into the next room, very much surprised at his way of doing business.

'If it please your Glory,' she began, overtaking him with difficulty, but he would not listen, and hurried on.

'I will settle with Rustan,' he said.

But in the room where he had left her, Zoë was leaning back in her chair alone, gazing at the sunlit window. At that very moment, so far as she knew, the gold was being counted out that was the price of her young life. In an hour she would be taken away in a closed litter, as she had been brought last night, she would be carried into another house, the slide would slip back, and she would be told to get down.

The voice would be a man's. Who was he? What was his name? What was she to be to him? He was a Venetian, she guessed by his dress, and she felt that his blood was gentle, like her own. But that was all, though she was already his property. It was dreadful; or, at least, it should be dreadful to think of! She felt that she ought to long for death now, a thousand times more earnestly than last night.

But she did not. For she was a most womanly woman already, though not nineteen, and there are few women of that intensely feminine temper who cannot judge at a first meeting with a man whether they can gain power over him or not. Moreover, this strength is greatest with men who are most profoundly masculine, because it is not the influence of one character over another, but the deeper, stronger, more mysterious power of sex over sex.

CHAPTER VI

Little Omobono's thin legs carried him up and down the stairs of Zeno's house at an astonishing pace during the next hour; for Carlo gave fifty orders, every one of which he insisted should be executed at once. It was not a small thing to instal a woman luxuriously in a house in which no woman had set foot since Carlo had lived there, and to do this within sixty minutes. It is true that the rich young merchant had great store of thick carpets and fine stuffs, and all sorts of silver vessels, and weapons from Damascus, and carved ivory chessmen from India; but though some of these things quickly furnished the upper rooms which Zeno set apart for the valuable slave's use while she remained under his roof, yet scimitars, chessmen, and heathen idols of jade were poor substitutes for all the things a woman might be expected to need at a moment's notice, from hairpins and hand-mirrors to fine linen pillow-cases, sweetmeats, and a lap-dog. Zeno's ideas of a woman's requirements were a little vague, but he determined that Zoë should want nothing, and he charged Omobono with the minute execution of his smallest commands.

He himself lived simply and almost rudely. He slept on a small hard divan with a little hard cushion under his head, and a cloak to cover him in cold weather. He hated hot water, scented soap, and all the soft luxuries of the Roman bath. There was no mirror in his room, no elaborate toilet service of gold and silver, such as fine young gentlemen used even then. He liked a good dinner when he was hungry, good wine when he was thirsty, and a wide easy-chair when he had worked all day; but it never had cost him a moment's discomfort to exchange such a home as he now lived in for the camp or the sea.

Women were different beings, however, so he made all allowances for them, and went to extreme lengths in estimating their necessities, as Omobono found to his cost. Yet with all his preoccupation for details, Zeno forgot that Zoë must have a woman to wait on her at once, and when he realised the omission, almost at the last minute, the future conqueror of the Genoese, the terror of the Mediterranean, the victorious general of the Paduan campaign, the hero of thirty pitched battles and a score of sea-fights, felt his heart sink with something like fear. What would have happened if he had not remembered just in time that Marco Pesaro's slave must have a maid? She should have two, or three, or as many as she needed.

'Omobono,' he said, as the little secretary came up the stairs for the twentieth time, 'go out quickly and buy two maids. They must be young, healthy, clean, clever, and silent. Lose no time!'

'Two maids?' The secretary's jaw dropped. 'Two maids?' he repeated almost stupidly.

'Yes. Is there anything wonderful in that? Did you expect to wait on the lady yourself?'

'The lady?' Omobono opened his little eyes very wide.

'I mean,' answered Zeno, correcting himself, 'the—the young person who is going to be lodged here. Lose no time, I say! Go as fast as you can!'

Omobono turned and went, not having the least idea where to go. Before he had reached the outer door, Zeno called after him down the stairs.

'Stop!' cried the merchant. 'It is too late. You must go and get the lady—the young person. Take two palanquins instead of one, and tell Rustan to let her choose her own slaves. You can put the two into one litter and bring them all together.'

'But the price, sir?' enquired Omobono, who was a man of business. 'Rustan will ask what he pleases if I take him such a message!'

'Tell him that if he is not reasonable he shall do no more business with Venetians,' answered Zeno, from the head of the marble stairs.

Omobono nodded obediently and followed his instructions. So it came to pass that before long he found himself within Rustan's outer wall with two palanquins and eight bearers, besides a couple of Zeno's trusty men-servants, well armed, for he carried a large sum of money in gold. The Bokharian and the secretary went into an inner room to count and weigh the ducats, but before this began Omobono delivered his message in full.

'I have the very thing,' said Karaboghazji. 'There are two girls who have waited on her and with whom she is much pleased. As for asking too high a price, forty ducats for the two is nothing. They are a gift, at that.'

'Forty ducats!' cried Omobono, casting up his eyes, and preparing to bargain for at least half an hour.

'If it is dear,' said Rustan, his face becoming like stone, 'may my tongue never speak the truth again!'

Considering attentively the consequences of such an awful fate Omobono did not think that the Bokharian risked any great inconvenience if the imprecation should take effect.

'It is far from me,' said the secretary, 'to suggest that your words are not literally true, according to your own light. But you must be aware that the price of maid-servants has fallen much since yesterday, owing to the arrival of a shipload of them from Tanais.'

Rustan shook his head and maintained his stony expression.

'They are worthless,' he said. 'Do you suppose I should not have bought the best of them? There has been a plague of smallpox in their country, and they are all pitted. They are as oranges, blighted by hail.'

As Omobono had invented the ship and its cargo, he found it hard to refute Rustan's argument, which was quite as good as his own.

'May my fingers be turned round in their sockets and close on the back of my hand, if I have asked one ducat too much,' said the Bokharian with stolid calm.

Omobono hesitated, for a new idea had struck him. Before he could answer, a door opened and Rustan's wife, who had put off her finery, ushered in Zoë, closely veiled and wrapped in the cloak she had worn on the previous night. It was, in fact, necessary that she should be delivered up in return for the gold, and the negress had supposed that the counting was almost over.

'My turtle dove,' said Rustan in dulcet tones, 'fetch those two girls who have waited on Kokóna Arethusa. The Venetian merchant will buy them for her.'

The negress grinned and went out. By this time Omobono had made up his mind what to say.

'My dear sir,' he began, in a conciliatory tone, consider that we are friends, and do not ask an exorbitant price. I beseech you to be obliging, by four toes and five toes.'

Omobono wondered what would happen after he had pronounced the mysterious words. Rustan looked keenly at him and was silent for a moment. Neither of them noticed that Zoë made a quick movement as she stood by the table between them. The Bokharian rose suddenly and went to shut the door.

'Where?' he asked as he crossed the small room.

Omobono's face fell at the unexpected and apparently irrelevant question. Instantly Zoë bent down and whispered three words in his ear. Before Rustan turned back to hear the clerk's answer, she was standing erect and motionless again, and he did not suspect that she had moved.

'Over the water,' answered Omobono, with perfect confidence.

'You may have the two for four-and-twenty ducats,' said Rustan. 'But you cannot expect me to take anything off the price of the Kokóna,' he added. 'I bargained with your master, and he agreed.'

'No, no! Certainly! And I thank you, sir.'

'I suppose,' said Rustan, 'that you would do as much for me.'

'Of course, of course,' answered Omobono. 'Shall we count the ducats?'

When the operation was almost finished, the negress returned with the two slave-girls, whose commonplace features were wreathed in smiles, and they began to kiss the hem of Zoë's cloak. Omobono inspected them critically.

'Are you pleased with them, Kokóna?' he enquired of Zoë. 'My master is very anxious that you should be satisfied.'

'Indeed I am,' Zoë answered readily. 'They are very clever little maids.'

The two were almost crying with delight, and only a meaning movement of the negress's hand to her girdle checked them. They were not out of her power yet. Omobono eyed them, and really thought them cheap at twelve ducats each, as indeed they were. He was paying four hundred for Zoë, but Rustan did not mean her to see the gold, and had covered it with one of his loose sleeves as she entered. He now begged his wife take the three slaves to the palanquins while he finished counting and weighing, and wrote out his receipt for the money. He called the negress his pet mouse, his little bird, and the down-quilted waistcoat of his heart, and but for her terrific appearance, and the weapon she carried in her girdle, Omobono would have laughed outright.

Rustan wrote on a strip of parchment, in bad Greek:—

In the name of the Holy Trinity, Constantinople, the Saturday before Passion Sunday, the second year of Andronicus Augustus Cæsar, and the fourteenth of the Indiction, I have received from the Most Magnificent Carlo Zeno, a Venetian, the sum of four hundred and forty gold ducats of Venice, for the following merchandise:—

For one Greek maid slave, slave-born, between seventeen and eighteen years old, answering to the name of Arethusa, without blemish, scar, or birthmark, having natural brown hair, brown eyes, twenty-eight teeth all sound, weighing two Attic talents and five minæ more or less, and speaking Greek, Latin, and Italian Ducats 400

For two maid slaves, from Tanais, slave-born, of fourteen and fifteen, answering to the names of Lucilla and Yulia, sound, healthy, never having been tortured or branded, each having black hair, black eyes, and twenty-eight teeth, trained to wait on a lady, and speaking intelligible Greek, besides a barbarous dialect of their own, warranted docile, and not given to stealing; at 20 ducats each Ducats 40—In all: Ducats 440.

RUSTAN KARABOGHAZJI, the son of Daddirján, Merchant. (Witness)—SEBASTIAN OMOBONO, of Venice, Clerk.

Omobono observed that the receipt acknowledged forty ducats as the price of the two girls, instead of twenty-four.

'Rustan Karaboghazji, surnamed the Truth-speaker, does not sell slaves at twelve ducats,' answered the Bokharian with dignity. 'Moreover, your employer will see that he has paid forty, and you can justly keep the sixteen ducats for yourself.'

'That would not be honest,' protested Omobono, shaking his neat grey beard.

Rustan smiled, in a pitying way.

'You Venetians do not really understand business,' he said, tightening the strings of the canvas bag into which he had swept the gold, and knotting them as he rose.

A few minutes later Omobono was trudging along after the two palanquins, wondering much at certain things that had happened to him during the last twenty-four hours and less. For he was curious, as you know, and it irritated him to feel that something was going on in the world, all about him and near him, of which he could not even guess the nature, manifesting itself in such nonsensical phrases as 'four toes and five toes,' and 'over the water,' which nevertheless produced such truly astonishing results. Since the previous afternoon he had met four persons who knew those absurd words,—the negress, her Bokharian husband, the sacristan to Saints Sergius and

Bacchus, and a Greek slave-girl, whom he was far from recognising as the beautiful creature he had seen yesterday in the ruined house in the beggars' quarter. She was so closely veiled to-day that he could not in the least guess what her face was like.

Since she not only knew the first password, but had whispered the second to him, he wondered why she had not used her knowledge to get her freedom. It was incredible that the people who knew the words should not be banded together in some secret brotherhood; but if they were brethren, how could they sell one another into slavery? Omobono was so much interested in these problems that he did not see where he was till the leading palanquin entered Zeno's gate.

Zeno himself was not to be seen. The servant at the door gave Omobono a slip of cotton paper on which the merchant had written an order. The secretary was to take his charges to what was now the women's apartment and leave them there. Zoë obeyed Omobono's directions in silence, still veiled, and the two maids tripped up the marble stairs after her, as happy as birds on a May morning, and taking in all they saw with wondering eyes; for they had never been in a fine house before.

'This is the Kokóna's apartment,' Omobono said, standing aside to let Zoë pass. 'If the Kokóna desires anything, she will please to send one of her maids to me. I am the master's secretary.'

He had been surprised when Zeno spoke of her as a 'lady,' but somehow, since she had whispered in his ear at the slave-dealer's house, and since he had seen her movement and carriage when she walked upstairs, he instinctively treated her and spoke to her as if she were his superior. She nodded her thanks now, but said nothing, and he went away. She looked after him and listened, but no key was turned after the door was closed, and she heard only his retreating steps on the marble stairs. Then she turned to the window, which was open, and she threw aside her veil and looked out upon the Golden Horn.

The two little maids at once began a minute examination of the rooms, which occupied more than half the upper story of the house, and were, if anything, too crowded with rich furniture, with divans, carved tables, hanging lamps, cushioned seats, and pillows of every size, shape, and colour. There were handsome wardrobes, too, full of the fine clothes Zoë was to wear. The girls touched everything and talked by signs, lest they should disturb Zoë's meditations. They told each other that the master of the house must be highly pleased with his slave, since he surrounded her with beautiful things; that these things were all new, which was a sign that there was no other woman in the house; and that they were very fortunate and happy to have been sold, after only a month of apprenticeship under the negress's merciless training. They also explained to each other that they were hungry, for it was past noon. The idea of running away had probably never occurred to either of them, even in Rustan's house. Where should they go? And besides, the fate of runaway slaves was before their eyes.

Meanwhile Zeno sat in his balconied room alone. Omobono had delivered the receipt and had simply told him that sixteen ducats had been saved on the bargain, though Rustan did not wish it known. Thereupon Zeno gave the secretary a couple of ducats for himself, which Omobono saw no reason for not taking.

Zeno was preoccupied and chose to be alone, so he dismissed his secretary with injunctions to rest after the labour of installing the new arrival, which had not been light, and he walked up and down his room in deep thought. He had acted on an impulse altogether against his own judgment, and now he was faced by the unpleasant necessity of justifying his conduct in his own eyes.

One thing was quite clear; so long as he did not draw from the house of Cornèr the money which Marco Pesaro had sent to the banker for the commission, the merchandise was his property, since he had paid for it. But he must make up his mind whether he meant to call it his own, or not. If he decided to keep Arethusa, he must at once set about finding another slave for Marco Pesaro, or else write to say that he declined to execute the commission.

In that case, Arethusa remained his. The reason why he had so suddenly determined to buy her was that he fancied she was a girl of good family whom some great misfortune had brought into her present distress. But she had calmly declared that she was a slave, and expected nothing better than to be sold.

If this were true he had paid four hundred ducats for a foolish fancy. She was perhaps the child of some beautiful slave, and had been carefully educated by her mother's owner; and the latter, needing money perhaps, had sent her to the market; or perhaps he had died and his heirs were selling his property.

All this was very unsatisfactory. If she was slave-born, Zeno's best course was to send Arethusa to Pesaro, as soon as the Venetian ship sailed, for he had not the least intention of wasting money in a futile attempt to free slaves whom the law regarded as born to their condition. Their position was a misfortune, no doubt, but they were used to it, and no one had then dreamed of man's inherent right of freedom, excepting one or two popes and fanatics who had been considered visionaries. To Zeno, who was a man of his own times, it seemed quite as absurd that every one should be born free, as it would seem to you that everybody should be born an English duke, a Tammany boss, a great opera tenor, or Crown Prince of the Empire. Moreover, in the case of a beauty, especially of one sold to live in Venice, there were palliations, as Zeno knew. Arethusa would live in luxury; she would also soon be the real dominant in Marco Pesaro's household, as favourite slaves very generally were in the palaces of those who owned them. They had not yet all the vast influence in Venice which they gained in the following century, but their power was already waxing balefully.

Zeno did not hesitate long; he never did, and when he had made up his mind he sent for one of Arethusa's maids.

'What is your name, child?' he asked, scrutinising the girl's commonplace features and intelligent eyes.

'Yulia, Magnificence,' she answered. 'If it please you,' she added diffidently, as if half-expecting that he would choose to call her something else.

'Yulia,' repeated Zeno, fixing the name in his memory, 'and what do you call your mistress?' he asked abruptly.

The girl was puzzled by the question.

'Her name is Arethusa,' she answered, after a moment's reflection.

'I know that. But when you speak to her, what do you call her? When she gives you an order, how do you answer her? You do not merely say, "Yes, Arethusa," or "No, Arethusa," do you? She would not be pleased.'

Yulia smiled and shook her head.

'We call her Kokóna,' she answered. 'Is not that the Greek word for young lady, your Magnificence?'

'Yes,' said Zeno, 'that is the Greek word for young lady. But Arethusa is only a slave as you are. Why do you give her a title? What makes you think she is a lady?'

'She is a different kind of slave. She cost much gold. Besides, if we did not call her Kokóna she would perhaps pull our hair or scratch our faces. Who knows? We are only ignorant little maids, but so much the big negress at the slave-prison taught us.'

'She taught you manners, did she?' Zeno smiled at the idea.

'She made us cry very often, but it was the better for us,' answered the maid, with philosophy beyond her years. 'We have fetched a good price, and we have a good master, and we are together, all because we waited cleverly on the Kokóna one night and one morning.'

'One night?' asked Zeno, in surprise.

'She was only brought to the slave-prison yesterday evening, Magnificence.'

'At what time?'

'It was the third hour of darkness, for the black woman sent the others to bed as soon as she was brought.'

Zeno thought over this information for a moment.

'Tell her,' said he, 'that I shall sup with her this evening. That is all.'

Yulia, who had kept her hands respectfully before her, made a little obeisance, turned quickly, and ran away, leaving the master of the house to his meditations. She found Zoë still sitting by the window, and the dainty dishes which Lucilla had received on a chiselled bronze tray and had placed beside her were untasted.

'The master bids me say that he will sup with you to-night, Kokóna,' said Yulia.

Zoë made a slight movement, but controlled herself, and said nothing, though the colour rose to her face, and she turned quite away from the maids lest they should see it. They stood still a long time, waiting her pleasure.

'Will it not please you to eat something?' asked Yulia timidly, after a time. 'You have eaten nothing since last night, and even then it was little.'

'I thought I ate all the sweetmeats,' answered Zoë, turning and smiling a little at the recollection of the girls' terror.

The hours passed and nothing happened. Some time after dinner she saw from her upper window that Zeno came out of the house and went down the marble steps to a beautiful skiff that was waiting there. As he stepped in, she drew far back from the window lest he should look up and see that she had been watching him. She heard his voice as he gave an order to the two watermen; their oars fell with a gentle plash, and when she looked again they were pulling the boat away upstream, towards the palace of Blachernæ and the Sweet Waters.

The maids, having eaten of the most delicious food they had ever tasted till they could eat no more, had curled themselves up together on a carpet not far from their mistress, and were fast asleep. The shadow of the house lengthened till it slanted out to the right beyond the marble steps upon the placid water, and the bright sunlight that fell on Pera and Galata began to turn golden; so, when gold has been melted to white heat in the crucible, it begins to cool, grows tawny, and is shot with streaks of red.

As the day waned in a purple haze and the air grew colder, the two maids awoke together, rubbed their eyes, and instantly sprung to their feet. Zoë had not even noticed them, but just then the even plashing of oars was heard again, and she saw the skiff coming back, but without Zeno. She looked again to be sure that it was the same boat, and a ray of hope flashed in her thoughts like summer lightning. Perhaps he had changed his mind, and would not come—not to-night.

The maids reminded her of his message, and she let them dress her again for the evening. They arranged her hair, and twined strings of pearls in it, which they had found in a sandal-wood box on the dressing-table. They took clothes from the wardrobes, fine linen, wrought with wonderful needlework, and pale silks, and velvet of faintest blue embroidered with silver threads; and when they had done their best they held two burnished metal mirrors before her and behind her, that she might admire herself. They had lighted many little lamps that were all prepared, for it was now dark out of doors, and they had spent two hours in arraying Zoë. And she smiled and patted their cheeks, and called them clever girls, for she was sure that Zeno had changed his mind. He would not come to her to-night.

But even as she repeated the words to herself, he came softly through the warm lamplight and stood before her, and her heart stopped beating.

For the first time since she had taken the final step, she felt the whole extent and meaning of what she had done. She was really a slave, and she was alone with her master.

CHAPTER VII

'Are you afraid of me?'

Zeno asked the question gently, for the colour had left her face; and she looked up at him with a frightened stare. He had once seen a like terror in the eyes of a startled doe, as if a clouded opal passed across its sight.

Zoë did not answer, but she moved instinctively, drawing herself together, as it were, and turning one shoulder to him. He heard her breathing hard.

It was a very new thing that he felt; for often, in fight, and often again, he had seen strong men turn pale before him, just when they felt that he was a master of the sword and was going to kill, but he had never seen a woman afraid of him in his life. In his narrow experience, they had always seemed glad that he should be near them, and should speak to them. Therefore, when he saw that Zoë was terrified, he did not know what to do or say, and he stupidly repeated his question,

'Are you afraid of me?'

Zoë dug her little nails into the palms of her hands, and looked round the room, as if for help; but the two maids had disappeared as soon as the master had entered, for so they had been taught to do by their trainer. She was quite alone with the man who had paid for her.

All sorts of confused thoughts crowded her brain, as Zeno sat down on a seat beside the divan. She wondered what would happen if she told him her story in a few words, and appealed to his generosity. She guessed that he was kind; at least, sometimes. But perhaps he was a friend of the new Emperor, and it would amuse him to know that he had bought Michael Rhangabé's daughter. Or he might send for Rustan, and insist on revoking the bargain, and Rustan might take her back to the beggars' quarter, and force poor Kyría Agatha to give up the money. Zoë knew at once little and much of the world of Constantinople, but of one thing she was certain, there would be neither mercy nor kindness for any of her name while Andronicus reigned in Blachernæ.

She was terrified by the presence of her master, but she was perfectly brave in her resolve; the sight of death itself before her eyes should not make her do anything whereby those for whom she had sold herself might suffer.

Zeno sat still and looked at her. It seemed to him that she was far more beautiful than he had at first realised. As she leaned sideways against the big cushions, turning her face away and her shoulder towards him, there was something in the line of her cheek and of her neck where it joined the ear, and in the little downy ringlets at the roots of her hair that stirred his blood, against his will. Also, the devil came and whispered to his heart that she was his personal property, as much as his horse, his house and his stores of merchandise. The laws about slaves were uncertain enough in Italy, but there was no doubt of the law in Constantinople. The slave Arethusa, weighing so many talents and minæ, having so many sound teeth, and other good points, was the absolute property of Carlo Zeno. He might kill her, if he liked, in any way he chose, and the law would not call it murder. There would be one slave less, and he would have thrown away four hundred gold ducats; but that would be all.

She seemed to him the most beautiful creature in the world, and the devil was not suggesting that he should kill her; not by any means.

For a long time, the man and his slave were silent, and scarcely moved, and neither of them afterwards forgot those minutes. In their thoughts each was struggling with what seemed an impossibility, a something which could never be done. The high-born girl, for the sake of a mother who was not her mother, and of brothers who were not of her blood, was resolved to be to the end what she had made herself to save their lives, the obedient slave of a merchant who had paid gold for her. It was worse than death, but if she did not die of it, she must live through it, lest the good she had done should be undone again.

The man who had the law's own right of life and death over her, and whose warm young blood her beauty stirred so profoundly, chose to resist and play that he was not the master after all. His lean face was calm enough in the quiet lamplight, as it would have been in raging battle; but within was that he would not care to feel again, nor perhaps to let others know that he had felt.

At last, wondering at the stillness, half-believing and quite hoping that he was no longer in the room, Zoë turned her head. His eyes were on her, but there was something in them that she could not fear.

'Tell me who you are,' he said quietly.

Of all questions she had least expected this one, which seemed so natural to him. She waited a moment before she spoke.

'Are you dissatisfied, sir?' she asked in a low voice. 'Has the Bokharian cheated you?'

'No! What a thought!'

'Then you know what I am, and I can tell you nothing more, my lord. Can a slave have a pedigree?'

'I do not believe that you were born a slave,' said Zeno, leaning forward a little and looking into her eyes.

After a moment, her lids drooped under his gaze, but she would not speak.

'Have you nothing to say?' he asked, disappointed at her silence.

Again the temptation seized her to tell him all, since he spoke so kindly; but still she thought of what might happen to Kyría Agatha.

'I am your bought slave,' she said, almost directly. 'I have nothing else to tell.'

'But you had a mother?'

'I never knew her.'

'Your father, then?'

'I never knew him.'

Zeno was not always patient, even with women, and there was no reason why he should be forbearing with his own property.

'I do not believe you,' he said in a tone of annoyance, and he rose and began to pace the room.

Now it chanced that Zoë had been able to answer his last two questions quite truthfully, for she had not the least recollection of her own father and mother, who had died of the plague when she was three months old.

'I will swear to you on all holy things that it is true,' she said, watching him.

He made an impatient gesture.

'A slave cannot take an oath,' he answered roughly.

Zoë lifted her beautiful head at once, and her eyes shone; but he did not see, for he had turned his back on her in his walk, and a moment later she resumed her former submissive attitude.

Zeno stopped near the door and clapped his hands; the two maids appeared.

'Bring supper,' he said.

As they went to obey he came back and sat down again beside the divan. There was just room to place a small table between him and Zoë. The girls came back and waited on them, but neither spoke. Zeno prepared a salad himself with ingredients brought ready for making it, and when it was dressed he helped Zoë to a little of it. She had watched him, for the Italian custom was new to her and she had never known how a salad was composed. Zeno poured Greek wine into her glass, a delicate white goblet from Murano, with faint blue lines round the stem. But she neither ate nor drank.

'Go,' said Zeno to the maids. 'I will call you.'

The two slipped away noiselessly. Zeno had forgotten his displeasure, and he felt her presence again.

'You must eat and drink,' he said gently. 'If there is anything you like, tell me. You shall have it.'

'You are kind,' she answered, but she did not lift her hand. 'I have no appetite,' she added, after a little pause.

I do not know why no man believes a woman when she says that she is not hungry. Zeno was annoyed, and by way of showing his displeasure he himself began to eat more than he wanted. Zoë looked on in silence while he finished another bird and all the salad he had made. She would not have been a woman if she had not seen that he felt a little shy, all at once, as the most fearless and energetic men may before a woman they do not understand. Then there was a change for the better in her own state; she breathed more freely, her heart beat more steadily, the weight that lay like lead on her chest, just below her throat, was lightened. When a woman sees that a man is shy with her, she is sure that sooner or later he will turn at her will; and though she is sometimes mistaken, the chances are that she is right.

Zeno had never been shy before; but now, when he wished to speak, he could find nothing to say, and Zoë knew it, and would not help him. It was strange that as her fear subsided she thought him handsomer than at first sight, in the morning. When he had finished eating, he drank some wine, set down the glass, and looked at her with an expression that was meant to show something like anger; for he already regretted the time—distant five minutes—when she had been afraid of him, and he had been master of the situation. He drew his brows together, set his lips, and glared at her, but to his amazement she did not seem frightened. He had lost the thread, for the time, and she had found it. She answered his look with one of gentle surprise.

'Have you finished supper already?' she asked sweetly.

A slight flush rose in his brown cheek, as he felt his shyness increase, but he kept his eyes steadily on her.

'You do not seem to be afraid of me any longer,' he said, by way of answer.

'Have I anything to fear from you?' she asked, in a trusting tone.

She risked everything on the question, or thought she did. She won. His face changed and softened, for by appealing to his generosity she had put him at ease.

'No,' he answered. 'You never were in danger from me. Besides,' he added, with something like an effort, 'I have not made up my mind what to do with you.'

Zoë sat up straight, resting one hand on the edge of the little table.

'The truth is,' he went on, 'I did not buy you for myself.'

Zoë made a quick movement in her seat. Then her tender mouth hardened in a look of contempt.

'So you are only another slave-dealer!' she cried scornfully. But Zeno laughed at the mere idea, and was glad to laugh. It was a relief.

'No,' he said, 'I am not a slave-dealer. I am a Venetian merchant, I believe. I have been a soldier, and I came near being a prebendary!'

'A priest!' Zoë's face showed her disgust.

'No, for I never was in orders,' answered Zeno, growing more sure of himself as she grew more angry. 'But as for you, a friend of mine, a rich gentleman of Venice, has asked me as a favour to send him the most beautiful slave to be had in Constantinople for the large price he named. As a matter of fact—'

But here he was interrupted, for Zoë turned from him and buried her face in the leathern cushion. Her body shook a little, and Zeno thought she was crying. She had grown almost used to him, and had begun to feel that she might have some power over him; and she was ashamed to own that he attracted her, though she meant to hate him. But the idea that he had only bought her like a piece of goods, to pass her on to an unknown man far away, was more than she could bear at first. Moreover, though the idea of eating sickened her, she was really weakened by need of food, and she had undergone within twenty-four hours as much as her nature could bear without breaking down in some way.

Zeno was distressed, and bent over her, rather awkwardly, anxious to soothe her. She turned her face to him suddenly, without warning, and he saw that her eyes were dry and her cheeks flushed.

'Venice is a beautiful city,' he said coaxingly. 'You will be a great person in my friend's house—he will give you—'

'When are you going to send me? To-morrow?' The girl had mastered herself a little.

'I have told you that I have not made up my mind about you,' Zeno answered. 'The money I gave the Bokharian was my own. I may keep you here after all.'

Zoë detested him in that moment. She longed to insult him, to strike him, to drive him away. There was something so condescending in what he said. He would make up his mind about her! He might keep her after all! He had paid his own money for her! It was not possible that she could have thought him handsome, that she could have been even momentarily attracted by his face, his manner, or his voice.

'I hate you!' she cried, shutting her teeth tightly as she spoke.

He was near her, and she drew back from him as far as she could against the cushions of the divan. He resumed his seat, for he saw how angry she was. He had purposely spoken as if she were really the slave she told him that she was, and against the natural instinct which bade him treat her as his equal.

'Indeed,' he said coldly, and he took a cracked walnut from the table and began to peel the kernel, 'it is not easy to know what will please you. You seem horrified at the idea of going to Venice and furious at the thought of staying here! Of course, there is a third possibility. I would not send my friend a slave who would be so discontented as to poison him and his family, and I shall certainly not keep one in my house who hates me and may take it into her head to cut my throat in my sleep. The only thing that remains will be to sell you back to the Bokharian at a loss. Should you like that?'

Zoë felt again that he was her master.

'You made me think you would be kind to me!' she said, and her voice quavered.

Zeno laughed, for he had been too much annoyed to yield at once to her appeal.

'That did not prevent you from saying that you hated me, a while ago,' he answered. 'You must not expect too much Christian virtue of me, for I am no saint. I never learned to love those that hate me!'

She liked him better now; as he threw back his head a little, looking at her from under his half-closed lids, she glanced at his brown throat and she did not think of cutting it, as he had suggested. But she was angry with herself for passing through so many phases of like and dislike in so short a time, and for not feeling relief at the thought of being sent on a long journey, which certainly would mean safety while it lasted, and perhaps a chance of freedom. She wondered, too, why she no longer wished to die outright now that she had saved Kyría Agatha. Her answer to his last speech was humble.

'You made me say it,' she said. 'I am sorry, sir.'

'At least, I have learnt that you would rather stay here than go back to Rustan Karaboghazji and that gentle wife of his—his red-haired dove!'

'Anything rather than that!'

Her tone was earnest, for it was the fate she feared most, both for herself and because she fancied that the dealer would in some way claim his money from Kyría Agatha. Zeno was apparently satisfied with her answer, for he looked more kindly at her and was silent for a time. Again he allowed his eyes to be delighted with her beauty.

'I will not send you back,' he said at last; and he held out his hand towards her, as if he were giving a promise to an equal.

She was grateful, but she thought that perhaps he was trying to make her betray her birth. No slave would take the master's hand familiarly in her own; she knew the ways of slaves, for there had been many in her adopted father's house, and she touched the tips of Zeno's fingers with her own and pressed her lips to the back of her own hand when she withdrew it. The action disconcerted him a little, for it was performed perfectly, with all the deference of born servitude.

'You were not long in Rustan's house, were you?' he asked, not seeming to be much interested in the answer, for he hoped to take her unawares.

If she told the truth, which he knew, he would show surprise and press her with another question; if she answered with an untruth he should gain that much knowledge of her character for future use. Quick-witted, she did neither.

'It pleased my lord to remind me a while ago that a slave's oath is never to be believed,' she said. 'It is the law that a slave must be tortured when giving evidence, is it not?'

'I believe it is,' answered Zeno, with a smile. 'But you are quite safe! I only ask you how long you were in Rustan's house.'

'One night and part of a day,' Zoë answered after a moment.

Zeno pretended surprise.

'So short a time! Then he only bought you yesterday?'

'Yesterday evening.'

'And of whom? Will you tell me that?'

Zoë reflected a moment and then smiled.

'Yes. I will tell you that. He bought me of a lady of Constantinople, in whose closest intimacy I was brought up. She is just of my own age and we are much alike.'

'I see,' said Zeno, completely deceived, and speaking almost to himself. 'Poor girl! The same father, I suppose—hence the—'

Zoë drooped her eyes and looked at the carpet.

'Yes—since you have guessed it, sir. We had the same father, though we never knew him. He died of the plague when we were a few months old.'

Zeno was perfectly satisfied with this logical explanation which entirely explained Zoë's aristocratic beauty, her nobility of manner, and the delicate rearing that was so apparent in all her ways, as well as the fearlessness which had made her turn upon him and tell him that she hated him. The only point he could not understand, was that Zoë should have smiled. But he thought, as was quite possible, that there might have been jealousy and even hatred between the mistress and her slave-born sister, and he would not enquire too closely yet, since all was so clear to him. Such unnatural doings were not rare in a city half-filled with slaves. Zoë's mistress had probably sold her in a fit of anger, or perhaps deliberately and with a cruel purpose, or even out of avarice, to buy a string of pearls.

The girl did not offer to say more, but she looked away from her owner and seemed to be thinking of the past, as indeed she was, though it was so different from that which his imagination was inventing for her.

He, on his side, peeled another walnut thoughtfully, and looked at her from time to time, sure that he knew the truth, and wondering what he ought to do, and above all what he really wished to do. He had believed her deeply wronged, and had paid a great sum to redress that wrong, almost without hesitating, because it was his nature to help any one in distress, and because he, who counted neither life nor limb when his cause was good, had never counted such stuff as gold in a like case.

But now, it was all clear. She was a slave, in spite of all appearances. She had suffered no injustice; her smile had told him that the change in her life had not been to greater unhappiness. That she should fear to be sent back to Rustan was only natural; she, who had no doubt always lived delicately in the great house where she had been born, must have felt the sordidness and the degradation of the slave-prison, in spite of the special care she had received in consideration of her beauty and value. Very likely, too, she had not much real feeling, in spite of her behaviour; slave women rarely have.

What should he do with her? He was passionate rather than material or pleasure-loving; he was consequently an optimist and an idealist where women were concerned, and was full of a vague belief in the romantic side of love. He could no more really love a slave-girl than he could have loved a hired maid, though she might be beautiful beyond comparison, for he was incapable of attaching himself to beauty alone. Only his equal could be his mate, and he never could care long or truly for any creature that was less. At twenty, the youth in him would have boiled up and over for a week, or a month; but he was verging on thirty, his thirty years that had been crammed with the deeds of many a daring man's whole life-time, and his nature had hardened in a nobler mould than his early youth had promised. He would not make a plaything of any woman now; and since he would not, he wondered what he should do with Zoë, now that she was his.

In this mood of uncertainty he rose to leave her, more or less resolved not to see her again until he had come to some conclusion as to her future; for in spite of all he still felt himself attracted to her, and the line of her cheek and throat when her face was half-turned away was of exquisite beauty. Standing beside her for a moment, he knew that if ever again in his life he stooped to take a woman for a toy, lovelessly, stupidly, contemptibly, the plaything would be this Arethusa whom he had bought of a scoundrelly Bokharian dealer.

'Good-night,' he said, looking down into her upturned eyes. 'If you need anything, if you want anything, send for Omobono, and you shall have it. Good-night, Arethusa.'

It was the first time he had called her by her name, as he knew it. He did not even hold out his hand. She looked up steadily.

'What shall you do with me?' she asked, very anxiously, surprised by his sudden leave-taking.

She was so lovely then that he felt a despicable impulse to take her into his arms, just for her loveliness, and close her sad eyes with kisses. Instead, he shook his head and turned away.

'I do not know,' he said, half-aloud. He reached the door. 'I do not know,' he repeated, as if the problem were very hard to solve; and he went out, not turning back to look at her.

Thus ended the first hour the slave spent with her master; and when he was gone she felt suddenly exhausted, as if she had fought with her hands; and strangely enough she knew all at once that she was weak from want of food, and that the thought of eating no longer disgusted her. Half-ashamed of herself, she glanced at the door through which Zeno had disappeared, as if she thought he might come back, and listened, as though expecting his footstep. Then, not seeing or hearing anything, she began to eat quickly, and almost ravenously, as if she were doing something to be a little ashamed of, and she hoped that the maids would not come in and see her.

She was soon satisfied, for it had been a nervous craving rather than anything else, and every woman who reads these lines knows precisely how Zoë felt, or will know one of these days; for in all that belongs to the instinctive side of life, women are much more alike than men are; whereas, because they are not led, pushed, or dragged through one average course of teaching, as most men are, but are left to think and above all, to guess at truth for themselves, they are much more unlike in their way of looking at things. This also is the reason why many gifted men and a good many really learned ones would rather talk to women than to men; for among men they hear the same things everlastingly, but women always have something new to say, which is flattering, pleasant, amusing, or irritating—perhaps, as they choose. Women have also a sort of mock-humble, wholly appealing way of asking the great man how it is possible that he can really care to talk with a poor, ignorant, little woman, when he might be engaged in a memorable conversation with the other great man, who is talking to the other poor, ignorant little woman with lovely eyes, on the other side of the room. In this way we learn that life is full of contradictions.

Zoë slept ten hours without dreaming, and awoke refreshed and rested, to wonder presently why her mood had changed so much. But Zeno was restless in the night, and dissatisfied with himself and with what he had done; when he lay awake he found fault with his impulsive action, but when he fell asleep for half-an-hour Zoë haunted his dreams. More than once he got up and walked barefoot on the marble mosaic pavement of his room, and he threw open the shutters and looked out. The night was calm and clear, and the air was almost wintry. To the left of Pera's towering outline the northern constellations shone bright and cold. Each time he looked he wondered at the slow motion of the Bear; the seven stars hung above the Pole, for it was springtime, and they hardly seemed to have moved a handbreadth to their westward sinking in a whole hour, when he looked again. When morning came his face was a little paler than usual, and he felt that he was in a bad humour.

Omobono only guessed it from a certain increase of his natural reserve, but that was enough for the experienced secretary, who was wonderfully careful not to speak unless Zeno spoke to him, and, above all, not to mention the existence of the women's apartment upstairs. On the other hand, although it was a Sunday, he had expected to be sent by his master to draw the money from the house of Cornèr, according to Pesaro's letter, of which he had thoroughly mastered the contents. But the order was not given, and as Zeno was neither forgetful of details nor slack in matters of business, Omobono began to wonder what had happened.

On Monday Zeno's mood had not changed, nor did he send for the money, and the secretary's curiosity grew mightily; on Tuesday it became almost unbearable. So far as he knew, and he knew most things that went on in the house, Zeno had only once gone upstairs, when he had supped with Zoë on Saturday evening, and had remained barely an hour. Since then he had not even asked after the slave, and no one had seen her except the two little maids, who came out upon the landing to receive the meals at regular hours, but never spoke to the men-servants. The secretary could have asked to see Zoë, to enquire if she needed anything, and she would certainly have received him; but he was afraid to do so without orders, and Zeno gave none, and might come in at the very moment when Omobono was there. The industrious secretary had fits of abstraction over his letters and accounts, and stared out of the window, stroking his neatly-trimmed grey beard very thoughtfully.

On Wednesday, a little before noon, Zoë was sitting in her window, and she again saw Zeno go down the steps to the water and get into his skiff. It was always there now, even at dawn, for since there had been women in the house Zeno had been rowed to another place for his morning plunge in the Golden Horn. To-day he was dressed with particular care, Zoë thought, as she caught sight of him, and she did not draw back from the window, as she had done the first time, but stayed where she was, and she wished in her heart that he would look up and see her. He did not even turn as he stepped into the boat, and she thought he held his head lower than when she had last seen him, and looked down, and raised his shoulders a little like a person determined not to look to the right or the left. Then the two men pulled the skiff away upstream, and she watched it till she could no longer distinguish it from many others that moved about on the water in the direction of the palace. She wondered where he went.

He had not been gone ten minutes when a man came to the gate of the fore-court on the other side of the house, and asked to see the secretary. He was simply dressed in a clean brown woollen tunic, that hung almost to the ground. It had wide sleeves, and they hid his joined hands as he stood waiting, in the attitude monks often take before a superior, or when reciting prayers before meals. But the man was not a monk, for he wore a broad belt of dark red leather, in which he carried a sheathed knife, a Syrian ink-horn, and a small cylindrical case of hammered brass, which held his reed pens. On his head he wore a tall felt cap, such as dervishes now wear.

The slave at the door looked at him attentively before admitting him. There was something unusual in his expression, though his features were not very marked, and he had the rather pasty complexion that is so common in the East. His eyes were perhaps a little longer and more almond-shaped than those of the average Greek or Bokharian, and he kept them half-closed. His scanty black beard had a few grey hairs in it. His nostrils curved sharply, but the nose was neither very large nor markedly aquiline. A commonplace face enough in Constantinople; but there was something oddly fixed in its expression, that made the slave feel uncomfortable and yet submissive. Many persons of all conditions came to the merchant's house on business during the day, and it was the rule to send them to Omobono. The slave's business was to keep out thieves, beggars, and suspicious characters; he stood aside, admitted the visitor to the court which separated the house from the street, and shut the gate again.

One of the free house-servants, of whom two or three were always waiting, came forward—a square-shouldered Venetian named Vito, who had been a sailor and had followed Zeno for years. He enquired the stranger's name and business.

'I am Gorlias Pietrogliant,' was the answer. 'My business with the secretary is private.'

The serving-man disappeared, and returned a moment later to conduct the visitor to the private room of the counting-house on the ground floor, where Omobono sat behind a high desk covered with papers and slips of parchment.

Omobono straightened himself on his stool and eyed the newcomer with a look of enquiry, at the same time drawing from his right arm the half sleeve of grey cotton which he always put on when he was going to write long, lest a spot of ink should stain the soft linen wrist-band which just showed below the tight cuff of his coat. He was a careful man. He looked at his visitor keenly, till he suddenly became aware that his scrutiny was returned with a rather disquieting fixedness.

'I am Gorlias Pietrogliant,' said the stranger.

Omobono bent his head politely, and wondered whether he should be able to repeat such an outlandish name.

'I am Messer Zeno's secretary,' he answered. 'What is your business, Master Porlias Dietroplant?'

'Gorlias,' corrected the other, quite unmoved. Gorlias Pietrogliant.'

'Master Gorlias—I beg your pardon.'

'I am an astrologer,' observed the visitor, seating himself on a high stool at Omobono's elbow, and relapsing into silence.

'You are an astrologer,' said the secretary tentatively, after a long pause, for he did not know what to say.

'Yes, I told you so,' replied Gorlias; and for a few seconds longer it did not seem to occur to him that there was anything else to be said.

There was something so oddly fixed in his look and so dull in his voice that Omobono began to fear that he might be a lunatic, which was indeed, in the secretary's opinion, much the same as an astrologer, for the Venetians were never great believers in the influence of the stars. But the visitor soon made him forget his suspicions by reviving his curiosity.

'The matter which brings me to you is of a very delicate nature,' said Gorlias, all at once speaking fluently and in a low voice. 'I have reason to believe that we are interested in the same business.'

'Are we?' asked the secretary in some surprise.

'I think we are. I think we are, by four toes and by five toes!'

'Over the water,' answered Omobono promptly, and hoping to learn more.

'Both salt and fresh,' returned Gorlias. 'By these tokens I shall trust to your fidelity and discretion.'

'Implicitly,' replied the Venetian, who was sure of being discreet, but wondered what the matter might be to which his fidelity was pledged beforehand. He inwardly hoped that his visitor was not going to ask him for money, for he suspected that some awful fate must be in store for those who refused a service when appealed to by the mysterious passwords, of which he had now learnt one more.

'Messer Carlo is gone out,' said Gorlias. 'By this time he is in the house of Messer Sebastian Polo, who wishes to marry him to his daughter. He will not come home till after dinner.'

Omobono stared at the speaker.

'You know more than I do,' he observed.

'Of course. I am an astrologer. You are in charge of the house and all it contains, and the servants and slaves are afraid of you because you have the master's ear, but they love you because you are kind to them. Therefore, whatever you do is right in their eyes. Upstairs there are three female slaves; one is Arethusa, the other two are called Yulia and Lucilla, and wait on her. You see, I know everything. Now, for the sake of that business in which we are both interested, you must take me up to their apartment, for I must speak with the one called Arethusa.'

Omobono wished that Gorlias had asked him for his coat, or his money, or anything that was his, rather than for such a favour; and he was about to risk refusing it, whatever the penalty might be, when a luminous idea revealed itself to him.

'There is only one condition,' he answered, after a moment's thought. 'I must be present while you talk with her.'

'That need not disturb you,' said Gorlias calmly. 'I have seen the room where she is by virtue of my knowledge of the stars. It has a small covered balcony with an outer lattice against the sun, on the south side. There I will talk with Arethusa, while you stand by the door and watch us. I will draw figures, and appear to explain them to her, so that the two girl-slaves may think that I have come to amuse her by setting up her horoscope. Even Messer Carlo could not object to that, and Arethusa can veil herself, so that I shall not be able to see her face.'

Omobono reflected a moment, but could now see no good reason for refusing the request, whereas he saw a prospect of learning something more about the mystery that interested him. Zoë herself had prompted him with the second password of the chain, in Rustan's house, and he was almost sure that in some way she knew the rest, and the meaning of them all.

The two went up the marble stairs to the second story, and Omobono tapped at the entrance to the women's apartment. There came a little pattering of slippered feet, and Lucilla opened the door just enough to put her head out, for it was not yet time for the mid-day meal, and she wondered what was wanted.

'Bid your mistress veil herself, my child,' said Omobono. 'Here is a famous astrologer come to tell her the future, which will help her to pass the time.'

Lucilla glanced at Gorlias with curiosity and smiled, showing all her teeth.

'Indeed it is very dull here,' she observed, and disappeared, shutting the door behind her.

While the two men waited Gorlias produced from the folds of his wide tunic a big roll of parchment, which he unrolled a foot or two, displaying a multitude of incomprehensible signs and figures; he also took out a large brass compass, a sheet of cotton paper from Padua, also rolled up, and an Arabic almanack with a silver clasp. Omobono surveyed these preparations with mingled curiosity and sceptical amusement, till Lucilla opened the door again and ushered both men into Zoë's presence. The astrologer made cabalistic signs with his right hand while he advanced, as if he were drawing imaginary figures in the air with his extended forefinger. Zoë's face was quite concealed in the double folds of a white gauze veil, but she seemed to watch him attentively as he came towards her.

CHAPTER VIII

Zoë and the astrologer sat in the covered balcony in full view of the secretary, who remained near the door, straining his sharp ears in vain to catch some words of the whispered conversation. The maids had been dismissed. From time to time Gorlias spoke aloud, pointing with his compass to different parts of the figure, but what he said only made it more impossible to guess at what he whispered. Zoë sat almost motionless, but she had opened the folds of her veil so as to uncover her mouth, and after her companion had been speaking some time she bent down and answered in his ear, pretending, however, to point to the figures on the paper, as if she were asking questions.

The substance of what Gorlias told her was that he and his friends were interested in a mighty enterprise, and had often tried to sound Carlo Zeno with regard to helping them to carry it out, but they had met with no success, for he either did not understand, or he would not. Messer Sebastian Polo, whose house he frequented, was a timid man, and was not to be trusted with such a secret; moreover, he was so extremely anxious to make Zeno marry his daughter, that he would certainly never allow him to run any risks.

All this he put very clearly, and Omobono might have been surprised to learn that he had not used any password. Then Zoë bent down to his ear.

'What is the name of Sebastian Polo's daughter?' she asked.

'Giustina,' whispered the astrologer. 'The sun near to mid-heaven,' he continued aloud, 'and in trine aspect to Mars, signifies fine horses and a retinue of servants.' He dropped his voice again. 'She is thirty, and has had the smallpox,' he whispered.

'The master has only been here once since I came,' said Zoë, bending to his ear again. 'I have no influence with him.'

Gorlias turned his face towards her in slow surprise.

'Had he not seen you before he bought you, Kokóna Arethusa?' he enquired.

'Yes, indeed!'

'Oh! I thought that you also might have had the smallpox,' was the whispered answer.

Zoë could not help laughing a little. The pretty notes, muffled by the veil, seemed to come from far away. It was the first time she had laughed naturally since many weeks. The astrologer bent nearer to her when she was silent again, and spoke aloud, pointing to his figure.

'Venus is in the Seventh House in benign aspect to the Moon,' he said aloud. 'You will be fortunate in love.' Then he whispered again, 'I will give you a philtre that has never failed. The next time he comes—'

Zoë shook her head decidedly, with something that looked like indignation.

'It is for a good matter, Kokóna,' Gorlias answered. 'If you will help us, you shall have pearls and diamonds, and gold and liberty.'

'Liberty? How?'

Gorlias thought that he had tempted her with that, at least.

'If you will promise your help with Messer Carlo, I will tell you.'

'How can I promise what is not mine to give?' asked the girl.

The astrologer was not discouraged, and after more talk about the planets, in a tone loud enough to be heard by the maids if they were listening at the door, he went on quickly again.

'Messer Carlo is a man who loves adventures, who has led desperate and forlorn hope to victory, both in Italy and Greece, who has the gift of the leader, if ever a man had it. Surely, you knew all this.'

'I know he has been a soldier,' Zoë answered, for Zeno had told her so.

'He also possesses some fortune, and has great connexions in Venice. Moreover, I can tell you, Kokóna, that this is no small matter. If he succeeds, he will earn gratitude of the Serene Republic and honour everywhere.'

'As much as that?' asked Zoë, looking attentively at the astrologer through her veil. 'How am I to believe you?'

'I thought I had spoken clearly enough,' Gorlias answered, 'but lest you should doubt my word and promise, take these.'

He had furtively slipped his hand into the bosom of his tunic, and when he withdrew it his fingers closed over something he held gathered in his palm. Cleverly turning the sheet of paper on which he had shown his astrological figures, so as to hinder Omobono from seeing, he disclosed to Zoë a short string of very large and beautiful pearls.

'In your nativity,' he rattled on, aloud, 'the beneficent influences altogether outweigh the malefic ones.'

He said much more to the same effect, and while he was speaking he let the pearls slip down upon the skirts of Zoë's over-garment on the side away from the secretary.

'They are yours,' he whispered. 'You shall have a hundred strings like them if you succeed.'

'Give such things to my maids,' Zoë answered, 'not to me! If you are in earnest make a sign, that I may know whence you come.'

'A sign?' repeated Gorlias, as if not understanding.

'Yes, where?' Her mouth was close to his ear as she whispered the question, and she turned her ear towards him for the answer.

He hesitated, and for the first time the dull fixedness of his expression was momentarily dispelled by a very faint look of surprise.

'I ask, where?' Zoë repeated, with strong emphasis, bending to him again.

'Over the water,' he answered at last.

'Both salt and fresh,' she replied instantly.

Gorlias looked at her veiled face long.

'Who are you?' he asked at length. 'Who taught you these things?' He glanced suspiciously at Omobono, who, as he had reason to believe, was acquainted with the secret.

Zoë shook her head.

'No,' she answered. 'One greater than he taught me what I know. You may go now, for your message is delivered. What I can do, I will do, and there is no more to say, for it is my own cause as well as his—the cause of justice, and God is with it.'

Gorlias spoke aloud again, and brought his explanation of the horoscope to a conclusion by informing Zoë that if she wished to know the smaller details of her wonderful future, she must consult him at intervals, as the phases of the moon had a great influence on her fate.

'When the Kokóna wishes to see me,' he said, rising, 'Messer Omobono will send for me, and I will come.'

Before Zoë realised that he had not picked up the string of pearls, he had made his obeisance and was at the door with Omobono, who bowed low to her, and ushered him out.

When she was alone she took the necklace from the folds of her dress, where it had lain, and looked at it a moment before she hid it in her bosom. For she would not allow the maids to see it, and was already debating how she should hide it till she could find an opportunity of giving it back. But when the cold pearls touched her flesh they sent a little chill to her heart, and she thought it was somehow like a warning.

She understood well enough what had happened, for she was quick-witted. Rustan, who had shown that he knew the secret, and his wife, who had spoken to him of Gorlias, had told the latter that Carlo Zeno was in love with a beautiful Greek slave, who could, of course, be easily induced by gifts to use her influence with her master. For Zeno's past deeds had already woven a sort of legend about his name, so that even the soldiers talked of him among themselves, and told stories of the desperate bravery and amazing skill with which he had kept a small Turkish army at bay in Greece with a handful of men for nearly a whole year, and many other tales, of which the most fantastic was less strange than much that afterwards happened to him in his life.

It must have seemed easy enough to the astrologer, and even to Omobono perhaps; but it looked strangely impossible to Zoë herself, when she remembered her only interview with the man whom she was now pledged to win over.

The whole situation was known to her. A conspiracy was on foot to take the Emperor Johannes from his prison and restore him to the throne, imprisoning his son Andronicus in the Amena tower in his stead. Thousands of John's loyal subjects recognised each other by passwords, and talked secretly of a great rising, in which some foresaw vengeance for the wrongs they had suffered, while others, like the Bokharian Rustan, hoped for fortune, reward, and perhaps honour. But the body of the army was not with them yet, the disaffected men lacked skill or courage to preach the cause of the lawful Emperor to their comrades, and the revolution had no guiding spirit. It is far easier to choose a general among soldiers than to pick out a leader of revolt amongst untried and untrained men.

Before he lost his liberty the Emperor had known Zeno, and though a weak man, had judged him rightly. In his prison he possessed means of communicating occasionally with his friends, and he had instructed them to ask Zeno's help; but so far his message had either not been delivered or Zeno had been deaf to the appeal, perhaps judging that the time was not come for the attempt, or that, after all, the cause was not a good one. Having failed to move him in all other ways, the revolutionaries had seized the unexpected opportunity that now presented itself.

The thought that such a man might turn the tide of history, restore the rightful sovereign to the throne, and avenge the awful death of Michael Rhangabé, had crossed Zoë's mind when she had first seen her purchaser in Rustan's house, for the born leader and fighting man generally has something in his face that is not to be mistaken; but to influence Carlo was another matter, as she had understood when he had supped with her. It would be as hard to induce him to do anything he was not inclined to do of his own accord as it would be impossible to hinder him from attempting whatever he chose to try. As for winning him to the cause by gentler means, the high-born girl blushed at the suggestion. He was certainly not in love with her at first sight; of that she was as sure as that she did not love him either.

Yet while she was thinking, she suddenly wondered whether Gorlias had spoken the truth about Giustina Polo. Was she really thirty, and was her face pitted like a cheese-grater, as Gorlias had told her? If she was ugly, why did Zeno go to Polo's house so often? For Zoë had no doubt but that he went there every time he was rowed up the Golden Horn in his pretty skiff. He was always carefully dressed when he stepped into his boat; it was not for old Polo that he wore such fine clothes.

She was very lonely now. During the first two days she had rested herself in her luxurious surroundings, not without the excitement of expecting another visit from Zeno, and she had thought with satisfaction of all the comfort her sacrifice must have brought to her adopted mother, to the little boys, and to poor old Nectaria. But now she wished she could at least be sure that all was well with them, though she was rather sadly conscious that she did not miss them as she had thought she must. During many months she had nursed Kyría Agatha most tenderly, and had helped the old slave to take care of the children; the last weeks had been spent in abject misery, the last days in the final struggle with starvation and sickness, and still she had bravely done her best. Yet she had long felt that Kyría Agatha had not much real affection for her, and would let her starve herself to death to feed her and the boys. It would have been otherwise if Rhangabé had lived; she would have willingly died of hunger for him, but he was gone, and though she had done and borne the impossible, it had not been for her own blood, but for the sake of the good and brave man's memory. He was in peace, after the agony of his death, his wife and his sons were provided for, so far as Zoë could provide by giving her freedom and her life for them. As far as she could she had paid her debt of gratitude to the dead, and the debt that was not wiped out was due to her; those who had murdered Rhangabé owed her his unspeakable sufferings and every precious drop of his heart's blood. They should pay. If she lived, they should pay all to the uttermost.

And now, fate had placed within her reach the instrument of vengeance, the bravest, rashest, wisest, most desperate of mankind. Her heart had silently and joyfully drunk in every word that Gorlias had said about the man who owned her as he owned the carpet under her feet, the roof over her head, and the clothes that covered her.

He was within her reach, but he was not within her power. Not yet. Her mood had changed, and for a while, not knowing what she dreamt of, she wished that she were indeed one of those Eastern enchantresses of whom she had often heard, without half understanding, who roused men to frenzy, or lulled their lovers to sleep and ruin, as they would; she wished she were that wicked Antonina, for whom brave, pure-hearted Belisarius had humbled himself in the dust; she wished she were Theodora, shamelessly great and fair, an imperial Vision of Sin, compelling to her heel the church-going, priest-haunted master of half the known world—Justinian. She knew the story of her adopted country. What had either of those women that she had not, wherewith to master a man?

Then the tide of shame came back, and she turned her face away from the empty room, as if it had guessed her thoughts; and then, to get away from them, she called her maids, clapping her hands sharply. They came running in and stood before her.

'Go, Yulia,' she said, 'find the secretary and beg him to come to me.'

While she waited, she made Lucilla arrange her veil again so that it hid her face, and this was scarcely done when Omobono was ushered in by the other girl. He bowed to Zoë and gravely stroked his pointed beard.

'What is the Kokóna's pleasure?' he asked, after a pause.

'Do you speak Latin?' Zoë enquired, in that language.

The little man drew himself up proudly, and cleared his throat.

'In my family we have been notaries for five generations,' he answered, in language that was comprehensible but would have filled an average Churchman with vague uneasiness, and would have made Cicero's ashes rattle in their urn.

Zoë was satisfied, however, for though her maids might understand Italian, she was quite sure that Latin was beyond them. She herself spoke it far more correctly than Omobono, though with a rather lisping Greek accent. She could not have helped saying 'vonus' for 'bonus,' 'eyo' for 'ego,' and 'Thominus' for 'Dominus.'

'Where is Thominus Carolus?' she enquired, so suddenly that the secretary was almost taken off his guard.

'He is—he is gone out,' he answered.

'Yes. He is gone to dine with Messer Sebastian Polo. He goes there two or three times a week.'

Zoë watched the secretary's face with amusement; his surprise was comical.

'Then the man is really an astrologer,' he said, in a wondering tone, 'and star-gazing is not all nonsense!'

'Sebastian Polo's daughter is young and beautiful,' observed Zoë, who apparently did not place implicit faith in astrology.

Omobono's face and gesture expressed a qualified assent, but he said nothing.

'Tell me at once,' said Zoë, 'that she is thirty, that her complexion resembles the dust when it is pitted by raindrops after a shower—'

'That would not be true,' cried the secretary. 'Giustina Polo is not supremely beautiful, but she is young and pretty, and as fresh as roses.'

'But she is very poor,' suggested Zoë. 'She has no dowry.'

'Who says so?' asked Omobono indignantly. 'The house of Sebastian Polo is as prosperous as any in Constantinople! He is as rich as any Venetian here except, perhaps, Marin Cornèr!'

'Then it is true that the master is going to marry his daughter,' Zoë replied, as if stating a fact that could no longer be denied.

She was rapidly working the secretary into a state of excitement in which his Latin grammar went to the winds.

'No, indeed!' he cried. 'It is altogether a lie! Who has told you such things?'

'She is young, pretty, fresh as roses, and very rich,' said Zoë, recapitulating. 'Did you not say so?'

'Yes—'

'And the master goes to dine in her father's house three times a week—'

'Perhaps—'

'Do you suppose that Polo would invite the master so often unless he wanted him for his daughter?'

'Perhaps not—'

'Or that the master would wilfully deceive Polo and the girl?'

'What are you saying?'

'Simply that Thominus Carolus is going to marry Thomna Justina.'

'But I tell you—'

'Either you are very simple, or you think I am,' interrupted Zoë, with crushing logic. 'Which shall it be, Master Secretary?'

Omobono thought her a terrible young person just then. He spread out his hands and looked up to the ceiling in despair, but still protesting.

'And meanwhile,' she continued, 'what is the master going to do with me? Am I to be locked up here for ever?'

If anything could further disturb Omobono's equanimity it was this question. His gentle temper was beginning to be ruffled.

'How can I tell?' he asked. 'He will do what he thinks best! Ask him yourself!'

After all, she was only a slave, he said in his heart, and he was the descendant of five generations of notaries. What right had she to cross-examine him? He was the more angry with her for asking the question, because his own curiosity had tormented him for days to find an answer to it.

'Omobono,' Zoë said, affecting a very grave tone, 'you know very well what the master means to do. Now I ask you solemnly, and you are warned that you must answer me—by four—'

'No, no!' cried the secretary, in sudden distress. 'Do not ask me by that!'

'I must, Omobono; and of course you have been told what you have to expect if you refuse to help a friend over the water.'

She emphasised the last words in a way that made him tremble.

'Yes, yes—I know—' he said feebly, though he had not the least notion of the penalty.

'You will be broken to pieces by inches with a small hammer, beginning at the tips of your fingers till there is not a whole bone in your body. That is only the beginning.'

Omobono's knees knocked together.

'Then your skin will be turned inside out over your head and your living heart will be cut out of your body, Omobono, and you will die.'

The secretary had already such belief in the power of those who knew the magic words that he turned pale and the cold sweat stood on his forehead.

'If all this were to be done to me now,' he faltered, 'I could not tell you what the master intends!'

She saw that it was the truth.

'Very well,' she said; 'then you must manage that he shall come here to-day as soon as he returns from Polo's house.'

'I will tell him that you have asked to see him—'

'No. Tell him that I shall fall ill if I am shut up in these rooms any longer, and that if he does not believe it, he had better come and see how I am. He will probably take your advice. I do not choose to show you my face, but I assure you I am very pale, and I have no appetite.'

'He will come,' said the secretary confidently.

'You can also do me another service, Omobono,' continued Zoë. 'I have learned that last Friday, when you went to find Rustan about buying me, you came upon him in the beggars' quarter, near the church of Saint Sergius and Saint Bacchus, at a house where some very poor people lived. This is true, is it not?'

Omobono nodded, wondering how she knew of the circumstance.

'A poor woman lay there ill, with children and a very old nurse, and Rustan gave them something. I wish to know how these poor people are, and where they live, if they have left that house. I am sure the master is charitable, and will let you give them something if they are still in need. There were two little boys, and there was a grown girl besides the sick woman and the other.'

'You know everything!' cried Omobono. 'The man must be a great astrologer! I will go myself to the beggars' quarter and do your bidding.'

Zoë had played her little comedy because she had by this time guessed the man's character, and wished to make sure that she could rely on his help in anything she decided to do; for it was clear that whenever Zeno was absent, the secretary was in charge of the whole establishment, and the servants would obey him without hesitation. As Gorlias had told him, whatever he did was right in their eyes.

That he was in haste to do her bidding she discovered before the afternoon was half over, for as she sat in her window she saw him go down to wait for his master at the marble steps, and he walked slowly on the strip of black and white pavement by the water's edge.

At last he stood still, and looked towards Blachernæ, for the skiff was in sight. Zoë drew her veil across her face and rested her head against the right-hand side of the open window as if she were very tired, and she did not move from this position as the boat came near. Zeno was leaning back in the stern, and could not help seeing her as he approached the house, but from her attitude he thought she did not see him, and he looked up at her steadily for two or three seconds. She was quite motionless.

Omobono stood by the water's edge as Zeno stepped ashore, and asked permission to say a few words to him at once. Zeno dismissed the boat by a gesture.

'Has anything happened?' he asked, glancing up at the window again.

Zoë had not moved, but she could see him through her veil. Then the two men walked up and down, while Omobono spoke in a low tone, but though she could not hear the words she knew what the substance was. Then came Zeno's voice, cold and clear.

'Certainly not,' he said decidedly. 'I shall do nothing of the sort! If she has no appetite send for a doctor. Do you take me for one? Send for old Solomon the Jewish physician. He is the best, and he is an old man. If he says the girl needs air, take her out in the boat, her and the maids, on fine mornings.'

A question from Omobono followed, which Zoë could not hear distinctly. Zeno was evidently annoyed.

'Omobono, you are a good man,' he said; 'but you have no more sense than a cackling hen! Never think! It is not your strong point. When you do just what I tell you, you never make a mistake.'

The secretary's voice was heard again, low and indistinct.

'No,' answered Zeno. 'You need not go and tell her what I have said, for she has probably heard every word of it herself, from the window. It is useless ever to tell women anything. They always know before they are told.'

Thereupon Zeno went in, apparently in a bad temper. If anything can make a woman angry when she is overhearing a conversation about herself, it is to hear it said that she is undoubtedly listening. Zoë had not hidden herself, and Zeno must have meant her to hear what he was saying, but she felt the more deeply insulted. Her cheek burned, and she drew back her veil to feel the cool air. So he had no intention of coming to see her again! A Jewish doctor and an airing in the boat, with Omobono for company! And she had been told that she had been listening—it was not to be borne! She threw her veil on one side, her silk shawl on the other, and then walked up and down the long room with restless steps, like a young wild animal in a cage.

The little maids picked up the things and watched her uneasily, for she had always seemed very gentle. They looked at her with wide eyes now, and their gaze irritated her, till she felt that she wanted to box their ears, and wished she had the negress's whip in her belt. Then, without any apparent reason, she threw her arms round the one that stood nearest and kissed the astonished girl a dozen times, almost lifting her from the floor. As she let her go, she laughed nervously at herself.

She was thirsty, and she drank off a tall glass of cold water at a draught; and all the time she was unconsciously repeating one phrase to herself.

'He shall pay me for this, he shall pay me for this!'

The words rang in her ears, to a sort of silly tune that would not go away. There is a vile natural hurdy-gurdy somewhere in our brains, and when we are angry, or in love, or broken-hearted, or otherwise beside ourselves, it plays its absurd little tunes at us till we are ready to go mad. I sometimes think that devil's music may have brought on the final fatal irritation against life, that has decided the fate of many half-mad suicides.

'He shall pay me for this!' She heard the words keeping time with her movements; she walked slower—faster, but it made no difference, for the infernal little notes took the beat from her steps.

She had not the least notion how Zeno was to pay for having made her so very angry, and that question did not obtrude itself on her thoughts till her temper was beginning to subside; then she suddenly felt how utterly helpless she was, and her wrath boiled up again. The only way of paying him out that suggested itself was to throw herself out of the window. Then he would be sorry for what he had done.

Would he? He would probably send Omobono to have her corpse taken away as quickly as possible. And the day after to-morrow he would go again to see Giustina Polo in her father's house, and she would have thrown herself out of the window for nothing. Besides, it would be wicked.

She realised how childish her thoughts were, and she sat down to think—'like a grown-up woman,' she said to herself. But just then she remembered Zeno's words to Omobono. 'Never think, for it is not your strong point,' he had said to his secretary; but he had of course meant it for her. Everything had been meant for her. She wished she could hold his brown throat in her hands and dig her little nails into it.

Appetite, indeed! Was it strange that she should not be hungry? How could any one eat who lived such a life, shut up between four walls?—with a tyrant downstairs who did not even take the trouble to come and look at her, but sent his silly old clerk to keep her company! He took trouble enough to go and see Giustina Polo!

This was thinking 'like a grown-up woman,' as she had proposed to do! She was disgusted with herself, and looked about for something to occupy her thoughts. There were sweetmeats, whole boxes of sweetmeats of every sort. Twice already they had been emptied and refilled with fresh ones, since she had been brought to the house. That was Zeno's idea of what a woman needed to occupy her thoughts and be happy! Sweetmeats! Preserve of rose-leaves! Figs in syrup! That was all he knew of her wants!

She lay back among her cushions, her brown eyes gleamed angrily, her lips were a little parted, and her nostrils quivered now and then as she drew a sharp breath. Presently, she called Yulia to her side.

'Go to the secretary,' she said, 'and tell him to send me a book.'

'A book?' repeated the slave stupidly, for she had never seen a woman who could read.

'Yes. A book in Greek, Latin, or Italian; it does not matter which. I am sick of doing nothing. Tell him to be quick, too,' she added, in a tone of authority.

The girl tripped away and found Omobono in the counting-house on the ground floor. He was in a bad humour too, but in his case it took the form of dignified sorrow. His master had compared him to a fowl, and to one that cackled.

'What does she want with a book?' he asked, in a dreary tone, looking up from his accounts.

'To read, I think, sir,' answered the little maid timidly; 'and she told me to beg you to let her have it soon.'

'As if a slave could read!' He looked about him in a melancholy way, and rose to take from the shelf above his head a good-sized volume bound in soft brown leather, with little thongs tied in slip knots, for clasps, to keep it shut.

'Take her that,' he said, thrusting the book into the girl's hands.

Yulia took it, and before she had left the room Omobono was gravely busy with his figures again; but each time he added up a column the sum seemed to be 'cackling hen,' instead of anything reasonable. But Yulia ran upstairs.

Zoë untied the thongs and opened the book in the middle. An exclamation of anger and disgust escaped her lips. The secretary, who did not believe she could really read, though she spoke Latin fluently, had sent an old volume of accounts in answer to her request. There were pages and pages of entries and columns of figures, all neatly written in his small, clear hand, on stout cotton paper. Here and there some one else had made a note, as if checking his work.

Zoë pushed the book away from her on the divan, and it fell over the edge and lay face downwards and open on the floor. Then the little tune began again in her head.

'He shall pay me for this!'

She wished he would open the door noiselessly and be all at once beside her, as on that first evening. That had been Friday, and to-day was Wednesday; five days had gone by. Counting Friday there were six, and six days were practically a week! She had been under his roof a whole week and he had only cared to see her face once.

'He shall pay me for this!'

The tune went on, and she quite forgot how she had longed for death, and how his first anticipated coming had been dreadful beyond anything she had ever suffered, beyond cold, starvation, and misery. Or if she remembered it at all, she told herself that the man she had seen was not the kind of man she had expected, and that she had nothing to fear from him. She was quite sure of that.

She turned on one side, as she half lay on the divan, till she could reach the account-book to pick it up. One of the maids jumped up from the carpet to help her.

'Go away!' she exclaimed crossly, for she had got hold of the cover and had drawn the volume over the edge of the divan. 'I will call if I want anything.'

The girls slipped away in silence and left her alone. She turned over the pages with a sort of angry curiosity, half expecting to find an entry concerning slaves bought and sold like herself. Just then she could have believed Zeno capable of anything.

But though she found a great many strange words which she did not understand, and which referred to tonnage, insurance, profit and loss, and all the complicated matters of an Eastern merchant's business, there was nothing which could possibly be interpreted to mean that Zeno had dealt in humanity, as most of the Venetians who lived in Constantinople certainly did. Sebastian Polo's name occurred very often. Large sums had been paid to him, and other large sums had been received from him. It was clear that the two men were in close relations of business, and constantly made ventures together, dividing the profits and sharing the losses.

That might account for Zeno's constant visits to his fellow-merchant, though Zoë was not inclined to admit such a view. On the contrary, she made herself believe that Zeno dealt with Polo solely in order to make an excuse for seeing more of the latter's daughter. He should pay for that, too! The little tune hammered away in her head at a great rate.

She clapped her hands.

'Take this back to the secretary,' she said, giving the book to Yulia. 'Tell him I am not a merchant's clerk, and that I want something to read.'

Again little Yulia tripped downstairs to the ground floor. But the counting-house was locked, and the men-servants told her that Omobono had gone out. She would not leave the book with them, for she had a superstitiously exaggerated idea of the value of all written things; therefore, after a moment's hesitation, she turned and carried it upstairs again, though she did not like the idea of facing her mistress.

At the first landing she almost ran against the master of the house, who asked her what she was carrying and where she was going. He spoke rather sharply, and Yulia was frightened and told him the whole story, explaining that Zoë seemed to be in a bad temper, and would be angry with her for bringing back the account-book, but that it was Omobono's fault. How could he dare to suppose that the Kokóna could not read? And why was he out? And if he was not out why had the men-servants told her that he was?

The little slave did as all slaves and servants naturally do when they wish to gain favour with the master; she hinted that all the other servants in the house were in league to do evil, and that she only was righteous. Zeno carelessly looked through the pages of the account-book as he stood listening to her tale.

'You talk too much,' he observed, when she paused. 'Go upstairs.'

Thereupon he turned his back on her and went in under the heavy curtain to his own room, taking the book with him and leaving Yulia considerably disconcerted. She looked at the curtain disconsolately for a few seconds, and then slowly ascended the second flight of steps to the women's apartments.

A few minutes later Zeno himself followed her, with another book in his hand. He knocked discreetly at the outer door, and Lucilla opened, for Yulia was still explaining to Zoë what had happened. The maid stood aside to let the master pass through the vestibule which separated the inner rooms from the staircase. Zeno raised the curtain and went in.

'I am no great reader,' he said, as he came forward towards the divan, 'but I have brought you this old book. It may amuse you. The man died more than fifty years ago, and I fancy he was mad; but there must be something in his poem, for it has been copied again and again. This was given me by the Emperor Charles when I was with him in Venice.'

Zoë had time to recover from her surprise and to study his face and manner while he spoke, and again she was convinced that he was a little shy in her presence. If she changed colour at all he did not see it, for though he glanced at her two or three times, he looked more often at the book he held. As he finished speaking he placed it in her hands and his eyes met hers.

Possibly Zoë had guessed that if she could make a stir in the house by sending messages to Omobono, the master would at last come in person; at all events she felt a little thrill of triumph when he was before her bringing his book and speaking pleasantly, as a sort of peace-offering for having neglected her so long.

'Thank you,' said she, very sweetly. 'Will it please your lordship to be seated?'

Yulia had pushed forward a large fold-stool, and Zoë motioned to her and her companion to sit down in a corner. Zeno thought she had sent them out of the room, and he looked round and saw them squatting on their carpet, side by side.

'Shall I send them away?' asked Zoë, with a sweet smile.

'They are not in the way,' Zeno answered coldly; for he felt that they might be if they understood, but nothing would have induced him to dismiss them just then.

A little pause followed, during which Zoë opened the manuscript and read the illuminated title-page.

'It is dull for you, here,' said Carlo awkwardly.

Zoë did not even look up, and affected to answer absently, while she turned over the pages.

'Oh no!' she said. 'Not in the least, I assure you!' She went back to the title and read it aloud. '"The Divine Comedy of Dante Alighieri"—I have heard his name. A Sicilian, was he not? Or a Lombard? I cannot remember. Have you read the poetry? The paintings are very pretty, I see. There is much more life in Italian painting than in our stiff pictures with their gilt backgrounds. Of course, there is a certain childlike simplicity about them, an absence of school, of the traditions of good masters, of reverence for the old art! But they mean something that is, whereas our Greek pictures mean something that never was. Do you agree with me?'

She had talked on in a careless tone, toying with the book, and only looking up as she asked a question without waiting for a reply. By the time she paused she had asked so many that Zeno only noticed the last.

'You would like Venice,' he said, 'but you would like Florence better. There are good pictures there, I believe.'

'You have not seen them yourself?'

'Oh yes! But I do not understand such things. This man Alighieri describes some of them in his book. He was a Florentine.'

As Zeno showed himself more willing to talk, Zoë seemed to grow more indifferent. She laid the book down beside her, leaned back, and looked out of the window, turning her face half away from him. It was the first time he had seen her by daylight since she had come, and the strong afternoon light glowed in her white skin, her eyes, and her brown hair. He could have seen on her cheek the very smallest imperfection, had it been as tiny as the point of a pin, but there was none. He looked at her tender mouth; and in the strong glare he could have detected the least roughness on her lips, if they had not been as smooth as fresh fruit. Moreover, the line from her ear to her neck was really as perfect as it had seemed at first sight. Her nervous, high-bred young hand lay on the folds of her over-garment, within his reach, and he felt much inclined to take it and hold it. He did not remember that any woman's near presence had disturbed him in the same way, nor had he ever hesitated on the few occasions in his life when he had been inclined to take a woman's hand. He had the fullest rights which the laws of the Empire could give him, for Arethusa, as he called her, was his property out-and-out, and if he died suddenly she would be sold at auction with the furniture. Yet, for some wholly inexplicable reason he did not quite dare to touch the tips of her fingers.

'I have heard that you are a hero,' Zoë observed, without looking at him. 'Is it true?'

Then she turned her eyes to him and smiled a little maliciously, he fancied, as if she had guessed his timidity from his silence.

'Who told you such nonsense?' Zeno asked, with a laugh, for her question had broken the ice—or perhaps had quenched the fire for a while. 'I am a man like any other!'

'That I doubt, sir,' answered Zoë, laughing too, though not much.

'You have no experience of men,' he said. 'They are all like me, I assure you. One sheep is not more like another in a flock.'

'I should not have taken you for one of the common herd. Besides, I know of your deeds in Italy and Greece, and how you fought a Turkish army for a whole year with a handful of men—'

'I have seen some fighting, of course,' Zeno replied. 'But that is all in the past. I am a sober, peace-loving Venetian merchant now, and nothing else.'

'It must be very dull to be a sober, peace-loving Venetian merchant,' said Zoë, faintly mimicking his tone.

'Making money is too hard work to be dull.'

'I suppose so. And then,' she added, with magnificent calm, 'I have always heard that avarice is the passion of old age.'

Zeno fell into the trap.

'Dear me!' he cried in astonishment. 'How old do you think I am?'

Zoë looked at him quietly.

'I have no experience of men,' she said, with perfect gravity, 'but from your manner, sir, I should judge you to be—about fifty.'

Zeno's jaw dropped, for she spoke so naturally and quietly that he could not believe she was laughing at him.

'I shall be twenty-nine in August,' he answered.

'Only twenty-nine?' Zoë affected great surprise. 'I should have thought you were much, much older! Are you quite sure?'

'Yes.' Carlo laughed. 'I am quite sure. But I suppose I seem very old to you.'

'Oh yes! Very!' She nodded gravely as she spoke.

'You are seventeen, are you not?' Zeno asked.

'How in the world should I know!' she enquired. 'Is not my age set down in the receipt Rustan gave you with me? How should a slave know her own age, sir? And if we knew it, do you think that any of us could speak the truth, except under torture? It would not be worth while to dislocate my arms and burn my feet with hot irons, just to know how old I am, would it? You could not even sell me again, if I had once been tortured!'

'What horrible ideas you have! Imagine torturing this little thing!'

Thereupon, without warning, he took her hand in his and looked at it. She made a very slight instinctive movement to withdraw it, and then it lay quite still and passive.

'I am sure I could never bear pain,' she said, smiling. 'I should tell everything at once! I should never make a good conspirator. I suppose you must have been wounded once or twice, when you were young. Tell me, did it hurt very much?'

He let her hand fall as he answered, and she drew it back and hid it under her wide sleeve.

'A cut with a sharp sword feels like a stream of icy-cold water,' he answered. 'A thrust through the flesh pricks like a big thorn, and pricks again when the point comes out on the other side. One feels very little, or nothing at all, if one is badly wounded in the head, for one is stunned at once; it is the headache afterwards that really hurts. If one is wounded in the lungs, one feels nothing, but one is choked by the blood, and one must turn on one's face at once in order not to suffocate. Broken bones hurt afterwards as a rule, more than at first, but it is a curious sensation to have one's collar bone smashed by a blow from a two-handed sword—'

'Good heavens!' cried Zoë. 'What a catalogue! How do you know how each thing feels?'

'I can remember,' Zeno answered simply.

'You have been wounded in all those different ways, and you are alive?'

Zeno smiled.

'Yes; and you understand now why I look so old.'

'I was not in earnest,' Zoë said. 'You knew that I was not. You need only look at yourself in a mirror to see that I was laughing.'

'I was not very deeply hurt by being taken for a man of fifty,' Zeno answered, not quite truthfully.

'Oh no!' laughed Zoë. 'I cannot imagine that my opinion of your age could make any difference to you. It was silly of me—only, for a man who has had so many adventures, you do look absurdly young!'

'So much the better, since my fighting days are over.'

'And since you are a sober, peace-loving merchant,' said Zoë, continuing the sentence for him. 'But are you so very sure, my lord? Would nothing make you draw your sword again and risk your life on your fencing? Nothing?'

'Nothing that did not affect my honour, I truly believe.'

'You would not do it for a woman's sake?' She turned to him, to watch his face, but its expression did not change.

'Three things can drive a wise man mad,—wine, women, and dice.'

'I daresay! Your lordship reckons us in good company. But that is no answer to my question.'

'Yes it is,' said Zeno with a laugh. 'Why should I do for a woman what I would not do for dice or wine?'

'But dice and wine never tempted you,' Zoë objected.

Zeno laughed louder.

'Never? When I was a student at Padua I sold everything, even my books, to get money for both. It was only when the books were gone that I turned soldier, and learned the greatest game of hazard in the world. Compared with that, dice are an opiate, and wine is a sleeping-draught.'

He only smiled now, after laughing, but there was a look in his face as he spoke which she saw then for the first time and did not forget, and recognised when she saw it again. It was subtle, and might have passed unnoticed among men, but it spoke to the sex in the girl, and made her young blood thrill. For worlds, she would not have had him guess what she felt just then.

'Fighting for its own sake would tempt you, if nothing else could,' she answered quietly.

'Ah—perhaps, perhaps,' he answered, musing.

'But you would need a cause, though ever so slight, and you have none here, have you?'

'None that I care to take up.'

'You may find something to fight for—over the water,' Zoë suggested, emphasising the words a little and watching his face.

The phrase meant nothing to him.

'Over the water?' he repeated carelessly. 'At home, in Venice, you mean. Yes, if Venice needed me, I should not wait to be called twice!'

It was quite clear that he attached no meaning to the words she had used, and this fact tallied with what the astrologer had told her in the morning as to his having been deaf to all advances made to him by the imprisoned Emperor's party.

Zoë leaned back in silence for a while, almost closing her eyes, and she saw that he watched her, and that an unmistakable look of admiration stole into his face. She was wondering whether it would ever turn into something more, and whether she should ever see the gleam of fight in his eyes, for her sake, that had flashed in them a moment ago at the mere thought of battle. What did women do, to make men love them? There is an age when girls believe that love need only be called, like a tame dove, and that he will fly in at the window; and there is an age when he comes to them uncalled-for. If only the ages were the same for all, much trouble might be spared. Zoë was perhaps between the two, but she still believed that there was some fixed rule on which clever women acted to make men fall in love with them, those wicked women who are described to young girls as 'designing,' and are supposed to know precisely the effect they can produce on men at any moment, to the very nicety of an eyelash.

Zeno broke the long silence with an unexpected speech which roughly awakened Zoë from her reflection.

'As for this Emperor John whom his son has locked up,' he said, 'his friends have done their best to interest me in his cause. He has even sent me messages, begging me to help him to escape. Why? What difference can it make to me whether he or his son dies in the Amena tower? They are poor things, both of them, and for all I care John may starve in his chains before I will lift a finger!'

Zoë sighed and bit her lip to check herself, for his voluntary declaration had dashed the palace of her hopes to pieces in an instant.

Then she was ashamed of having even dreamt that he might love her, since he despised the very cause for which she had wished to win his love. But this state of mind did not last long, either. She was too brave to let such a speech pass, as if she agreed with it.

'You are wrong,' she said, quite forgetting that she had set herself to play the part of the slave. 'You ought to help him, if you can—and you can, if you will.'

Zeno looked at her in surprise. There was something like authority in her tone, and the two little maids, whom he had forgotten in their corner behind him, stared in astonishment at her audacity. Not a word of the conversation had escaped them.

'I mean,' continued Zoë, before he could find an answer to her plain statement, 'if you are a true Venetian you should wish to put down the man whom the Genoese and the Turks have set on the throne. Johannes is your friend and your country's friend, though he is a weak man and always will be. Andronicus is an enemy to Venice and a friend to her enemies. He is even now ready to give the island of Tenedos to them—the key to the Dardanelles—'

'What?' asked Zeno in a loud and angry tone. 'Tenedos?'

His manner had changed, and he almost rose from his seat as he bent forwards and seized her wrist in his excitement. She was glad, and smiled at him.

'Yes,' she answered, 'the Genoese demand it as the price of their protection, and they will force him to give it to them. But it may not be easy, for the governor of the island is loyal to Johannes.'

'How do you know these things?' asked Zeno, still holding her wrist and trying to look into her eyes.

'I know them,' Zoë answered. 'If I am not telling you the truth, sell me in the market to-morrow.'

'By the Evangelist,' swore Zeno, 'you will deserve it.'

CHAPTER IX

A month had passed, and yet, to all outward appearance, Zeno's manner of living had undergone no change. He rose early and bathed in the Golden Horn on fine days. He attended to his business in the morning, and dined with Sebastian Polo twice a week, but generally at home on the remaining days; and he rode out in the afternoon with a single running footman, or stayed indoors if it rained. Even his own servants and slaves hardly noticed any change in his habits, and only observed that he often looked preoccupied, and sometimes sat on his balcony for an hour without moving, his eyes fixed on the towers of the Blachernæ palace.

They did not know how much time he spent with his beautiful Greek slave; and they found that the two little maids, Yulia and Lucilla, were not inclined to gossip when they came downstairs on an errand. Omobono probably knew a good deal, but he kept it to himself, and stored the fruits of his lively curiosity to enjoy alone the delicious sensation of the miser gloating over his useless gold. On the whole, therefore, life in the Venetian merchant's house had gone on much as usual for a whole month after Zoë had fired a train which was destined to produce momentous results when it reached the mine at last.

Zeno saw her every day now, and often twice, and she had become a part of his life, and necessary to him; though he did not believe that he was in love with her, any more than she would have admitted that she loved him.

For each was possessed by one dominant thought; and it chanced, as it rarely chances in real life, that one deed, if it could be performed, would satisfy the hopes of both. Zeno, born patriot and leader, saw that the whole influence of his country in the East was at stake in the matter of Tenedos; Zoë thirsted to revenge the death of Michael Rhangabé, her adopted father and the idol of her childhood.

If the imprisoned Emperor Johannes could be delivered from the Amena tower, both would certainly obtain what they most desired. Johannes would give Tenedos to Venice, in gratitude for his liberty, and the people of Constantinople would probably tear Andronicus to ribands in the Hippodrome, on the very spot where Rhangabé had suffered.

They would rally round their lawful sovereign if he could only be got out of the precincts of the palace, where the usurper was strongly guarded by his foreign mercenaries, mostly Circassians, Mingrelians, Avars, and Slavonians. The people would not rise of themselves to storm Blachernæ, nor would the Greek troops revolt of their own accord; but as they all feared the soldiers of the foreign legion, they hated them and their master Andronicus, and the presence of Johannes amongst them would restore their courage and make the issue certain.

Such a leader as Carlo Zeno might indeed have successfully besieged Andronicus in his palace; but he knew, and every man and woman in Constantinople knew well enough, that Andronicus would make an end of his father and of his two younger brothers in prison, at the first sign of a revolution, so that there might be no lawful heir to the throne left alive but he himself.

Therefore it was the first and the chief object of the patriots to bring Johannes secretly from his place of confinement to the heart of the city, or to one of the islands, beyond the reach of danger, till the revolution should be over and his son a prisoner in his stead; though it was much more probable that the latter would be summarily put to death as a traitor.

All this Zeno had understood before Zoë had spoken to him about it; but he had not known that the Genoese had demanded Tenedos of Andronicus as the price of their protection against the Turks; for the negotiations had been kept very secret, and at first Carlo had not believed the girl, and had deemed that the tale might be a pure invention.

He had come again to see her on the following day, and again he had vainly tried to find out who she was, and in what great Fanariote house she had been brought up. It was impossible to get a word from her on this subject; and she warned him that what she had told him must not be repeated in the hearing of any Genoese, nor of any one connected with the Court. The Genoese meant that no one should know of the treaty till it was carried out, and until Tenedos was theirs; for the place was very strong, as they afterwards found by experience, and Andronicus needed their help too much to risk losing their favour by an indiscretion.

These injunctions of silence made Carlo still more doubtful as to the veracity of Zoë's story, and he frankly told her so and demanded proof; but she only answered as she had at first.

'If it is not true,' she said, 'brand me in the forehead, as they brand thieves, and sell me in the open market.'

And again he was angry, and swore that he would do so by her indeed if the story was a lie; but she smiled confidently, and nodded her assent.

'If you do not save the Emperor,' she said, 'you Venetians will be driven out of Constantinople before many months; and if Genoa once holds Tenedos how shall you ever again sail up the Dardanelles?'

Many a time she had heard Michael Rhangabé say as much to his friends, and she knew that it was wisdom. So did Zeno, and he wondered at the knowledge of his bought slave. So he came and went, turning over the great question in his brain; and she awaited his coming gladly, because she saw that he was roused, and because the longing for just revenge was uppermost in her thoughts. Thus were the two drawn together more and more, fate helping. Yet he told her nothing of the steps he took so quickly after he had once made up his mind to act.

She no longer asked him what he meant to do with her; she did not again send for the secretary to complain that her existence was dull; she no longer was impatient with her maids; she seemed perfectly satisfied with her existence.

She went out when she pleased to go, in the beautiful skiff, in charge of Omobono, and always with one of the girls; and she sat in the deep cushioned seat as the great ladies did when they were rowed to the Sweet Waters, and as she had sat many times in old days, beside Kyría Agatha. The secretary sat on a little movable seat in the waist of the boat, which was built almost exactly like a modern Venetian gondola without the hood, and the slave-girl sat in the bottom at her mistress's feet. Zoë, the adopted daughter of the Protosparthos, had gone abroad with uncovered face, but Arethusa, the slave, was closely veiled, though that was not the general custom. And often, as she glided along in the spring afternoons, she passed people she had known only a year ago, or a little more, who wondered why she hid her features; or told each other, as was more or less true, that she was some handsome white slave, whose jealous master would not suffer her beauty to be seen. For it was clear that Omobono was only a respectable elderly person placed in charge of her.

The two generally conversed in Latin, and the secretary told her of his search for Kyría Agatha, the children, and old Nectaria. She had never shown him her face since she had been a slave, and she believed that he did not connect her with the ragged girl he had seen bending over the sick woman's bed in the beggars' quarter. She had enjoined upon him the greatest discretion in case he found the little family, and with Omobono such an injunction was quite unnecessary, for outward discretion is the characteristic quality of curiosity, which is inwardly the least discreet of failings. People who look through keyholes, listen behind curtains, and read other people's letters are generally the last to talk of what they learn in that way.

As yet, the secretary's search had been fruitless, but he had long ago made up his mind that Zoë was Kyría Agatha's daughter. The bandy-legged sacristan of Saint Bacchus had helped him to this conclusion by informing him that Rustan Karaboghazji had not come to perform his devotions in the church for some time; never, in fact, since that Friday afternoon on which Omobono had inquired after him.

The secretary had searched the beggars' quarter in vain. He remembered the ruined house very well, and the crazy shutters with bits of rain-bleached string tied to them for fastenings. There were people living in it, but they were not the same beggars; it was now inhabited by the chief physician of the beggars himself, whose business it was to prepare misery for the public eye, at fixed rates. For among those who were really starving there lived a small tribe of professional paupers, who displayed the horrors of their loathsome diseases at the doors of the churches all over Constantinople. The physician was skilful in his way, and though he preferred a real cripple, or a real sore for his art to improve upon, he could produce the semblance of either on sound limbs and a whole skin, though the process was expensive. Yet that increased cost was balanced by the ability of his healthy patients to go alone to a great distance, and thus to vary the scene of their industry. They thus picked up the charity which should have reached the real poor, most of whom could hardly crawl as far as the great thoroughfares more than once or twice a week, at the risk of their lives. The sham beggar always has a marvellous power of covering the ground, but you must generally seek the real one in the lair where he is dying. Omobono had learnt much about beggars which he had not known before then, and he had found no trace whatever of the people whom he was seeking.

They seemed very far away when Zoë thought of them. She wondered whether any of them missed her, except Nectaria, now that they had warm clothes and plenty to eat. The sacrifice had been very terrible at first,—it did not seem so now; and she knew that on that very afternoon when she went home after being out in the boat, she would listen for Zeno's footstep in the vestibule, and think the time long till he came.

But Omobono had gathered a good deal of information about her from his acquaintance, the sacristan, whom he strongly suspected of being in league with Rustan to inform him when there was anything worth buying in the beggars' quarter; for the Bokharian was a busy man, and had no time to spend in searching for unusual merchandise, nor, when there was any to be had, would it have been to his advantage to be seen often in its neighborhood. So he paid the sacristan to quarter the ground continually for him, while he was engaged elsewhere. It is to the credit of Rustan's splendid business intelligence that the system he employed has not been improved on in five hundred years; for when the modern slave-dealers make their annual journeys to the centres of supply they find everything ready for them, like any other commercial traveller.

Having understood Rustan's mode of procedure, Omobono had extracted from the sacristan such information as the latter possessed about Zoë and Kyría Agatha, but that was not very much after all. They had lived three or four weeks in the ruined house, or perhaps six; he could not remember exactly. At first they all came to the church, but they had sold their miserable clothes and their wretched belongings. The last time the girl had come, she had been alone, and she had worn a blanket over her shoulders to keep her warm. That had been at dusk. Then Rustan had bought her, and soon afterwards they must have gone away, since the beggars' physician was now installed in the house. Why should the sacristan take any interest in them? They were gone, and Constantinople was a vast city. No, the woman had not died, for he would have known it. When people died they were buried, even if they had starved to death in the beggars' quarter.

Zoë thanked Omobono for the information, and begged him to continue her search. He wondered why she did not burst into tears, and concluded that she was either quite heartless, or was in love with Zeno, or both. He inclined to the latter theory. Love, he told himself with all the conviction of middle-aged inexperience, was a selfish passion. Zoë loved Zeno, and did not care what had become of her mother.

Besides, he knew that she was jealous. She had heard of Giustina, and was determined to see her. She insisted that the boat should keep to the left, going up the Golden Horn, and she made the secretary point out Sebastian Polo's dwelling. It was a small palace, a hundred yards below the gardens of Blachernæ, and it had marble steps, like those at Zeno's house. A girl with dyed hair sat in the shade in an upper balcony; her hair was red auburn, like that of the Venetian women, and her face was white, but that was all Zoë could see. She wished she had a hawk's eyes. Omobono said it might be Giustina, but as the latter had many friends, it might also be one of them, for most Venetian women had hair of that colour.

Farther up, they neared Blachernæ, and came first to the great Amena tower, of which the foundations stood on an escarped pier in the water. Zoë looked up, trying to guess the height of the upper windows from the water, but she had no experience, and they were very high—perhaps a hundred palms, perhaps fifty—Zeno would know. Could he get up there by a rope? She wondered, and she thought of what she should feel if she herself were hanging there in mid-air by a single rope against the smooth wall. Then in her imagination she saw Zeno half-way up, and some one cut the line above, for he was discovered, and he fell. A painful thrill ran down the back of her neck and her spine and through her limbs, and she shrank in her seat.

It was up there, in the highest story, that Johannes had been a prisoner nearly two years. The windows needed no gratings, for it would be death to leap out, and no one could climb up to get in. The pier below the tower sloped to the stream, and its base ran out so far that no man could have jumped clear of it from above—even if he dared the desperate risk of striking the water. Bertrandon de la Broquière saw it, years afterwards, when Zeno was an old man, and you may look at a good picture of it in his illuminated book.

A solitary fisherman was perched on the edge of the sloping pier, apparently hindered from slipping off by the very slight projection of the lowest course of stones, which was perpendicular. His brown legs were bare far above the knee, he wore a brown fisherman's coat of a woollen stuff, not woven but fulled like felt; a wide hat of sennet, sewn round and round a small crown of tarred sailcloth, flapped over his ears. He angled in the slow stream with a long reed and a short line.

Zoë looked at him attentively as the boat passed near him, and she saw that he was watching her, too, from under the limp brim of his queer hat.

Her left hand hung over the gunwale of the skiff, and when she was opposite the fisherman she wetted her fingers and carelessly raised them to her lips as if she were tasting the drops. The man instantly replied by waving his rod over the water thrice, and he cast his short line each time. She had seen his mouth and chin and scanty beard below the hanging brim of his hat, and she had fancied that she recognised him; she had no doubt of it now. The solitary fisherman was Gorlias Pietrogliant, the astrologer.

Omobono had scarcely noticed him, for his own natural curiosity made him look steadily up at the high windows, on the chance that the imperial prisoner might look out just then. He had seen him once or twice before the revolution, and wondered whether he was much changed by his long confinement. But instead of the handsome bearded face the secretary remembered, a woman appeared and looked towards Pera for a moment, and drew back hastily as she caught sight of the skiff; she was rather a stout woman with red cheeks, and she wore the Greek head-dress of the upper classes. So much Omobono saw at a glance, though the window was fully ninety feet above him, and she had only remained in sight a few seconds. He had always had good eyes.

But without seeing her at all Zoë had understood that communication between the prisoner and the outer world was carried on through Gorlias, and that by him a message could be sent directly to the Emperor. She did not speak till the boat had passed the whole length of the palace and was turning in the direction of the Sweet Waters.

'That astrologer,' she said, 'do you remember him? Why has he never come again?'

Omobono promised to send for him the very next day. After that there was silence for a while, and the skiff slipped along upstream, till the secretary spoke again, to correct what he had last said.

'He had better not come to-morrow. I will tell him to come the next morning.'

'Why?' Zoë asked, in some surprise.

'To-morrow,' said Omobono, 'Messer Sebastian Polo comes to dine with the master. There will be confusion in the house.'

'Confusion, because one guest comes to dinner?' Zoë spoke incredulously.

'I believe,' said Omobono rather timidly, 'that he will not be the only guest.'

'He brings his daughter with him, then?' Zoë felt that she changed colour under her veil.

'I do not know,' the secretary said smoothly; 'but there will be several guests.'

Zoë turned towards him impatiently.

'You will have orders to keep me out of the way while they are in the house,' she said. 'I shall receive through you the master's commands not to show myself at my window!'

'How can you think such a thing?' cried Omobono, protesting. 'Rather than put you to such inconvenience I am sure the master will beg his guests to enter by the other side of the house.

If it was his object to exasperate her, he had succeeded, but if he expected her to break out in anger he was mistaken. She was too proud, and she already regretted the few hasty words she had spoken. Moreover, her anger told her something that surprised her, and wounded her self-respect. She understood for the first time how jealous she was, and that she could feel no such jealousy if she were not in love. She was not a child, and but for misfortune she would have been married at least two years by this time. This was not the dreamy and slowly stealing dawn of girlhood's day; her sun had risen in a flash amidst angry clouds, as he does in India in mid-June, when the south-west monsoon is just going to break and the rain is very near.

When Omobono had spoken she leaned back in her seat and drew the folds of her mantle more closely round her, as if to separate herself from him more completely, and she did not speak again for a long time. On his side, the secretary understood, and instead of feeling rebuked by her silence, he was pleased with himself because his curiosity had made another step forward in the land of discovery.

It occurred to him that it would be very interesting to bring Zoë and Giustina within sight of each other, if no nearer. Zeno had not said that his guests were to come by land instead of by water; the secretary had only argued that he would request them to do so, to avoid their seeing Zoë if she happened to be at her window. Omobono had power to do whatever he thought necessary for keeping the house and the approach to it in repair without consulting any one. That was a part of his duty.

It was usual to repair the road in the spring. Omobono chose to have the work done now, sent for a gang of labourers, and gave a few simple orders. Before Zeno knew what was going on the way to the main entrance was quite impassable, though a narrow passage had been left to the door of the kitchen for the servants and slaves. The secretary had suddenly discovered that the road was in such a deplorable condition as to make it necessary to dig it out to the depth of a yard here and there, where the soil was soft, thus making a series of pits, over which no horse could pass.

'What in the world possessed you to do this now?' asked Zeno, with annoyance, 'I told you that Messer Sebastian and his daughter were coming to dine with me to-morrow, as well as other friends.'

'They will see nothing, sir,' answered the secretary imperturbably. 'The guests always come by water, they dine on that side of the house, and they go away by water. How could they see the road, sir? It is beyond the court!'

Zeno did not choose to explain that he had especially begged Polo and the others to come by land, and he now concealed his displeasure, or believed that he did. But when Omobono had gone to his own room Zeno sent for the running footmen and bade them go to each of the invited guests early the next morning to say that the road was torn up and that they must be good enough to come in their boats.

Then he went upstairs, for he had not seen Zoë all day, and it pleased him to sup with her. As soon as he entered the room and saw her he felt that something was wrong, but he made as if he noticed nothing, and sat down in his usual place.

'We will have supper together,' he said in a cheerful tone, settling himself in his big chair, and rubbing his hands, like a man who has finished his day's work and looks forward to something pleasant.

As a matter of fact he had done nothing in particular, and had set himself a rather disagreeable task; for he did not wish Messer Sebastian to know that Zoë or any other woman was in the house, and he was reduced to the necessity of telling the girl not to show herself. She was legally his chattel, and if he chose he might lock her up in a room on the other side of the house for a few hours, or in the cellar. He told himself this; and for the hundredth time he recalled her own story of her birth and bringing up, which was logical and clear, and explained both her gentle breeding and the careful education she had evidently received. But logic is often least convincing when it is most unanswerable, and Zeno remained in the belief that the most important part of Zoë's story was still a secret.

She said nothing now in answer to his announcement, but she beckoned to Yulia to bring supper, and the maid disappeared. Being out of temper with him at that moment, she was asking herself how she could possibly be jealous of Giustina Polo; she mentally added that she would no more think of sitting at the window to see her go by, than of looking at her through a keyhole. Also, she wished Zeno would sit where he was for an hour or two, and not utter a word, so that she might show him how utterly indifferent she was to his presence, and that she could be just as silent as he; and women much older than Zoë have felt just as she did then.

But Zeno, who was uncomfortable, was also resolved to be cheerful and at his ease.

'It has been a beautiful day,' he observed. 'I hope you had a pleasant morning on the water.'

'Thanks,' Zoë answered, and said no more.

This was not encouraging, but Zeno was not easily put off.

After a few moments he tried again.

'I fear you do not find my secretary very amusing,' he said.

Zoë was on the point of asking him whether he himself considered Omobono a diverting person, but she checked herself with a little snort of indignation which might have passed for a laugh without a smile. Zeno glanced at her profile, raised his eyebrows, and said nothing more till the slave-girls came with the supper. While they brought the small table and set it between the two, he leaned back in his carved chair, crossed one shapely leg over the other, and drummed a noiseless tattoo with the end of his fingers on his knee, the picture of unconcern. Zoë half sat and half lay on her divan, apparently scrutinising the nail of one little finger, pushing it and rubbing it gently with the thumb of the same hand, and then looking at it again as if she expected to observe a change in its appearance after being touched.

The maids placed the dishes on the table and poured out wine, and Zoë began to eat in silence, without paying any attention to Zeno. That is one way of showing indifference, and both men and women use it, yet it still remains surprisingly effective.

'What is the matter with you?' Zeno asked, suddenly.

Zoë pretended to be surprised and then smiled coldly.

'Oh! you mean, because I am hungry, I suppose. I have been in the open air. It must be that.'

She at once took another mouthful, and went on eating.

'No,' answered Zeno, watching her. 'I did not mean that.'

She raised her beautiful eyebrows, just as he had raised his a few minutes earlier, but she said nothing and seemed very busy with the fish. Carlo took another piece, swallowed some of it deliberately, and drank a little before he leaned back in his chair and spoke again.

'Something has happened,' he said at last with great conviction.

'Really?' Zoë pretended surprised interest. 'What?' she asked with affected eagerness.

'You understand me perfectly,' he replied with a shade of sternness, for he was growing tired of her mood.

She glanced at him sideways, as a woman does when she hears a man's tone change suddenly, and she is not sure what he may do or say next.

'You do not make it easy to understand you, my lord,' she said after an instant's hesitation.

'The matter is simple enough. I find you in a bad humour—'

'Oh no! I assure you!' Zoë broke in, with a woman's diabolical facility in interrupting a man just at the right moment for her own advantage. 'I was never in a better temper in my life!'

To prove this, she took a bird and some salad, and smiled sweetly at her plate, leaving him to prove his assertion, but he did not fall into the trap.

'Then you are not easy to live with,' he observed bluntly. 'I am glad it is over.'

'Do take some of this salad!' suggested Zoë. 'It is really delicious!'

'To-morrow,' Zeno said, without paying any attention to her recommendation, 'I shall have a few guests at dinner.'

'I should advise you to give them a salad exactly like this,' answered Zoë. 'It could not be better!'

'I am glad you like it. I leave the fare to Omobono. It is about another matter that I have to speak.'

'You need not!' Zoë laughed carelessly. 'I know what you are going to say. Shall I save you the trouble?'

'I do not see how you can guess what it is—'

'Oh, easily! You do not wish your friends to see me and you are going to order me not to look out of the window when they come. Is that it?'

'Yes—more or less—' Zeno was surprised.

'Yes, that is it,' laughed Zoë. 'But it is quite useless, sir. I shall most certainly look out of the window, unless you lock me up in another room; and as for your doing that, I will yield only to force!'

She laughed again, much amused at the dilemma in which she was placing him. And indeed, he did not at first know how to answer her declaration of independence.

'I cannot imagine why you should be so anxious to show yourself to people you do not know,' he said. 'Or perhaps you fancy they may be friends—you think that if they recognise you—but that is absurd. I have told you that if you have friends in the world you may go to them, and you say you have none.'

Zoë's tone changed again and became girlishly petulant.

'It is nothing but curiosity, of course!' she answered. 'I want to see the people you like. Is that so unnatural? In a whole month I have never seen one of your friends—'

'I have not many. But such as I have, I value, and I do not care to let them get a mistaken impression of me, or of the way I live.'

'Especially not the women amongst them,' Zoë added, half interrogatively.

'There are none,' said Zeno, as if to cut short the suggestion.

'I see. You do not want your men friends to know that there are women living in your house, do you? They are doubtless all grave and elderly persons, who would be much shocked and grieved to learn that you have bought a pretty Greek slave. After all, you came near being a priest, did you not? They naturally associate you in their minds with the clergy, and for some reason or other you think it just as well for you, or your affairs, that they should! I have always heard that the Venetians are good men of business!'

'You are probably the only person alive who would risk saying that to me,' said Zeno, looking at her.

'What do I risk, my lord?' asked Zoë, with a sort of submissive gravity.

'My anger,' Zeno answered curtly.

'Yes sir, I understand. Your anger—but pray, my lord, how will it show itself? Shall I be beaten, or put in chains and starved, or turned out of your house and sold at auction? Those are the usual punishments for disobedient slaves, are they not?'

'I am not a Greek,' said Zeno, annoyed.

'If you were,' answered Zoë, turning her face from him to hide her smile, 'you would probably wish to tear out my tongue!'

'Perhaps.'

'It might be a wise precaution!' she laughed.

Zeno looked at her sharply now, for the words sounded like a threat that was only half-playful. She knew enough to compass his destruction at the hands of Andronicus if she betrayed him, but he did not believe she would do that, and he wondered what she was driving at, for his experience of women's ways was small.

'Listen,' he said, dropping his voice a little. 'I shall not beat you, I shall not starve you, and I shall not sell you. But if you try to betray me, I will kill you.'

She raised her head proudly and met his eyes without fear.

'I would spare you the trouble—if I ever betrayed you or any one.'

'It is one thing to talk of death, it is another to die!' Zeno laughed rather incredulously, as he quoted the old Italian proverb.

'I have seen death,' Zoë answered, in a different tone. 'I know what it is.'

He wondered what she meant, but he knew it was useless to question her, and for a few moments there was silence. The lamps burned steadily in the quiet air, for the evenings were still and cool, and the windows were shut and curtained; through the curtains and the shutters the song of a passing waterman was heard in the stillness, a long-drawn, plaintive melody in the Lydian Mode, familiar to Zoë's ears since she had been a child.

But Zeno saw how intensely she listened to the words. She clasped her hands tightly over her knee, and bent forwards to catch each note and syllable.

The waters are blue as the eyes of the Emperor's daughter, In the crystal pools of her eyes there are salt tears. The water is both salt and fresh. Over the water to my love, this night, over the water—

The voice died away, and Zoë no longer heard the words distinctly; presently she could not hear the voice at all, yet she strained her ears for a few seconds longer. The boat must have passed, on its way down to the Bosphorus.

For a whole month she had sat in the same room at that hour, and many times already she had heard men singing in their boats, sometimes to that same ancient Lydian Mode, but never once had they pronounced those meaning words. Often and often again she had passed within sight of the Amena tower, but not until to-day had she seen a solitary fisherman sitting at the pier's edge below it, and he had waved his rod thrice over the water when she passed by. And now in a flash of intuition she guessed that the singer was the fisherman and none other, and that the song was for her, and for no one else; and it was a signal which she could understand and should answer if she could; and there was but one way of answering, and that was to show some light.

'It is hot,' she said, beckoning to Yulia. 'Open the large window wide for a few minutes and let in the fresh air.'

Yulia obeyed quickly. The night was very dark.

'Besides,' Zoë continued carelessly, as Zeno looked at her, 'that fellow has a fine voice, and we shall still hear him.'

And indeed, as the window was opened, the song was heard again, at some distance—

Over the water to my love, she is awake to-night, I see her eyes amongst the stars. Love, I am here in the dark, but to-morrow I shall see the day in your face, I shall see the noon in your eyes, I shall look upon the sun in your hair. Over the water, the blue water, the water both salt and fresh—

Once more the voice died away and the faint plash of oars told Zoë that the message was all delivered, and that Gorlias was gone, on his way downstream.

Zeno, whose maternal tongue was not Greek, could not be supposed to understand much of the song, for unfamiliar words sung to such ancient melodies can only be caught by native-born ears, and sharp ones at that. At a signal from Zoë, the maid shut the window again, and drew the curtains.

'Could you understand the fellow?' Zeno asked, glad in reality that the conversation had been interrupted.

'Yes,' Zoë answered lightly, 'as you would understand an Italian fisherman, I suppose. The man gave you a message, my lord. Shall I interpret what he said?'

'Can you?' He laughed a little.

'He tells you that if you will not try to force Arethusa to keep away from the window to-morrow, she will probably do as you wish—probably!'

'Your friend must have good ears!' Zeno smiled. 'But then he only said "probably." That is not a promise.'

'Why should you trust the promise of a poor slave, sir? You would not believe a lady of Constantinople in the same case if she took oath on the four Gospels! Imagine any woman missing a chance of looking at another about whom she is curious!'

'Who is the other?' asked Zeno, not much pleased.

'She is young, and as fresh as spring. Her hair is like that of all the Venetian ladies—'

'Since you have seen her, why are you so anxious to see her again?'

'Ah! You see! It is she! I knew it! She is coming to-morrow with her father.'

'Well? If she is, what of it?' asked Zeno, impatiently.

'Nothing. Since you admit that it is she, I do not care to see her at all. I will be good and you need not lock me up.'

Thereupon she bent towards the table and began to eat again, daintily, but as if she were still hungry. Zeno watched her in silence for some time, conscious that of all women he had ever seen none had so easily touched him, none had played upon his moods as she did, making him impatient, uneasy, angry, and forgiving by turns, within a quarter of an hour. A few minutes ago he had been so exasperated that he had rudely longed to box her little ears; and now he felt much more inclined to kiss her, and did not care to think how very easy and wholly lawful it was for him to do so. That was one of his many dilemmas; if he spoke to her as his equal she told him she was a slave, but when he treated her ever so little as if she were one, her proud little head went up, and she looked like an empress.

She had never been so much like one as to-night, he thought, though there was nothing very imperial in the action of eating a very sticky strawberry, drawn up out of thick syrup with a forked silver pin. She did it with grace, no doubt, twisting the pin dexterously, so that the big drop of syrup spread all round the berry just at the right moment, and it never dripped. Zeno had often seen the wife of the Emperor Charles eating stewed prunes with her fingers, which was not neat or pleasant to see, though it might be imperial, since she was a genuine empress. But it was neither Zoë's grace nor her delicate ways that pleased him and puzzled him most; the mystery lay rather in the fearless tone of her voice and the proud carriage of her head when she was offended, in the flashing answer of her brave eyes and the noble curve of her tender mouth; for these are things given, not learnt, and if they could be taught at all, thought Zeno, they would not be taught to a slave.

He let his head rest against the back of his chair and wished many things, rather incoherently. For once in his life he felt inclined for anything rather than action or danger, or any sudden change; and in the detestable natural contradiction of duty and inclination it chanced that on that night, of all nights, he could not stay where he was to idle away two or three hours in careless talk, till it should be time to go downstairs and sleep. The habit of spending his evenings in that way had grown upon him during the past month more than he realised; but to-night he knew that he must break through it, and perhaps to-morrow, too, and for long afterwards, if not for ever. That was one reason why it had annoyed him to find Zoë out of temper.

He rose with an effort, and with something like a sigh.

'I must be going,' he said, standing beside the divan. 'Good-night.'

Zoë had looked up in surprise when he left his seat, and now her face fell.

'Already? Must you go already?' she asked.

'Yes. I have to keep an appointment. Good-night.'

'Good-night, Messer Carlo,' answered Zoë softly and a little sadly.

She had never before addressed him in that way, as an equal and a Venetian would have done, and the expression, with the tone in which it was uttered, arrested his attention and stopped him when he was in the act of turning away. He said nothing, but there was a question in his look.

'I am sorry that I made you angry,' she said, and she turned her face up to him with one of those half-pathetic, hesitating little smiles that ask forgiveness of a man and invariably get it, unless he is a brute.

'I am sorry that I let you see I was annoyed,' he answered simply.

'If I had not been so foolish, you would not go away so early!'

Her tone was contrite and regretfully thoughtful, as if the explanation were irrefutable but humiliating. Eve was, on the whole, a good woman, and is believed to be in Paradise; yet with the slight previous training of a few minutes' conversation with the serpent she was an accomplished temptress, and her rustic taste for apples has sent untold millions down into unquenchable fire. It was a mere coincidence that Eve should have been always called Zoë in the early Greek translations of Genesis, and that Zoë Rhangabé should have inherited a dangerous resemblance to the first beautiful—and enterprising—mother of men.

'I would stay if I could,' Zeno said. 'But indeed I have an appointment, and I must go.'

'Is it very important, very—very?'

Zeno smiled at her now, but did not answer at once. Instead, he walked to the window, opened the shutters again, and looked out. The night was very dark. Here and there little lights twinkled in the houses of Pera, and those that were near the water's edge made tiny paths over the black stream. After his eyes had grown used to the gloom Zeno could make out that there was a boat near the marble steps, and a very soft sound of oars moving in the water told him that the boatman was paddling gently to keep his position against the slow current. Zeno shut the window again and turned back to Zoë.

'Yes,' he said, answering her last speech after the interval, 'it is very important. If it were not, I would not go out to-night.'

He was going out of the house, then. She knew that he rarely did so after dark, and she could not help connecting his going with the invitation he had given to Polo and his daughter for the next day. Zoë's imagination instantly spun a thread across the chasms of improbability, and ran along the fairy bridge to the regions of the impossible beyond. He was to be betrothed to Giustina to-morrow, he was going now to settle some urgent matter of business connected with the marriage-contract; or he was betrothed already; yes, and he was to be married in the morning and would bring his bride home; Zoë, in her lonely room upstairs, would hear the noisy feasting of the wedding-guests below—

When the thread broke, leaving her in the unreality, her lip quivered, and she was a little pale. Zeno was standing beside her, holding her hand.

'Good-night, Arethusa,' he said in a tone that frightened her.

The words sounded like 'good-bye,' for that was what they might mean; he knew it, and she guessed it.

'You are going away!' she cried, springing to her feet and slipping her hand from his to catch his wrist.

'Not if I can help it,' he answered. 'But you may not see me to-morrow.'

'Not in the evening?' she asked in great anxiety. 'Not even after they are gone?'

'I cannot tell,' he replied gravely. 'Perhaps not.'

She dropped his wrist and turned from him.

'You are going to be married,' she said in a low voice. 'I was sure of it.'

'No!' he answered with emphasis. 'Not that!'

She turned to him again; it did not occur to her to doubt his word, and her eyes asked him the next question with eager anxiety, but he would not answer. He only repeated the three words, very tenderly and softly—

'Good-night—Arethusa!'

She knew it was good-bye, though he would not say it; she was not guessing his meaning now. But she was proud. He should not see how hurt she was.

'Good-night,' she answered. 'If you are going away—then, good-bye.'

Her voice almost broke, but she pressed her lips tight together when the last word had passed them, and though the tears seemed to be burning her brain she would not shed them while his eyes were on her.

'God keep you,' he said, as one says who goes on a long journey.

Again he was turning from her, not meaning to look back; but it was more than she could bear. In an inward tempest of fear and pain she had been taught suddenly that she truly loved him more than her soul, and in the same instant he was leaving her for a long time, perhaps for ever. She could not bear it, and her pride broke down. She caught his hand as he turned to go and held it fast.

'Take me with you!' she cried. 'Oh, do not go away and leave me behind!'

A silence of three seconds.

'I will come back,' he said. 'If I am alive, I will come back.'

'You are going into danger!' Her hand tightened on his, and she grew paler still.

He would not answer, but he patted her wrist kindly, trying to soothe her anxiety. He seemed quiet enough at that moment, but he felt the slow, full beat of his own heart and the rush of the swelling pulse in his throat. He had not guessed before to-night that she loved him; he was too simple, and far too sure that he himself could not love a slave. Even now he did not like to own it, but he knew that the hand she held was not passive; it pressed hers tighter in return, and drew it to him instead of pushing it away, till at last it was close to his breast.

'Oh, let me go with you, take me with you!' she repeated, beseeching with all her heart.

He was not thinking of danger now, he had forgotten it so far that he scarcely paid attention to her words or to her passionate entreaty. Words had lost sense and value, as they do in battle, and the fire ran along his arm to her hand. It had been cold; it was hot now, and throbbed strangely.

Then he dropped it and took her suddenly by her small throat, almost violently, and turned her face up to his; but she was not frightened, and she smiled in his grasp.

'I did not mean to love you!'

He still held her as he spoke; she put up her hands together and took his wrists, but not to free herself; instead, she pressed his hold closer upon her throat, as if to make him choke her.

'I wish you would kill me now!' she cried, in a trembling, happy little voice.

He laughed low, and shook her the least bit, as a strong man shakes a child in play, but her eyes drew him to her more and more.

'It would be so easy now,' she almost whispered, 'and I should be so happy!'

Then they kissed; and as their lips touched they closed their eyes, for they were too near to see each other any longer. Her head sank back from his upon his arm, for she was almost fainting, and he laid his palm gently on her forehead and pushed away her hair, and looked at her long.

'I had not meant to love you,' he said again.

Her lips were still parted, tender as rose-leaves at dewfall, and her eyes glistened as she opened them at the sound of his voice.

'Are you sorry?' she asked faintly.

He kissed the question from her lips, and her right hand went up to his brown throat and round it, and drew him, to press the kiss closer; and then it held him down while she moved her head till she could whisper in his ear:—

'It was only because you were angry,' she said. 'You are not really going out to-night! Tell me you are not!'

He would not answer at first, and he tried to kiss her again, but she would not let him, and she pushed him away till she could see his face. He met her eyes frankly, but he shook his head.

'It must be to-night, and no other night,' he said gravely. 'I have made an appointment, and I have given my word. I cannot break it, but I shall come back.'

She slipped from his hold, and sat down on the broad divan, against the cushions.

'You are going into danger,' she said. 'You may not come back. You told me so.'

He tried to laugh, and answered in a careless tone:—

'I have come back from far more dangerous expeditions. Besides, I have guests to-morrow—that is a good reason for not being killed!'

He stood beside her, one hand half-thrust into his loose belt. She took the other, which hung down, and looked up to him, still pleading.

'Please, please do not go to-night!'

Still he shook his head; nothing could move him, and he would go. A piteous look came into her eyes while they appealed to his in vain, and suddenly she dropped his hand and buried her face in the soft leathern pillow.

'You had made me forget that I am only a slave!' she cried.

The cushion muffled her voice, and the sentence was broken by a sob, though no tears came with it.

'I would go to-night, though my own mother begged me to stay,' Zeno answered.

Zoë turned her head without lifting it, and looked up at him sideways.

'Then much depends on your going,' she said, with a question in her tone. 'If it were only for yourself, for your pleasure, or your fortune, you would not refuse your own mother!'

Zeno turned and began to walk up and down the room, but he said nothing in reply. A thought began to dawn in her mind.

'But if it were for your country—for Venice—'

He glanced sharply at her as he turned back towards her in his walk, and he slackened his pace. Zoë waited a moment before she spoke again, looked down, thoughtfully pinched the folds of silk on her knee, and looked up suddenly again as if an idea had struck her.

'And though I am only your bought slave,' she said, 'I would not hinder you then. I mean, I would not even try to keep you from running into danger—for Venice!'

She held her head up proudly now, and the last words rang out in a tone that went to the man's heart. He was not far from her when she spoke them. The last syllable had not died away on the quiet air and he already held her up in his arms, lifted clear from the floor, and his kisses were raining on her lips, and on her eyes, and her hair. She laughed low at the storm she had raised.

'I love you!' he whispered again and again softly, roughly, and triumphantly by turns.

She loved him too, and quite as passionately just then; every kiss woke a deep and delicious thrill that made her whole body quiver with delight, and each oft-repeated syllable of the three whispered words rang like a silver trumpet-note in her heart. But for all that her thoughts raced on, already following him in the coming hours.

With every woman, to love a man is to feel that she must positively know just where he is going as soon as he is out of her sight. If it were possible, he should never leave the house without a ticket-of-leave and a policeman, followed by a detective to watch both; but that a man should assert any corresponding right to watch the dear object of his affections throws her into a paroxysm of fury; and it is hard to decide which woman most resents being spied upon, the angel of light, the siren that walketh in darkness, or the semi-virginal flirt.

Zoë really loved Zeno more truly at that moment, because the glorious tempest of kisses her speech had called down upon her willing little head brought with it the certainty that he was not going to spend the rest of the evening at the house of Sebastian Polo. This, at least, is how it strikes the story-teller in the bazaar; but the truth is that no man ever really understood any woman. It is uncertain whether any one woman understands any other woman; it is doubtful whether any woman understands her own nature; but one thing is sure, beyond question—every woman who loves a man believes, or tells him, that he helps her to understand herself. This shows us that men are not altogether useless.

Yet, to do Zoë justice, there was one other element in her joy. She had waited long to learn that Zeno meant to free Johannes if it could be done, and he had met all her questions with answers that told her nothing; she was convinced that he did not even know the passwords of those who called themselves conspirators, but who had done nothing in two years beyond inventing a few signs and syllables by which to recognise each other. Whether he knew them or not, he was ready to act at last, and the deed on which hung the destinies of Constantinople was to be attempted that very night. Before dawn Michael Rhangabé's death might be avenged, and Kyría Agatha's wrongs with Zoë's own.

'I want to help you,' she said, when he let her speak. 'Tell me how you are going to do it.'

'With a boat and a rope,' he answered.

'Take me! I will sit quite still in the bottom. I will watch; no one has better eyes or ears than I.'

'More beautiful you mean!'

He shut her eyes with his lips and kissed the lobe of one little ear. But she moved impatiently in his arms, with a small laugh that meant many things—that she was happy, and that she loved him, but that a kiss was no answer to what she had just said, and that he must not kiss her again till he had replied in words.

'Take me!' she repeated.

'This is man's work,' he answered. 'Besides, it is the work of one man only, and no more.'

'Some one must watch below,' Zoë suggested.

'There is the man in the boat. But watching is useless. If any one surprises us in the tower, I can get away; but if I am caught by an enemy from the water the game is up. That is the only danger.'

'That is the only danger,' Zoë repeated, more to herself than for him.

He saw that she had understood now, and that she would not try to keep him longer, nor again beg to be taken. She went with him to the door of the vestibule without calling the maids, and she parted from him there, very quietly.

'God speed you!' she said, for good-bye.

When he reached the outer entrance and looked back once more, she was already gone within, and the quiet lamplight fell across the folds of the heavy curtain.

CHAPTER X

Zeno left his house noiselessly half an hour later, after changing his clothes. He was now lightly clad in dark hose and a soft deerskin doublet with tight sleeves, a close-fitting woollen skull-cap covered his head, and he had no weapon but one good knife of which the sheath was fastened to the back of his belt, as a sailor carries it when he goes aloft to work on rigging. The night was cool, and he had a wide cloak over his shoulders, ready to drop in an instant if necessary.

It was intensely dark as he came out, and after being in the light he could hardly see the white marble steps of the landing. He almost lost his balance at the last one, and when he stepped quickly towards the boat, to save himself, he could not see it at all, and was considerably relieved to find himself in the stern sheets instead of in the water.

'Gorlias!' he whispered, leaning forwards.

'Yes!' answered the astrologer-fisherman.

The light skiff shot out into the darkness, away from the shore, instead of heading directly for Blachernæ. After a few minutes Gorlias rested on his oars. Zeno had grown used to the gloom and could now see him quite distinctly. Both men peered about them and listened for the sound of other oars, but there was nothing; they were alone on the water.

'Is everything ready?' Zeno asked in a low tone.

'Everything. At the signal over eight hundred men will be before Blachernæ in a few minutes. There are fifty ladders in the ruined houses by the wall of the city. The money has had an excellent effect on the guard, for most of them were drunk this evening, and are asleep now. In the tower, the captain is asleep too, for his wife showed the red light an hour ago. She took up the package of opium last night by the thread.'

'And Johannes himself? Is he ready?'

'He is timid, but he will risk his life to get out of the tower. You may be sure of that!'

'Have you everything we need? The fishing-line, the tail-block, and the two ropes? And the basket? Is everything ready in the bows, there?'

'Everything, just as you ordered it, and the rope clear to pay out.'

'Give way, then.'

'In the name of God,' said Gorlias, as he dipped his oars again.

'Amen,' answered Zeno quietly.

The oars were muffled with rags at the thole-pins, and Gorlias was an accomplished oarsman. He dipped the blades into the stream so gently that there was hardly a ripple, and he pulled them through with long, steady strokes, keeping the boat on its course by the scattered lights of the city.

Zeno watched the lights, too, leaning back in the stern, and turning over the last details of his plan. Everything depended on getting the imprisoned man out of the Amena tower at once, and he believed he could do that without much difficulty. At first sight it might seem madness to attempt a revolution with only eight hundred men to bear arms in the cause, against ten or fifteen thousand, but the Venetian knew what sort of men they were, and how profoundly Andronicus was hated by all the army except his body-guard. The latter would fight, no doubt, and perhaps die to a man, for they had everything to lose, and expected no quarter; but for the next two hours most of them would be still helplessly asleep after their potations, and if they woke at all they would hardly be in a condition to defend themselves. Money had been distributed to them without knowledge of their officers, purporting to be sent to them from Sultan Amurad, now in Asia Minor. It had pleased the Turk more than once to keep the guards in a good humour towards him, and the soldiers were not surprised. Besides, they cared very little whence money came, provided it got into their hands, and could be spent in drink, for they were not sober Greeks or Italians; most of them were wild barbarians, who would rather drink than eat, and rather fight than drink, as the saying goes.

For nearly twenty minutes Gorlias pulled steadily upstream. Then he slackened speed, and brought the boat slowly to the foot of the tower.

The windows were all dark now, and the great mass towered up into the night till the top was lost in the black sky. During the hours Gorlias had spent in fishing from the pier he had succeeded in wedging a stout oak peg between the stones; he found it at once in the dark, got out and made the boat fast to it by the painter. His bare feet clung to the sloping surface like a fly's to a smooth wall; he pulled the boat alongside the pier, holding it by the gunwale, and held up his other hand to help Zeno. But the Venetian was in no need of that, and was standing beside his companion in an instant. It was only then, a whole second after the fact, that he knew he had stepped upon something oddly soft and at the same time elastic and resisting, that lay amidships in the bottom of the boat, covered with canvas. The quick recollection was that of having unconsciously placed one foot on a human body when getting out. He had taken off his shoes, but the cloth soles of his hose were thick, and he could not feel sure of what he had touched. Besides, he had no time to lose in speculating as to what Gorlias might have in the skiff besides his lines and his coil of rope.

Gorlias now got the end of the fishing-line ashore, and took it in his teeth in order to climb up the inclined plane of the pier on his hands and feet, ape-fashion. In a few seconds he had found the end of a string that hung down from the blackness above, with a small stone tied to it to keep it from being blown adrift. To this string he bent the fishing-line. Until this was done neither of the men had made the least sound that could possibly be heard above, but now Gorlias gave a signal. It was the cry of the beautiful little owl that haunts ruined houses in Italy and the East, one soft and musical note, repeated at short and regular intervals. The bird always gives it thus, but for the signal Gorlias whistled it twice each time, instead of once. No living owl ever did that, and yet it was a thousand to one that nobody would notice the difference, if any one heard him at all, except the person for whom the call was meant.

He had not been whistling more than a quarter of a minute when he felt the twine passing upwards through his fingers, and then the line after it. He let the latter run through his hand to be sure that it did not foul and kink, though he had purposely chosen one that had been long in use, and he had kept it in a dry place for a week.

Zeno had dropped his cloak in the stern of the boat before getting out, and he now sat at the water's edge with his hands on the moving line ready to check the end when it came, in case it were not already fast to the rope that was to follow it. But Gorlias had done that beforehand, lest any time should be lost, and presently Zeno felt the line growing taut as it began to pull on the rope itself.

This had single overhand knots in it, about two feet apart, for climbing, and instead of coiling it down, Gorlias had ranged it fore and aft on the forward thwarts so that it came ashore clear.

Whatever the astrologer's original profession had been, it was evident that he understood how to handle rope as well as if he had been to sea. Moreover Zeno, who was as much a sailor as a soldier, understood from the speed at which the rope was now taken up, that there was a tolerably strong person at the other end of it, high up in the topmost story of the tower. The end came sooner than he expected, and a slight noise of something catching and knocking against the inner side of the boat brought Gorlias instantly to the water's edge.

'The tail-block is fast to the end,' he whispered; 'and the other line is already rove, with the basket at one end of it. When you are aloft, you must haul up the climbing rope and make the block fast—you understand.'

'Of course,' Zeno answered, 'I have been to sea.'

'Whistle when you are ready and I will answer. As he comes down I can check the rope with a turn round a smooth stone I have found at the corner of the tower. You must come down the climbing rope at the same time, and steer the basket as well as you can with your foot.'

'Yes. Is all fast above?'

Gorlias listened.

'Not yet,' he whispered. 'Wait for the signal.'

It came presently, the cry of the owlet repeated, as Gorlias had repeated it. Zeno heard it and began to climb, while Gorlias steadied the rope, though there was hardly any need for that. The young Venetian walked up with his feet to the wall, taking the rope hand over hand, as if he were going up a bare pole by a gant-line.

When he was twenty feet above the pier and was fast disappearing in the darkness, something moved in the boat, and a white face looked up cautiously over the gunwale. It was a woman's face. Zeno had stepped upon her with his whole weight when he was getting ashore, but she had made no sound. Her eyes tried to pierce the gloom, to follow him upwards in his dizzy ascent. Soon she could not see him any longer, nor hear the soft sound of his cloth-shod feet as he planted them against the stones.

Up he went, higher and higher. Gorlias steadied the end below, keeping one foot on the block lest it should thrash about on the stones and make a noise. He could feel each of Zeno's movements along the rope; and though he had seen many feats in his life, he wondered at the wind and endurance of a man who could make such an ascent without once crooking his leg round the rope to rest and take breath. But Carlo Zeno never stopped till his feet were on the slight projecting moulding of the highest story, and his hands on the stone sill.

As he drew himself up with a spring his face almost struck the chest of a large woman who was standing at the window to receive him. He saw her outline faintly, for there was a little light from one small lamp, placed on the floor in the farthest corner of the oblong room. The tower was square, but the north side of the chamber was walled off to make a space for the head of the staircase and a narrow entry. The single door was in this partition. Zeno looked round while he took breath, and he was aware of a tall man with a long beard who stood on one side of the window, and seemed inclined to flatten himself against the wall, as if he feared being seen from without, even at that height and in the dark.

The woman moved a step backwards, and Carlo put one leg over the window-sill and got in. He took his skull-cap from his head and bowed low to the imprisoned Emperor before he spoke to the woman in a whisper.

'I will haul up the basket,' he said, and he laid his hands on the knotted rope to do so.

But the tall man with the beard touched him on the shoulder, and spoke in a low voice.

'We must talk together,' he said.

Zeno hardly turned his head, and did not stop hauling in the rope. Below, Gorlias was steering the tail-block clear of the wall, lest it should strike the stones and make a noise.

'This is no time for talking,' Zeno said. 'When your Majesty is free and in safety we can talk at leisure.'

The knotted rope was coming in fast; Zeno threw it upon the floor behind him in a wide coil to keep it clear.

'Stop!' commanded the Emperor, laying one hand on the Venetian's arm.

Zeno set his foot on the rope to keep it from running out, and turned to the prisoner in surprise.

'Every moment is precious,' he said. 'If we are discovered from outside the tower the game is up, and we shall be caught like rats in a trap. I have a basket at the end of this rope in which you will be quite safe from falling, if that is what makes you hesitate. Fear nothing. We are two good men, I and my companion below.'

'You are a good man indeed, to have risked your life in climbing here,' answered Johannes.

He made a few steps, bending his still handsome head in thought. He limped slightly in his walk, and he was said to have only four toes on his left foot.

Zeno at once continued hauling up the rope, but a moment later the Emperor stopped close beside him.

'It is of no use,' he said; 'I cannot go with you.'

Zeno was thunderstruck, and stood still with the rope in his two hands.

'You will not go?' he repeated, almost stupidly. 'You will not be free, now that everything is ready?'

'I cannot. Go down your rope before there is an alarm. Take God's blessing for your generous courage, and my heartfelt thanks. I am ashamed that I should have nothing else to offer you. I cannot go.'

'But why? Why?'

Carlo Zeno could not remember that he had ever been so much surprised in his life, and so are they who gather round the story-teller and listen to his tale. But it is a true one; and many years afterwards one of Carlo Zeno's grandsons, the good old Bishop of Belluno, wrote it down as he had heard it from his grandsire's lips. Moreover it is history. The imprisoned Emperor Johannes refused to leave his prison, after Zeno had risked life and limb to prepare a revolution, and had scaled the tower alone.

'Andronicus has my little son in the palace,' said the prisoner; 'if I escape he will put out the child's eyes with boiling vinegar, and perhaps mutilate him or kill him by inches. Save him first, then I will go with you.'

There was something very noble in the prisoner's tone, and in the turn of his handsome head as he spoke. Zeno could not help respecting him, yet he was profoundly disappointed. He tried one argument.

'If you will come at once,' he said, 'I promise you that we shall hold the palace before daybreak, and the little prince will be as free as you.'

Johannes shook his head sadly.

'The guards will kill him instantly,' he said; 'the more certainly if they see that they must fight for their lives.'

'In short, your Majesty is resolved? You will not come with me?'

'I cannot.' The Emperor turned away, and covered his face with his hands, more as if trying to concentrate his thoughts than as if in despair. 'No, I cannot,' he repeated presently. 'Save the boy first,' he repeated, dropping his hands and turning to Zeno again, 'then I will go with you.'

Zeno was silent for a moment, and then spoke in a determined tone.

'Hear me, sire,' he said. 'A man does not run such risks twice, except for his own blood. You must either come with me at once, or give up the idea that I shall ever help you to escape. The boy may be in danger, but so are you yourself, and your life is worth more to this unhappy Empire than his. To-night, to-morrow, at any moment, your son Andronicus may send the executioner here, and there will be an end of you and of many hopes. You must risk your younger boy's life for your cause. I see no other way.'

'The other way is this; I will stay here and risk my own. I would rather die ten deaths than let my child be tortured, blinded, and murdered.'

'Very well,' answered Zeno; 'then I must go.'

He let the knotted rope go over the sill again till it was all out, and he sat astride the window mullion ready to begin the descent.

'Cast off the rope when I whistle,' he said, 'and let it down by the line, and the line after it by the twine.'

He spoke to the big woman, who was the wife of the keeper, himself a trusted captain of veterans. She nodded by way of answer.

'For the last time,' Zeno said, looking towards Johannes, 'will you come with me? There is still time.'

The Emperor looked prematurely old in the faint light, and his figure was bent as he rested with one hand on the heavy table. His voice was weak too, as if he were very tired after some great effort.

'For the last time, no,' he answered. 'I am sorry. I thank you with all my heart—'

Zeno did not wait for more, and his head disappeared below the window almost before the prisoner had spoken the last words. Five minutes had not elapsed since he had reached the chamber.

Below, Gorlias had been surprised when he felt the second rope slack in his hand, and when the basket and block, which had been half-way up the wall, began to come down again. The astrologer could only suppose that there was an alarm within the tower, and that Zeno was getting away as fast as he could. The last written message, lowered by the yarn at dusk that evening, had been to say that the Emperor was ready, and that a red light would be shown when the captain was asleep, under the influence of the drug his wife had given him. It could not possibly occur to the astrologer that Johannes would change his mind at the very last moment.

'Take care!' Gorlias whispered quickly to the woman at his elbow, as soon as he was sure of what was happening. 'He is coming down again.'

'Alone?' The anxious inquiry answered his words in the same breath.

'Alone—yes! He is on the rope now, he is coming down, hand under hand.'

The woman slipped down the inclined surface, almost fell, recovered her foothold, and nearly fell again as she sprang into the boat, and threw herself at full length upon the bottom boards. Zeno was half-way down, and before she covered herself with the canvas she glanced up and distinctly saw his dark figure descending through the gloom.

She had scarcely stretched herself out when she was startled by a loud cry, close at hand.

'Phylaké! Aho—ho—o! Watch, ho! Watch, ho!'

A boat had shot out of the darkness to the edge of the pier. In an instant three men had sprung ashore, and were clambering up the sloping masonry towards Gorlias. The woman stood up in Zeno's skiff, almost upsetting it, and her eyes pierced the gloom to see what was happening.

Gorlias threw himself desperately against the three men, with outstretched arms, hoping to sweep them altogether into the water from a place where they had so little foothold. The woman held her breath. One of the three men, active as a monkey, dodged past the astrologer, caught the knotted rope, and began climbing it. The other two fell, their feet entangled in the line-rove through the tail-block, and with the strong man's weight behind them they tumbled headlong down the incline. With a heavy splash, and scarcely more than one for all three, Gorlias and his opponents fell into the water.

There was silence then, while the other man climbed higher and higher.

The woman watched in horror. In falling, the men had struck against the stem of the skiff, dragging the painter from the peg. The other boat was not moored at all, and both were now adrift on the sluggish stream. The woman steadied herself, and tried to see.

The man climbed fast, and above him the dark figure moved quickly upwards. But Zeno's pursuer was fresher than he, and as quick as a cat, and gained on him. If he caught him, he might crook his leg round the knotted rope to drag Zeno down and hurl him to the ground.

Still he gained, while the boats began to drift, but still the woman could make out both figures, nearer and nearer to each other. Now there were not ten feet between them.

A faint cry was heard, a heavy thud on the stones, and silence again. Zeno had cut the rope below him. The woman drew a sharp breath between her closed teeth. There was no noise, now, for the man that had been as active as a cat was dead.

But an instant later one of the other three was out of the water, and on the edge of the pier, panting for breath.

The woman took up one of the oars, and tried to paddle with it. She thought that the man who had come up must be Gorlias, and that the other two were drowned, and she tried to get the boat to the pier again; she had never held an oar in her life, and she was trembling now. High in mid-air Zeno was hanging on what was left of the rope, slowly working his way upwards, fully fifty feet above the base of the tower.

The skiff bumped against the other boat alongside, and the woman began to despair of getting nearer to the land, and tried to shove the empty boat away with her hands. The effect was to push her own skiff towards the pier, for the other was much the heavier of the two. Then, paddling a little, she made a little way. The man ashore seemed to be examining the body of the one who had been killed; it lay sprawling on the stones, the head smashed. The living one was not Gorlias; the woman could see his outline now. She was strong, and with the one oar shoved her skiff still farther from the other boat, and nearer to the pier. The man heard her, got upon his feet, and slipped down to the water's edge again.

'Hold out the end of the oar to me,' he said, 'and I will pull the boat in.'

It was not the voice of Gorlias that spoke, and the woman did not obey the instructions it gave. On the contrary she tried to paddle away, lest the man should jump aboard. Strangely enough the skiff seemed to answer at once to her will, as if some unseen power were helping her. It could not be her unskilled, almost helpless movements of the oar that guided it away.

But the man rose to his feet, on the lowest course of the stones, where there was a ledge, and he sprang forwards, struck the water without putting his head under, and was at the stern of the boat in a few seconds.

The woman seemed fearless, for she stepped quickly over the after thwart, taking her oar with her, and a moment later she struck a desperate blow with it at the swimmer, and raised it again. She could not see him any more, and she knew that if she had struck his head he must have sunk instantly; but she waited a little longer in the stern, the oar still uplifted in both her hands.

At that moment, the repeated call of the owlet came down from far above. It could only mean that Zeno had reached the upper window in safety. Then the boat rocked violently two or three times, and the woman was thrown down, sitting, in the stern sheets; she saw that a man was getting in over the bows, and was already on board.

'That was well done, Kokóna,' said the voice of Gorlias, softly.

Zoë sank back in the stern, half-fainting with exhaustion, pain, and past anxiety.

'Is he safe?' she managed to ask.

'That was his call. He has reached the window again, but it was a narrow escape.'

She could hardly breathe. Gorlias had taken the oars, and the skiff was moving.

CHAPTER XI

Zeno found the two occupants of the room terrorstruck, and standing on one side of the window, from which they had not dared to look out after the cry of alarm had been given from below. Indeed they were in a dangerous pass, unless all three of the men who had attempted to stop Zeno were dead, or if the first cry had roused the sleeping captain and guards of the tower from their drugged sleep.

But Zeno's own situation was quite as bad. It was out of the question to shout to Gorlias, on the mere chance of his being still alive and on the pier. No communication was possible, and the rope was cut below. It was true that the whole of the fishing-line still lay coiled on the floor of the room, but even if it were long enough to double it would hardly bear the man's weight; and Carlo guessed that he had cut off nearly three-quarters of the knotted rope below him.

There was no time to be lost either. He did not know the number of his assailants, and though he gave his signal when he reached the window, on the mere chance of being heard, he would not have trusted the answer to it if it had come. Any one could imitate such a sound after hearing it once. If he let down the remaining length of the rope by the fishing-line, and if his enemies were on the pier instead of Gorlias, they would have wit enough to knot the rope where it had been cut, and to send it up again, for him to come down by, and he would drop into their very midst.

He understood all this in an instant, and without hesitation he cast off everything above, and dropped the rope and the fishing-line out of the window. He knew Gorlias well enough to be sure that he would come back before daylight and land if there were no one on the pier, and remove all traces of the attempt.

'We are all lost!' moaned the big woman.

'My hour has come,' said the Emperor Johannes in solemn terror.

Thereupon he began to say his prayers, and paid no more attention to the others. Zeno took the woman by the wrist.

'We are not lost unless your husband is awake,' he said. 'Take me to him.'

The captain's wife stared at him.

'There is no other way. If he is awake, you will tell him that I got into the tower, and that you have betrayed me into his hands. You will be safe at least, and I will take my chance. If he is asleep I have nothing to fear.'

He drew her to the door and began to unbar it himself. She had understood that he was right, so far as her own safety was concerned, and she helped him. A horn lantern stood on the stone floor in the entry at the head of the stair, where she had left it when she had last come up. Before going down she barred the door outside as usual, and then led the way.

At the first landing she opened a door as softly as she could and went in, leaving Zeno on the threshold. It was the sleeping room, and Zeno heard the captain's stertorous breathing with relief. He went in and looked at the sleeping man's face, which was congested to a dark red by the powerful drug, and Zeno thought it doubtful whether he would ever wake again. The woman, ignorant of the effects of much opium, was afraid her husband might open his eyes, and she plucked at Zeno's sleeve, anxious to get him away; but the Venetian smiled.

'He is good for twelve hours' sleep,' he said. 'Give me his cloak and helmet. If I find no one awake I will leave them at the outer gate. Otherwise I will send them to the tower in a clothes-basket to-morrow morning.'

The captain's wife obeyed, less frightened than she had been at first; Zeno muffled half his face in the big cloak, and threw the end over his shoulder whence it hung down, displaying the three broad stripes of gold lace that formed the border distinctive of a captain's rank in the guards. The bright helmet had a gilt eagle for a crest, scarcely differing from that of the modern German Gardes du Corps regiment.

'Now show me the way,' Zeno said.

Under the folds of the cloak he had the short broad sheath-knife ready in his grasp, and it was no bad weapon in the hand of such a fighter as Carlo Zeno. The captain's wife led the way with the lantern.

At the foot of the next flight of stairs she almost stumbled over the sentinel, half-seated on the lowest step in a drunken sleep; his shaggy head had fallen forwards on his breast, and his legs stuck straight out before him, wide apart, like the legs of a wooden doll. His hands lay open with the palms upwards, one on his knee, the other on the step beside him; and his helmet, which had rolled off his head, had happened to stop just between his feet, the right side up, and facing him, as if it were watching him in his slumber like a living thing.

The story they had now reached contained the living room of the captain and his wife, and no sentinel was needed higher up in the tower. An iron door, fastened on the inside, cut off the descent, and had to be opened for Zeno to pass. But being constantly in use the lock was well oiled, and the bolts slipped back almost without noise. Nevertheless, as he followed his companion down the next flight, Zeno drew up the folds of the cloak on his right arm till the edge barely covered the drawn knife in his hand.

They reached the next story below, where the upper guard-room was. The door was half-open, and a lamp was burning within, but as the window was over the great court of Blachernæ no light had been visible from the water. Zeno heard voices, and caught sight of two guards carousing at the end of an oak table. At the sound of footsteps one of the men rose quickly, but staggered when he tried to walk to the door.

'Who goes there?' he called out, steadying himself by the door-post, and looking out.

The captain's wife had the presence of mind to hold up the lantern, so that the light fell full upon the helmet Zeno wore. Instantly the soldier tried to straighten himself to an attitude of attention, with his hands by his sides. But this was too much for his unstable balance, and he reeled backwards half across the room within, till he struck the table behind him, and tumbled down with a clatter of accoutrements and a rattling of the horn drinking-cups that were thrown to the ground. His companion, who was altogether too drunk even to leave his seat, broke into a loud idiotic laugh at his accident.

'You have done your share well, Kyría,' said Zeno, as he followed her again. 'The Emperor's friends could have brought him down by the stairs in triumph without being stopped.'

'You are not out of the palace precincts yet,' answered the captain's wife in a warning tone.

She went on, treading more softly as she descended, and carrying the lantern low lest she or her companion should stumble over another sleeping sentinel; but the staircase and the door that led into the court were deserted, for the captain was a very exact man, and had his supper at the same hour every evening, and went to bed soon afterwards like an honest citizen, after setting the watch and locking the iron door of his own lower landing. In two years he had never once come down the tower after sunset. The consequence was that the guards, who were mostly rough barbarians from the Don country and the shores of the Black Sea, did as they pleased, or as their lieutenant pleased; for he found it pleasant to spend his nights in another part of the palace, and was extremely popular with his men, because they were thus enabled to go to bed like good Christians and sleep all night.

All this the captain's wife knew well enough. Her apprehension was for what might happen to Zeno between leaving the tower and passing the great gate, which was the only way to get out of the fortified precincts. The wide courtyard was very dark, but there were lights here and there in the windows of the buildings that surrounded it on three sides, the great mass of the palace on the right, the barracks of the guards along the wall to the left, and the main post at the great gate in front with the buildings on each side of it, some occupied by slaves and some used as stables.

Zeno wished that he had stripped one of the sleeping soldiers and had put on his dress, for he had been informed of the captain's habits, and knew that the disguise was no longer a safe one after leaving the tower. Indeed it was a chief part of the captain's duty never to go out after dark, on any excuse, and he apparently made sure of obeying this permanent order by going to bed early and getting up late. For the rest, he had always left the personal care of his prisoner to his wife, judging that her stout middle-age and fiery cheeks sufficiently protected his domestic honour. She had been young and very pretty once, it was true, but the captain did not know that Johannes had even seen her then, much less did he guess that many years ago, when the Emperor was a handsome young prince and she was a lovely girl in the old Empress's train, she had worshipped him and he had condescended to accept her admiration for a few weeks. But this was the truth, as Zeno's grandson the bishop very clearly explains.

She left her lantern just inside the door and came out with Carlo into the open air. After walking a few steps she laid her hand on his arm, stopped, looked round, and listened. As yet they had not exchanged two words about the situation, and were far from sure that the watch which had detected Carlo from the water and had failed to catch him, had not come round by land to the palace gate to give the alarm.

Zeno slipped the cloak from his shoulders and wrapped it round the helmet, so that the captain's wife could carry both conveniently.

'It is hopeless,' she whispered, as she took them. 'This morning he promised that he would leave the prison if you could bring him out. He has often spoken to me as he spoke to you this evening—he loves the boy dearly; but I was sure that he had made up his mind to risk everything, else I would not have shown the red light.'

'After all,' Zeno observed, 'it is just as well that he would not come, since we were seen, though I really believe Gorlias was too much for the men who almost caught us. He and I together could certainly have settled them all—there were only three. I saw them distinctly when they first jumped ashore, and one was killed by the fall when I cut the rope. Gorlias silenced the other two, for if they were alive there would have been an alarm here by this time.'

'Yes,' the woman answered. 'But some one must have betrayed us. We cannot try that way again.'

'I shall not try that, or any other way again!' Zeno said with emphasis. 'In the name of the Evangelist, why should I risk my neck to free a man who prefers to be a prisoner?'

'The wonder is that you are alive this time!'

'It will not even be safe to communicate by the thread again. Will you take him a message?'

'As well as I can remember it.'

'Tell him that the next time he asks my help he must send me, by the same messenger, a deed giving Tenedos to Venice, signed and sealed. Otherwise I will not stir!'

'Shall I tell him that?'

'Yes. Tell him so from me. And now, go back, Kyría, and thank you for your guidance and your lantern in those dark stairs.'

'How shall you pass the gate?' asked the captain's wife.

She spoke anxiously, for Zeno was a handsome man, and she had seen how brave he was.

'I do not know,' he answered, 'but one of two things must happen.'

'What things?'

'Either I shall get out or I shall never see daylight again! I shall not let myself be taken alive to be impaled in the Hippodrome, I assure you. Thank you again, and good-night.'

She drew back into the shadow of the tower door and watched the handsome young man with the peculiar half-motherly, half-sentimental anxiety of the middle-aged woman, who was a flirt in her youth and turned the heads of just such men, who knows that she is grown fat and ugly and can never turn the head of another, but who has preserved many tender and pleasant recollections of all the sex.

Zeno did not walk straight towards the gate, though it was easily distinguished from the adjacent buildings by the greater number of its lights. He crossed the wide court diagonally to the right, in the direction of the stables, till he was near enough to see distinctly any one who chanced to come under the rays of one of the scattered lamps that burned here and there in doorways and open windows. Before long he saw a trooper of the guards emerging rather unsteadily out of the darkness into one of these small circles of light. Zeno could not help smiling to himself at the idea that there was hardly one sober man awake among the guards that night, and that they had all drunk themselves stupid with his money.

He overtook the man in half-a-dozen strides, and spoke to him in a low voice.

'Hi! comrade! You who are still perfectly sober, help a friend who is very drunk!'

The man stopped, steadied himself, and answered with ponderous gravity.

'Perfectly—hic—hic—sober!'

'I wish I were!' replied Zeno. 'The truth is, I am exceedingly drunk, though I do not show it. Wine only affects my brains, never my legs or my tongue. It is a very strange thing!'

'Very—cu—hic—rious!' responded the soldier, trying to see his interlocutor clearly, by screwing up his eyes.

'Extraordinarily cuhicrious, as you justly observe,' Zeno answered gravely. 'But the fact is—'

'Excuse me—hic,' interrupted the soldier. 'Are you one man—hic—or two men?'

'One man,' Zeno answered. 'Only one, and so drunk that I have quite forgotten the password.'

'Sec—hic—ret,' hiccoughed the man. 'Password secret,' he repeated, with a tremendous effort.

'Here is a gold piece, my dear friend. You will help a comrade in trouble.'

The man took the money eagerly, and tried to put it into his wallet. To do so he had to bend his head down so as to see the thongs that fastened it. It took a long time to find them.

'Just give me the password before you do that,' Zeno said in a coaxing tone.

'Password?' The man looked up stupidly.

The effort of undoing the thongs had been too much for him, and had sent the blood to his head. He staggered against the Venetian, and tried to speak. After many efforts he got the words out suddenly.

'Drunk, by Moses!' he cried, quite distinctly, as he fell in a heap at Zeno's feet.

In his vexation Zeno could have kicked the stupid mass of humanity across the great yard, but he was far too wise to waste his time so unprofitably. Instead of kicking him he stepped across him, thrust his hands under the unconscious man's armpits, hove him up like a sack of flour, got him over his shoulder, and carried him to the open door of the nearest stable, whence the light came. Five horses stood or lay in their stalls, but the sixth stall was vacant, and there was fresh straw in it. Zeno threw the man down there, and looked round, to see that no one else was in the place. He hesitated a moment as to whether he should shut the door, but decided that to do so might attract the attention of a sober man, if there were any about, which was doubtful.

The trooper was now sound asleep, and it was the work of a few moments to pull off his boots of soft leather and slip them on, for Zeno had left his own in the boat, and had walked in his cloth hose; he took off the soldier's sword-belt and tunic next, the latter of rich scarlet cloth trimmed with heavy silver lace, the belt being entirely covered with silver scales. The drunken sleeper grunted with satisfaction when he felt himself relieved of his useless clothes, and settled himself comfortably in the straw while Zeno put on the tunic over his own buff jerkin and drew the belt tight round his waist, settled the man's tall Greek cap on his own head at the proper angle, as the troopers wore it, and threw the military cloak over his arm.

He could now easily pass himself for a trooper at the gate, and a man who has been a soldier is rarely at a loss amongst soldiers, especially if he wears a uniform. In consideration of what he had taken, Zeno, who was an honest man of business, left the man his wallet with the piece of gold and anything else it might contain, and after carefully removing a few wisps of straw that clung to his clothes, he went towards the door of the stable.

His plan was to saunter to the gate and loiter there till a chance offered of opening the small night-postern in the great door, which he had noticed in passing the palace when the gates were open. The fact of his being sober when almost every one else was more or less intoxicated, would give him a great advantage.

But as he turned from the sleeper and walked along the line from the empty stall, which was the last, his eye fell on the saddles and bridles, neatly arranged on stout pegs that projected from the walls, each set opposite the stall of the horse to which it belonged. He peered out into the wide court, and listened for the sound of voices. From very far away he heard the echo of a drinking chorus, less loud than the noise made behind him by one of the horses that had a fancy for a mouthful of hay just then, and was chewing it conscientiously as only animals can chew.

All was very quiet outside. Zeno changed his plan, turned back into the stable, and began to saddle the horse farthest from the door. He did not mean to ride far, else he would have picked out his mount with all the judgement he possessed. There was but a dash to make, and it was far more important that no passing trooper should see him in the act of putting on saddle and bridle than that he should have the best horse under him afterwards. Besides, they were all big, hay-fed animals, sleek and sleepy, mostly white Tunisians, and much more fit for a procession than a campaign.

When he had finished, he led the charger past the other stalls, stopping just before he reached the door to put out the oil lamp that hung by the entrance. This done, he slipped his arm through the bridle and left the stable. He struck across the deserted court towards the palace, until he was almost in the middle of the yard, and opposite the great gate, towards which he looked steadily for some seconds, trying to make out, by the uncertain light that dimly illuminated it from within, whether the doors under the arch were open or shut. There was just a possibility that they might be open. It was worth trying for; and after all, if they were barred, he was sure that he could impose upon the sentinels to open them. A man accustomed to command does not doubt that he must be obeyed when he asserts himself.

Zeno mounted the big horse, which was as quiet as any old circus hack in the Hippodrome, trained to let a dancing-girl skip the rope on his broad back. His rider put him from a walk to a canter, and from a canter to a thundering gallop that roused echoes all round the court.

As he came near he saw that the doors were shut, but he did not slacken speed till he was almost upon the startled sentinels. Then he drew rein suddenly, as was the practice of horsemanship in those days, and the great Tunisian threw himself back on his haunches with outstretched forefeet, while Zeno called out to the watch.

'On the Emperor's service!' he shouted. 'The gates, and quickly!'

The sentinels were tolerably sober, for they were not to get their full share of the flood of wine that was flowing till their guard was relieved. But they could hardly be blamed for obeying Zeno's imperative command. It was not likely that a guardsman of their troop who wished to slip out of barracks for a night's amusement would dress himself in full uniform and come galloping and shouting to the gate, nor that any trooper would dare to pretend that he rode on the Emperor's business if it were not true.

The two sentinels therefore did not hesitate, but set their long cavalry lances upright against the walls on either side, took down the bar, and laid hold of the ponderous gates, each man taking one and throwing himself backwards with all his weight to move it. When once started, the doors swung slowly but easily backwards. Zeno sat motionless in the saddle, ready to dash forward as soon as there was room for him to pass. He had halted just far enough away to allow the doors to swing clear of his horse's head as they were pulled inward. It was an anxious moment.

A second more and there would be space between the yawning gates. But that second had not yet passed when a tall officer in scarlet rushed shouting from the open door of the guard-house, and seized Zeno's bridle.

'Stop him!' yelled the lieutenant. 'Shut the gates!'

The two soldiers did their best to obey instantly, but the leaves of the gate were of cypress wood four inches thick, and covered with bronze, and were swinging back faster now under the impulse they had received. It was impossible to check them suddenly, and the order was hardly spoken when Zeno saw that there was room to ride through.

He would have given his fortune for a pair of Arab spurs at that moment, but he struck the corners of his heels at the horse's sides with all his might, and almost lifted him by the bridle at the same time. The big Tunisian answered the call upon his strength better than the rider had dared to hope; he gathered himself and lifted his forequarters, shaking his head savagely to get rid of the hands that grasped the off rein close to the bit, and then he dashed forwards, straight between the doors, throwing the officer to the ground and dragging him violently away in the powerful stride of his heavy gallop.

Seeing what had happened the sentinels started in pursuit at full speed, following the sound of the charger's shoes on the cobble-stones rather than anything they could see, for it was as dark as pitch outside.

The officer, who was very active and seemed indifferent to the frightful risk he ran, still clung to the bridle, regained his feet, ran nimbly by the side of the galloping horse, and seemed about to spring up and close with Zeno to drag him from the saddle. Zeno had no weapon within reach now, for his knife was in his own belt, under the belted tunic he wore over his clothes, and he could not possibly get at it. But the officer was unarmed, too, as he had sprung from his couch, and was at a great disadvantage on foot.

They dashed on into the darkness of the broad street. Zeno bent down, and tried to get at his adversary's collar with his right hand, but the officer dodged him and jerked the bridle with desperate energy, bringing the Tunisian to a stand after one more furious plunge. At the same instant Zeno heard the footsteps of the two guardsmen running up behind, and he realised that the odds were three to one against him, and that he had no weapon in his hand. The troopers, of course, had their Greek sabres. If he could not escape, he must either be taken alive or cut to pieces on the spot, with no defence but his bare hands.

He did not hesitate. The officer, dragging down the charger's head by his weight to stop him, was almost on his knees for a moment, on the off side, of course, and the soldiers had not yet come up. Zeno dropped the reins, sprang from the saddle, and ran for his life.

CHAPTER XII

Zoë sat in the dark just within the open doorway of Zeno's house, before the marble steps. She was shivering with cold, now that the danger to herself was over, and she was bent with pain, though she scarcely knew she was hurt; for she was conscious only of her anxiety for Zeno. If he got out of the tower and reached his home, he would certainly come in by that door, since he had left it open, and the one on the land side was barred; and there was a way of coming round the house to the water's edge without entering the gate or passing through the fore-court.

Zeno had unconsciously stepped upon her body with his whole weight in getting out, when she lay hidden in the bottom of the boat, but she would rather have died than have made a sound or winced under the pressure. And now her side hurt her, and the pain ran down to her knee and her foot, so that she had hardly been able to walk after Gorlias had helped her ashore.

It had been impossible to hinder her from getting in, when she had run down to the landing while Zeno was changing his clothes; there had not been time, and she had not waited to argue the question, but had simply whispered to Gorlias that she was going, and that he must hide her as well as he could, and say nothing. He was not a man to be easily surprised, and he reflected that as she was in the secret, and as it was her influence that had decided Zeno to act at last, she might possibly be useful; as indeed she afterwards proved herself to be. Besides, Gorlias thought it likely that Zeno had told her all his plans, although he did not wish to take her with him; for the astrologer was not at all clear as to the relations existing between the master and the slave.

She sat alone and shivering in the dark. Gorlias had left her and had hastened back to the foot of the tower to remove all traces of the unsuccessful attempt before daybreak, by throwing the dead body into the water with a weight, and carrying off the gear that had been left lying on the sloping pier. Zoë thought he must be of iron. He had been some time in the water in his clothes, and had probably been more or less bruised in the struggle, and in rolling down the stones, if not by the fall at the end. But he seemed as calm and collected as ever, and apparently had no idea of drying himself before morning.

Zoë thought of him only very vaguely as of a person connected with Zeno, round whom alone the whole world had moved since she had known that he loved her; and in her imagination she followed him on after he had reached the tower window the second time and had whistled the call that told her he was safe so far.

It was agonising to think of his danger. She did not believe that he could possibly escape from within the prison through the palace precincts; in some way or other he must succeed in climbing down the wall again, and Gorlias would find him and bring him home. But when she had said this to the astrologer, he had shaken his head. There were good reasons why Zeno should not attempt the perilous descent that night, when there had just been an alarm from below of which it was not possible to let him know the result. Moreover, no one knew whether the man whom Zoë had struck had sunk and was drowned, or had parried the blow with his arm and had succeeded in swimming ashore. Neither Gorlias nor Zoë knew that yet, and they might never know it.

She waited, but not a sound disturbed the silence of the chilly night. Within the house every one was sleeping; the two little slave-girls, curled up on their carpet in the corner, where Zoë had left them, would not wake till dawn; Omobono slept the sleep of the just in his small bedroom behind the counting-house, dreaming of the mysteries of four toes and five toes, and quenching his insatiable curiosity at last in the overflowing fountain of fancy. As for the servants and slaves, all slumbered profoundly, after the way of their kind.

But Zeno did not come. Zoë crouched in the doorway, and drew the skirts of her long Greek coat round her little white feet more than half instinctively, for she did not care if she died of the cold, since he did not come.

A mad longing seized her to go out into the city to look for him in the dark and silent streets; he might be lying somewhere, wounded and alone, perhaps left for dead; if she did not come upon him she would push on to the great gate of Blachernæ; and she was sure that she could find the way, though it was far. She would slip in, unnoticed by the sentries; she would pass herself for a woman of the palace, where she had often been taken by Kyría Agatha in the happy days; she remembered where the great tower stood in the corner of the palace yard, the farthest corner to the right, and she could almost see its door, though indeed she had never noticed one. He was somewhere behind it, somewhere in there, above or below ground, caught in the trap, waiting for the dawn of his dying day. For Andronicus would not let him live. If he was taken, his hours were numbered. He must die the death Michael Rhangabé had died; there was none more cruel.

As she thought of it, there alone in the cold, a sharp pain bit at her heart, and in the gloom she could no longer make out the white marble steps, the chequered black-and-white pavement, nor the last unextinguished lights of Pera reflected in the water; she saw nothing, and she sank back against the step behind her, fainting and unconscious.

She lay there alone, quite still; but he did not come. When she opened her eyes again she thought she had fallen asleep, and was angry with herself at the thought of having rested while he was in danger of his life. She would go out to find him, come what might. Then she tried to get upon her feet, and was startled to find that she could not. Chilled to the bone and bruised as she was, she could not move her limbs, and she wondered in terror whether she were paralysed. But she was brave still, and after a time she managed to turn on one side, and with her hands on the cold step she laboriously got upon her knees. Sensation came back and pain with it, and presently she was able to raise herself by holding the edge of the door, first on one knee, then on her feet. But that was all, and she knew that she could do no more. Perhaps she might crawl upstairs by and by, after resting a little.

She stood still a long time, holding the door and hesitating, for in her intense anxiety it seemed impossible to think of giving up and going to bed. He must come. It would be late, it might be daylight, but he must come; for if he came not, that could only mean that he was taken, and if he was taken he must die.

Again the pain bit savagely at her heart, but she set her lips and grasped the door with both hands, and refused to let herself faint.

She could at least rouse Omobono and the household to go out and search for the master. She had almost let go of the door to make the first step forward, when the counter-thought checked her. The attempt to free the Emperor had been made very secretly; if she called the secretary, the servants, the slaves, she would be revealing that secret, and if, by some miracle, Zeno were still free and safe, some one might betray him. Some one must have betrayed him already, else the watch would not have come upon him exactly at the most critical moment. The three men had been lurking near, waiting till he was on the rope the second time, and expecting to catch him in the very act of bringing out the prisoner. Who was the traitor? Most probably some one in the house. It would not be wise to call the servants, after all.

The hopelessness of it all came over the lonely girl now, and she almost let herself sink down again upon the steps to wait till daylight, if need be, for the awful news that was sure to reach her only too soon. Gorlias would bring it, and no one else.

But she was too proud to give way altogether, unless she fainted outright. It was torture, but she would bear it, as he would if he were taken. Perhaps at that very moment they were questioning him before Andronicus, twisting his handsome limbs till the joints cracked, or holding red-hot irons close to his blistering feet. He would set his teeth and turn white, but he would not speak; he would be torn piecemeal and die, but his tormentors would not get a word from him, not a syllable. Again and again, she felt the pain in imagination; but she wished that she could indeed feel it for him, and be in his place at that moment, if he were suffering. The pain would be less, even the pain of the rack and the glowing irons, than the agony of being powerless to help him.

Now, the time seemed endless; now, again, an hour passed quickly in a waking dream, wherein Zeno was vividly before her, and she lived again the moments that had taught her the truth in the touch of his lips. Then, the world was dark once more and she was alone and shivering, and mad with anxiety for the one living thing she loved.

He did not come. The northern stars sank to the west and he did not come; they touched the horizon, yet he did not come; an icy breath foreran the coming dawn, and still he came not, but still Zoë waited.

Then the stars faded, and the sky was less black, and she thought day was coming; but it was the faint light of the waning moon rising above the Bosphorus. It was not light, now, but the thick darkness had become transparent; it was possible to see through it, and Zoë saw a skiff come silently alongside the landing. It was Gorlias; he moored the craft quickly and came up the steps. Zoë had recognised his outline, because she expected him, and she made a step to meet him, though it hurt her very much to move. He came quickly and securely, as men do who can see at night, like cats and wild animals; when he was near, Zoë even fancied that his eyes emitted a faint light of their own in the dark, but her imagination was no doubt disturbed by her bodily pain and terrible mental anxiety.

'Has he not come yet?' Gorlias asked in a low tone.

The question could only mean that Zeno was taken, and Zoë grasped the astrologer's arm in sudden fear.

'He is lost!' she exclaimed. 'They will kill him to-morrow!'

'It is not easy to kill Carlo Zeno,' answered Gorlias, rubbing his stiffened hands, and then slowly pulling each finger in succession till the joints cracked. 'He is not dead yet,' he added.

'Not yet!' echoed Zoë despairingly.

'No,' said Gorlias, 'for he got out of the palace.'

'Got out? You are sure?' Zoë could have screamed for joy; the revulsion was almost too sudden.

'Yes, I am sure of that. There is a search for him in all the quarters about the palace. When I had cleared everything away below the tower, I dropped downstream to a quiet place I know, and went ashore to learn what I could. The great gate of Blachernæ was open, the court was full of lights, and the guards had been called out. Half of them were reeling about, still very drunk, but I met many that were more sober, searching the streets and lanes with lanterns. I lingered till the same party found me twice and looked at me suspiciously, and then I slipped away again and came here. I do not believe any of them know whom they are looking for; they have only been told that some one has broken out of the palace, I suppose. That made me think that Zeno had come quietly home, quite sure that he had not been recognised.'

Gorlias told his story in the low, monotonous tone peculiar to him, which seemed to express the most perfect indifference to anything that might happen. But Zoë cared nothing for his way of telling what was just then the best possible news. Zeno was not safe yet, but she knew him well enough to feel sure that if he had not been taken within the palace, he had little to fear. Sooner or later he would come home, as if nothing had happened. Gorlias understood her sigh of relief.

'You must go in and rest, Kokóna,' he said, and he quietly pushed her towards the door. 'I will watch till daylight in the boat, in case he should come and need anything.'

She could hardly walk, and he now noticed her lameness for the first time, and asked the cause of it.

'He stepped on me when I was lying under the canvas,' she answered. 'But it is nothing,' she added quietly. 'I hardly felt anything at first.'

'I will carry you,' said Gorlias.

Before she could prevent him, he had lifted her in his arms and was carrying her into the house. He knew the way up to her apartment, having been to see her there, and he stepped easily and surely with his burden, his bare feet hardly making any sound on the marble steps. She lay across his arms like a thing without weight, borne along as a maid carries a fresh gown that she is afraid of ruffling. But the man's arms and clothes were wet and cold, and even his breath chilled her.

Her nerves were overwrought, and she was foolishly frightened now. The stairs were very dark, and the touch of the man who carried her was like that of a wet monster of night, cold and horribly strong, holding her and carrying her in his vast arms as the autumn night wind whirls the leaves along. He never paused for breath, he never stopped to try and see the steps under his feet; he only went on and up, up, up, till she fancied she was not in Zeno's house, but in some high and mysterious tower to which she had been suddenly transported by an awful being from another world who was taking her to the top and would hurl her from the highest turret into space.

But now Gorlias stood still and set her on her feet at her own door, steadying her by her shoulders, and guiding her in, for he could see the ray of light that crept out between the curtain and the doorpost of the inner entrance.

He lifted the heavy stuff and still supported her with his other hand. After being so long in the dark the light of the little lamps was dazzling, though they were burning low. Three or four of them had already gone out, and the acrid smell of the burnt-out olive-oil and the singed wicks hung in the air.

Gorlias watched Zoë while she limped over the thick carpet to the divan, and he saw her sink down there exhausted, and draw a heavy silk shawl across her body.

'Thank you,' she sighed, as her weary head pressed the pillow at last.

But he had already dropped the curtain again and was gone, and almost at the same instant she shut her eyes and fell asleep.

Gorlias reached the bottom of the stairs without waking any one, closed the door, which he could not fasten, and got into his boat to wait for Zeno until daybreak, and also to watch lest any one should try to enter the house.

But no one came, neither Zeno, nor any messenger from him, nor any stealthy thief; and at last the dawn rose behind Constantinople and dissolved the night, and the poor waning moon had not much light left and almost went out altogether as the day broke. Then Gorlias drew his oars inboard, and laid them across the boat before him, leaning his elbows on them and resting his chin upon his folded hands, like a man in deep thought; and he let the craft drift slowly away towards the Bosphorus, into the morning mist.

Also, the dawn crept into the house between the half-closed shutters of Zoë's room and made the lingering flame of the last lamp seem but a smoky little yellow point in the cold clearness; and the girl's pale face, that had taken a golden tinge from the lamplight, now turned as white as silver.

Also, the coming sun waked Omobono, and he sat up in bed and gravely rubbed his eyes, quite unaware that anything had happened during the night; and it roused the slaves and the servants, and presently all the house was astir; and Yulia and Lucilla got up too and came softly and stood beside Zoë, who did not stir, and they wondered at her deep sleep and at the weariness of her face, and at the look of pain all about her mouth.

But where Zeno was the light did not enter; for dawn and sunset, and noon and midnight were all alike there.

CHAPTER XIII

When Zeno slipped from his borrowed charger and ran for his life towards that part of the square that looked darkest, he had no time to choose the direction he would afterwards take, nor to think of anything but covering the ground at the greatest possible speed without stumbling over an unseen obstacle. On those singular occasions when a perfectly brave man has no choice but to run, there is not much time to spare.

The young Venetian strained his strength and his wind to get as far as he could from his pursuers in the shortest possible time, and he was so successful that he was out of their reach almost before they were aware that he had fled.

At first he had run straight across the wide open space before Blachernæ; he had then found the entrance to a street which he had followed for about fifty yards, and he had turned a corner to his left without meeting any one; he had rushed on without pausing till he judged it time to double again and had then turned to the right. A few steps farther on, he stopped short and listened, believing himself alone and not at all sure where he was.

Suddenly a light flashed in his face, very near him.

'Is it time?' asked a low voice in Greek, and the lantern was closed again, leaving him dazzled.

Accident, or his fate, had taken him into the very midst of the men he had enlisted in the cause of the revolution, to storm the palace before daybreak. They had waited two hours and were impatient, and even before Zeno answered the question they saw that matters had gone ill with him.

'There is an alarm,' he said hurriedly. 'I barely got away. Disperse quickly, and get to your quarters, all of you! I will let you know when we can do it.'

A murmur of discontent came from the invisible crowd of soldiers. Zeno knew them to be a desperate crew, who would hold him responsible for failure, and would not thank him for success.

'We must separate at once,' he said calmly. 'I thank you for having been ready. If possible, we will meet a week from to-night.'

He did not choose to let them know that Johannes himself had refused to quit the tower, and he was about to leave them, meaning to find his way home alone, when the sound of feet moving behind him, and of men whispering together told him that he was surrounded on all sides by the soldiers. Then some one spoke in a tone of authority.

'You must stay with us,' the voice said. 'You have our lives in your hand, and we cannot let you go. It might suit your interests to give us up to the Emperor any day.'

Seeing his liberty threatened, Zeno laid his hand to the knife at the back of his belt and was about to try and break his way through. In the dark, a man with a drawn weapon in his hand easily inspires terror in a crowd. But it was clear that the soldiers had determined beforehand what to do, for they closed in upon him instantly, and his arm was caught by a dozen hands when he was in the very act of drawing his knife. He was held by twenty men, as it seemed to him, who all took hold of him and lifted him from the ground, not very roughly, but irresistibly. He had no chance against so many; Gorlias Pietrogliant himself could have done nothing, and he was far stronger than Zeno, stronger perhaps than any man in Constantinople.

Zeno knew that it would be worse than useless to shout for help; at his first cry he would most likely be strangled by men whose own lives were more or less at stake. They carried him quickly along the street and through unfamiliar and narrow ways which he could hardly have recognised even in broad daylight, much less at night. They turned sharp corners to the right, to the left, to the right again, and he thought he could distinguish the broken outlines of a ruined wall against the faint greyness of the ink-and-water sky.

Then all was dark for an instant, and he felt that his bearers were pausing at some obstacle or difficulty. The lantern flashed again, and he saw a rough vault above him; there was a big cobweb just above his head, and a loathsome fat spider jumped out of a crevice and ran along the threads till it disappeared as if by magic in the very middle of the web. He saw it in an instant in the sudden light as some one held up the lantern to show the way. Such things take hold of the memory and stick to it afterwards, as little burs fasten themselves upon one's clothes in autumn fields. Besides, though Zeno was one of the bravest men of any age, he detested fat spiders, and was very nearly afraid of them.

He felt himself carried down an inclined plane at a swinging rate; the air smelt of dry earth, and presently it grew much warmer, though it was not at all close. It seemed a long time until the men stopped, set him on his feet, and left their hold on him. The man who had acted as the leader now pushed the others aside, and stood before him, a broad-shouldered Tartar with a huge tawny beard, dressed in leather and wearing a breastplate embossed with the Roman eagle. Zeno knew him well; he was a Mohammedan, like many soldiers of fortune in the Greek army at that time, his name was Tocktamish, and he had been with Zeno in Patras. He spoke a barbarous dialect, compounded of Greek and Italian.

'Messer Zeno,' he said, 'we are not going to hurt you, but we think it better for your own safety to keep you here for a while, till everything is quiet again. Do you understand?'

'Perfectly,' Zeno answered, with a laugh. 'Nothing could be clearer! You naturally suppose that if I found myself in danger I would turn evidence against you to save myself, and you propose to make that impossible.'

Tocktamish pretended to be hurt.

'How can you think that I could take my old leader for a traitor, sir?' he asked.

'The idea would occur naturally to a man of your intelligence,' Zeno answered, laughing again. 'Listen to me, man. I am a soldier, and I do not take you for a flight of angels or heavenly doves settling round me for my consolation. You are an infernal deal more like a pack of wolves! So let us be plain, as wolves generally are when they are hungry. You joined me because you hoped to be plundering the palace by this time. As that has failed, you want something instead. You know very well that I am not the man to betray a comrade, and that if I am free I shall probably get Johannes out of his prison in the end. But you expect something now. How much do you want?'

The Tartar looked down sheepishly and passed his thumb round the lower edge of his corselet, backwards and forwards, as if he were slowly polishing the steel.

'Come,' continued Zeno, 'what is the use of hanging back? As I could not succeed in turning you all into patriots to-night and regenerators of your country, you have, of course, turned yourselves into bandits; you have got me a prisoner, and you want a ransom. How much is it to be?'

Tocktamish still hesitated, feeling very much ashamed of himself before his old captain.

'Well, sir, you see—there are eight hundred of us—and—'

'And if any one gets less than the rest he will sell all your skins to Andronicus for the balance,' laughed Zeno. 'Quite right, too! I love justice above all things.'

'Then give us ten ducats each,' cried the clear voice of a Greek from the background.

'Ten ducats apiece will make eight thousand,' said Zeno. 'I am sorry, but I have not so much money at my disposal.'

'You can borrow,' answered the Greek.

'I am afraid not, my friend.' He turned to the Tartar leader again. 'You are a fool, Tocktamish,' he said calmly. 'As long as you keep me here I cannot get money at all. Do you suppose that we merchants put away thousands of ducats in strong boxes under our beds? If we did that, you would have broken into our houses long ago, to help yourselves!'

'What promise will you make, sir?' inquired the Tartar, beginning to waver.

But half-a-dozen voices protested.

'No promises!' they cried. 'Let him send you for the money!'

'You hear them?' said Tocktamish.

'Yes,' answered Zeno, 'I hear them. Their nonsense will not change facts. If you had the souls of mice in your miserable bodies,' he continued, turning to the men with a contemptuous little laugh, 'you would come with me now and seize the palace. The gates are open, and the guards are all beastly drunk. There will be more than eight thousand ducats to divide there!'

The men were silent; many shook their heads.

'The moment is passed,' answered the Tartar, speaking for them. 'The whole city is roused by this time.'

'We shall have so many more good men to help us, then,' Zeno said. 'Not that we need any one. A handful could do the work.'

'Send for the money!' cried the voice of the Greek again.

'I have told you that I have not got it,' Zeno answered. 'If you have nothing more sensible to say, go to your quarters and let me sleep.'

'Pleasant dreams!' jeered the Greek; and several men laughed.

'I hope my dreams will be pleasant, for I am extremely sleepy,' Zeno answered carelessly. 'If you cut my throat before I wake you will get nothing at all, not even my funeral expenses! Now good-night, and be off!'

'We had better leave him,' Tocktamish said, pushing the nearest men away. 'You will get nothing at present, and it is impossible to frighten him. But he cannot get out, as you know. It is for our own safety, sir,' he added, changing his tone as he addressed Zeno. 'We cannot let you out till the city is quiet again, but you shall lack nothing. There are two cloaks for you to sleep on and for covering yourself, and I will bring you food and drink, and anything you want, in the morning.'

Zeno had found time to look about him during the conversation, as far as the light of the lanterns and the men who crowded upon him allowed him to see. He had understood very soon that he was not in the cellar of a ruined house, as he had at first supposed, but in one of those great disused cisterns, of which there are several in Constantinople, and of which two may still be seen. Centuries had passed since there had been water in this one, and the dust lay thick on the paved floor. Two or three score columns of grey marble supported the high vaulted roof, in which Zeno guessed that there was no longer any visible opening to the outer air. Yet air there was, in abundance, for it entered by the narrow entrance through which Zeno had been carried in, and probably found its way out through the disused aqueduct which had once supplied the water, and which still communicated with some distant exit. Zeno could only guess at this from his experience of fortresses, which always contained some similar cistern; every one he had seen was provided with openings, almost always both at the top; a few had staircases in order that men might more conveniently go down to clean them when they were empty.

His captors left him reluctantly at the bidding of their chief. They set one lantern against a pillar and filed out, carrying away the other. Zeno listened to their departing footsteps for a moment, when the last man had gone out, and then he went quickly to the entrance and listened again. In two or three minutes he heard what he expected; a heavy door creaked and was shut with a loud noise that boomed down the inclined passage. Then came another sound, which was not that of bolt or bar, and was worse to hear. The men were rolling big loose stones against the door to keep it shut—two, three, more, a dozen at least, a weight no one man could push outward. Then there was no more noise, and Zeno was alone.

His situation was serious, and his face was very thoughtful as he went back to the lantern and picked up one of the two cloaks Tocktamish had left him. He put it on and drew it closely round him, for he was beginning to feel cold in spite of the heavy guardsman's tunic he wore over his own clothes.

He thought of Arethusa, as he called Zoë; she had been in his mind constantly, and most of all in each of the moments of danger through which he had passed since he had left her. He thought of her lying awake on her divan in the soft light of the small lamps, waiting to hear his footsteps on the landing below her window, then falling gently asleep out of sheer weariness, to dream of him; starting in her rest, perhaps, as she dreamt that he was in peril, but smiling again, without opening her eyes, when the vision changed, and he held her in his arms once more. He little guessed what that yielding something beneath the canvas had been, on which he had pressed his foot so heavily when he had stepped ashore. She was happily ignorant, he fancied, of the succession of hairbreadth escapes through which he had passed unhurt so far. What weighed most on his mind, after all, was the thought that when he met her he should have to tell her that he had failed.

But he was not thinking of her only as he sat there, for his own situation stared him in the face, and he could not think of Arethusa without wondering whether he was ever to see her again. He had heard those big stones rolled to the door, and something told him that neither Tocktamish nor his men would bring the promised bread and water in the morning. They did not believe that he was unable to pay the ransom they demanded, and they meant to starve him into yielding. But he had spoken the truth; he had not such a sum of money at his command. The question was, what the end would be. For the present they had not left him so much as a jug of water, and he suddenly realised that he was thirsty after his many exertions. He could not help laughing to himself at the idea that he might die of thirst in a cistern.

But it was not in him to waste time in idly reflecting on the detestable irony of his fate, when there was any possibility that his own action might help him. He rose again and took up the lantern to make a systematic examination of his prison. After all, Tocktamish and his soldiers must have acted on the spur of the moment, and though they evidently knew the entrance to the cistern, and had probably been aware that it had a door which could be shut, it was not impossible that there might be another way out which they had overlooked in their haste.

But Zeno could find none, and the place was not so large as he had at first supposed. He counted eight columns in each direction, which gave sixty-four for the whole number, and he guessed the cistern to be about one hundred feet square. The walls were covered with smooth cement, to which the dust hardly adhered, and which extended upwards to the spring of the vault, at the same level as the capitals of the columns. There was no opening to be found except the one entrance. Zeno followed the steep inclined passage upwards till he reached the closed door which, as he well understood, must be at a considerable distance from the cistern. It was made of oak, and though it might have been in its place a couple of hundred years it was still perfectly sound. The lock had been wrenched off long ago, probably to be used for some neighbouring house, but Zeno had heard the stones rolled up outside the door, and even before he tried it, he knew that he could not make it move.

He wondered whether Tocktamish had set a watch, and he called out and listened for an answer, but none came; he shouted, with the same result. Then he took up his lantern and went down again, for it was clear that the soldiers thought him so safely confined that it would not be necessary to guard the entrance. Since that was their opinion, there was nothing to be done but to agree with them. Zeno lay down in the dust, rolled himself in the spare cloak, placing a doubled fold of it between his head and the base of a column, and he was soon fast asleep.

CHAPTER XIV

There was consternation in little Omobono's face the next morning when he learnt that his master had gone out during the night, and had not come home. The secretary would not believe it at first, and he went himself to Zeno's bedroom and saw that the couch had not been slept on; he could tell that easily, though it was not a bed but a narrow divan covered with a carpet; for the two leathern pillows were not disturbed, and the old dark red cloak which Zeno always used as a covering was neatly folded in its place. It had been with him through the long campaign in Greece, and he had the almost affectionate associations with it which men of action often connect with objects that have served them well in dangerous times.

Zeno had not slept at home, and he had changed his clothes before going out. Questioned by Omobono, Vito could not say with any certainty what the master had put on; in fact, he could not tell at all. All the cloth hose and doublets and tunics were in their places in the cedar wardrobes and chests of drawers, except those he had taken off, which lay on a chair. It looked, said the servant, as if the master had gone out without any clothes at all!

Omobono felt that if he had been a bigger man he would have boxed the fellow's ears for the impertinent suggestion. But it was not quite safe, for the man was a big Venetian gondolier and sailor. Besides, as he went on to explain, the master had often gone down to the marble steps at dawn for a plunge and a swim, with nothing but a sheet round him, coming back to dress in his room. Perhaps he had done so now, and perhaps—

The man stopped short. Perhaps Zeno was drowned. He looked at Omobono, but the secretary shook his head, and pointed to the undisturbed couch. Zeno would certainly not have gone out bathing before going to bed. Neither of them thought of looking into the small military trunk which stood in a dark corner, and from which Zeno had taken the leathern jerkin and stout hose which he had put on for the expedition.

Omobono had, of course, already questioned the slave-girls. They told what they knew, that the master had supped upstairs, and had dismissed them. When they came back to the room he was gone, they said; and this was true, since they had slept all night. The Kokóna was now asleep, they added; but they did not say that she was sleeping dressed as she had been on the previous evening, and looked very tired, for that was none of the secretary's business.

Omobono went up and down the stairs almost as often that morning as on the day of Zoë's first coming, and again and again he instructed Yulia to call him when her mistress awoke. The answer was always the same: the Kokóna was still asleep, and the secretary should be called as soon as she rose. At last he began to think that she, too, had left the house, and that the girls were in the secret, and he threatened to go in and see for himself. To his surprise Yulia stood aside to let him pass, laying one finger on her lips as a warning to make no noise; for the little slave saw well enough that he suspected her of lying, and she was afraid of him in Zeno's absence. Seeing that she did not oppose him, he was convinced, and did not go in.

He would not send out messengers to ask for his master at the houses of the Venetian merchants, or at their places of business, for he had a true Italian's instinct to conceal from the outer world everything that happens in the house. Yet he found himself in a dilemma; for Zeno had invited Sebastian Polo, his wife and his daughter, and other friends to dinner, and they would come, and be amazed to find that he was not there to receive them. Yet if word were sent to them not to come, Zeno might return in time and be justly angry; and then he would call the poor secretary something worse than a cackling hen. It was a terrible difficulty, and all the servants and slaves downstairs were chattering about it like magpies, except when the secretary was just passing. The cook sent to ask whether he was to prepare the dinner.

'Certainly,' answered Omobono. 'The master is no doubt gone out on pressing business, and will be back in plenty of time to receive his friends.'

He tried to speak calmly, poor man, but he was in a terrible stew. Anxiety had brought out two round red spots on his grey cheeks; for once his trim beard was almost ruffled, and his small round eyes were haggard and bloodshot.

As the time for the arrival of the guests drew near, he felt his brain reeling, and the rooms whirled round him, till he felt that the universe was going raving mad, and that he was in the very centre of it. Still Zoë slept, and still the master did not come.

At last there was but half an hour left. Omobono strained every nerve he possessed, and determined to meet the tremendous difficulty in a way that should elicit Zeno's admiration. He would receive the ladies and gentlemen as major-duomo, he would make an excuse for his master, he would instal them in their places at table, and would direct the service. Of the cook and the cellar the little man felt quite sure, and that was a great consolation in his extremity. If he gave Zeno's friends of the best, and made a polite apology, and saw that nothing went wrong, it would be impossible to ask more of him or to suggest that he had failed in his duty. When the guests were gone he would go to bed and have an attack of fever; of that he felt quite sure, but then the terrible ordeal would be over, and it would be a relief to lie on his back and feel very ill.

He retired and dressed himself in his best clothes. His cloth hose were of a dark wine colour, but were now a little loose for his legs. He looked at them affectionately as he examined them in the light. They recalled many cheerful hours and some proud moments; they remembered also the days when his little legs had not been so thin. Yet by pulling them up almost to the tearing point they lost in width what they gained in length, and made a very good appearance after all, for he secured them by an ingenious contrivance of belt and string. It was true that when he walked he felt as if he were being lifted from the floor by the back of his waistband, but that only made him feel a little taller than he was, and forced him to hold himself very straight, which was a distinct advantage.

Now in all this trouble it never occurred to him that his master was in any great danger or trouble, much less that he might have been killed in some mad adventure. Carlo Zeno had lived through such desperate perils again and again, that Omobono had formed the habit of believing him to be indestructible, if not invulnerable, and sure to fall on his feet whatever happened. The secretary only wished he would not choose to disappear on the very day when he had asked five friends to dine with him.

Omobono stood in his fine clean shirt and his wine-coloured hose, combing and smoothing his beard carefully with the help of a little mirror no bigger than the bottom of a tumbler. The glass was indeed so small that he could only get an impression of his whole face by moving the thing about, from his chin to his nose, from one cheek to the other, and from his forehead to his thin throat, round which he admired the neatly fitting line of the narrow linen collar. But this last effort required a good deal of squinting, for the point of his beard was in the way.

While he was thus engaged some one tapped at his door, and a small voice informed him that Kokóna Arethusa was now awake, and wished to see him instantly. Though the door was not opened by the speaker, Omobono hastily laid down his glass and his comb, and struggled into his tunic as if his life depended on his getting it on before he answered; for he was a very modest man, and the voice was a girl's; moreover, he was aware that the device of belt and strings by which his hose were drawn up so very tightly must present a ridiculous appearance until covered by his over-garment; then, however, the effect would be excellent. So he got on his tunic as fast as he could, and then answered with the calmness of perfectly restored dignity through the closed door.

'Tell the Kokóna that I am at her service,' he said; 'and that I shall be with her immediately.'

'Yes, sir,' said the small voice, and he heard the girl's retreating footsteps immediately after she had spoken.

A few moments later he was going up the stairs as fast as the tremendous tension of his hose would allow, and as he went he reflected with satisfaction that as major-duomo he could not by any possibility be called upon to sit down in the presence of his master's guests.

One of the slave-girls ushered him into Zoë's presence. The latter was seated on the edge of the divan, looking anxiously towards the door when he entered, and for the first time since she had been in the house he saw her face uncovered. It was very pale, and there were deep shadows under her eyes. Her beautiful brown hair was in wild disorder, too, and fell in a loosened tress upon one shoulder. The hand that rested on the edge of the divan strained upon a fold of the delicate silk carpet that covered the couch. She spoke as soon as Omobono appeared.

'Have you heard from him?' she asked anxiously. 'Is he coming?'

It did not seem strange to the secretary that she should already know of Zeno's absence, since no one in the house could think or talk of anything else. On his part he was resolved to maintain the calm dignity becoming to the major-duomo of a noble house.

'The master will doubtless come home when he has finished the urgent business that called him away,' he answered. 'In his absence, it will be my duty to make excuses to his guests—'

'Are they coming? Have you not sent them word to stay away?'

Omobono smiled in a sort of superiorly humble way.

'And what if the master should return just at the hour of dinner?' he asked. 'What would he say if I had ventured to take upon myself such a responsibility? The Kokóna does not know the master! Happily I have been in his service too long not to understand my duty. If it pleases him to come home, he will find that his friends have been entertained as he desired. If he does not come, he will be glad to learn afterwards that the proper excuses were offered to them for his unavoidable absence, and that they were treated with the honour due to their station.'

Zoë stared at the secretary, really amazed by his calmness, and almost reassured by his evident belief in Zeno's safety. It was true that he knew nothing of the facts, and had not seen his master hanging by the end of a rope, fifty feet above the ground, within twelve hours. It would have been hard to imagine Omobono's state of mind if he had spent the night as Zoë had. But nevertheless his assurance rested her, and restored a little of her confidence in Zeno's good fortune. Of his courage and his strength she needed not to be reminded; but she knew well enough that unless chance were in his favour, he could never leave Blachernæ except to die.

'Do you really think he is safe?' Zoë asked, glad to hear the reassuring words, even in her own voice.

'Of course, Kokóna—'

But at this moment the sound of oars in the water, and of several voices talking together, came up through the open window from the landing below.

All Omobono's excitement returned at the thought that he might not get down the stairs in time to receive the guests at the marble steps just as the boats came alongside. Without another word he turned and fled precipitately.

Zoë had heard the voices too, and had understood; and, in spite of her anxiety, a gentle smile at the secretary's nervousness flitted across her tired face. The two slave-girls had run to the window to see who was coming, and as they had always been told not to show themselves at windows, they crouched down in the balcony and looked through the open-work of marble which formed the parapet.

Zoë rose to cross the room. In the first rush of memory that came with waking, she had almost forgotten that she had been hurt, and now she bit her lip as the pain shot down her right side. But she smiled almost instantly. She would rather have been hurt unawares by the man she loved, than that he should not have touched her at the very moment of going into danger. The memory of his crushing weight upon her for that instant was something she would not part with. Women know what that is. She thought how tenderly he would have stooped to kiss her, if he had known that she was lying there under the canvas. Instead, he had stepped upon her body; and it was almost better than a kiss, for that would have left nothing of itself; but now each movement that hurt her brought him close to her again.

She had received no real injury, but she limped as she walked to the window. Then she stood still just within it, where she could not see down to the steps below, but could talk with the slave-girls in a whisper. Doubtless, since Zeno had not wished her to be seen, she would not have shown herself; but she was quite conscious that she looked ill and tired, and by no means fit to face a rival who had been described to her as fresher than spring roses; so that the sacrifice was, after all, not so great as it might have been.

'Tell me what you see,' she said to the maids.

Lucilla turned up her sallow little face.

'There are three,' she answered. 'There is a Venetian lord, and his lady, and a young lady. At least, I suppose she is young.'

'I should think you could see that,' Zoë said.

'Her face is veiled,' Lucilla replied, after peering down; 'but I can see her hair. It is red, and she has a great deal of it.'

'Red like Rustan's wife's hair?' asked Zoë.

'Oh no! It is red like a lady's; for it is well dyed with the good khenna that comes from Alexandria. Now they are getting out—the old lady first—she is fat—the secretary and her husband help her on each side. She is all wrapped in a long green silk mantle embroidered with red roses. She is like a dish of spinach in flames. How fat she is!'

Lucilla shook a little, as if she were laughing internally.

'What does her daughter wear?' asked Zoë.

'A dark purple cloak, with a broad silver trimming.'

'How hideous!' exclaimed Zoë, for no particular reason.

'The secretary bows to the ground,' Lucilla said. 'He is saying something.'

She stopped speaking, and all three listened. Zoë could hear Omobono's voice quite distinctly.

'By a most unfortunate circumstance,' he was saying, 'Messer Carlo Zeno was obliged to go out on very urgent business, and has not yet returned. I am his secretary and major-duomo, as your lordship may deign to remember. In my master's absence I have the honour to welcome his guests, and to wait upon them.'

Sebastian Polo said something in answer to this fine speech; but in a low tone, and Zoë could not hear the words. Then a peculiarly disagreeable woman's voice asked a question. Zoë thought it sounded like something between the croaking of many frogs and the clucking of an old hen. 'We hope you will give us our dinner, whatever happens,' said the lady, who seemed to be of a practical turn of mind.

'Is that the girl's voice?' asked Zoë of Lucilla, in a whisper.

The maid shook her head.

'The mother,' she answered. 'Now they are going in. I cannot hear what Omobono says, for he is leading the way. They are all gone.'

Zoë did not care who else came, and now that the moment was over she was much less disturbed by the fact that Giustina was under the same roof with her than she had expected to be. She did not believe that Zeno had ever kissed Giustina, and he had certainly never stepped on her.

She let her maids do what they would with her now, hardly noticing the skill they showed in helping her to move, and in smoothing away the pain she felt, as only the people of the East know how to do it. As she did not speak to them they dared not ask her questions about the master's absence. They had left him with her when they had been sent away; they had slept till morning; when they awoke they had found Zoë lying on the divan asleep in her clothes, and the master had gone out of the house unseen and had not returned. That was as far as their knowledge went; but they were sure that she knew everything, and they hoped that if they pleased her even more than usual she would let fall some words of explanation, as mistresses sometimes do when their servants are particularly satisfactory. Most young women, when they are in a good humour, let their maids know what they have been doing; and as soon as they are cross the maids revenge themselves by telling the other servants everything. In this way the balance of power is maintained between the employer and the employed, like the hydrostatic equilibrium in the human body, which cannot be destroyed without bringing on a syncope.

But though Zoë felt very much less pain after Yulia and Lucilla had bathed her and rubbed her, and had gently pulled at all her joints till she felt supple and light again, she said nothing about Zeno; and though they dressed her so skilfully that she could not help smiling with pleasure when they showed her to herself in the large mirror they held up between them, yet she only thanked them kindly, and gave them each two spoonfuls of roseleaf preserve, which represented to them an almost heavenly delight, as she well knew, and which she herself did not at all despise. That was all, however; and they were a little disappointed, because she did not condescend to talk to them about the master's disappearance, which was the greatest event that had happened since they had all three lived under Zeno's roof.

Meanwhile Omobono was playing his part of major-duomo downstairs, and had installed the guests at the table set for them in the large hall looking over the Golden Horn. After Polo and his wife, another Venetian merchant had arrived, the rich old banker Marin Cornèr, long established in Constantinople, and a friend of Sebastian Polo. The fifth person invited did not appear, so that two seats were vacant, the sixth being Zeno's own; and behind his high carved chair Omobono installed himself, to direct the servants, quite an imposing figure in his dark purple tunic and the handsome silver chain, which he had put on to-day to indicate his high office in the establishment. Poor Omobono! He little dreamt of what was in store for him that day.

The three older guests were moderately sorry that Zeno was not present. In their several ways they were all a little afraid of their eccentric countryman, about whom the most wild tales were told. Though in truth he was extremely punctual in meeting his financial engagements, both Sebastian Polo and Marin Cornèr had always felt a little nervous about doing business with a young man who was known to have kept an army at bay for a whole winter, who was reported to have slain at least a hundred Turks with his own hand, and whose brown eyes gleamed like a tiger's at the mere mention of a fight. It would be so extremely awkward if, instead of meeting a bill that fell due, he should appear at Cornèr's bank armed to the teeth and demand the contents of the strong box. On the whole the two elderly merchants ate with a better appetite in his absence.

But Giustina was inconsolable, and the good things did not appeal to her, neither the fresh sturgeon's roe from the Black Sea, nor the noble palamit, nor the delicate quails, nor even the roasted peacock, whose magnificent tail rose out of a vast silver dish like a rainbow with spots on it.

She was a big, sleepy creature with quantities of handsomely dyed hair, as Lucilla had told Zoë. She had large and regular features, a perfectly colourless white skin, and a discontented mouth. She often turned her eyes to see what was going on, without turning her head at all, as if she were too lazy to make even that small effort. Her hands were well shaped, but heavy in the fingers, and they looked like new marble, too white to be interesting, too cold to touch.

She was terribly disappointed and deeply offended by what seemed to her a deliberate insult; for she did not believe a word of Omobono's polite apology. The truth was that Zeno had only invited the party because her mother had invited herself in the hope of bringing him to the point of offering to marry Giustina. As a matter of fact nothing had ever been farther from his thoughts. Sebastian Polo, urged by his wife, had entered into the closest relations of business with Zeno, and had again and again given him a share in transactions that had been extraordinarily profitable. He had rendered it necessary for Zeno to see him often, and had made it easy by his constant hospitality; in these things lay the whole secret of Zeno's visits to his house. But seeing that matters did not take a matrimonial direction as quickly as she had expected, Polo's wife had adopted a course which she intended to make decisive; she had asked herself and her daughter to dine with Zeno. From this to hinting that he had compromised Giustina, and thence to extracting an offer of marriage, would be easy steps, familiar to every enterprising mother, since the beginning of the matrimonial ages. And that was a long time ago—even before Solomon's day, when the horseleech's two daughters cried, 'Give, give!' Zeno's value as a possible husband lay less in his fortune than in his very magnificent connections at home, and in the fact that the Emperor Charles had been his godfather and afterwards his friend and patron.

Giustina understood her thoughtful parent's policy; she was therefore unhappy, and would eat no peacock, a circumstance which greatly distressed Omobono. Happily for him, the young woman's abstention was fully compensated by the readiness of the elder guests to partake of what she obstinately refused, even to something like repletion.

While they ate, they talked; that is to say, Sebastian Polo and Marin Cornèr compared opinions on business matters such as the value of Persian silks, Greek wines, and white slaves, without giving away to each other the least thread of information that could be turned into money. And Polo's wife, who had an eye to the main chance, croaked a few words now and then, encouraging Cornèr to talk more freely of his affairs; perhaps, thought she, he might betray the secret of his wonderful success in obtaining from the Caucasus certain priceless furs which no merchant but he had ever been able to get. But though the fat dame lured him on to talk and made signs to have his glass filled again and again with Chian wine, and though the colours of a most beautiful sunset began to creep up his thin nose and his high cheek bones, as the rich evening light climbs in the western sky, Marin Cornèr's speech was as quiet and clear as ever, and what he said was, if anything, a trifle more cautious than before.

And meanwhile Giustina stared across her empty plate at the boats on the Golden Horn, and nursed her wrath against the man she wished to marry.

'My child,' croaked her mother, 'we fully understand your disappointment. But you should make an effort to be cheerful, if only for the sake of Messer Marin Cornèr, your father's valued friend.'

'I beg you to excuse my dulness, Madam,' answered the daughter dutifully, and with all the ceremony that children were taught to use in addressing their parents. 'I shall endeavour to obey you.'

'Come, come, Donna Giustina!' cried Cornèr. 'We will drink your health and happiness in this good—'

The sentence remained unfinished, and his lips did not close; as he set down the untasted wine, his eyes fixed themselves on a point between Omobono and Polo, and the sunset effects faded from his nose, leaving a grey twilight behind.

The fat dame thought it was an apoplexy, and half rose from her seat; but Giustina's eyes followed the direction of his look and she uttered a cry of real fear. Sebastian Polo, who sat with his back to the sight that terrified his daughter, gazed at the other three in astonishment. But Omobono turned half round and gasped, and seized the back of Zeno's empty chair, swinging it round on one of its legs till it was between him and the vision.

Tocktamish stood there, grinning at the assembled company in a way to terrify the stoutest heart amongst them. He was magnificently arrayed in his full dress uniform of flaming yellow and gold, and his huge round fur papakh was set well back on his shaggy head. His right hand toyed amidst a perfect arsenal of weapons in his belt, and his blood-shot eyes rolled frightfully as he looked from one guest to the other, showing his shark's teeth as he grinned and grinned again.

It was certainly Tocktamish, the Tartar; and Tocktamish was not perfectly sober. He was the more pleased by the impression his appearance had produced. He at once came forward to the empty place of the absent guest, which was next to Giustina's.

'I see that you have kept a place for me,' he said in barbarous Greek. 'That was very kind of you! And I am in time for the peacock, too!'

Thereupon he sat down in the chair, looked round the table, and grinned again.

The fat lady collapsed in a fainting fit, the two elderly merchants edged away from the board as far as they could, and Giustina uttered another piercing shriek when the Tartar leered at her.

'Who is this person?' her father tried to ask with dignity, meaning the question for Omobono.

But Omobono had vanished, and the servants had fled after him.

CHAPTER XV

Tocktamish poured half a flagon of Chian wine into a tall Venetian beaker and drank it off by way of whetting his appetite.

'The master of the house is unavoidably absent,' he observed, when he had smacked his lips noisily. 'He has sent me to beg that you will excuse him and make yourselves at home.'

By this time Dame Polo was beginning to revive, and the two men were somewhat reassured as to the Tartar's intentions. When he had entered he had looked as if he meant to murder them all, but it was now evident from his manner that he wished to produce a pleasant impression. He drew the peacock towards him, and at once took all the best pieces that were left on the dish, using his fingers to save trouble. Giustina watched him without turning her head, and judged that, after all, he had only meant to show his admiration for her beauty when he had leered so horribly. She was in reality the least timid of all the party, though she had shrieked so loudly, and she remembered a fairy story about a frightful monster that had loved a beautiful princess. She was already pondering on the means of making a similar conquest.

'Are we to understand,' asked Marin Cornèr, politely, but in a shaky tone, 'that you come from Messer Carlo Zeno?'

Tocktamish grunted assent, for his mouth was full, and he nodded emphatically.

'Messer Carlo Zeno is in need of a large sum of money without delay,' he said, when he was able to speak again.

Sebastian Polo looked at Marin Cornèr significantly; and Marin Cornèr looked at Sebastian Polo. The fat lady pricked her ears, figuratively speaking, for indeed they were much too deeply embedded in their exuberant surroundings of cheek and jowl to suggest that they could ever prick at all. The Tartar crammed his mouth full again, and his great beard wagged with his jaws in the inevitable silence that followed. In her heart Giustina compared him to a ravenous lion, but her father thought he resembled a hungry hyena.

Finding that his throat was not cut yet, and learning that there was to be a question of money, Marin Cornèr felt that the colour was returning to his nose and the warmth to his heart.

'Why does Messer Carlo not come home himself and get the money he needs?' he asked.

By this time Omobono had recovered from his fright enough to creep into the room behind Tocktamish. He was already making anxious gestures to the two Venetian gentlemen to enjoin caution. The Tartar drank again before he answered the question.

'He happened to be so busy that he preferred to send me to get the money for him,' said the soldier. 'You see we are old friends. We fought together in Greece.'

Then Omobono's voice was heard, quavering with anxiety.

'There is no money in the house!' he cried, winking violently at Polo and Cornèr. 'There is not a penny, I swear! There were large payments to make yesterday.'

The poor little secretary was so anxious to be heard that he had come within arm's length of the Tartar, though behind him. Tocktamish turned his big head, and put out his hand unexpectedly, and Omobono felt himself caught and whirled round like a child till he was close to the table and face to face with the tipsy giant. He was sure that he felt his liver shrivelling up inside him with sheer fright.

'What is this little animal?' the Tartar asked, cocking one eye in a knowing way and examining him with a sort of boozy gravity.

But Omobono really could not find a word. His captor shook him playfully.

'What is your name, you funny little beast?' he enquired, and he roared with laughter by way of answering himself.

Giustina, strange to say, was the only one to join in his mirth, and she laughed quite prettily, to the inexpressible surprise of her parents, who were shocked and grieved, as well as scared almost to death.

'Come, come!' laughed the Tartar, shaking the little man like a bean-bag. 'If you cannot speak, you can at least give up your keys, and I will see for myself if there is any money!'

Thereupon he seized the bunch of keys which the secretary wore at his belt, and wrenched it off with a pull that snapped the thong by which it hung. Again Giustina laughed, but a little more nervously now; her mother sat transfixed, open-mouthed, with an almost idiotic expression. Again the two merchants glanced at each other, and then both looked towards the door.

Between his fright and the terrible indignity of having his keys torn from him, Omobono had never been nearer to fainting in his life.

'Robbery!' he gasped. 'Rank robbery!'

Tocktamish sent him spinning into the nearest corner by a turn of the wrist, after which the ruffian took another mouthful of meat, and slowly filled his glass while he was disposing of it. Omobono had steadied himself in the corner, but his face was deadly white, and his lips were moving nervously in a delirium of terror.

'Messer Carlo needs ten thousand ducats before sunset,' observed the Tartar before he drank.

Polo and Cornèr started to their feet; to their commercial souls the mere mention of such a demand was more terrifying than all the crooked weapons that gleamed in Tocktamish's broad belt.

'Ten thousand ducats!' they repeated together in a breath.

'Yes!' roared the Tartar, in a voice that made the glasses on the table shake together and ring. 'Ten thousand ducats! And if I do not find the money in the house, you two must find it in yours! Do you understand?'

They understood, for his voice was like thunder, and he had risen too, and towered above them with his full glass in one hand and Omobono's keys in the other. Then, being already tolerably drunk, he solemnly raised the keys to his lips, thinking that he held the glass in that hand, and rolled his eyes terribly at the two merchants; and he set the glass down with an emphatic gesture, as if it had been the bunch of keys, and it broke to pieces, and the yellow wine splashed out across the table and ran down and streamed upon the mosaic floor.

A terrific Tartar oath announced that he had realised his mistake, and as he at once made up his mind that the Venetians were responsible for it, his next action was to hurl the foot of the broken glass at Polo's head; and he instantly seized the empty silver flagon and flung it at Cornèr's face. The lighter weapon missed its aim and broke to atoms against the opposite wall, but the jug struck Cornèr full on the bridge of his thin nose with awful effect, and he fell to the floor and lay there, a moaning, bleeding heap.

Polo looked neither at his wife nor at his daughter, but fled through the open door at the top of his not very great speed. His wife fainted outright, and in real earnest now, and with a final croak rolled gently from her chair, without hurting herself at all. Omobono flattened his lean body against the wall, trembling in every joint, and gibbering with fear; and Tocktamish, seeing that he had so satisfactorily cleared the field, proceeded to address his attentions to Giustina, who had not fainted, but was really much too frightened to rise from her seat or try to escape.

The Tartar drew his chair nearer to hers, and suddenly smiled, as if he had done nothing unusual, and was only anxious to make himself agreeable. He had been drinking since early morning, but he would be good for at least another gallon of wine before it made him senseless. He addressed Giustina in the poetic language of his native country.

'Come, pet parrot of my soul!' he began, coaxingly. 'Fill me a cup and let me hear your ravishing voice! Tocktamish has cleared the house as the thunderstorm clears the hot air from the valley! Drink, my pretty nightingale, and the golden wine shall warm your speech in your little throat, as the morning sunshine melts the icicles in my beard when I have been hunting all night in winter! Drink, my fawn, my spring lamb, my soft wood-pigeon, my white bunny rabbit! Drink, sweet one!'

The Tartar's similes were in hopeless confusion, possibly because he translated them into Greek, but he was convinced that he was eloquent, and he was undeniably as strong as a bear. He had filled a fresh glass and was evidently anxious to make Giustina drink out of it before him, for he held it to her lips with his left hand while his right tried to take her round the waist and draw her to his knee.

But this was much more than she was prepared to submit to. In the fairy story, Beast was less enterprising in the presence of Beauty, and collapsed into obedience at the mere lifting of her finger. Giustina was a big creature, usually sleepy and not inclined to move quickly; but she was capable of exerting considerable strength in an emergency. The instant she felt Tocktamish's hand at her waist, she rose with a quick, serpentine motion that unwound her, as it were, from his encircling hold, and almost before he knew that she was on her feet she had fled from the room and slammed the door behind her.

Tocktamish tried to follow her, but he stumbled successively over the still unconscious dame and the still moaning Cornèr, so that when he reached the door at last his purpose had undergone a change, and, as he thought, an improvement. Women never ran out of the house into the street, he argued; therefore Giustina was now upstairs and would stay there; hence it would be wiser to finish the peacock and anything else he could lay hands on before going to pay her a visit. For Tocktamish found the food and the wine to his liking, and such as were not to be had every day, even by a Tartar officer with plenty of money in his wallet. He was tolerably steady still, as he made his way back towards his seat.

His eye fell on Omobono, flattened against the wall and still in a palsy of fear; for all that has been told since Cornèr had fallen and Polo had run away had occupied barely two minutes.

Tocktamish suddenly felt lonely, and the little secretary amused him. He took him by the collar and whirled him into Giustina's vacant chair at the table.

'You may keep me company, while I finish my dinner,' he explained. 'I cannot eat alone—it disturbs my digestion.'

He roared with laughter, and slapped Omobono on the back playfully. The little man felt as if he had been struck between the shoulders by a large ham, and the breath was almost knocked out of his body; and he wondered how in the world his tight hose had survived the strain of his sitting down so suddenly.

'You look starved,' observed the Tartar, in a tone of concern, after observing his face attentively. 'What you want is food and drink, man!'

With a sudden impulse of hospitality he began to heap up food on Giustina's unused plate, with a fine indifference to gastronomy, or possibly with a tipsy sense of humour. He piled up bits of roast peacock, little salt fish, olives, salad, raisins, dried figs, candied strawberries, and honey cake, till he could put no more on the plate, which he then set before Omobono.

'Eat that,' he said. 'It will do you good.'

Then he addressed himself to the peacock again, with a good will.

Omobono would have got up and slipped away, if he had dared. Next to his bodily fear, he was oppressed by the terrible impropriety of sitting at his master's table, where the guests should have been. This seemed to him a dreadful thing.

'Really, sir,' he began, 'if you will allow me I would rather—'

'Do not talk. Eat!'

Tocktamish set the example by tearing the meat off a peacock's leg with his teeth.

'You need it,' he added, with his mouth very full.

The poor secretary looked at the curiously mixed mess which his tormentor had set before him, and he felt very uncomfortable at the mere idea of tasting the stuff. Then he glanced at the Tartar and saw the latter's bloodshot eye rolling at him hideously, while the shark-like teeth picked a leg bone, and terror chilled his heart again. What would happen if he refused to eat? Tocktamish dropped the bone and filled two glasses.

'To Messer Carlo Zeno!' he cried, setting the wine to his lips.

Omobono thought a little wine might steady his nerves; and, moreover, he could not well refuse to drink his master's health.

'Good!' laughed Tocktamish. 'If you cannot eat, you can drink!'

Just then Cornèr groaned piteously, where he lay in a heap on the floor. His nose was much hurt, but he was even more badly frightened. The Tartar was not pleased.

'If that man is dead, take him out and bury him!' he cried, turning on Omobono. 'If he is alive, kick him and tell him to hold his tongue! He disturbs us at our dinner.'

Omobono thought he saw a chance of escaping, and rose, as if to obey. But the Tartar's long arm reached him instantly and he was forced back into his seat.

'I thought you meant me to take him away,' he feebly explained.

'I was speaking to the slaves,' said Tocktamish gravely, though there was no servant or slave within hearing.

The unfortunate merchant, who was not at all unconscious, and had probably groaned with a vague idea of exciting compassion, now held his peace, for he did not desire to be kicked, still less to be taken out and buried. The Tartar seemed satisfied by the silence that followed. After another glass he rose to his feet and took Omobono by the arm; considering his potations he was still wonderfully steady on his legs.

'Where is the strong box?' he asked, dragging the secretary towards the door opposite to the one through which Giustina had gone out.

'There is no money in the house,' cried Omobono, in renewed terror. 'I swear to you that there is no money!'

'Very well,' answered the Tartar, who had taken the keys from the table. 'Show me the empty box.'

'There is no strong box, sir,' answered the secretary, resolving to control his fear and die in defending his master's property.

The difficulty was to carry out this noble resolution. Tocktamish grabbed him by both arms and held him in the vice of his grasp.

'Little man,' he said gravely. 'There is a box, and I will find the box, and I will put you into the box, and I will throw the box into the water. Then you will know that it is not good to lie to Tocktamish. Now show me where it is.'

Omobono shrank to something like half his natural size in his shame and fear, and led the way to the counting-house. Once only he stopped, and made a gallant attempt to be brave, and tried to repeat his queer little prayer, as he did on all the great occasions of his life.

'O Lord, grant wealth and honour to the Most Serene Republic,' he began, and though he realised that in his present situation this request was not much to the point, he would have gone on to ask for victory over the Genoese, on general principles.

But at that moment he felt something as sharp as a pin sticking into him just where his hose would naturally have been most tight, and where, in fact, the strain that pulled them up was most severe; in that part of the human body, in short, which, as most of us have known since childhood is peculiarly sensitive to pain. There was no answer to such an argument a posteriori; the little man's head went down, his shoulders went up, and he trotted on; and though he could not be put off from finishing his prayer he had reached the door of the counting-house when he was only just beginning to pray that he might have strength to resist curiosity, a request even more out of place, just then, than a petition for the destruction of the Genoese. A moment later he and Tocktamish entered the room, and the Tartar shut the door behind him.

Neither of the two had heard two little bare feet following them softly at a distance; but when the door was shut Lucilla ran nimbly up to it and quickly drew the great old iron bolt which had been left where it had once been useful, at a time when the disposition of the house had been different. Lucilla knew that all the windows within had heavy gratings, and that neither Omobono nor his captor could get out.

Giustina had fled upstairs, as women generally do to save themselves from any immediate danger. They are born with the idea that when a house has more than one story the upper one is set apart for them and their children, as indeed it always was in the Middle Ages, and they feel sure that there must be other women there who will help them, or defend them, or hide them. For it is a curious fact that whereas women distrust each other profoundly where the one man of their affections is concerned, they rely on each other as a whole body, banded together to resist and get the better of the male sex, in a way that would do credit to any army in an enemy's country. Therefore Giustina went upstairs, quite certain of finding other women.

Now there was but one door on the upper landing, and that was Zoë's, and it was open; and just outside it Lucilla was hiding in the curtain, listening to the strange sounds that came up from below; but when Giustina ran in without seeing her, the little slave stayed outside and slipped downstairs noiselessly, listened again at the dining-room door, watched the Tartar and the secretary from a place of safety, and then ran nimbly after them on purpose to lock them in, as she did, for she was a clever little slave and remembered the bolt.

Meanwhile Giustina rushed on like a whirlwind till she fell panting on the divan beside Zoë, hardly seeing her at all, and staring at the door, through which she expected every moment to see the burly Tartar enter in pursuit; so that Yulia, who guessed the danger, ran and shut it of her own accord.

Then Giustina drew a long breath and looked round, and she met Zoë's eyes scrutinising her face with a look she never forgot.

'That monster!' she exclaimed, by way of explanation and apology.

Zoë had heard nothing, for the house was solidly built, and she had not the least idea who had frightened Giustina. It occurred to her that Gorlias might be in the house, and that on being seen by the Venetians it had suited him to terrify them in order to get out again without being questioned.

'You are Giustina Polo,' she said. 'I am Arethusa, Messer Carlo Zeno's slave. Will you tell me what has happened?'

Giustina had now recovered herself enough to see that this Arethusa was very lovely, and she momentarily forgot the danger she had escaped.

'You are his slave!' she repeated slowly, and still breathing hard. 'Ah—I begin to understand.'

'So do I,' Zoë answered, looking at the handsome, heavy face, the dyed hair, and marble hands.

There was something like relief in her tone, now that she had examined her rival well.

'When did Carlo buy you?' asked Giustina, growing coldly insolent as she recovered her breath and realised her social superiority.

'I think it was just five weeks ago,' Zoë answered simply. 'But it seems as if I had always been here.'

'I have no doubt,' said Giustina. 'Five weeks! Yes, I understand now.'

Then a fancied sound waked her fear of pursuit again, and her eyes turned quickly towards the door. Yulia was standing beside it, listening with her ear to the crack; she shook her head as she met Giustina's anxious glance. There was nothing; no one was coming.

'You had better tell me what has happened,' Zoë said. 'You met some one who frightened you,' she suggested.

Giustina saw that Zoë was in complete ignorance of the Tartar's visit, and she told what she had seen and heard downstairs. As she went on, explaining that Tocktamish demanded ten thousand ducats in

Zeno's name, Zoë's expression grew more anxious, for she gathered the truth from the broken and exaggerated narrative. After failing in his attempt to free Johannes, Zeno had fallen into the hands of the soldiers he had won over to the revolution; they demanded an enormous ransom, and if it was not forthcoming they would give him up to Andronicus.

It was bad enough, yet it was better than it might have been, for it meant that Zeno was still alive and safe, and would not be hurt so long as his captors could be made to wait for the money they asked.

'Ten thousand ducats!' Zoë repeated. 'It is more than can ever be got together!'

'My father could pay twice as much if he pleased,' answered the rich merchant's daughter, vain of his immense wealth. 'But I hardly think he will give anything,' she added slowly, while she watched Zoë's face to see what effect the statement might have.

'Messer Carlo has many friends,' Zoë answered quietly. 'But if he is alive it is very probable that he may come home without paying any ransom at all. And if he does, he will certainly repay the soldiers for the trick they have played him.'

'You do not seem anxious about him,' said Giustina, deceived and surprised by her assumed calmness.

'Are you?' Zoë asked.

At that moment Yulia opened the door, for she had been listening from within and had heard her companion's bare feet on the pavement outside. Lucilla slipped in, almost dancing with delight at her last feat, and looking like a queer little sprite escaped from a fairy tale.

'I have locked them up in the counting-house, Kokóna!' she cried. 'The Tartar giant and the secretary! They are quite safe!'

She laughed gleefully and Yulia laughed too. Giustina suddenly recollected her mother, who had fainted in the dining-room. As for her father, her knowledge of his character told her that since there had been danger he was certainly in a place of safety. She did not care what became of Marin Cornèr, whom she detested because he had once dared to ask for her hand, though he was a widower of fifty. But her mother was entitled to some consideration after all, if only for having brought into the world such a wonderful creature as Giustina really believed herself to be. Yet in her heart the young woman felt a secret resentment against her for having grown so enormously fat; since it very often happens that as daughters grow older they grow more and more like their mothers, and Giustina was aware that she herself was already rather heavy for her age. It would be a terrible thing to be a fat woman at thirty, and it would be her mother's fault if she were. Many daughters are familiar with this argument, though they may cry out and rail at the story-teller in the bazaar who has betrayed it to the young men.

Giustina rose with much dignity now that she was fully reassured as to the safety of the house. Zoë was questioning Lucilla, who could hardly answer without breaking into laughter at the idea of having imprisoned Omobono and the terrible Tartar. The little secretary had never been unkind to any one in his life, but once or twice, when the master had been out and he had been on his dignity, he had found the slave-girls loitering on the stairs and had threatened them with the master's displeasure and with a consequent condign punishment if they were ever again caught doing nothing outside their mistress's apartment; and it was therefore delightful to know that he was shut up with Tocktamish, in terror of his life, and that his tremendous dignity was all gone to pieces in his fright.

'You are a clever girl,' said Zoë. 'I only hope the door is strong.'

'I called the servants and the slaves before I came upstairs,' Lucilla answered. 'I left them piling up furniture against the door. A giant could not get out now.'

'Poor Omobono!' Zoë exclaimed. 'How frightened he must be.'

Giustina meanwhile prepared to go away, settling and smoothing the folds of her gown, and pressing her hair on one side and the other. Yulia brought her a mirror and held it up, and watched the young lady's complacent smile as she looked at her own reflection. When she had finished she barely nodded to Zoë, as she might have done to a slave who had served her, and she went out in an exceedingly stately and leisurely manner, quite sure that she had impressed Zoë with her immeasurable superiority. She was much surprised and displeased because Zoë did not rise and remain respectfully standing while she went out, and she promised herself to remember this also against the beautiful favourite when she herself should be Carlo Zeno's wife.

But at a sign from Zoë, Lucilla followed her downstairs since there was no one else to escort her; and a few minutes later Yulia saw the little party come out upon the landing below. The fat lady in green silk was in a very limp condition, the embroidered roses seemed to droop and wither, and she was helped by three of Zeno's men; Marin Cornèr was holding a large napkin to his injured nose, so that he could not see where he put his feet and had to be helped by the door porter. As for Sebastian Polo, his wife and daughter well knew that he was by this time safe at home, and was probably recovering his lost courage by beating his slaves.

'They are gone,' said Yulia, when the boat had shoved off at last.

Zoë rose then, and went slowly to the window. She stood there a few moments looking after the skiff, and in spite of her deep anxiety a faint smile played round her tender mouth as she thought of her meeting with Giustina; but it vanished almost at once. Her own situation was critical and perhaps dangerous.

She knew that although she was a slave she was the only person in the house who could exercise any authority now that Omobono was locked up in the counting-house, and that it would be impossible to let him out without liberating Tocktamish at the same time, which was not to be thought of. If the Tartar got out now he would probably murder the first person he met, and every one else whom he found in his way; indeed, Zoë thought it not impossible that he was already murdering Omobono out of sheer rage.

'Come,' she said to Lucilla. 'We must go downstairs and see what can be done.'

CHAPTER XVI

Neither Tocktamish nor his victim knew that Lucilla had slipped the bolt after them, for Omobono was too terrified to hear anything but the Tartar's voice, and the latter was just in that state of intoxication in which a man perceives nothing that is not closely connected with the idea that possesses him for the time being; it is a state of mind familiar to those whose business it is to catch men, or to cheat them.

The strong box stood against the wall at the farther end of the room, and close to the high desk at which Omobono usually worked. When he came to it the secretary stood still, and Tocktamish bent down and began to fumble with the keys.

The box had three locks, each having a hasp that closed with a strong spring when the lid was shut down, and each requiring a separate key. It was a large chest, completely covered with sheet-iron and heavily bound with iron straps, the whole being kept bright by daily polishing.

Tocktamish could not make the keys fit, and desisted with an oath.

'Open it!' he commanded, seizing the trembling secretary by the collar and forcing him to his knees before the chest.

It would have been death to disobey, in the Tartar's present mood. Omobono put each key into the lock to which it belonged, turned each three times, and the middle one a fourth time, which had the effect of drawing back all the springs at once; at the same time he raised the heavy lid a little with one hand, and then opened it with both.

Tocktamish began to throw the contents out on the floor with eager haste, seizing upon the money-bags first; but these were not many, nor were they very heavy, for the young merchant's capital was invested in many enterprises and was rarely lying idle, and as for spare cash he had taken out a goodly sum within the past two days to be given away to the guards at the palace. The Tartar soon saw that there were not a thousand gold ducats in the chest, and there was but a little silver. The rest of the contents consisted of accounts, papers, and parchments, many of which represented wealth, but could not be turned into gold by a thief. Tocktamish had an ignorant barbarian's primitive idea of riches, and being profoundly disappointed he at once became furiously angry.

'Where is the treasure?' he roared, and his face grew purple.

He shook Omobono like a rat, as he repeated his question again and again. The wretched secretary felt that his hour was indeed come, and though he tried to speak and protest he really made no sound. Then Tocktamish remembered his own words.

'I said I would drown you in the box!' he cried. 'And by the sun and moon, full and new, I will! I will, by the vine, the wine, and the drinkers, you rat, you miserable Italian flea, you skinny little bag of bones!'

Thereupon he hove up Omobono sideways by one arm and one leg and dropped him, fainting, into the empty money-chest, of which he instantly shut the lid. It closed with a loud snap as the three springs simultaneously fell into the slots in the three hasps. At the same moment Omobono lost consciousness; his last impression had been that he was killed and was to wake up in purgatory, and he had made one wild attempt to say a prayer when Tocktamish whirled him off his feet, but he could only remember the last words—

'... strength to resist curiosity.'

Then everything was dark, the big locks snapped above his head and he knew nothing more. Having successfully accomplished this brave feat, the tipsy giant gravely sat down on the chest to think, for he had already forgotten that he had meant to throw it into the Golden Horn, and besides, even in his condition, he knew very well that four men could hardly have moved such a weight. As he sat he stooped down and drew the scattered contents of the chest towards him, and picked the small bags from the heaps of documents. Then it occurred to him that it would be more convenient to put all the coin into one sack which he could fasten to his belt. It would not be a very heavy weight, and it was not possible to cram all the bags into his wallet. A thousand gold ducats only weighed about twenty pounds, by goldsmiths' weight.

When he had put all together in a soft leathern sack which he found empty, he got upon his feet, with the idea of going back to rifle the house since he had not found what he expected in the safe. It was familiar work to him, for after he had left Greece he had been a robber before he had turned respectable by taking service with the Emperor. He kicked the strong box before he went away.

'Good-bye, little man!' he laughed.

But there was no answer, and at the idea that Omobono was such a fragile creature as to have died of fright, he laughed louder and slapped his huge thigh with his hand. It seemed quite inexpressibly funny to him that any one should actually die of fear, of all disorders in the world.

He had fastened the leathern sack securely to his belt, and he went to the door to let himself out. When he found it fastened he looked at it curiously, and scratched his big head, trying to remember whether he had locked it after him or not, for he recollected that he had shut it lest any one should come upon him suddenly. But there was no key in the lock on the inside. He might have dropped it, or slipped it into his wallet, and he began to look for it, going round and round the room and kicking the papers and account-books hither and thither. It was not to be seen, and the windows were heavily grated; but he did not doubt his strength to break the door down. That was a mere trifle after all.

He shook it violently, struck it, kicked it, and shook it again, but to his stupefaction it would not budge an inch. The servants had pushed a heavy marble table against it, and had piled up half a ton of furniture; he might as well have tried to break through the wall. Then it occurred to him that Omobono might have taken the key. He would open the box, though it was a pity to disturb a dead man in such an excellent coffin.

But the box could not be opened any more than the door, for the springs had snapped, and he did not understand the complicated locks. He tried again and again, but failed each time. Perhaps the secretary was not dead after all. Tocktamish would speak to him, and ask him how to open the safe.

'Little man,' he said, 'I will let you out if you will tell me how to use the keys.' But the little man did not answer. If he was alive and heard, he had no desire to be let out while his tormentor was in the house. At the thought that he could perhaps hear, but would not speak, Tocktamish went into a paroxysm of fury.

He seized the high stool that stood beside the desk and swung it with terrific force, bringing it down on the strong box, so that it flew into splinters with an appalling din. He raged, he foamed at the mouth, he bawled and yelled, and he smashed one piece of furniture after another on the heavy iron without producing the smallest impression on it, and without getting the least answer from Omobono, who was still half-unconscious, happily for his nerves, and was dreaming that he had taken refuge in a baker's oven during a terrible thunderstorm.

The stool was reduced to kindling wood, two large chairs had followed it, and Tocktamish was in the act of heaving up the desk itself, sending inkstand, pens, and papers flying to the four corners of the room, and determined to crack the strong box with one tremendous blow, when a musical voice spoke gently through the window nearest to him. Zoë and her maids were there, and the whole household of men-servants and slaves were behind them. The three girls were standing on the broad stone seat that ran round the outside of the house in the Italian way, and they could easily look through the bars. In her haste Zoë had not veiled herself, and when the Tartar caught sight of her beautiful face at the window, the effect on his susceptible sentiments was instantaneous. The vision was a hundred times more lovely than the handsome Giustina who had escaped him. He had never seen any one like Zoë as she stood outside in the quiet afternoon sunshine. For a moment or two he was almost sober; the desk fell from his hands upon the iron chest, and was not even broken, and Tocktamish's hands hung down by his sides while he stared in stupid wonder.

Zoë was glad that there were iron bars between him and her, for she had never seen a human being more like a raging wild beast. She had looked anxiously for Omobono, but as there was no trace of him nor of any blood, she at once decided that he had been able to get out by some secret way, after Lucilla had barred the door.

'Where is Messer Carlo?' were the words which arrested Tocktamish in the act of smashing the desk.

He stood gazing at Zoë stupidly, and as he did not answer she repeated her question, watching him quietly so that he should understand that he was completely in her power. When he heard her voice again he made a sort of instinctive attempt to smooth himself, as the peacock spreads his tail before the female; he pulled out his immense moustaches, drew his shaggy beard through his two hands, settled his fur papakh on his head, and smiled complacently as he approached the window, prepared, in his own estimation, to win the heart of any woman in Constantinople. The exercise of breaking up the furniture had probably done him good, for he walked quite steadily, with his eyes wide open and his big head a little on one side.

'Messer Carlo is quite safe and very well,' he answered when he was near the grating. 'He has sent me to get him a little money, which he greatly needs.'

'You have a singular way of executing his commission,' observed Zoë, looking at the splinters of the smashed furniture.

Tocktamish felt that the havoc round him must be explained.

'I have been killing the rats,' he said. 'It is extraordinary how many rats and mice get into counting-houses!'

'Where is Messer Carlo?' Zoë asked a third time.

'Sweet woolly ewe-lamb of heaven,' said Tocktamish, leaning on the window-sill and bringing his face close to the bars, 'if you will only give me one little kiss, I will tell you where Carlo is!'

Zoë stepped to one side along the stone seat on which she stood, for she saw that he was going to slip one of his hands through the grating to catch her; and even with the bars between them he looked as if he could twist one of her arms off if she resisted him. Indeed, she was hardly out of his reach in time. He laughed rather vacantly as he grasped the air. The grating projected several inches beyond the window, like the end of a cage, as the gratings generally do in old Italian houses; and though Zoë was on one side, Tocktamish could still look at her.

'If you will come inside, I will tell you what you wish to know, my little dove,' he said with an engaging leer, for he did not really believe that any woman could resist him.

'Thank you,' Zoë answered. 'I will not come in, but I will warn you. If you will not tell me where Messer Carlo is, I shall have you shot with the master's crossbow, like a mad dog.'

'Shall I get the bow?' asked the voice of Carlo's man, the Venetian gondolier, who was an excellent shot, and had won a prize at the Lido.

But Tocktamish laughed scornfully.

'Your crossbow cannot shoot through the shutters,' he said, for they were very heavy ones, at least three inches thick. 'Besides,' he added, 'I can sit on the floor under the window, and you will not even see me.'

'If we cannot shoot you, we can starve you,' retorted Zoë.

'Little ewe-lamb,' said the Tartar, 'the heart of Tocktamish is fluttering for you like a moth in a lamp. For one kiss you shall have anything you ask!'

'Do you understand that I mean to starve you?' Zoë asked sternly.

'Oh no, my beautiful pink-and-white rabbit! You will not be so hard-hearted! And besides, if you will not let me out and give me a kiss, my men will come presently and burn Carlo's house down, and I shall carry you away! Ha ha! You had not thought of it! But Tocktamish is not caught in the trap like a cub. He is an old wolf, and knows the forest. My men know I am here, and if I do not go back to them within this hour they will come to get me. That was agreed, and I can wait as long as that. Then sixty of them will come, and before night we shall take Carlo to the Emperor and give him up, and tell all we know; and to-morrow morning he will be on a stake in the middle of the Hippodrome, and it will be the third day before he is quite dead! Ha ha! I remember how we watched that old scoundrel Michael Rhangabé! I and my men were on duty at that execution!'

Zoë's cheeks turned ghastly white, and her eyes gleamed dangerously. If there had been a weapon in her hand at that moment she could have aimed well through the grating, and Tocktamish's days would have ended abruptly. But on the other side of the bars the drunken Tartar was laughing at his own skill in frightening her, for he thought she turned pale from fear.

'Can no one silence this brute?' she cried in a tone that trembled with anger.

'It is easily done,' said a voice she knew.

She turned and looked down from the little elevation of the stone seat, and she saw the impassive face of Gorlias Pietrogliant looking up to her.

'Come into the house, Kokóna,' he said, holding up a hand to help her down. 'We will send him a pitcher of Messer Carlo's oldest wine to help him pass an hour before his men come to burn the house down!'

Zoë understood the wisdom of the advice; Tocktamish would drink himself into a stupor in a short time.

'The astrologer is right,' she said to the servants. 'Come in with me, all of you.' She led the way, but Gorlias lingered a moment, stepped upon the stone seat, and spoke to the prisoner in a low voice.

'They will be here in half an hour,' he said. 'Meanwhile I will send you wine to drink. Are you hungry?'

'Hungry?' Tocktamish laughed at the recollection of the peacock. 'I never dined better! But send me some wine, and when we divide, I will have that white-faced girl for my share. The men may have the money here. Tell them so.'

He slapped the well-filled leathern sack at his girdle as he spoke.

'As you please,' Gorlias answered indifferently.

He stepped to the ground again and reached the door in time to enter with the last of the train that followed Zoë. In the dining-hall things had been left as they were when Tocktamish and Omobono went out. The table was in confusion, and flooded with wine that had run down to the floor, and two or three chairs were upset. Gorlias filled a silver pitcher with Chian; but when he turned towards the window Zoë was the only one who saw him empty into the wine the contents of a small vial which he seemed to have had ready in the palm of his hand. He called Carlo's man.

'Take it to him,' he said. 'You can easily pass it through the bars.'

'It is not much wine,' observed the man doubtfully. 'He will drink that at a draught.'

'If he asks for more, fill the pitcher again,' answered Gorlias. 'If he falls asleep, let me know.'

The man went off.

'Clear away all that,' said Zoë to the men-servants who stood looking on. 'The master must not find this confusion when he comes home.'

Her tone and her manner imposed obedience, and besides, they knew that Tocktamish was safe for a while. They began to clear the table at once, and Zoë left the room followed by Gorlias and her two maids, who had been silent witnesses of what had passed.

Upstairs, they left her alone with the astrologer, and disappeared to discuss in whispers the wonderful things that were happening in the house.

'Where is he?' asked Zoë, as soon as the maids were gone.

'He is in a dry cistern near the north wall of the city.'

'Hiding?'

'No—a prisoner. In escaping last night he ran among the soldiers who were to have helped us, and they held him for a ransom. The Tartar came to extort the money. You know all.'

'At least, he is safe for the present,' Zoë said, but very doubtfully, for she did not half believe what she said.

'No,' Gorlias answered; 'he is not safe for long, and we must get him out. They demand a ransom, but they know well enough that even if they get it they will not dare to let him go free, since he could hang them all by a word.'

'What will they do?'

'If they can get the money they will let him starve to death in the cistern. If they do not, they will give him up to Andronicus for the reward. The Emperor has proclaimed that he will give ten pounds of gold to any one who will bring him Carlo Zeno, dead or alive. That is not enough.'

'The Emperor knows it was he?' asked Zoë with increasing anxiety.

'Yes.'

'How?'

'I do not know. Some one has betrayed us.'

'Us all?'

'I fear so.'

'But you yourself? Do you dare go about?'

'I have many disguises, and they who know the fisherman do not know the astrologer.'

'But if you should be taken?'

'A man cannot change his destiny. But look here. I have something from Johannes already. He has changed his mind; he regrets not having let us take him out last night, and he sends me this by the captain's wife.'

Gorlias produced a parchment document.

'What is it?'

'The gift of Tenedos to Venice.'

'Ah! If Messer Carlo were only free!'

'Yes—if!' Gorlias shook his head thoughtfully. 'It will not be easy to send an answer to this,' he went on. 'The woman brought it to me at the risk of her life, and said it would be impossible for her to come again. The guard is doubled, and a very different watch will be kept in future. I do not believe that we can bring Johannes out, as we might have done in spite of those fellows last night. Yet I am sure that if Messer Carlo were at liberty he would try. He would at least send word, in answer to this. But the days are over when we used to send letters up and down by a thread—the tower is watched from the river now.'

'Can you not get in by a disguise?'

'No. There is not the least chance of gaining admittance at present.'

'I could,' said Zoë confidently. 'I am sure I could! If I went in carrying a basket of linen on my head and dressed like a slave-girl in blue cotton with yellow leathern shoes, I am sure they would let me go to the captain's wife.'

'What if your basket were searched and the letter found?'

'I would put it into my shoe. They would not look for it there.'

'You would run a fearful risk.'

'For him, if it were of any use,' Zoë answered. 'But it will not help him at all, and if anything happened to me he would be sorry. Besides, why should we send a message that pretends to come from Messer Carlo when he himself is a prisoner?'

'This is the case,' Gorlias answered. 'The soldiers will never let him out till they feel safe themselves; and the only way to make them sure that there is no danger is really and truly to bring Johannes out and set him on the throne again. So long as Andronicus reigns and may take vengeance on them, they will keep Messer Carlo a prisoner to give up at any moment, or to starve him to death for their own safety—unless they murder him outright. But I do not believe that any ten of them would dare to set upon him, for they know him well.'

Zoë smiled, for she was proud to love a man whom ten men would not dare to kill.

'Then the only way to save him is to free Johannes?' she said. 'Yes,' she went on, not waiting for an answer, 'I think you are right. Even if we got them their ten thousand ducats they would not let him out as long as Andronicus is at Blachernæ.'

'That is the truth of it,' Gorlias answered. 'Neither more nor less. Messer Carlo's life depends upon it.'

'Then it must be done, come what may. Thank God, I have a life to risk for him!'

'You have two,' said Gorlias quietly. 'You have mine also.'

'You are very loyal to Johannes, even to risking death. Is that what you mean?'

'More than that.'

'For Messer Carlo, then?' Zoë asked. 'You owe him some great debt of gratitude?'

'I never saw him until quite lately,' Gorlias answered. 'You need not know why I am ready to die in this attempt, Kokóna Arethusa.'

Some one knocked at the outer door; Zoë clapped her hands for her maids, and one of them went to the entrance. The voice of Zeno's man spoke from outside.

'The Tartar is fast asleep already,' he said, 'and I can hear the secretary moaning as if he were in great pain; but I cannot see him through the window. He must be somewhere in the room, for it is his voice.'

Zoë made a movement to go towards the door, but Gorlias raised his hand.

'I will see to it,' he said, 'I will have the fellow taken back to his quarters.'

Zoë bit her lip for she knew that it would be cruel and cowardly to hurt even such a ruffian as Tocktamish, while he was helpless under the drug Gorlias had given him. But the words he had spoken rankled deep, and it was not likely that she should forget them.

'Do as you will,' she said.

Half an hour later poor little Omobono was in his bed, and Zeno's man was giving him a warm infusion of marsh-mallows and camomile for his shaken nerves. The money-bags and the papers had been restored to the strong box in the counting-house, and Tocktamish the Tartar, sunk in a beatific slumber, was being carried to his quarters in a hired palanquin by four stalwart bearers.

That was the end of the memorable feast in Carlo Zeno's house.

But Zoë sat by the open window, and her heart beat sometimes very fast and sometimes very slow; for she understood that the plight of the man she loved was desperate indeed.

CHAPTER XVII

The position of Zeno was quite clear to Zoë now, and a great wave of happiness lifted her and bore her on with it as she realised that she might save his life just when his chances looked most hopeless, and that whether she succeeded or failed her own must certainly be staked for his. Heroism is nearer the surface in women than in most men, and often goes quite as deep.

Zoë had understood very suddenly how matters stood, and that Tocktamish and his men meant to let Zeno perish, simply because he might ruin them all if he regained his liberty; or, if it were found out that he was taken, they intended to hand him over to Andronicus. It was not at all likely that they would set him free even if they got the great ransom they demanded.

But if by any means Johannes could be brought suddenly from his prison, all Constantinople would rise in revolution to set him on the throne, and it would be as dangerous to keep his friend Zeno in confinement as it now seemed rash to his captors to let him out. The first thing to be done was to reach Johannes himself and warn him, and this could only be accomplished by a woman. Gorlias knew the soldiers, and had as much influence with them as any one, perhaps, and whatever could be done from without he would do; yet it was quite certain that the men could not be got together again unless Johannes were actually free.

The difficulty lay there. To reach him was one thing, and was within the bounds of possibility; to bring him out would be quite another. But Zoë had confidence in the devotion of the captain's wife, of whom Gorlias had told her, and believed that in such a case two women could do more than ten men.

Yet she saw that it might be fatal to let the imprisoned Emperor know that Zeno was himself a prisoner. To prevent this she conceived the plan of writing a letter in the Venetian's name, accepting on behalf of the Republic the gift of Tenedos, and promising instant help and liberty. Zeno had given his word that he would renew the attempt for the sake of Tenedos, though for nothing else; this condition being accepted, she knew that nothing could hinder him from keeping his word if he were free. She would therefore only be writing for him what he himself would write if he could; and besides, if she needed a more valid excuse, it would be done to save his life.

Her learning stood her in good stead now as she carefully penned the answer on stout Paduan paper. She made Zeno thank the Emperor on behalf of the Serene Republic for his generous gift, and say that he was ready, that not a moment should be lost, and that in an hour the sovereign should be restored to his people, or Carlo Zeno would die in the attempt.

This last phrase, as it ran from her pen, seemed to her a little too theatrical to be Zeno's own, but she determined to let it stand for the sake of the impression it should make on Johannes. Zeno would no more have mentioned such a trifle as the risk of life and limb in anything he meant to do than seamen would stop to talk of danger when ordered to shorten sail in a dangerous gale. Such things are a part of the game. No sailor will spin a yarn about a storm unless he has seen the Flying Dutchman or the Sea Serpent or the Man in the Top; he is in danger half his life. But the average modern soldier, who may be under fire three or four times in his career, repeats the story of his battles to any one who will listen. Zoë did not know whether Johannes had ever seen Zeno's handwriting or not, but that mattered little in those days, when many fine gentlemen could not write their own letters. She folded the sheet neatly in a small square, and placed it in her shoe by way of experiment, to see whether it would stay there while she walked.

She did all this while Gorlias was gone, and before he came back the afternoon was half over, though the spring days were growing long. He told her that the Tartar was safe in his quarters, where he would probably sleep till midnight at the very least, to the infinite rage and disgust of his men. They had expected him to return laden with gold or with the secure promise of it, and he had come back not only empty-handed, but hopelessly drunk; and as they knew him well, but did not know that he had swallowed a dose of opium that would have sent a tiger to sleep, they meditated in gloomy thirst on the quantity of strong wine he must have absorbed during an absence which had only lasted two hours. What he had told Zoë of their coming to fetch him if he stayed too long had been a pure invention to frighten her; they did not even know where he had been, for he had merely announced his intention of going out to collect Zeno's ransom from the Venetian merchants, and his reputation for strength and ferocity was such that they had not dreamed of his needing help.

Thus much Gorlias had found out, and he had also ascertained that the men were in a thoroughly bad temper in consequence of the turn affairs had taken, and much more inclined to murder Zeno than to let him out. As for his whereabouts, Gorlias only knew that he was in one of the many dry cisterns, which existed under old Constantinople, and which had never been in use since the crusaders had cut the aqueducts and sacked the city more than a hundred and seventy years earlier. The men who had shut up Zeno knew where he was, but it was very likely that they had not told their comrades. In those last days of the Empire the foreign mercenaries were little better than bands of robbers, half-trained at that, who preyed on the peasant part of the population, obeying their officers only when it was worth the trouble, and not even practising thieves' honour in the division of plunder. Not a day passed then without brawl and bloodshed amongst the soldiery; hardly a night went by without some act of violence and depredation for which they were responsible. They had stolen under Johannes, they robbed under Andronicus; under Johannes restored, they would steal again. And they drank perpetually. If Sultan Amurad had been the man that Mohammed the Conqueror turned out to be, the Turks would have been in possession of Constantinople fully eighty years before they actually stormed it, and with a tenth of the loss.

If Zeno had relied on the eight hundred soldiers who had agreed to make a revolution for Johannes, he had done so because he knew they could be trusted to rise if there was a chance of plundering the palace and of cutting the throats of a few hundred of their divers countrymen who had been preferred before them as a body-guard, and were therefore their sworn enemies. But the instant those delightful prospects disappeared they cared no more who was Emperor than a cur cares who throws him a bone; the existing condition of things was good enough for them, and they would risk nothing to change it, unless change meant wine, women, and loot. Many of them were in reality Mohammedans like Tocktamish, and looked upon all Christians, including their employers, as their lawful prey—as dogs, moreover, and no great fighters at that, but mostly cowardly curs. It was agreeable to live amongst them because one could beat them and drink wine without the disapproval of the greybeards; but as for respecting them, a Tartar like Tocktamish would as soon have thought of fearing them.

Zoë knew all this, and so did Gorlias, and they agreed that unless Johannes could be brought visibly before the soldiers there was little chance of success, and none of saving Zeno. The difficulty lay in the fact that Johannes was kept in a place even more inaccessible than Zeno's cistern. The whole matter was a vicious circle. He could not be set free unless the troops rose for him; but the troops would not rise unless they saw him in their midst; and if there were no rising Zeno would be starved to death in the well. Gorlias Pietrogliant was a man of resources, but the problem completely baffled him.

He stood silent and in thought at Zoë's window; she sat quite motionless on the great divan, watching him and thinking too. Her knees were drawn up almost to her chin, and her folded hands clasped them while she looked straight at the astrologer's back with unwinking eyes. Neither he nor she knew how long they kept silence; it might have been five minutes, or it might have been half an hour. Time plays queer tricks when people are in great danger or in great distress.

Then Zoë's expression began to change very slowly, as an idea dawned upon her. It was as if she saw something between her and Gorlias, something that took shape by degrees, something new and unexpected that presently grew to be a whole picture, and from a picture became a real scene, full of living people, moving and talking; the tender mouth opened a little as if she were going to speak, and the delicate nostril quivered, the colour spread like dawn in her pale cheeks, and a deep warm light came into her eyes.

When the scene was over and the vision disappeared, she nodded slowly, as if satisfied that in her waking dream she had dreamed true.

'I have thought of a way,' she said at last.

Gorlias turned, crossed the room, and stood beside her to listen; but he did not think she had any practicable scheme to propose, and at first, while she was speaking, he was much more inclined to follow his own line of thought than hers. Then, all at once, he felt that she had received one of those inspirations of the practical sense which visit women who are driven to extremities, and which have been the wonder of men since Jacob's mother showed him how to steal his father's blessing. It is quite certain that it was a woman who showed Columbus the trick with the egg, when he himself was trying to balance one on its point. Only a woman could have thought of anything so simple.

And now, after Gorlias had vainly racked his ingenious brain for an idea, it was the girl that suggested the only possible one. He grasped it easily.

'It is a daring plan, and it could not succeed in broad daylight,' he said, when she had finished, 'but it may at dusk.'

'It must,' Zoë said emphatically. 'If it fails, we shall not see each other again.'

'Not unless it occurs to Andronicus to crucify us together,' Gorlias answered, rather gravely. 'Very much depends on our timing ourselves as exactly as possible.'

'Yes. Let it be a little more than half an hour after sunset, just when the dusk is closing in. Have you everything you need?'

'I can get what is lacking. We have three good hours still before us.'

'Go, then, and do not be late. You know what will happen to me if you do not come just at the right time.'

'You are risking more than I,' Gorlias said.

'I have more to lose, and more to win,' Zoë answered.

She was thinking of Zeno,—of life with him, of life without him, and of the life she would give for his. But Gorlias wondered at her courage, for it was held nothing in those days to tear a living man or woman to shreds, piecemeal, on the mere suspicion of treason, and that would surely be her fate if he could not carry out precisely and successfully the plan she had thought of. A delay of half an hour might mean death to her, though it would not of necessity affect the result so far as Johannes and Zeno were concerned.

Gorlias left her to make his own preparations. When he was gone Zoë sent Yulia for Zeno's own man, Vito, the Venetian boatman. He came and stood on the threshold while she spoke to him, out of the maids' hearing, and in Italian, lest they should creep near and listen.

'Vito,' said Zoë, 'how is the secretary?'

'Excellency,' the Venetian answered, 'fear is an ugly sickness, which makes healthy men tremble worse than the fever does.'

He either forgot that he was supposed to be speaking to a slave who had no more claim to be called 'Excellency' than he had himself, and less, if anything; or else he had made up his mind that this beautiful Arethusa whom he had to-day seen for the first time, was not a slave at all, but a great lady in disguise.

'You are never frightened, are you, Vito?' she asked with a smile.

'I?' Vito grinned. 'Am I of iron, or of stone? Or am I perhaps a lion? When there is fear I am afraid.'

'But the master is never frightened,' suggested Zoë. 'Is he of stone, then?'

'Oh, he!' Vito laughed now, and shrugged his shoulders. 'Would you compare me with the master? Then compare copper with gold. The master is the master, and that is enough, but I am only a sailor man in his service. If there is fighting, I fight while I see that I am the stronger, but when I see that I may die I run away. We are all thus.'

'But surely you would not run away and leave Messer Carlo to be killed, would you?'

'No,' Vito answered quite simply. 'That would be another affair. It would be shame to go home alive if the master were killed. When one must die, one must, as God wills. It may be for the master, it may be for Venice. But for myself, I ask you? Why should I die for nothing? I run away. It is more sensible.'

'You need not risk being killed if you do what I am going to ask,' Zoë said, for after talking with the man she liked his honest face, and thought none the less of him for his frankness. 'It is a very simple matter.'

'What is it, Excellency?'

'You need not call me that, Vito,' answered Zoë. 'I want you to row me at sunset to the landing which is nearest to the palace gate. It must be the dirty little one on this side of the Amena tower, is it not?'

'That is it. But without the master's orders—'

Vito looked at her doubtfully, for he had been reminded that she considered herself a slave, and it occurred to him that she meant to escape in Zeno's absence.

'Messer Carlo would wish me to go, if he were here,' said Zoë quietly, and not at all as if she were insisting, for she saw what was the matter.

'I have no doubt it is as you say,' Vito answered. 'But I have no orders.'

'There is a message from the master to some one in the palace,' Zoë explained. 'No one but I can deliver it.'

'That is easily said,' observed Vito bluntly. 'There are no orders.'

Zoë felt the blood rising to her forehead at the man's rudeness and distrust of her, but she controlled herself, for much depended on obtaining what she wished.

'It is not a message,' she said; 'it is a letter.'

'Where is it?' asked Vito incredulously.

'I will show it to you,' Zoë answered, but she first turned to the maids, who waited at the end of the room. 'Go and prepare me the bath,' she said.

The two disappeared, though they did not believe that their mistress really wished to bathe again so soon. When they were gone, she stooped and took the letter from her shoe, unfolded it, and spread it out for Vito to see. The effect it made upon him was instantaneous; he looked at it carefully, and took a corner of it between his thumb and finger.

'This is the paper on which the master writes,' he said, as if convinced.

It did not occur to him that the slave Arethusa could write at all, nor any one else in the house except Omobono; and as for the latter, if he had written anything he must have done so under Zeno's orders. Writing of any sort commanded his profound and almost superstitious respect.

'This is certainly a letter from the master,' he said, satisfied at last, after what he considered a thoroughly conscientious inspection.

'And he wishes me to deliver it,' Zoë said. 'If I am to do that, you must be good enough to take me to the landing in the boat. There is no other way.'

'I could take the letter myself,' Vito suggested.

'No. Only a woman will be allowed to pass, where this must go.'

Vito began to understand, and nodded his head wisely.

'It is for Handsome John,' he said, with conviction, and fixing his eyes on Zoë's. 'It is for the other Emperor, whom the master wishes to set free.'

'Yes—since you have guessed it,' Zoë answered. 'Will you take me now?'

'You will take one of your slaves with you, as you do when you go out in the boat with the secretary, I suppose?'

Vito still felt a little hesitation.

'No. I must go alone with you. And I myself shall be dressed like a slave, and I shall have a basket of things to carry on my head to the wife of the gaoler.'

'I see,' said Vito, who really loved adventure for its own sake, and was much less inclined to run away from danger than he represented. 'Did you say you wished to go at sunset?'

'Yes.'

'I shall be ready. But it will be better to take an old boat, and I will put on ragged clothes, to look like a hired boatman.'

'Yes; that will be better.'

Vito went away, delighted with the prospect before him. He was too young and too true a Venetian not to look forward with pleasure to rowing the beautiful Arethusa up the Golden Horn, though he was only a servant and she was the master's most treasured possession. He felt, too, some manly pride in the thought of possibly protecting her, for he meant to follow her ashore and look on from a distance, to see whether she got safely into the tower, and he would wait until she came out. The master would expect that much of him, at least.

As yet, neither Vito nor any member of the household, except Zoë, knew that Zeno was a prisoner, held for ransom. It had pleased him to go out of his house during the previous night, and some important business detained him; that was all. When he was at leisure he would come home. The men-servants who had waited on the guests and had heard Tocktamish's words, to the effect that Zeno had sent him for money, looked upon the statement as a clumsy trick which the half-drunken robber was trying to play in Zeno's absence, and as nothing more. But they had been far too badly frightened to stay and listen, as has been seen. To Vito, who was, nevertheless, by far the best of them, it had been a matter of utter indifference whether the Tartar cut the throats of the four guests or not, compared with the urgent necessity of keeping out of his reach. If the master had been present another side of their character would have come into play, but as he was absent they had thought of their own safety first.

CHAPTER XVIII

The sun had set, and the wide court of Blachernæ was filled with purple light to the wall tops, like a wine-vat full to the brim; and everything that was in the glow took colour from it, as silver does in claret, the polished trappings of the guards' uniforms, the creamy marble steps of the palace, the white Tunisian charger of the officer who rode in just then, and the swallows that circled round and round the courtyard. The world moved in that short deep dream that comes just when the sun has slipped away to rest, when the light is everywhere at once, so that things cast no shadows on the ground, because they glow from within, as in fairyland, or perhaps in heaven.

The officer rode in on his charger, and after him entered a girl slave, dressed in coarse blue cotton, and carrying on her head a small round basket, which was covered with a clean white cloth. The four corners of the napkin hung down, and one of them would have flapped across her face if she had not held it between her teeth to keep it down. It partly hid her features, and her head was tied up in a blue cotton kerchief passed twice round and knotted upon her forehead. She limped a little as she walked. What could be seen of her face was pale and quiet, and had a rather fixed look.

She was walking boldly through the gate, without slackening her pace, when one of the two sentinels stopped her, and asked where she was going. She stood still, and one hand steadied the basket on her head, while the other pointed to the Amena tower.

'My mistress sends some fine wheat bread and cream cheese to the wife of the captain who keeps the tower,' said Zoë, affecting the mincing accent very common with female slaves and Greek ladies' maids.

The second sentinel, returning on his short beat, now came up and stood on her other side. He was a big Bulgarian, and he lifted one corner of the cloth and looked down into the basket, merely for the sake of detaining the girl. He saw the wheaten loaves and the cream cheese neatly disposed on a second napkin, and the cheese was nested in green leaves to keep it fresh. Both the soldiers at once thought of tasting it with the points of their daggers, but at that moment the officer of the watch strolled out of the guard-house, a magnificent young man in scarlet and gold. The two sentinels at once turned their backs on the cheese and Zoë, and marched away in opposite directions on their beats, leaving her standing in the middle. The officer was far too high and mighty a person to look at a slave-girl or her basket, and Zoë therefore went on without turning her head, taking it for granted that she was now free to enter. In her baggy blue cotton clothes, and with her face almost covered by the napkin, there was nothing about her to attract attention, unless it were her slightly limping gait; and she instinctively made an effort to walk evenly, for she could not help feeling ashamed of being suddenly lame, as perfectly sound and healthy people do. But she realised that the folded letter was in the wrong shoe and increased her lameness, whereas if she had carried it in the other it might have made walking easier.

She went from under the great gate into the liquid purple light in the court, and it was pleasant to be in it. But then again it made her think of yesterday, when she had sat in her window at sunset, not dreaming of all that was to happen to her in one night and one day. It made her think of the man she loved so dearly, imprisoned somewhere under the great city, starving and thirsting no doubt, and face to face with thoughts of death; and it was to save him that she was crossing the courtyard of Blachernæ disguised as a household slave. It was because there was no other way; and if Gorlias Pietrogliant failed her, or came too late, the end would overtake her in a few hours, or perhaps quite suddenly, which would be more merciful. She knew what she was doing, and she did not deceive herself. They would put out her eyes first; but that would be the least of the cruel things they would do to her, if Gorlias failed.

She was only a weak girl, after all, and once or twice, when she thought of the pain, a sharp little shiver ran down her back to her very heels, and things swam before her for an instant in the deep sea of colour; but that only lasted for a moment, and when she reached the foot of the tower and went in under the archway that led to the door, she was thinking of Zeno again, and of nothing else.

It was as Gorlias had told her. A very different watch was set there since the attempt of the previous night, and she found herself face to face with an obstacle she had not anticipated. The iron door was shut and was guarded by two huge Africans in black mail armour, who stood on either side with drawn scimitars.

They looked over her head as she approached them, and they seemed to take no notice of her existence. She thought she had never seen such expressionless faces as theirs; the features were as shiny and motionless as bronze, and the purple haze of the sunset without filled the deep arch and lent them an unnatural colour which was positively terrifying.

'If you please, kind sirs,' Zoë began as she stood still, 'my mistress sends some fine wheat bread and fresh cream cheese to the wife of the captain.'

She might as well have spoken to statues; neither of the negroes paid the slightest attention. But she was not to be put off so easily.

'If you please,' she repeated with pleading emphasis and more loudly, 'my mistress—'

She stopped speaking in the middle of the sentence, suddenly scared by the immobility of the two black men, and by their size, and by the purple glare that was reflected from their great polished scimitars, of which one noiseless sweep could sever her head from her body. They were like the genii in one of those tales of the Arabian Nights which Greek story-tellers were then just learning from the Persians, and from the Tartar merchants of Samarcand and Tashkent. Zoë had listened to them by the hour when she was a little girl, and now she suddenly felt an irrational conviction that she had dreamed herself into one of them, and that the imprisoned Emperor was guarded by supernatural beings.

However, when she looked at the motionless features and at the broad, polished blades, she did not feel that painful shiver which had run down her when she had thought of being tortured by the people of the palace, and she soon took courage again and began to speak a third time.

'If you please,' she said, but she got no further, for she had gently plucked at the mailed sleeve of the man on her right, to attract his attention, and he moved at once, and bent down a little.

He touched his ear with his left forefinger and shook his head slowly to show that he was deaf, and pointed to his companion and back to his own ear and shook his head again; and then, to Zoë's horror, he opened his enormous mouth just before her eyes, and she saw that it was empty. He had no tongue.

Johannes was guarded by deaf mutes, and Zoë knew Constantinople and the ways of the palace well enough to understand that they were placed there to make an end of any one, man or woman, who should attempt to pass.

She tried signs, now. She took her basket from her head and set it down on the step between the sentinels, and crouched on her heels to uncover it and show the contents. The men saw and nodded, and then inclined their heads to one side in that peculiar way which means indifference all over the East. And indeed they did not care whether the basket held cheese or sweetmeats, and their faces grew stony again as they looked outwards, over her head.

She covered up her little basket disconsolately and rose to her feet. The glow was beginning to fade in the courtyard, and she felt her heart sink as the shadows deepened. It was absolutely necessary to the success of the dangerous enterprise on which she and Gorlias had embarked, that Johannes himself, or at least the captain's wife should be warned of what was to take place in less than half an hour. If this could not be done, everything might go wrong at the last minute, their cleverly concerted trick would fail and be exposed, and she and Gorlias, and Zeno himself, would probably pay for their audacity with their lives.

The closed door between the sentinels was covered with iron and studded with big nails. It was perfectly clear that it must be opened from within, if at all, and that the men themselves would have to knock or make some other signal by sound in order to obtain entrance for any one who was really authorised to go in. It was also clear that if the men on the other side of the door were stone deaf like the two guards, they could not hear any such knocking, and no entrance would be possible at all except when those within opened for some reason of their own or at fixed hours. Again, thought Zoë, it followed that there was probably some one near who could hear sounds from without, and there was always a bare possibility, in such times, that this person might be a secret friend to the prisoner, though supposed to be one of his gaolers.

All these thoughts flashed across her mind in a few seconds, while she was covering her basket. She therefore took rather more time over this than was necessary, and as the mutes did not show signs of driving her away, she at once began to sing, quite sure that they could not hear her. It was a forlorn hope, indeed, but anything was worth trying. Her voice sounded loud and clear under the archway:—

Over the water to my love, for the hour is come! The water, the blue water, the water salt and the water fresh! Open, my very dear love, open thy door to me, For I have come swiftly over the water—

At this point, to Zoë's inexpressible amazement and delight, the door really opened, and she almost choked for sheer joy.

The captain's wife appeared in the dim evening light, standing well within, and Zoë recognised her at once from the description Gorlias had given of her. The sentinels, being perfectly deaf, did not at first know that the door had been opened, as they stood looking straight before them. The stout woman spoke in a low voice.

'By four toes and by five toes,' she said, by way of answer to the words Zoë had sung.

The girl lost no time, for there was none to lose, and though there was little light she saw that there were four or five more armed Ethiopians in the small chamber, so that it would be impossible to deliver her letter.

'Tell him from Carlo Zeno to be ready at once,' she said quickly, 'and not to show surprise at anything that happens.'

The deaf mutes outside now perceived that she was speaking with some one, and that the entrance behind them was open. She had just handed her basket to the captain's wife when the two turned together to see who had opened, but almost at the same instant the heavy iron door swung quickly on its hinges again and shut with a clang that echoed out to the courtyard. Zoë sprang back hastily lest the door itself should strike her as it closed, and the quick movement hurt her a little, for she made a false step on the foot with which she limped, turning it slightly as her weight came upon it.

That one step nearly cost her life, for though the sentinels were deaf and dumb they were not blind. She thought they were going to let her go away unhindered, and she was already almost out of the archway when she felt herself seized by the arms from behind.

When she had stumbled, her low shoe had turned a little, and the folded letter, now useless, had fallen out. As it was white, the guards had seen it instantly on the dark pavement, and one of them had picked it up while the other had caught her.

Zoë instinctively struggled with all her might for a few seconds, but the dumb man twisted one of her arms behind her till it was agony to move, and she was powerless. Her captor now handed her over to his companion, who had sheathed his scimitar and had placed the letter inside his steel cap. She could not look round, but she felt that the grip on her twisted wrist changed, and she was pushed out into the courtyard and made to walk in the direction of the palace. She could not help limping much more than before, and in the grasp of the big Ethiopian she felt what a small weak thing she would be in the tormentors' hands if Gorlias did not come in time.

The purple light had almost faded below, and the grey dusk was creeping up out of the ground, though the high upper story of the marble palace was still bathed in the evening glow, and still a few swallows circled round the eaves. Zoë looked up to the vast cornices and at the fleecy pink clouds that floated in the sky, and as she was forced along, almost as fast as she could walk, she wondered whether she should ever again see the bright noonday sun. It would not take long to kill her if Gorlias did not come in time.

There were many men coming and going now, and there were guards in scarlet, drawn up at the entrance to the palace as if they were waiting. Some slaves, hastening away, paused a moment to watch Zoë go by, smooth-faced creatures who lived among the Emperor's women.

'There goes five hundred ducats' worth!' laughed one, in a voice like a girl's.

'What has she done?' asked another, of the dumb Ethiopian.

The speaker was a newcomer in the palace, and the others jeered at him for not knowing that the man was one of the mutes.

And he pushed and dragged Zoë along without noticing them. She looked straight before her now, at the palace door, and as she went, she was in a kind of dream, and she wondered what the room to which she was being taken would be like, the place where she was presently to be tortured if Gorlias did not come in time; she wondered whether it would be light or dark, and what the colour of the walls would be.

The African hurt her very much as he forced her along, though she made no resistance; but she did not think of the pain she felt, nor of the pain she would surely be made to feel presently. It was as if she were detached from her own personality, and could speculate about what was going to happen to her, and about the men who would ask her questions, and about the queer-looking instruments of torture that would be brought, and even the colour of the executioner's hair. She fancied him a red-haired man with ugly, yellow eyes and bad teeth that he showed. She did not know whether it were fear or courage that so took her out of herself.

But all the time she was listening for a distant sound that might come, or that might not; and her hearing grew so sharp that she could have heard it a mile away, and the distance between her and the palace door grew shorter very quickly, and the ruthless mute urged her along faster and faster, though she limped so badly.

Then her heart leapt and stood still a moment, and the Ethiopian's grasp relaxed a little, and he slackened his pace. Not that he heard what she heard, for he was stone deaf; but the guards who stood about the door had begun to range themselves in even ranks on either side, and a tall officer made signs to the African to stand out of the way. The air rang with the music of distant silver trumpets, there was a subdued hum of many voices and the trampling of many horses' hoofs on the hard earth outside the court.

'The Emperor comes!' cried the officer, again motioning the mute and his prisoner away.

The man understood well enough, and dragged her aside quickly and roughly out of the straight way, but not out of sight; and the sounds grew louder, and the trumpet-notes clearer, as the imperial cavalcade passed in under the great gate. First there rode a score of guards on their white horses; six running footmen came next, in short hose and red tunics that fitted close to their bodies and glared in the twilight; then two officers of the household on their chargers; and young Andronicus himself rode in on a bay Arab mare between two ministers of state, followed by many more guards who pressed close upon him to protect him from any treacherous attack. He was dressed all in cloth of gold, and his tall Greek cap was wrought with gold and jewels; but the day had gone down, and neither the metal nor the stones gave any light, while the scarlet uniforms of the guards and footmen surged about him like waves of blood in the gathering dusk.

The Ethiopian held Zoë pinioned by the arms and looked over her head as the Emperor came near. Andronicus had pale and suspicious eyes that searched every crowd for danger, and saw peril everywhere. He hung his head a little, his jaw was heavy, his lip was loose, and his uneasy glance wandered continually hither and thither. There was still plenty of light near the palace, and Zoë saw every little thing; and the cloth of gold he wore was lit up again by the reflexion from the marble walls.

He saw the girl, too, but though her hands were behind her, he did not see at once that the African held them, for she stood quite still and met his gaze. Then he perceived that the face was the most lovely he had ever seen, and he made a motion in the saddle that was like the rising of the snake when its prey is near, and his pale eyes gleamed, and his loose lower lip shook and moved against the upper one.

He drew rein and spoke in a low tone to the minister on his right, a Greek with a fawning face, who instantly made a sign to the girl to come nearer; and the Ethiopian mute saw the gesture, and pushed her forward with one hand, close to the Emperor's stirrup, and with the other hand he took his steel cap very carefully from his head, drawing it down close to his head and over his ear so that the letter should not fall out; then, still grasping Zoë's wrist, he held the helmet up like a cup, so that Andronicus might see what was in it.

The action needed no explaining, for the young usurper had himself ordered that his father should be guarded by the dumb Ethiopians after the alarm of the previous night. The Emperor looked down at the girl's beautiful white face, but he took the letter from the soldier's steel cap and spread it out, and read it quickly, and then passed it to the minister at his elbow, who read it too.

He looked at Zoë again, but in his eyes her beauty was all gone at once. She was one of those monsters that were always conspiring against him, against his throne and his life; she was one of those thousands whom he saw nightly in his dreams of fear, stealing upon him when he was alone and helpless, to blind him and kill him, and to bear his crowned father to the throne high on their shoulders. Zoë might have been as lovely as Aphrodite herself, just wafted from the foam of the sea by the breath of spring; to Andronicus she would have been but one of the countless evil beings who for ever plotted his destruction.

But this one was in his power. He sat on his horse and looked down at her, and his loose lips smiled; yet her face was still and proud, and in her poor blue cotton slave's dress she faced him like a young goddess.

'Who sent you with this?' he asked in the deep silence, and every man there listened for her answer.

'Since you have read it, you know,' she answered, and there was no tremor in her voice.

'Take care! Where is this Venetian, this Zeno?'

'I do not know.'

'Take care, again! I ask, where is he?'

Zoë was silent for a moment, and though she did not take her eyes from the young Emperor's face she listened intently for a distant sound that did not come.

'I do not know where he is,' she said at last, 'but I think you will see him before long, for he is coming here.'

'Here?' Andronicus was taken by surprise. 'Here?' he repeated in wonder.

'Yes, here,' Zoë answered, 'and soon. He has business here to-night.'

'The girl is mad,' said the Emperor, looking towards the ministers.

'Quite mad, your august Majesty,' said one.

'Evidently out of her mind, Sire,' echoed the other. 'It will be well to put out her eyes and let her go.'

The one who had spoken first, the fawning Greek, made a sign to an officer near him, and the latter gave an order to one of the running footmen who stood waiting. The latter instantly ran in through the great open doorway of the palace. Where Andronicus was, the torturer was never hard to find.

'And pray,' asked the Emperor, with an ugly smile, 'what possible business can a Venetian merchant have here at this hour? Will you please to tell us?'

'A business that will be soon despatched, if God will,' answered Zoë.

She could not look away from the man who had murdered Michael Rhangabé, and though she knew what she was risking if she did not gain time, the longing for just vengeance was too strong for her, so that she could not control her speech, and in her clear young voice Andronicus heard an accent that struck terror to his heart.

'She is not mad!' he exclaimed in sudden anxiety. 'She knows something! Make her speak!'

While the words were on his lips the running footman returned, and after him another man came quickly, carrying a worn leathern bag. He was very tall and thin, and he stooped, he had the face of a corpse and there was no light in his eyes. Zoë did not see him, but he came and stood behind her, close to the Ethiopian, and he fumbled in his bag; and all around the uniforms of the guard were as red as blood in the twilight.

'I am not afraid to speak, since I am caught,' Zoë said, answering the Emperor's words, 'and what I say is true. For what you owe me, you owe to many and many more, and the name of that debt is blood!'

'She is raving!' cried Andronicus in an unsteady voice.

'No, I am not mad,' Zoë answered, speaking loud and clear. 'Your reckoning has been due these two years, and a man is coming within the hour to claim it, and you shall pay all, both to others and to me, whether you will or not!'

'Who is this creature?' asked the Emperor, but his cheeks were whiter now.

Not a sound broke the silence, and the man with the leathern bag crept a little nearer to the defenceless girl, and the Ethiopian's grip tightened on her wrists. From somewhere beyond the walls of the courtyard the neighing of a horse broke the stillness.

'Who is this girl that dares me within my own gates?' Andronicus asked again, turning to his ministers and officers.

The Greek with the fawning face bent in his saddle towards the young Emperor as if he were prostrating himself, and he spoke in a very low voice.

'Your Majesty would do well to have her tongue torn out before she says more.'

'Who is she, I say?' cried the sovereign, suddenly furious, as cowards can be.

No one spoke. The corpse-faced man crept nearer to Zoë, his dull eyes fixed on her features. Beyond the wall and far off the unseen horse neighed again. It was growing darker, but all around the scarlet tunics of the guards were as red as blood.

Then the answer came. The twisted lips of the tormentor moved slowly, and words came from them in a thin, harsh voice, like the creaking of the rack.

'She is Michael Rhangabé's daughter.'

'The Protosparthos?' The Emperor's voice shook again.

The corpse-faced man nodded twice in assent, and his thin lips writhed hideously when Zoë's eyes fell on him.

'I saw her at the prison when I took him out to die,' he said.

His bony hand, all knotty and stained from his horrid work, took the girl's delicate chin, forcing her to turn her full face to him; and she quivered from head to foot at his touch. He knew well the convulsive shiver that ran through the victim he touched for the first time; he could feel it in his fingers as the musician feels the strings; he was familiar with it, as the fisherman's hand is with the tremor and tension of his rod when a fish strikes; and he smiled in a ghastly way.

'Yes,' he said, 'it is she.' And he laughed.

He held her by the chin and wagged her beautiful head to right and left.

Since the Emperor had spoken no sound had been heard but the torturer's discordant voice; but now the outraged girl's shriek of fury split the air.

'Wretch!'

Her small hands suddenly slipped through the Ethiopian's capacious hold. Before he could catch her she had wrenched herself free from both men and had struck a furious blow full in the torturer's livid face; and though she was but a slender girl her anger gave her a man's strength, and her swiftness lent her a sudden advantage. The man reeled back three paces before he could steady himself again.

'Hold her!' cried Andronicus, for he feared she might have a knife hidden on her, and both her hands were free.

But only for that instant. Though the African was huge, he was quick, and he was behind her. Almost before the Emperor had called out, Zoë was a prisoner again, and the man she had struck was close to her with his battered leathern bag. He looked up to Andronicus for a command before he began his work.

'Make her tell what she knows,' the Emperor said, reassured since she was again fast in the African's great hands.

He leaned forward a little, the better to hear the words which pain was to draw from Zoë's lips, and the Greek minister settled himself comfortably in the saddle to enjoy the rare amusement of seeing a beautiful and noble girl deliberately tortured before half a hundred men. Some of the guards also pressed upon each other to see; but there were some among them who had served under Rhangabé, and these looked into one another's faces and spoke words almost under their breath, that all together swelled to a low murmur, such as the tide makes on a still night, just when it turns back from the ebb.

The sunset had faded, but there was light enough to see the dark bruise across the corpse-like face where Zoë had struck it with all her might.

The man opened his old leathern bag, and his stained hands fumbled in it, amongst irons that were brown but not rusty, and thongs plaited with wire, and strangely shaped tools in which there were well-greased screws that turned easily.

But all these his knotty fingers rejected. He knew each by the touch. They were good enough for ordinary slaves, or perhaps for a double-dealing steward, or even a lying courtier. For a highborn maiden victim he had an instrument far more refined and exquisitely keen than any of these things, and he treasured it as a very rare possession which never left him day or night; for it had been sent to him from very far away in the south as a present of great value; and it was alive, and needed the warmth of his body constantly lest it should die. But there was something in the bag that belonged to it and must be found before it could be taken from its little cage of silver filigree in the bosom of the corpse-faced man.

He found it. His stained hand drew from the bag a dry walnut. With the point of the knife he wore at his belt he split it carefully, and turned the nut out of one of the half shells, tossing the other into the bag.

The Greek minister watched him with the deepest interest, but Andronicus drummed impatiently with his gloved fingers on the high gilt pommel of his saddle. Yet it was all very quickly done, and though there was less light there was still enough; and while he waited the Emperor again read the letter Zoë had dropped.

But she watched him, calm and fearless, and ready to face death if need be; she wondered what sort of hold Carlo Zeno would take on his neck, when all was known. And she saw red all round him and behind him and beside him up to his knees, the red of the guards' tunics that were like scarlet stains in the twilight air.

Once more the restless horse neighed, far off, and another answered him.

Then the man was ready. He took his knife and ripped Zoë's blue cotton tunic from her throat to her left shoulder and down her side, and she tried not even to shudder, for she did not know what was coming but she would die bravely; and when she was dead Zeno would come, and Gorlias, and they would avenge her. Death was but death, even by torture, and there were worse things in life which had been spared her.

Furthermore, if she died, it would be for a good cause, as well as to help Zeno to be free. Therefore, now that it was all decided, she looked a last time at the face of Andronicus, loose-lipped and cruel, and then shut her eyes and prayed God that she might neither flinch nor utter one word that could hinder the end, if it was at hand, as she still hoped.

She felt the chilly air on her shoulder and side, and then something small and hard was pressed against her, just under her arm; and hands that felt like horns, but were horribly quick and skilful, put a bandage round her and drew it tight, and it kept the thing in its place.

But under that thing, which was the half walnut shell, something small was alive and moved slowly round and round. There was no real pain at first, but she felt that the slow and delicate irritation might drive her mad.

Then, suddenly, a thrill of wild agony ran through her and convulsed her body against her will, but many hands held her now and she could not move. The horrible borer-beetle had begun to work its way into her flesh, under the walnut shell.

The corpse-faced man had watched her attentively, and when he saw her start his creaking voice was heard in the stillness.

'She will speak before you can count ten score,' he said.

CHAPTER XIX

Zoë had closed her eyes to bear the pain better, and a tiny drop of blood slowly trickled from the lip she had bitten in the first moment of the torture. It made a thin, dark line from her mouth downward, a little on the left side, over her white chin. Her breath came in deep and quivering sobs, drawn through her clenched teeth, but no other sound escaped her in those awful seconds. She was praying that death might come soon, but she did not ask for strength to be silent; that she had, for Carlo Zeno's sake, and for the sake of the just vengeance that would overtake Andronicus when she was dead, if only he were not warned of what was perhaps so near. She thought she might die of the pain only; she was sure that she must faint away if it lasted many moments longer.

The Emperor bent down in his saddle to see her agonised white face more clearly in the gathering gloom, and to catch the least syllable she might speak; and his loose lip moved, for he was counting to himself, counting the ten score, after which she would be able to bear no more and would tell him where the danger was. For the corpse-faced man knew his business, and his experience had been wide and long, and the Emperor knew that he never made a mistake. Moreover, the Greek minister smiled with sheer pleasure at the sight, and hoped that his master would command them to put the girl to death by very slow torments.

The guards, too, crowded upon each other to see, but they were not all silent now; for there were brave men amongst them, savage adventurers from the wild mountains beyond the Black Sea, who feared neither God, nor Emperor, nor man; and they did not like the sight they saw, and they said words one to another in strange tongues which the Greeks could not understand.

Andronicus counted slowly to twenty, and then still more slowly to forty, and the tortured girl's sharp breathing irritated him.

'Speak!' he cried, in a tone that was low and angry. 'Tell me where the danger is, or the thing shall eat out your heart!'

Then the answer came, but not in Zoë's voice, nor by one voice, but by many, loud and deep; and though the words were confused, some could be heard well enough; and they told the loose-lipped cowardly youth where the danger was, for it was upon him.

'Johannes! Johannes reigns! God and the Emperor! Emperor Johannes!'

That was what the voices shouted from the gate, as the multitude swept in, driving the sentinels and guards before them as the gale drives dry leaves. With but one breathing-space for thought and resolve, the guards in their scarlet tunics closed round Andronicus like waves of blood in the deep dusk, and he went down under them, and heard them answer the coming people—

'Johannes reigns! Emperor Johannes!'

Zoë heard the cry through her torment and forgot the pain for one moment, and the next, the dumb Ethiopian who had held her, slit the torturer's bandage and plucked the walnut shell from under her arm, with its living contents, and threw them away; for he had seen Andronicus go down, and knew that there was a new master. Then some of the men, who remembered it afterwards, saw the corpse-faced man grovelling on the ground and searching for his treasure, which could make the toughest victim speak before one could count ten score; for he served the Emperor, whoever he might be, as he and his father before him had served many. No one ever killed the torturer. So he went amongst the trampling feet on his hands and knees, feeling nothing, if so be that he might find his pet and get it back safely into its cage in his bosom. And when he found it still in the walnut shell, by the strange chance that protects all evil, he laughed like a maniac and slipped between the guards' legs on all fours, like a hideous white-faced ape, and ran away into the palace.

Zoë had opened her eyes, and the pain was gone, leaving only a throb behind, and she gathered her torn tunic to her neck with one hand as best she could and slipped out of the turmoil; and only she, of all those that heard the first shout, knew how it was that the people were cheering for the delivered Emperor, while Johannes was still shut up in the tower and guarded by the deaf-and-dumb Africans; and in the glorious triumph of her plan she forgot everything else but the man she loved, and he was safe now, beyond all doubt. Was he not the friend of the restored Johannes? The soldiers would not dare, on their lives, to keep him a prisoner now, not for one hour, not for one moment.

And there he rode, surely enough, in the front rank of the multitude, on the right hand of Emperor John. She knew him, though the last grey light was fading from the sky. She would have known him in the dark, it seemed to her that if she had been blind she would have known that he was near; and her joy rose in her throat, after the torture she had endured, and almost choked her, so that she reeled unsteadily and gasped for breath.

He was on the right hand of the Emperor John, 'Handsome John,' whom the people had once loved and whom they were now ready to love again, having tasted of the scorpions with which Andronicus had regaled them. 'Handsome John,' with his splendid brown beard—the light of torches flashed upon it now—and his cloth-of-gold cloak drawn closely round him like a bishop's cope, so that it hid his hands and half his bridle on each side, and covered the back of his head, too, and a great part of his cheeks; he wore the tall imperial head-dress also, and it shaded his eyes. The people had recognised him more by his fine beard and his cloth of gold than by his face, but the beard was unmistakable; and besides, there were men with him who scattered coins to the multitude, and those coins were good. But the followers who were nearest to him and Zeno, and who pressed round them both to defend them, if need be, were almost all sailors, Venetian shipwrights and workmen from the docks, though Tocktamish's Tartars were close behind, making a tremendous shouting, and striking their long tasselled spears against each other after their manner, with a clatter of wood like a monstrous rattle; and other soldiers had joined them by hundreds, and after them pressed the artisans of Constantinople, the Bulgarian blacksmiths, the Italian stone-cutters and masons, the Moorish armourers and the Syrian sword-smiths from Damascus, the Sicilian rope-makers, the Persian silk-weavers, and the Smyrniote carpet-weavers, and the linen-weavers from Alexandria with many others; and every man who was not a soldier had something in his hand for a weapon—a hammer, a mallet, or a carpet-maker's staff, or only a stout cudgel. And they ran, and pushed, and forced their way through the gate, spreading out again within the court, cheering and yelling for Johannes in a dozen languages at once.

The Emperor John sat quite still on his horse, wrapped in his cloak, but Zeno rode forward, till he was almost upon the knot of the guards who had pulled down Andronicus, and he threw up his hand, crying out to the men not to kill, in a voice that dominated the terrific din; and he was but just in time, for he was only obeyed because he offered a reward.

'Ten pounds of gold for Andronicus alive!' he shouted.

For that was the price Andronicus had set on his head that morning, and what was enough for Zeno was enough for an Emperor. So half a dozen of the guards dragged the man alive into the palace, and bound him securely with his hands behind him, and stripped off his jewels and his gold, and kicked him into a small secret room behind the porter's lodge, and shut the door. There the corpse-faced man was squatting in a dark corner, blowing some coals to a glow in an earthen pan, because he might soon be called to do more work, and unless the vinegar was really boiling hot the fumes of it would not put out the eyesight. As Andronicus lay on the floor he could see the man.

But outside, the confusion grew and the noise increased as the people poured into the vast courtyard and pressed behind upon those who had entered before them.

Then the door of the tower in the corner was opened from within, and the African mutes came out and joined the other soldiers, and from an upper window the captain and his wife looked down, and by the help of what she told him he understood that it was time to set his prisoner free, if he did not mean to risk being torn to shreds by the people, though he could not at all understand who it was whom he saw on horseback in the torchlight, dressed in cloth of gold, with the imperial head-dress on his head, for he knew well enough that so long as the key of the upper prison hung at his own belt, Johannes could not get out. Yet there was no mistaking the cry of the people, and his wife urged him not to lose time.

The crowd was surging towards the tower now, led by Zeno and the Emperor, and they and their sailors and dockmen kept in front of the crowd to be the first to dismount and enter the tower, and then the sailors kept the throng back, telling them that Johannes had gone in to free his youngest son, and the two men who had the deep bags of money threw lavish handfuls to the people, to amuse them while they waited.

But when Zeno and the Emperor came out again, Johannes' face was all uncovered, and the cloth-of-gold cope hung loosely on his shoulders; and by the glare of many torches every one knew that it was Johannes himself, and none other, and men cheered and yelled till they were hoarse.

After the Emperor and Zeno came a man whom no one had seen go in with them, and he had a very scanty dark beard and was dressed in quiet brown, though he wore a horseman's boots, and he was Gorlias Pietrogliant, who had acted so well the part which Zoë had imagined for him.

But Zeno knew nothing of Arethusa, yesterday his slave, and since last night the woman of his heart, for in the haste and stress of that tremendous half-hour, Gorlias could tell him nothing, except that he was Gorlias and not the Emperor, and that the deed giving Tenedos over to Venice was signed and in his bosom; and Zeno supposed that he had devised all the wonderful scheme, which looked so simple as soon as it began to be carried out. Arethusa, he thought, was safe at home; sleepless, worn out with waiting, trembling with anxiety, perhaps, but safe. Now that the deed was done, now that Andronicus was bound, and Johannes, his father, was restored to the throne, Carlo Zeno thought only of leaving Constantinople without delay, before the Emperor could take back his word, and revoke the cession of Tenedos. For Zeno did not put his trust in Oriental princes, and feared the Greeks even when they offered gifts. With a swift Venetian vessel and a fair wind, the coveted island could be reached in two days, or even less; its governor had always at heart been faithful to Johannes, and would obey the deed which Gorlias had thrust into Zeno's hand in the tower, and if once the standard of St. Mark were raised on the fort there was small chance that any enemy would be able to tear it down.

Therefore, just when the soldiers were lifting Johannes from his horse to carry him to the throne-room with wild triumph and rejoicing, Zeno slipped from the saddle to escape notice, elbowed his way to the outskirts of the crowd, and was on the point of making for the gate when Gorlias found him again.

'Arethusa asks you to come to her,' Gorlias said.

'I am going—'

'No. She is here. It was all her plan; she risked her life for it, we were a few moments late, and she has been tortured. Come quickly!'

Zeno's face changed. Gorlias saw that, even in the dim light of the now distant torches. It was the change that comes into a master swordman's face when he makes up his mind to kill, after only defending himself because his adversary has tried some dastardly murderous trick of fence. But Zeno said nothing as he strode swiftly by his companion's side.

Gorlias had found her and had brought her into the lower chamber of the tower, now deserted by the guards. The captain's wife had been standing at the door, not daring to go out amongst the half-frantic soldiers. She might have fared ill at their hands if she had been recognised just then as the wife of the Emperor's gaoler. So she had stood under the archway, watching and listening, and Gorlias had given Zoë half-fainting into her care while he went to find Zeno.

She had taken the girl on her knees like a child, while she herself sat on the narrow stone bench that ran round the wall, for there was no furniture of any sort there. Zoë's head lay upon the shoulder of the big woman who gently smoothed and patted the soft brown hair, and rocked the light figure on her knees with a side motion as nurses do. She did not know what was the matter, but she recognised the girl who had brought the message and who had been caught outside the door.

Then Zeno came, and in a moment he was close beside Zoë; resting one knee on the stone bench, bending down, and very tenderly lifting the lovely head into his own arm.

She knew his touch, she turned her face up with a great effort, for she had hardly any strength left, and her lids that were but half-closed like a dying person's, quivered and opened, and for one instant her eyes were full of light. Her voice came to him from far off, almost from the other world.

'Safe! Ah, thank God! It was worth the pain!'

Then she fainted quite away in his arms, but he knew that she was not dying, for he had seen many pass from life, and the signs were familiar to him.

He gathered her to him and carried her lightly through the open door, where Gorlias was ready; and Gorlias knew where Vito was waiting with the skiff at the old landing not far below the tower, and he helped the boatman to row them home.

Thus ended that long day, which had so nearly been Zoë's last and Zeno's too; and when she opened her eyes again and found herself lying on her own divan under the soft light of the lamps, and looked into his anxious, loving face, all the weariness sank away from her own, and for an instant she felt as strong as if she had freshly waked from rest; then she put up her arms together, though it hurt her very much to lift the left one, and she clasped her hands round his handsome brown neck and drew him down to her without a word.

It was only for a moment. Her strength failed her again, and he felt her little hands relax; so he knelt down by the divan and laid his cheek upon the edge of her pillow, so that he could look into her face, and they both smiled; and his smile was anxious, but hers was satisfied. He did not know what they had done to her, but he was sure that she needed care.

'You are suffering,' he said. 'What shall I do? Shall I send for a physician?'

'No. Stay with me. Let me look at you. That is all I need.'

Her speech came in short, soft phrases, like kisses from lips half-asleep, when there is a little dream between each sentence and the next. But even when she was asleep he still knelt beside her, and now and then her body quivered, and she drew a sharp breath suddenly as if the pain she had borne ran through her again, though more in memory than in real suffering now.

CHAPTER XX

Zeno left her when she was breathing quietly, after ordering the two little maids to watch her by turns, or at least to go to sleep very near her, in case she should wake and call. He himself was worn out with fatigue and hunger, for he had not tasted anything since he had supped with Zoë on the previous evening. He went down to his own rooms, where Vito had prepared him food and wine, which he had asked Gorlias to share with him. But the ex-astrologer was gone, and the master ate and drank alone that night, smiling now and then at the recollection of the dark hours in the dry cistern, and giving orders to Vito about the journey which was to be begun on the morrow, if possible. And Vito gave him a detailed account of what had happened in his absence.

Now that Zoë was safe he was supremely happy. In his heart the fighting man had detested the peaceful merchant's life he had chosen to lead for more than two years, and already, in imagination, his hands were on the helm, the salt spray was in his face, and his ship was going free on her course for the wonderful Isles of Adventure.

But by the orders he gave while he ate his supper, Vito understood that he was not going alone. When had Carlo Zeno ever taken rich carpets, soft cushions, silver basins, and delicate provisions to sea with him, except as merchandise, packed in bales and stowed below? A camp-bed ashore, a hammock at sea, were enough for his comfort. Vito mentally noted each order, and when the time came he had forgotten nothing; but he asked no questions.

Early in the morning, when Zeno had learned that Zoë was still asleep, he went down to the harbour and found that Sebastian Cornèr's ship was to sail the next day at dawn, the same vessel that had brought the letter from Venice which had led him to buy Arethusa; the very galley by which she should have been carried to Marco Pesaro, if Zeno had not thought better of the matter before drawing the three hundred ducats.

Now Sebastian Cornèr was a brave captain, as well as a man of business, and could be trusted; and when Zeno had shown him the deed which gave Tenedos to the Serene Republic he did not hesitate, but promised to help Carlo to take possession of the island within three days, before Johannes could change his mind. So that matter was settled, and Zeno departed, saying that he would send his baggage on board during the day.

When he came home he found the secretary waiting with his tale of woe. Omobono looked and felt like an elderly sick lamb, very sorry for himself and terribly anxious not to be blamed for what had happened, while equally afraid of being scolded for talking too much. He had passed through the most awful ordeal of his peaceful life very bravely, he believed; and if Zeno had called him a cackling hen that morning the shock might have unsettled his brain, and would certainly have broken his heart.

But Zeno had been informed by Vito of the events that had disturbed his household, and knew that Omobono had done his best, considering what his worst might have been, he being of a timid temperament.

'You did very well,' said the master. 'In ancient days, Omobono, those who died for their faith were indeed venerated as martyrs, but those who suffered and lived were afterwards revered as confessors. That is your position.'

This piece of information Zeno had acquired, with more of the same kind, when he had expected to be made a canon of Patras. Omobono's heart glowed at the praise.

'And the confessor, sir, has the advantage of being alive and can still be useful,' he ventured to suggest, though with some diffidence.

'Precisely,' Zeno assented. 'A live dog is better than a dead lion. I mean a watch-dog, of course, Omobono,' he added rather hastily, 'a faithful watch-dog.'

Omobono's appearance that morning did not suggest the guardian of the flock, the shepherd's shaggy friend. Not in the least; but he was pleased, and when he was told that he was to pack his belongings and make ready to leave Constantinople for a trip to Venice his delight actually brought a little colour into his grey cheeks.

'And may I enquire, sir,' he began, 'about the—' he paused and looked significantly at the ceiling, to indicate the upper story of the house,—'about the lady?' he added, finishing his question at last.

'She goes with us,' answered Zeno briefly.

'Yes, sir. But may I ask whether it will be part of my duty to be responsible for her?'

'You?' Zeno looked at the little man in undisguised astonishment.

'I mean, sir, on Messer Marco Pesaro's account. I had understood—'

'No,' said Zeno, 'you had not understood.'

'But then, sir—'

'Omobono, I have often warned you against your curiosity.'

'Yes, sir. I pray every day for strength to withstand it. Nevertheless, though I know it is a sin it sometimes leads me to learn things which are of use. I do not think that if you knew what I know, sir, you would contemplate the possibility of disposing of—'

'You talk too much,' said Zeno. 'If you have anything to say, then say it. If you have nothing to say, then say nothing. But do not talk. What have you found out?'

Thus deprived of the pleasure of telling a long story, Omobono conscientiously tried to impart his information in the fewest possible words.

'The lady is not called Arethusa, sir. Before she sold herself to Rustan to save her people from starvation she was called Zoë Rhangabé, the daughter of the Protosparthos who was executed by Andronicus—'

'Rhangabé?' repeated Zeno, not believing him; for it was a great name, and is still.

'Yes, sir. But that was not her name, either, for he and his wife had adopted her because they had no children, but afterwards two boys were born to them—'

'Confound their boys!' interrupted Zeno. 'Who is she?'

'Her real name is Bianca Giustiniani; she is a Venetian by birth, and her father and mother died of the plague here soon after she was born. You see, sir, under the circumstances, and although the lady called herself a slave, such a commission as Messer Marco Pesaro's—'

'Omobono,' said Zeno, interrupting him again, 'get a priest here at once. I am going to be married.'

'Married, sir?' The little secretary was aghast.

'Send Vito for the priest!'

And before Omobono could say more, Zeno had left the room.

He found Zoë standing by the open window, and the morning sun was still streaming in. Her hair was not taken up yet, but lay like silk all over her shoulders, still damp from the bath. She was a little pale, as a flower that has blossomed in a dark room, and the rough white silk of the robe she drew closely round her showed by contrast the delicate tint and texture of her skin, and the sweet freshness of the tender and spiritual mouth.

He took her hand and looked at her earnestly before he spoke. Only a night, a day and a night, had passed since he had understood what had hidden itself in his heart for weeks. That same truth had stolen into hers, too, but she had known what it meant.

'You kept your secret well,' he said—'too well!'

She shook her head, thinking he spoke of her love.

'You knew it long ago,' she answered. 'And what you did not know, you guessed. You kept yours better far.'

'I kept that one from myself, as best I could,' said he, understanding what she meant. 'I could not keep it for ever! But since we know that we love, our life begins here, and together. Together, because you saved mine—I know everything, for they have told me; and so my life is yours, and yours is mine, because we were born to mate, as falcons mate with falcons, doves with doves, and song-birds with song-birds.'

'Say falcons!' laughed Zoë. 'I like the brave bird better!'

'I do, too,—and so my little falcon, Arethusa, we must wing it together to a safer nest before Tocktamish or some other barbarian stirs up a counter-revolution. Will you come with me?'

She smiled and laid her hand in his.

'Am I not your bought slave?' she asked. 'I must obey.'

'That is not enough. We are Christian man and maid. You shall go with me in honour to my own people.'

'A gentleman of Venice cannot marry a slave,' she objected, though she smiled.

He laughed, happily, and drew back from her a little.

'A gentleman of Venice may do what seems good in his own eyes, if it be not treason,' he said. 'I publish the banns of marriage between Messer Carlo Zeno, of Venice, bachelor, and Arethusa—'

'Of Rustan Karaboghazji's slave market, spinster!' suggested Zoë, laughing with him. 'It is a noble alliance for the great Doge's house, sir!'

'Oh! You talk of Doges? Then I will put it in another way, as the priest will say it presently, for I think he is waiting downstairs by this time, and Omobono is teaching him his lesson.'

'How shall you put it?'

'Bianca Giustiniani, wilt thou take this man to be thy wedded husband?'

She was taken by surprise, and for a moment the words would not come.

'Wilt thou take this man?' he asked again, but more softly now, and nearer to her lips, though he did not see them; for he thought he saw her soul in her brave brown eyes, and as for her answer, he knew it.

Now the rest of Zeno's life, with much of what the story-teller has told here, is extant in very bad Latin, written by one of his grandsons, the good bishop Jacopo Zeno of Belluno: how he sailed down the Dardanelles, and made good the Emperor John's gift of Tenedos to the Republic; and how the Genoese tried hard to take it from him; and how he fought like the hero he was, with a handful of men against a host, and drove them off and saved the island; and also how he lived to save Venice herself from them when all seemed lost, and broke their power for ever afterwards; and how he did many other glorious and great things, all after he had taken Bianca Giustiniani to wife.

Francis Marion Crawford was born in Bagni di Lucca, Italy on 2nd August, 1854, the only son of the American sculptor Thomas Crawford and Louisa Cutler Ward. His aunt was Julia Ward Howe, the American poet, most famous for the words to 'The Battle Hymn of the Republic'.

After his father's death in 1857, his mother remarried to Luther Terry, with whom she had Crawford's half-sister, Margaret Ward Terry.

Crawford's education began at St Paul's School, Concord, New Hampshire and then went on to Cambridge University, the University of Heidelberg and finally the University of Rome.

In 1879, Crawford went to India to study the ancient language of Sanskrit and to edit Allahabad, The Indian Herald.

Returning to America in February 1881, he enrolled at Harvard University for a year to continue his studies in Sanskrit. Crawford had no real career path at this time although for two years he contributed to various periodicals, mainly The Critic.

Early in 1882, Crawford established a close, lifelong friendship with Isabella Stewart Gardner, a noted and eccentric heiress from Boston who over the years built up a large and eclectic collection of art.

Crawford lived most of his time in Boston with his Aunt Julia and Uncle Sam. The family were concerned by his lack of ambition, prospects in general, and his financial ones in particular.

His mother had hoped he might train in Boston for a career as an operatic baritone based on his private renditions of Schubert lieder. With that in mind it was, in January 1882, that George Henschel, the conductor of the Boston Symphony Orchestra, was called in to assess young Crawford's talents. Henschel was direct and to the point. Crawford would 'never be able to sing in perfect tune'. His Uncle Sam, knowing that Crawford was keen on literary pursuits, proposed that his years in India might be good source material to write about. Crawford agreed. He set to work. Uncle Sam also set about developing contacts with a number of New York publishers.

Events moved very quickly. By December of that year Crawford had completed his first novel, 'Mr Isaacs', based on modern Anglo-Indian life flavoured with a touch of Oriental mystery. It was an immediate success. Crawford set about writing a second novel and the result was 'Dr Claudius' in 1883.

In October 1884 he married Elizabeth Berdan, the daughter of the Civil War Union General Hiram Berdan. The marriage would produce two sons; Harold and Bertram, and two daughters; Eleanor and Clara.

Crawford, buoyed by his excellent start, now decided to return to Italy and to live there permanently.

The couple initially went to Sorrento and lived at the historic Hotel Cocumella during 1885 before moving permanently to Sant' Agnello, where the purchase of the Villa Renzi would now be rededicated as Villa Crawford.

As a writer Crawford had more than his fair share of detractors but, perhaps due to the physical distance between author and these detractors, they did not distract from his prolific output.

Each year seemed to bring a new F. Marion Crawford novel. His popularity was evident although some works, such as 1896's offering 'Adam Johnstone's Son', was described by his left-wing English contemporary, George Gissing, as "rubbish". Over half of his novels are set in Italy. He also wrote three long historical studies of Italy and was nearing completion on a history of Rome in the Middle Ages when he died.

His 'Saracinesca' series are considered his best works. The third in the series, 'Don Orsino' (1892) was told against the background of a real estate bubble and is especially effective. The volume immediately after was 'Corleone' (1897), and the first major treatment of the Mafia in literature.

Crawford himself was fondest of 'Khaled: A Tale of Arabia' (1891), a story of a genie who becomes human. 'A Cigarette-Maker's Romance' (1890) was dramatized, and had considerable popularity on the stage as well as in its novel form.

Towards the end of the 1890's Crawford ventured down another path with his writing. He began his historical works. 'Ave Roma Immortalis' was published in 1898, followed by 'Rulers of the South' (1900), and 'Gleanings from Venetian History' (1905). Most were re-titled with longer more explanatory titles for the American market. Within them all his careful and precise knowledge of the local Italian history together with his literary talents combined to great effect.

Whilst on an American Lecture tour in the winter of 1897-1898 Crawford was researching and gathering technical information for his historical work 'Marietta' (published 1901), that describes glass-making in late medieval Venice. Whilst visiting a glass-smelting plant in Colorado he suffered a severe lung injury when he inhaled toxic gasses. This would eventually contribute to his death a decade or so later.

Crawford's commercial popularity and appeal at the time was such that in 1901, the American Macmillan firm began a deluxe uniform edition of his novels as his works came up for re-printing. In 1904 the P. F. Collier Company in New York was authorized to publish a 25-volume edition (which was later expanded to 32 volumes).

In 1902 he wrote a stage play 'Francesca da Rimini', that was produced in Paris by his friend and legendary actress Sarah Bernhardt.

Towards the end of his life Hollywood had begun to realise that his works were a valuable source of stories and ideas and several were turned into movies and continued to be so for decades after his death.

Crawford also had a gift for pulling off excellent short stories. Several, such as 'The Upper Berth' (1886), 'For the Blood Is the Life' (1905, a vampiress tale), 'The Dead Smile' (1899), and 'The Screaming Skull' (1908), are among the most anthologized classics of the horror genre. After his death several collected volumes were published from various sources.

After most of his fictional works had been published, most had the view that he was a gifted narrator; and his books of fiction, were full of historic vitality and energy as well as dramatic characterization. He was widely popular among readers to whom literature was more for escapism than a confrontation with reality or pages of subjective analysis. In 'The Novel: What It Is' (1893), Crawford was both resolute and disarming in defending his literary approach, self-conceived as a combination of romanticism and realism, defining the art form in terms of its marketplace and audience. The novel, he wrote, is "a marketable commodity" and "intellectual artistic luxury" that "must amuse, indeed, but should amuse reasonably, from an intellectual point of view .... Its intention is to amuse and please, and certainly not to teach and preach; but in order to amuse well it must be a finely-balanced creation ...."

Francis Marion Crawford died at Sorrento on Good Friday 1909 at Villa Crawford of a heart attack.

F. Marion Crawford – A Concise Bibliography

Novels

Mr. Isaacs: A Tale of Modern India (1882)
Dr. Claudius (1883)
To Leeward (1884)
A Roman Singer (1884)
An American Politician (1884)
Zoroaster (1885)
A Tale of a Lonely Parish (1886)
Saracinesca (1887)
Marzio's Crucifix (1887)
Paul Patoff (1887)
With the Immortals (1888)
Greifenstein (1889)
Sant' Ilario (1889); sequel to Saracinesca
A Cigarette-Maker's Romance (1890)
Khaled: A Tale of Arabia (1891)
The Witch of Prague (1891)
The Three Fates (1892)
Don Orsino (1892); sequel to Sant' Ilario
The Children of the King (1893)
Pietro Ghisleri (1893)
Marion Darche (1893)
Katharine Lauderdale (1894)
The Upper Berth (1894); with "By the Waters of Paradise"
Love in Idleness (1894)
The Ralstons (1894); sequel to Katharine Lauderdale
Casa Braccio (1895); related to Katharine Lauderdale and The Ralstons.
Adam Johnstone's Son (1896)
Taquisara (1896)
A Rose of Yesterday (1897)
Corleone (1897)
Via Crucis (1899)
In the Palace of the King (1900)

Marietta (1901)
Cecilia (1902)
Man Overboard! (1903)
The Heart of Rome (1903)
Whosoever Shall Offend (1904)
Soprano (1905); U.S. title: Fair Margaret.
A Lady of Rome (1906)
Arethusa (1907)
The Little City of Hope (1907)
The Primadonna (1908); sequel to Soprano/Fair Margaret
The Diva's Ruby (1908); sequel to The Primadonna
The White Sister (1909)
Stradella (1909)
The Undesirable Governess (1910)
Wandering Ghosts; British title: Uncanny Tales.

Non-fiction

Our Silver (1881)
The Novel: What It Is (1893)
Constantinople (1895)
Bar Harbor (1896)
Ave Roma Immortalis (1898)
Rulers of the South (1900; 1905 in the U.S. as Southern Italy and Sicily and The Rulers of the South)
Gleanings from Venetian History (1905; in the U.S. as Salvae Venetia and in 1909 as Venice; the People and the Place)

Drama

In the Palace of the King (1900) with Lorrimer Stoddard.
Francesca da Rimini (1902) The piece was adapted into an opera by Franco Leoni in 1904.
Evelyn Hastings (1902) Unpublished typescript discovered in 2008.
The White Sister (1909) with Walter C. Hackett.

Filmography

A Cigarette-Maker's Romance, directed by Frank Wilson (UK, 1913, based on the novella)
The White Sister, directed by Fred E. Wright [it] (1915, based on the novel)
In the Palace of the King [it], directed by Fred E. Wright [it] (1915, based on the novel)
Whosoever Shall Offend, directed by Arrigo Bocchi (UK, 1919, based on the novel)
Il cuore di Roma, directed by Edoardo Bencivenga (Italy, 1919, based on the novel)
A Cigarette-Maker's Romance, directed by Tom Watts (UK, 1920, based on the novella)
Saracinesca [it], directed by Gaston Ravel (Italy, 1921, based on the novel)
Sant' Ilario [it], directed by Henry Kolker (Italy, 1923, based on the novel)
The White Sister, directed by Henry King (1923, based on the novel)
In the Palace of the King, directed by Emmett J. Flynn (1923, based on the novel)
Son of India, directed by Jacques Feyder (1931, based on the novel Mr. Isaacs)
The White Sister, directed by Victor Fleming (1933, based on the novel)

The Screaming Skull, directed by Alex Nicol (1958, named after the short story)
The White Sister, directed by Tito Davison (Mexico, 1960, based on the novel)